The Wall Outside

The Xun Ove Series: Book 1

Step Across The Barrier

James William Peercy

To Penny,
Hope you enjoy.
Jenn W. P...
9/17/21

ThreeSidedCoin.com

The Wall Outside

The Xun Ove Series: Book 1

Step Across The Barrier

2nd Edition

Published by arrangement with the author.

For information contact:

Three Sided Coin Publishing PO Box 2695 Sherman, TX 75091-2695
ThreeSidedCoin.com

Manufactured in the United States of America

Library of Congress Cataloguing-in-Publication Data
Peercy, James William
The Wall Outside/James William Peercy
Library of Congress Control Number: 2018903078

ISBN: 1-937491-02-1
ISBN-13: 978-1-937491-02-4

DEDICATION

For my wife, who liked the book from the very first read. She was its inspiration.

In memory of Travis James Curry, who passed away at the age of 47 due to lung cancer.

In memory of Dorothy Phillips, my grandmother, whose whimsical ways helped to mold the image of Dorothy, Queen of the Pixies.

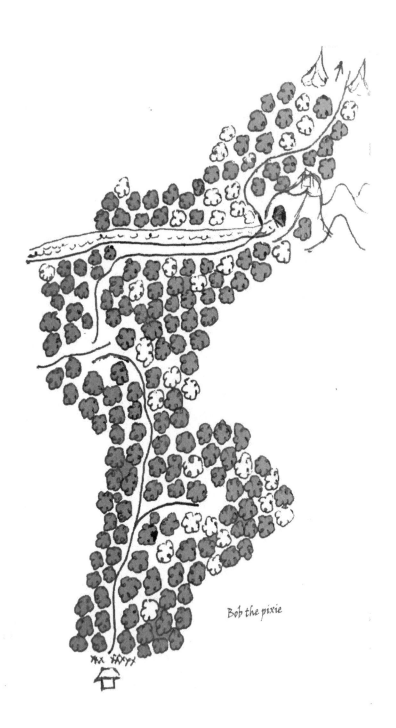

Bob the pixie

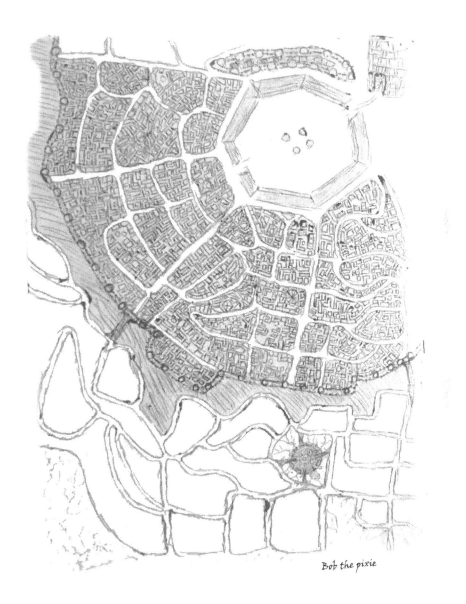

Bob the pixie

ACKNOWLEDGMENTS

I wish to express sincere appreciation to family and friends. In particular: Claudette Peercy for putting up with me when I've said, "Come look at this..."; Clifford and Dianne Peercy, who never set limitations on what I could become; Brian Miller and Darrell Miller, with whom I used to swap stories and dreams as we rode to school on the bus; Elizabeth Mendoza, whose excellence in photography is equal to her personality and friendship; Arash Mahboubi for reading and commenting (to the point of asking, "When is the next one?"); and Lana Bernardin for her enthusiasm to utilize her promotional skills. Thanks to Frank Hall with Hydra Publications for the first printed edition and Lynn Calvert with Otherworld Publications for the first Kindle printing.

To all of you, highest commendations.

PROLOGUE

"What do you see?" a little girl asked.

Jonna jumped, turning from the well. A moment ago, there had been no one beside him.

Her hair shone golden, glistening in the sun. A smile lit her face, which was full of life. She wore a circlet of daisies around her head.

"I see a face in the water." Jonna's eyes lit up. "She looks like a queen."

"Maybe she is." The little girl laughed, sending shivers up his spine. "Want to play?"

"Jonna," the boy's mother called from the back of their home. It was over the creek and up the hill. "Time for supper!"

"I've got to go." He turned around. "Maybe we can—" The little girl was gone. He looked into the water, but the face had vanished, too.

"Jonna!" his mother called again.

Jonna took off, heading for home.

CHAPTER 1
DOUBLE WINDOWS, BLOWING RAIN, DARK WOOD ELVES

Jonna sighed. "So much for taking a walk." He watched as the rain splattered against the window, at first sporadic but then with increasing speed.

Stephanie looked up from her book. "What was that?"

"I said—" He raised his voice, covering the thunder that shook the house. "So much for taking a walk."

"You don't have to yell." She rolled her eyes playfully, tilting her head as the thunder echoed away. "I can hear you just fine." She looked around. "When did it begin to rain?"

He laughed. "While you were reading."

She raised the book to start again, but noticed something in his tone. She looked at him. "Am I ignoring you? I'm sorry. I didn't mean to." She placed the book beside her.

"No." He raised a hand. "You're not ignoring me. I guess I'm just a little disappointed that it's raining on our vacation."

"We can go up to the bedroom and snuggle while I read." Her eyes brightened. "That would be fun."

The thought of a midmorning snuggle sounded nice. After all, most snuggles turned into a little more fun.

A burst of wind hit the cabin. One of the shutters slammed against the outside wall.

"What was that?" Stephanie jumped, losing her grip on the book but finding it quickly. Her attention was definitely not on snuggling. She looked toward the window. "That's not just rain. It feels more like a storm." The shutter slammed again.

"I better get that," Jonna said, sounding unhappy. He went to the closet and pulled out his jacket. It was not exactly a raincoat, but it would have to do. Pulling the hood over his head, he zipped the jacket tight.

"Be careful." Stephanie looked worried. She pulled a blanket tighter around her. "I'll wait here until you get back."

"See you shortly."

The sound of rain hitting the cabin echoed in the room. He opened the front door, stepped out onto the wooden porch through a blast of wind and water, and closed the door behind him. Raising his head, he could see the water running off the top of the overhang in streams. "So much for the weather report."

Jonna had checked it three times—or was it four?—to make sure that nothing like this would happen. On the radio on the way up, they'd heard the first bad news.

"A storm, moving in from the west, is approaching the coast of Washington State."

From that point on, all he could do was watch. At first light gray, the clouds had become darker by the moment, culminating in the splatter of rain against the cabin window. At least they had reached the cabin before the storm hit.

Boom, crash, slam. A flash brightened the sky.

The shutter slammed again. He located its direction, turned left, and gazed down the cabin's side. Off the porch, directly in front of him, the shutter that protected the kitchen window was swinging in the wind.

For a brief moment, Jonna saw the silhouette of a tiny man hanging from the shutter's slide bolt. He rubbed his eyes and blinked. Was the figure trying to close the shutter?

Lightning flashed. The silhouette vanished. Jonna stared at where it had been. "Trick of the light, no doubt."

The rain fell in buckets, bringing his attention back to the weather. Coat or not, he was about to get wet. He tightened the hood on his jacket and stepped out.

The ground was already saturated. He could hear the squish under his boots. It would take days to dry this out; once the rain decided to stop, that is. Unfortunately, by that time, they would be heading home.

The wind hit, shoving him toward the side of the house. The shutter slammed, and he heard a distinctive grunt. Jonna reached up and caught the shutter as a flash of lightning lit the sky. He blinked, seeing spots, while simultaneously closing the shutter and tying it off. Who makes shutters that have to be tied, anyway, especially from the outside? And where were the shutter dogs?

A sheet of rain struck, driving him against the house. He ducked his head, then dared to peek out from under his hood as he tried to find the porch overhang.

With one hand placed on the side of the house, he reached up to find the kitchen shutter. Lightning flashed again. The same tiny man silhouette appeared right in front of him. Startled, Jonna jumped and slipped.

"Dang—" Jonna stifled an expletive he did not intend to say. He hit the ground, pants soaked, his clothes becoming wetter by the moment. A sigh escaped his lips, but he refused to jump to his feet. Vacation was, most certainly, not turning out fun.

As if in sympathy, the sheet of rain gave way to a light drizzle. Looking up, he saw that the silhouette had disappeared once more. Trees in the area could have easily cast the image, and with the lightning at play—

Taking in his surroundings, he remembered the fence that bordered their cabin yard. The trees outside the perimeter thickened in all directions. If only the sun were shining, he could be walking through those trees right now, hand in hand with Stephanie. Blinding light flashed. What he thought to be a shadow from beyond the fence took on the shape of a man.

Jonna blinked, and it vanished. The cool wetness, along with the aggravation, had to be playing tricks on him. He studied the area. The longer he watched, the more he knew his imagination had been running away. It was easy to explain. The shadow of a larger tree had created this visual effect. Maybe its trunk was more knotty than the rest.

He got up and turned toward the porch, but stopped and looked back at the tree once more. Despite his reasonable explanation, a nagging doubt sprouted at the back of his mind. Oh, why not? He was soaked already. Once he got inside, he could take a nice warm shower.

The fence had a rough look. Whoever built it had chosen to use the forest's small natural trees without removing the bark. The unusually large tree casting the man-like shadow stood nearer the fence than the others, probably not removed due to its size.

Approaching it, he continued to watch the light play with the shadowy apparition. The knots did give the impression of a man—a thin man, but a man nonetheless. It depended on the angle.

Jonna climbed over the fence, using the overhanging branches to hold himself steady on the wet wood. Stepping down on the other side, he noticed that the low-hanging branches had formed an umbrella above him. He ran his hand over the knots. How cool! If nothing else came from this trip, he would have to get a picture of this before they left for home.

Lightning flashed several more times. In that instant, he could see most of the cabin. A sense of being out of place overwhelmed him. The builders had tried to make the cabin look like it belonged but could not. Something about it, something man-made, did not fit in with the forest. Jonna grabbed the fence, placed a tentative foot up, and paused, looking back at the tree.

When lightning flashed again, the face of a light-skinned humanoid with blond hair appeared. Jonna lost his grip.

He scrambled to grab something, anything, but it was too late. He hit the ground, groaning. Soft ground or not, these falls were beginning to get annoying. From out of nowhere, a small-boned hand extended, grasped his arm, and hauled him up with unusual strength.

"Art thou hurt?"

Though the accent sounded thick, Jonna could still understand the words. He stared at the person before him, mouth agape. When he realized what he was doing, he closed it.

"Green," he finally managed to say, but shook his head when he heard it. "I mean, yeah. I mean, who are you?"

The rain stopped. The sun tried to peek through the clouds.

"Green?" The man spoke curiously. "Thou hast an odd form of welcome." He looked down and caught sight of his own clothes. "Of necessity they be green—the queen's royal green." The man in green shook his head. "Methinks thou hit thy head."

Jonna reached up and felt the back of his head. "Nothing hurts." He glanced toward the cabin, then back at the man in green. "Who are you?"

"Sir Verity." The man in green bowed. "Lead guard and protector of the queen's forest. An' thou art?"

"I—Jonna." Jonna's voice faltered a moment. "Jonna McCambel."

"McCambel? Hmm." Sir Verity placed his hand under his chin. "I canst not think of such a name. From whence came thou?"

"Why, the cabin, of course." Jonna pointed over the fence. When he held out his hand, the sun warmed it. Curiously, the storm clouds were gone.

"I see," Sir Verity answered, though something in his voice remained unspoken. Was it Jonna's imagination or was it getting easier to understand the man in green? At first, he heard *thee* and *thou*. Now it sounded more normal.

"Perhaps you should go to your cabin." Sir Verity's voice held a little cautiousness mixed with urgency. He turned his head to the right and listened.

"You hear something?" Jonna strained to hear it, too, but nothing hit his ears. "What do you hear?"

"The approaching of horses." Sir Verity spoke as if far away in his thoughts. "Dost thou not hear it?" He studied Jonna.

Jonna shook his head. The sun heating up the hood of his jacket made his head uncomfortably warm. He slid it off.

Sir Verity stepped back, a bow and arrow coming from nowhere. "Thou art human!"

Jonna's hands snapped up in front of him. "Hold it. I'm no threat to you."

The man demanded, "How didst thou see me? Speak now, and preserve thy life!"

"I don't know," Jonna pleaded quickly. "I was standing by the cabin in the rain, and a flash of lightning showed you to me."

"Rain? The rain hath been gone a fortnight." Sir Verity stomped the ground. "Even the ground is dry." He stopped and stared at Jonna. "And yet, thou dost have water dripping off thee even as we speak." Sir Verity searched around him. "This be pixie magic."

Now even Jonna could hear the horses.

"Down." Sir Verity grabbed him by the arm and forced him beside the tree. Off to their right, two riders, both dressed in clothes like Sir Verity's but wearing the colors of blue and tan, rode by. They disappeared down a split in the trail.

"The king's men." The man sighed, answering Jonna's unspoken question. "Until the duel, there can be no peace."

"You are at war?"

Sir Verity gave Jonna a funny look but then shook his head. "This is the fault of the pixies." He raised his fist to the sky. "You should not have interfered."

"Interfered?" Jonna looked around but saw no one. "Who interfered?"

"The pixies, of course." Sir Verity sighed again. "They think the queen needs help from beyond our borders and are afraid she will lose the duel." He turned back to Jonna. "You have lost your accent."

"Me?" Jonna blinked. "How are you now speaking normal

English?"

"English?" The man looked offended. "I speak the language of the queen."

Jonna frowned. "Maybe I did hit my head." It was easier for him to check without the hood. Nope, there was no bump or blood.

"Well," Jonna said after a pause. "I guess I should let you go to whatever duel you need to go to."

"Nay."

"That's better," Jonna said aloud by mistake before continuing the rest in his head. *Now he sounds more like when we met.*

"Then you agree?" Sir Verity looked grave. "It is not a light thing to accept."

Jonna paused, not sure what he was agreeing to.

Sir Verity accepted his silence as consent. "Good. 'Tis settled. But first, we must present you to the queen."

"What," Jonna said slowly, "did I just settle?" He tried to make sense of the last few exchanges but still could not figure them out.

"You've accepted the position of dueling for the queen."

Things were beginning to get out of hand, not that they didn't already seem crazy. "I did *what?*"

"Why else do you think the pixies sent you?"

Jonna shook his head. "I don't even know a pixie."

"They knew you," the man said with confidence. "And that is all that matters. Why do you think one of my caliber would be scouring the countryside in search of a hero? Though I must admit, the queen may be surprised you're human."

"And you're not?" Jonna stepped back as Sir Verity's previous reaction to him sank in. "What are you?"

Sir Verity removed his cap, gave a polite bow, and showed his pointed ears. "A woodland elf, of course."

"Of course." Had Stephanie been listening, she would have known something was wrong in Jonna's voice. However, only Sir Verity stood by, and he paid no attention.

"This way." Sir Verity headed further into the forest, following a path that opened as he walked.

Jonna glanced back at the cabin. Though the ground around it seemed dry, he could still see small drops of water falling from the overhang.

This was crazy. This was madness. For all he knew, he had hit his head on a rock and was lying in the rain drowning. Jonna shook himself. What a horrible thought! Somehow, some way, this appeared to be happening. If he jumped the fence and ran to the cabin, would the whole thing disappear?

His practical side said yes. However, his curiosity had risen. If this was a dream, what would it hurt?

"Are you coming?" Sir Verity raised his voice. The elf had already stepped out of sight. How had the elf's language so quickly turned into English?

This was silly. There were no such creatures as elves, pixies, or whatever else his imagination might have dreamed up. He put his foot on the fence, grabbed it with both hands, and hopped over.

CHAPTER 2
WHISPERINGS AT THE DOOR

The clouds were back, but the rain had stopped. Strangely, the ground became wetter as Jonna neared the cabin.

Stepping onto the porch, he stomped his feet, cleaning them as best he could. The dried clods of dirt crumbled off without fuss. *Dried, hmm.* Jonna turned around, spotting where he had fallen by the shutter, and then followed the path to the fence with his eyes. He brushed a hand against his pants. They, too, were dry.

Shaking his head, he went to the front door. It closed behind him with a click as he walked in, but just to be safe, he locked the bolt behind him.

"You were gone awhile." Stephanie looked up from her book, smiling. "A whole two minutes."

"Two minutes?" Jonna distinctly remembered more time than that passing.

"I think the rain stopped before you got out the door, or maybe I was caught up in my book. Anyway, ready to go upstairs? I might be persuaded to stop reading." Her eyes sparkled.

"That sounds great to me." Jonna's thoughts drifted back to the man in green, but he shook the image away. No, nothing had taken place. It couldn't have. This was not the time to let Stephanie think he was crazy. "Let's go!" He took a step forward.

"My, my, aren't we in a hurry?" Stephanie laughed. Placing a marker in the book, she laid it on the table. "I wonder if this sofa might not be more comfy." She let one foot show, teasing him.

"Mayyybe." He drew out the word with a grin.

"No?" She pretended not to hear him. "Hmm, just a little more, perhaps?" She slid one long leg out and around, making a circle in the air. He followed it with his eyes until she slowly pulled it back.

She blinked with innocent eyes. "Still maybe?"

Jonna forgot to breathe. She was in a playful mood. The upstairs bedroom sounded better by the moment.

A tiny knock sounded at the door, almost undetectable. It snapped him back to the here and now. "Who is that?" Had the elf followed him here? Surely not! Elves and pixies did not exist.

"Who is what?" Stephanie looked around. "I didn't hear anything."

The tiny knock repeated, this time catching Stephanie's attention. She laughed. "Sounds like a woodpecker to me."

He loved her laugh; it helped him to relax, though the tension would not entirely go away. He smiled as her long blonde hair tumbled over one shoulder. "Sure, that's it."

Rubbing behind his ear, he tried to get a hold of himself. He heard the knock again but pretended to ignore it. Instead, he focused on her, prompting with an inviting smile, "Ready to go upstairs?"

"I might be persuaded." She played with the end of the cover. "If you carry me."

He bowed before her like a prince. "It would be my pleasure, m'lady."

She rose to her feet and curtsied. "M'lord."

Jonna moved closer, swept her up, and held her in his arms. He kissed her softly on the lips, held the moment, and then released slowly, making his way to the stairs.

"Oh, what big, strong muscles you have," Stephanie said playfully.

"Careful." Jonna laughed. The events outside the cabin were being pushed—no, shoved—out of his mind. "You'll make me drop you."

"Oh, really? Let me try that again."

"Stop." Jonna leaned against the wall, laughing. "This isn't as easy as it looks."

"Well," she said with mock hurt as he let her feet touch the ground. "I should be offended." Standing, she threw him a sexy smile. "But I'm not." She intertwined her fingers with his and led him into the bedroom.

With his other hand, Jonna pushed the door. It swung quietly from his touch, heading toward the doorframe. With a satisfying click, it closed, cutting off the tiny knock.

Stephanie laughed. "What are you doing? No one's going to peek in."

"Better safe than sorry," he said with a nod, stressing the point. He released her hand as she turned to face him with her back toward the bed. Her fingers softly traced up his arm as he added under his breath, "Who knows what might drop by."

A quizzical look crossed her face. "Did you say *what*?"

"I did, didn't I?" It was a Freudian mistake, but he still tried to cover. "I mean, er, who."

She shook her head, playing with him. "I highly doubt anyone will be coming to visit." Stephanie reached up, pulling him close. He let her, smelling her sweetness and tasting the touch of her lips before they came together.

Their lips met lightly at first and then gradually pressed into a long kiss. As they released, Jonna relaxed, moving his arms around her. He played his right hand up her back, ending at her long, soft hair. They moved gently toward the bed, gazing into each other's eyes.

"You're wonderful," she purred.

He sighed. "You're my magnificent love."

"I like that, you know."

"Like what?"

"The sparkle in your eyes when you look at me." Her smile brightened. "It makes me think you love me."

He could not help but smile. "I do love you, silly. That's why I suggested this in the first place. We needed to get away from the rush of the city."

She beamed, looking at him lovingly. "It was a good idea."

Stephanie was right. They had each grown up in the country, so being at the cabin relaxed them. After a while, the rush of the city seemed to drain them dry. Although, for some reason, Stephanie had put up quite a battle when she learned where he had planned to go. Stepping from his thoughts, he added, "I told you it would be fine."

"I know." She stretched, wrapping her arms around him. With a deep breath of the woodsy air held within the cabin, she toyed with the buttons on his shirt. He felt her finger push against his chest. "This has been on long enough. And look at the dirt on your clothes! Tsk, tsk, leave you alone for two minutes—"

He put a finger to her soft lips and then kissed them with his own.

She paused. "That was nice."

"I bet there is something else we could do that's even nicer." He slowly started kissing her neck, finding the buttons on her blouse.

She sighed with pleasure, giving a small giggle. "That's nice, too."

Between kisses, he whispered, "Don't worry. It gets better."

She felt his nibble. "Oooo."

This reality, he liked. Goodbye, imagination.

CHAPTER 3
PIXIES AND CHOCOLATE

Buzzing. Was there a fly in the room?

Jonna's eyes remained shut. To his right, he could hear Stephanie's slow breathing, but the buzzing kept his attention. He opened his eyes to see a swarm of glowing fireflies forming a sphere above his head.

In the middle of the mass hovered a tiny glowing person. From her, angry sparks shot off in random directions, fading away into the air. What was she sprinkling over his head?

As his eyes gained focus, his ears translated the buzzing into words. Was he being chewed out by a pixie?

Jonna moved, hitting his skull on the headboard. He muzzled an expletive just in time to keep from making more noise. Then he heard the words, "Who do you think you are? Running out when the queen needs you most!"

"I—you're not real." Jonna waved his hand. "Go away." He closed his eyes. When the buzzing didn't go away, he opened them again slowly. Sure enough, the tiny female was still floating above his face.

"Not a real pixie, am I? We'll see about that!" She raised her tiny wand.

He spotted something building at the end of the wand. "Hold it."

A strange violet enveloped his body, and he was lifted into the air. The cover slipped off. *Oh no! Where are my shorts?* He spotted them on the edge of the bed, grabbed them quickly, and pulled them on while still floating up. After the initial shock, floating did not seem too bad, at least until he realized he could not get down.

"Uh." He tried to think of a respectful way to address the pixie. "I don't believe that we've been properly introduced." He turned over to look at her.

"Believe me now, do you?" She smiled triumphantly, crossing her arms. "They always do."

"Um." He frowned, taking in the sizable number of fireflies. "Do you often come into other people's houses and make them float?"

She chuckled, daring him to contradict. "Only when invited."

"And how—" Jonna moved his hands, trying to express the words. "By chance, did we invite you?"

She motioned with a tiny hand toward the barely open window.

"I see. Might you tell me what this is about?" Imagination or no, he might as well ask.

Those were the wrong words. If pleasantries had been in order, they were gone now. "Young man, you know exactly what this is about!"

"Look who's calling who young." It came out before he caught his tongue.

The pixie glared. "I'll have you know, I'm over two thousand years old, and not a day younger."

Apparently, this was a sore point. "I see. Two thousand years would definitely make you my elder."

Still steamed, she continued, "It's not the size that counts, you know!"

"Yes, ma'am."

"And don't you be ma'amming me!"

That was a sore point too? "Yes, ma—I mean, what should I call you?"

"Dorothy!"

"Dorothy?"

"Yes, Dorothy! Officially, Queen Dorothy of the pixies, but you haven't any time for formalities right now!"

"Okay. Um, uh, Dorothy, wouldn't it be easier to have a civilized human to pixie conversation sitting down?"

Dorothy gave him a suspicious look. "If this is a trick—"

"No, no. No trick. Just a simple, friendly conversation between two, er, persons."

She considered him slowly. "Well, I guess we could—"

"Of course we could. It would be great. Just you and me and, well, maybe the fireflies? What do you say?" Jonna gave an encouraging smile.

Dorothy bobbed her head back and forth, thinking as if they had all the time in the world. Jonna glanced toward Stephanie. What would happen if she woke up and saw him like this?

This did not seem to be working. Dorothy was taking way too long. Surely he could offer something else? Food, perhaps? A drink? What had he seen in the kitchen cabinets? "Over hot chocolate?"

Her eyes lit up. "That might be nice."

Jonna descended, thankfully, at a very slow rate. He reached the bed with not so much as a bump and slid out quietly. Grabbing his pants, he spotted Dorothy watching. He whispered, "Do you mind giving me a little privacy?" *She didn't seem to be that old.*

Dorothy giggled but turned her head while he slipped on the rest of his clothes. He found his keys, billfold, and pocketknife, stashing them in the appropriate pockets. When finished, he tiptoed to the bedroom door and opened it silently.

All the fireflies and Dorothy followed him out, although they did wait a moment for a smaller firefly to catch up. As the door closed behind him, Stephanie continued to sleep. He spotted the kitchen entrance, hoping that there really was hot chocolate.

"Now then," Jonna began a little while later. In front of him were three cups of cocoa: one for him, one for the fireflies, and one for Dorothy. He had started to make only two cups, but Dorothy had insisted he not share with the fireflies. Who was he to argue?

"Tell me about the queen."

"The queen." Dorothy hummed but went no further, caught up in other thoughts. This went on for quite a while.

Finally, Jonna dared to ask, "Uh, Dorothy?"

"Yes?" She looked around as if she'd forgotten where she was. "Oh, sorry." She blushed. "Indulged in a few little memories, I did."

"I see."

"The queen," she began. "She is far older than you or me."

"Then she's old?" He tilted his head more toward her.

"Yes." She caught his look. "I mean, no. Yes in years, but so beautiful that her people fall madly in love with her forever."

That didn't fit what Sir Verity had said. "If her people fall madly in love with her forever, what's this I hear about the king?"

"Oh, that." Dorothy shook her head. "Such a silly thing, really. You know how love is. Hate can be just as strong. It seems the two had a falling out over an elvish girl—"

"I think I've heard enough." Jonna nodded. "The wandering eye syndrome."

"No." Dorothy flew back in surprise. "Not at all. This girl is their daughter, and—"

Jonna sighed and shook his head. "That's far worse."

"Will you stop that?" Dorothy waved her wand menacingly.

He sat up straighter.

"That's better. Now this girl, their daughter, decided she did not want to be"—she dropped her voice very low—"queen." He barely heard the last part. The pixie's eyes grew round.

15

"Queen?" he echoed at a normal tone.

"Shh!" Dorothy looked around. "That's not something commonly known to the average elf. It is only privy to the upper ranks. And, of course, we pixies know."

"I see." This conversation was taking an awfully long time, and at any moment he expected Stephanie to awaken. "How about we skip to the part about the duel?"

"That's an easy one." Dorothy sipped a little more hot chocolate. She looked at the cup. "This is so delicious."

"Thank you."

Dorothy sighed. "Now, the duel." She paused as if waiting for something unseen to happen.

After a moment, Jonna prompted, "Duel?"

"Shh," she answered, looking up. "There. I see it now."

He glanced around but did not see anything. "I thought—"

A soap bubble formed above Dorothy, growing to the size of a crystal ball. As it steadied, images crossed its surface: men on horseback, elves carrying spears, and burning trees casting orange glows. The scene changed, opening up to a field of battle. On one side, humans stood with weapons ready. On the other side, elves stood, the green of their uniforms working as camouflage. The bubble popped, and Jonna jumped.

"So you see," Dorothy admonished, "you must stop the war. You must fight the duel."

"Dorothy—" He picked his words carefully. "You still haven't told me what the duel is."

"Oh, that." She sipped the last of her hot chocolate, licking her lips. "Thank you so much!"

"You're welcome." He smiled, though it was somewhat forced. "About the duel?"

"I can't tell you that. That would take away all the fun!" Dorothy giggled, flew up into the air, and waved her magic wand. Little gold glitters dropped down all around the kitchen.

Jonna tried to scoot back from under them but was unsuccessful. In a terrified voice, he asked, "What did you do?"

A smug, pleased look crossed her face. "Why," she said with a grin, "I'm giving you a pixie blessing, of course." She laughed. "You're not bad for a human. I see why she likes you."

"Who?"

"Er, Stephanie, of course."

"You know my wife's name?"

"Of course. What type of pixie would I be if I didn't know everybody's name?"

He sat back and stared. "I have no idea."

Dorothy's voice took on a serious tone, and her eyes narrowed. "Be ready, Jonna McCambel. There are those around you who would see you fail." As Dorothy faded away, the fireflies vanished one by one.

Jonna stared at the empty kitchen—so much for her answering his questions.

"Jonna," Stephanie called from the upstairs bedroom, yawning. "Are you downstairs?" A creak came from above him. She had to be by the door, pulling it slightly open. By the tone of her voice, she was about to come down. The cups! Shoot!

Jonna went to stand. His knee whammed into the underside of the table. He fell back into the chair, gritting his teeth to keep from crying out. The floor upstairs groaned again.

He massaged his knee while grabbing the three cups and slid around the table toward the sink. There was no time to wash them. He put them in, ran the water, and rinsed. How was he going to explain this?

Her voice grew louder. She must have stuck her head through the doorway. "Jonna, are you coming back?"

"Right now, love." Jonna fought to keep his voice normal, looking back and forth to make sure all evidence of his meeting was gone. Maybe she wouldn't notice the wet cups?

A tiny voice whispered in his ear, "You have a surprise."

Jonna froze, not sure who had spoken.

"Say it," the voice whispered again.

"I'm bringing you a surprise," Jonna translated, while still trying to keep normalcy in his voice. By the sound of the floor, she had returned to the bed.

"Now," the small voice whispered. "Hold your hands out, palms up."

Jonna did, trying to figure out where the voice was coming from. It seemed to bounce from one shoulder to the other. Tiny sparkles materialized above the palms of his hands. A tray with two steaming mugs of hot chocolate appeared.

"Go," the tiny voice finished.

Jonna moved out of the kitchen, half-afraid to look back. He mounted the stairs, stepped into the bedroom, and closed the door behind him.

"You're so sweet." Stephanie's eyes sparkled as she laughed. "I guessed you were up to something!"

He grinned—if she only knew.

"For you, love." He moved to her side, placing the hot chocolate on the small table to her right.

She sniffed the air above the cup. "Smells good." Picking it up, she took a tentative sip. "Not too hot. Not too cold. Who would have known you could make the perfect cup of hot chocolate?"

Jonna paused, thought, and then nodded. "It took some magic."

"I bet." She reached over and kissed him, touching his arm with her soft fingers. "I'm sorry I did not want to come to the cabin. After I left my parents' country home, I never cared to go back. You've made it very romantic."

Puzzled, he crossed his eyebrows. "I never understood why you did not like the forest."

"It's not the forest—exactly." Stephanie looked thoughtful. "Sometimes we avoid things for the people we love."

"I don't understand."

She laughed. "Nor should you. Maybe someday I'll tell you." A woodsy breeze blew through the room, and Stephanie shivered. "That's cold."

"It does seem to be getting cool." Jonna looked around and spotted the problem. What had been a barely open window now stood wide open.

Stephanie pulled the covers around herself. Her voice trembled with a touch of fear. "Can you close that for me, honey?"

"Sure, love." His brows furrowed. She would not look in the open window's direction. Why had the wind triggered fear in her? He quickly moved to close it.

"No," a tiny voice whispered before he got there.

Jonna mumbled back, "I have to."

"Did you say something?" Stephanie asked, reaching for the hot chocolate.

"No," the voice pleaded again. "You'll lock me in for sure!"

Jonna covered. "I'm really glad you like the hot chocolate." He glanced toward Stephanie with a smile, moved next to the window, and closed off most of it, leaving a tiny temporary gap.

"Thanks." The voice sighed. "I've never been cooped up before."

The more Jonna listened, the more this voice sounded male.

"I take it Dorothy sent you?" Jonna prompted in a whisper. He looked out the window at the forest as a cover.

"Well, no, actually. I was just sort of curious, you doing the duel and all."

Jonna's voice rose. "Does everybody know I'm doing this duel?"

"Shh," the voice from nowhere answered. "She'll hear you!"

"You mean she'll think I'm crazy!"

"Shh," the voice answered again. "You'll be okay. Just stick with me."

"And you are?" Jonna fought to lower his voice, catching Stephanie's reflection in the window. Her book was in her hands.

"I'm Bob, short for—"

Jonna's eyes widened in fear. "Her book was downstairs."

"Yes, I—"

"She's going to suspect."

"No, she won't. It's all part of the magic."

"You have to get out of here!"

Bob squinted at Jonna. "Stop it!"

"Ouch!" Jonna slapped his ear. Did Bob just pinch him?

"You have to let me finish a sentence," Bob declared. "I'm here to help, you know!"

Stephanie put the book on the table. "What is so interesting about that window? Surely not more than me?" She blinked her eyes innocently, and Jonna relaxed. With the window mostly closed, her playfulness had returned.

"Er, the rain has stopped. The forest looks so peaceful."

Stephanie frowned. "I know you had your heart set on walking today. Maybe we can do that tomorrow—after it dries a little."

There it was. Though she did not say it, she always came up with a reason for why she could not walk in the woods. Even on the drive to the cabin, she had kept the window closed.

"See," Bob stated. "I told you I'd take care of it."

"Out," Jonna ordered quietly.

Bob sounded hurt. "What do you mean?"

"Out," Jonna ordered again. "You see that crack. Out the window you go."

"But you need me!"

19

"At the duel, I'll need you. This is time with my wife."

Bob made a poor excuse for a French accent. "Ah, to be in love! Oh, very well." He appeared beside the windowsill wearing green pants and a shirt with a brown belt. His outfit was almost identical to Sir Verity's. "See ya later." Sparkles materialized above him falling toward his feet. He took on a cartoon, frozen-in-place position and vanished. Jonna turned back toward Stephanie.

"You look nervous." Stephanie smiled. "I don't bite." She pretended to be coy. "At least, not usually."

He laughed. The tension melted away. Jonna backed up against the window, closing it completely and hearing the lock fall into place.

"Maybe I like it when you bite," he teased. Moving to the bed, he dropped down beside her. "Finally alone."

A faraway look crossed her face. "We are, aren't we? This place is nothing like the city: no cars, no people, and no smog. There are only stars and the forest as far as the eye can see." Her expression turned dreamy. It was strange, especially given her reaction just moments before. Did she believe in pixies and elves?

He shook his head—if she only knew. Jonna closed his eyes, remembering. "Like when I was a boy. I remember running through a forest and seeing an image in the water—" He sat up. Why did that particular memory come back now?

"Jonna?" She looked concerned. "What's wrong?"

He gave a nervous laugh. "Not a thing." His eyes swept around the room, expecting to see a firefly. "What shall we have tonight? A roaring fireplace or dinner by candlelight?"

"A roaring fire," Stephanie chose, a sly smile creeping across her face. "We can have candlelight tomorrow."

"Done." Jonna reached over, stroked her cheek, and kissed her. "It's two in the afternoon. I better go check on the firewood. If the cabin's proprietor didn't cut any, I might have to do it myself."

"Well—" She glanced at him, a mischievous glint in her eye. "If you're getting up, I should, too." Stephanie slipped out of the covers. His eyes never left her lithe form.

"That's not the way to get me outside." He leaned toward her.

"No, no, no." She put a finger on his forehead and gently pushed him back. "You have to wait till after dinner. I'm going to take a shower."

Jonna's eyes lit up. "Shower?"

20

"No, you don't." She laughed lightly. "Go cut your wood or whatever you need to do."

Sighing, Jonna rose and pulled himself toward the door. Why had he suggested a fire? At the moment, all good reasons escaped him.

He found the axe in the kitchen, shuffled around for a log splitter, and headed out the back door. He did recall what Stephanie had told him before their marriage. She, too, had been raised in the country and later headed to the city. Though she never said it, he suspected her childhood held some sort of bad memory. It took almost a year to convince her that a vacation here would be good for both of them. According to her own words, the cabin was not far from where she grew up.

A stock of tinder had already been prepared in a large wooden box. Beside it was a flat area with a small overhang for storing logs. Unfortunately, all the logs were gone.

Jonna hefted the axe with his right hand, letting it lie on top of his shoulder. Beside the tinder box was a small wooden wagon. He grabbed the cart's handle and headed toward a gate in the fence.

Cutting down trees was not his thing. Even as a boy, that never sat well. Instead, he decided to check the trail that led from the gate. He was certain there would be branches and trees already knocked down by the storm.

The gate snapped shut behind him. As it did, a feeling of euphoria came over him, followed by a wave of warmth. He shivered at the abrupt change in temperature. Was it a result of the trees forming a wind barrier? He found himself whistling as he headed down the path.

As soon as the gate was out of view, he found his fallen tree. At first, it looked like one brought down during the last storm, the branches snapping on impact with the ground. However, the closer he came, the more he saw that was impossible. The wood appeared dry and cracked. In places, the bark had fallen from it. It had lain there for quite some time.

Jonna stopped and listened to the silence. No fireflies appeared. No pixie voices spoke next to his ear. The previous events could have happened in his imagination. Some sort of hallucination brought on by his earlier disappointment? He would be perfectly happy if it all went away.

Removing the splitter from the wagon, Jonna spotted the best location to start chopping the trunk. He stepped up, raised the axe above his head—

A female voice shrieked, "How could you?"

Jonna froze, still holding the axe high. "How could I what?" Though he peered about, he could not see anyone.

"How could you cut down that tree? You are an awful human!" There was that word again: human.

Jonna lowered the axe, searching carefully for the voice. To his right, in the shadow of an oak, stood a female form. She looked quite shocked, her eyes wide, her lips quivering.

"I didn't cut down this tree," Jonna countered, annoyed. "I don't cut down trees."

"Oh yeah?" the voice challenged. She pointed. "Then what are those marks?"

His eyes followed her slim dark-brownish hand to the place she indicated. She was correct. A storm had not downed this tree. It had been cut. "You're right." He nodded. "Someone did chop it down." He turned to face her. "But that person wasn't me. I'm just getting wood for the fireplace."

The female sobbed uncontrollably, and Jonna hesitated. He had been prepared to go right back to chopping. Instead, he laid the axe on the wagon and stepped closer. "Ma'am—" He paused, unable to get a clear view of her because of the shadows. "I—I'm sorry."

Okay, idiot, Jonna thought. *Come up with something else brilliant to say.* Perhaps he could distract her. "But why are you crying?"

"The tree." She sobbed. "He was my boyfriend."

Jonna looked from her to the tree. Apparently, crazy was not limited to his imagination. "The tree was your boyfriend?" Jonna took a step back. "The *tree?*"

"Not the tree. The sprite who lived in the tree." The female sniffled with an extra-long boohoo. "And now he's gone away."

"I must be back." Jonna shook his head, looking around. "Where are the pixies and elves this time?"

The wood sprite looked confused. "What?"

"You wouldn't mind confirming where we are, would you?" He searched the undergrowth, listening for the sounds of pixies.

"What?" she repeated, still looking confused.

He volunteered, "This is the queen's forest?"

"Oh, yes." Abruptly, the weeping vanished. "The elves are wonderful to us." She smiled. "We help each other."

22

"Couldn't they tell you who cut down the tree?"

"I never thought of that." She gazed lovingly up at the sky. "Thank you. What a nice human you are! For that, you may have the fallen tree."

"Why, thank you." He bowed. "You are most kind." If he could quickly chop the wood and make it back to the cabin, he could get out of this madness.

The wood sprite giggled, watching as he took the axe and raised it above his head. She asked in a quiet voice, "What are you going to use the wood for?" The question halted the start of his downward stroke.

"My wife and I have a romantic meal planned." Jonna brought the axe down the rest of the way, hitting his mark. A deep cut scarred the surface of the trunk.

The wood sprite groaned. "Ouch." With her eyes going wide, she brought her hand to her mouth. "Oops, I'm sorry."

He paused, turning toward her. "It might be better if you don't watch."

The wood sprite nodded and smiled, turning her back to Jonna. However, he had the distinct impression she kept stealing peeks, though how, he could not figure out. No matter. He raised the axe up and brought it down. At the impact, the trunk shook.

"Oooo." She grimaced again.

Her reaction grated on his nerves. Maybe it would be better to pick up some branches. Jonna laid the axe on the wagon.

"You haven't finished the tree." Disappointment filled her voice. "What's wrong?"

Jonna laughed, sure this was what she wanted all along. "How can I cut a tree you loved? Would it be better if I pick up the branches?"

"Would you?" she pleaded, her eyes dancing with excitement. "I know my boyfriend's gone, but I—"

"I would be honored." He reached down, brought up a small twig, and handed it to her. "This is for you to remember him by."

"Oh—" Sap-like tears flowed down her cheeks. "You are so thoughtful and kind." The wood sprite took the stick from him, hiding it somewhere near her tree just out of sight. "And for your kindness—" Her voice was jubilant as she turned to face him. "I have a gift for you, but you must come closer to receive it."

"A gift?" Jonna stepped closer. For the first time, he noticed her long brownish hair falling in curls down to her waist. It waved and blew even with no wind to stir it. Combined with her delicate face and slim body, the look was quite alluring.

CHAPTER 4
A SPRITE WITHOUT SPITE

The wood sprite took one of his hands, turning it palm up. She stared into his eyes.

"Three are one, and one will hold. The forest of the queen will bless. This human who has traveled far will in these woods now find his rest." She stroked his hands softly. "There," she finished, placing three small twigs within his hand and forcing his fingers to grasp them. "Use these wisely, and they will be a protection in all your endeavors."

"Thank you." He nodded as a peaceful calm drifted over him. Something resonated in the air, a sweetness he had not heard before. The wind—the wind sang through his fingers like branches on the trees.

As he gazed into her eyes, they drew him in, covering him, hiding him within the softness of her touch. Her flowing hair, the delicate fingers—before his eyes, his skin darkened.

Sir Verity appeared behind Jonna. "Snovipa, what do you think you're doing?"

"He's mine." Snovipa dared him to interfere. "He has come to me freely."

"Nay," Sir Verity countered. "He is new to these woods and does not know your tricks. Tell him the truth of the fallen tree."

Snovipa stood firm, refusing to speak.

"Tell him, or we'll cast judgment on your own tree."

Snovipa's eyes widened. "You wouldn't!"

"I would," the elf warned.

"Very well." She looked back toward Jonna. He heard the exchange but seemed frozen to the earth. "I'm sorry." Her pouting voice sounded more like singing. "The fallen tree was not my boyfriend. I did not know him at all."

Something released Jonna when he heard the truth, and he realized what she had been trying to do.

"You attempted to turn me into a tree?" He stepped back, his skin returning to normal as the darkness faded away.

Snovipa stared at the ground, still pouting. "I was lonely."

"But you have all these other trees!" Jonna waved his hand, pointing them out.

"I know. But you were so kind, and—" Her words dropped off. "I really am sorry." She gave him a puppy dog look with her large brown eyes. "It's just my nature."

Jonna glanced toward Sir Verity.

The elf nodded. "She is sorry. Though mischievous, she is not evil. She does like you."

Jonna sighed. He felt more like himself with every passing moment, but the sprite's magic still lingered. "All right." He breathed. "I forgive you."

Snovipa's face brightened into a smile.

"But only if you promise not to do it again." He gave her a stern look.

She nodded, her eyes bright. "I promise!"

He started to hand the three twigs back.

"No, no. They are a gift. Keep them, and they will aid you in your endeavors."

"What endeavor? To get wood? Are you sure?" He looked to the elf. "Sir Verity?"

"She has no more power over you," the elf reassured. "Now you know her name."

"He's right, you know." She winked at him mischievously. "But I'm glad you do know. Now you can visit me without fear, and here you will always have a friend." Her eyes twinkled in the sunlight.

Though Jonna was sure he would be cautious if he ever met her in the future, he nodded. "Thank you."

"A wise human," Sir Verity stated as both he and Jonna turned away. "The spells of sprites are not easily resisted. You did well."

"What do you mean? She caught me!"

"Nay." The elf shook his head. "If she had, you would have already been a tree instead of only changing into one as I found you. You delayed her magic."

That made him feel better—not.

They passed the wagon with the axe still lying on top as they moved down the trail.

"Are you ready to meet the queen?"

Jonna swallowed. "The queen. I almost forgot. Um, Sir Verity, I realize you see me as some sort of dueling hero—"

Verity became adamant. "That's what the pixies say. It must be so."

To Jonna, it seemed like Verity was trying to convince himself.

26

"Well, okay. I'm not questioning the pixies, but I have a wife and wood to gather for tonight, and—"

With one finger, Sir Verity made a circle in the air. From nowhere, three elves emerged, taking the wagon with them.

"Your wood is taken care of. You will be back in time to see your wife. Are there any other reasons why the queen should be *put off*?"

"Put off?" Jonna did not like that implication, although he knew Sir Verity was right.

"Not many have the gall to make the queen wait."

"She's waiting for me?" Jonna swallowed. "Why me?" He stopped. "Oh yeah, the pixies said so." His mind said *walk away*. Whatever these creatures were, they had to be nuts. However, they obviously weren't going to let him go right now.

Verity nodded, pointing to a side trail. It was narrower than the one they were on, and they were forced to move in a single file as the elf took the lead.

"What weapon are you proficient with?" the elf asked, following the weaving path.

"Weapon?" That was a thought. Maybe he should have a weapon. The only things in his pocket were keys, his billfold, a pocketknife, and three sticks. Unfortunately, the knife was too small. He'd have to throw it at them to do any damage.

"Yes, weapon. How else are you to do the duel?"

Jonna stepped over a branch, catching another that Sir Verity released. "That's a good question. To be honest, I really don't know. I'm more of a hand-to-hand type guy."

"You used the axe well."

"That was chopping wood. I did that a lot when I was a boy."

"Hmm." Verity ducked a branch, and Jonna did the same. At the next bend, a clearing appeared with elven smiths hard at work. The amount of noise they made should have been heard for miles but did not go beyond the clearing.

Seeing the question on his face, Sir Verity volunteered, "The trees and the wind protect us. This is something most humans cannot understand." He looked for something in Jonna's face. "If you are to win this duel, you must know what we fight for."

"I think I do." The back of Jonna's mind tickled as if struggling to release a thought. He could almost grab it, but not quite.

Sir Verity shook his head. "Not yet, but the time will come. Then, you must choose."

"Choose what?" Sir Verity's tone spoke of things unsaid. Was it a hidden message or a warning?

"We will talk later." Verity turned to face one of the elven smiths. "Show me your weapons."

The smith bowed, backed away from the forge, and disappeared into a tent. When he returned, he carried a long, wrapped-up cloth. Placing it on the ground, he unrolled the cloth to reveal a large assortment of weapons.

Verity looked to Jonna. "Choose."

Jonna's eyes traced the long line of weapons. There were swords, halberds, spears, and more, each with its own pocket that held it secure to the cloth, but none of these weapons caught his eye. "I do not see one."

Sir Verity huffed. "These weapons have been forged by the greatest of the elven smiths. How can you deny their worth?"

Jonna gazed at them again. He went down the line one by one, shape by shape, but shook his head. "None of these are a weapon I can use."

"Tradition states a warrior is to present his weapon to the queen and swear an oath of loyalty." Verity looked disgusted. "How can you do this without one?"

It was a good question, and Jonna had no idea how to answer. The noise in the camp stopped. All eyes gazed upon him as he gave Verity a thin smile and shrugged.

"Hmm." Sir Verity's eyes narrowed, and he snapped in an icy tone, "Let us proceed to the queen."

The smith nodded nervously. He rolled up the cloth and hurried into the tent.

The trail stopped at the far side of the clearing. The only way out appeared to be the same path they had taken in. Jonna turned to look this way and that. "Where now?"

"You think too limited, Jonna McCambel." The elf's tone melted only a tiny bit as he pointed a finger up.

As Jonna followed it with his eyes, he forgot to breathe. In the furthest heights of the trees, a city sparkled like diamonds. The light of the sun bounced from building to building and platform to platform. A basket with a curved top for a covering and windows in the side, large enough for a group of five, dropped down in front of them. Sir

Verity stepped inside, waving Jonna to follow. Watching the transport glimmer, Jonna did.

"Where's the rope?" Leaning out a window, Jonna tried to get a better view. From a side angle, he could make out a series of thin, near-transparent cords, twisted together, holding the basket up.

"It is a special elven rope made from spider thread." Sir Verity watched Jonna's face. "Do not fear. Though it is thin, it will not break."

"Breaking never crossed my mind." However, the words did make Jonna look down as they ascended, which was not the best choice. It appeared to be a long way to the bottom.

The basket came to a landing and stopped. Jonna stepped out and immediately grabbed the handhold.

Sir Verity chuckled. "Most humans act that way their first time here."

That raised some interesting questions. Jonna held the first one ready. "You've brought other humans here?"

"Upon occasion." Sir Verity did not smile. "You are one of the few to be welcomed."

And that answered most of the others. "Then I am privileged." He bowed slightly to the elf.

"You are," Sir Verity assured, chin still a tad in the air. "Show respect and all will be well."

Jonna could not help but respond to the warning. "That has a slightly ominous ring." He observed elves assembling to watch on the platforms and walkways around them at various levels through the trees' branches. Not all looked happy. In fact, some even looked mad. "Are you sure I should be here?"

Sir Verity took the lead, his hand staying near his weapon. "It is at the queen's request."

Okay, so not all the elves liked humans. Then again, he remembered the first time he met Sir Verity. The arrow in his bow had not been a toy.

Jonna looked to the right and saw a small elven boy poking his head between his parents and trying to get a better view. Jonna smiled. The boy ducked back. "Skittish, aren't they?"

"Most of the children have never seen a human."

"How odd—" *Well, come to think about it, how many humans had ever seen an elf?*

"Sir Verity, is there currently a war with the humans?"

"Not officially." The elf turned to the left, choosing a larger path. The route angled around the present tree. It hit several intersections and moved toward the largest building. There was no way to tell how far they walked, and the forest below gave no clues.

One of the citadel guards stepped forward. "Stop, by order of the queen!"

Sir Verity stood his ground. "This is the one. Let the human pass."

"It is forbidden. No human may enter the queen's citadel. No human is allowed to see its secrets."

Sir Verity glared at them, and his voice boomed. "Do you doubt the word of the pixies?" The ferocity was enough to make a person cower. "Move back. It is the queen's command."

Both guards stood their ground despite their nervous twitches.

On the wind, a soft, delicate female whisper stirred the heart and soul, cutting through the tension. "Enough."

With no more argument, the guards returned to their places, ignoring the presence of both Sir Verity and Jonna.

The female voice continued, "Let the human wait in the foyer. I would speak with Sir Verity alone." This had to be the elven queen Dorothy had spoken of. Jonna could still hear the pixie's words in his head.

Past the doors, Sir Verity motioned for him to step into a small room just off the main hall. "Wait here."

Bright white cushions threaded with gold adorned benches that held ornate pictures sown in a way Jonna could only guess. A carafe and water bowl sat on a table to his right. Around the bottom of both, a border of mystical creatures danced in a tribute to joy.

A musical female voice called out, "Please, be seated."

He saw no one as he entered, yet the voice came from somewhere in the room.

"Would you like something to drink?"

"Water, please." Jonna glanced around but still could not catch sight of the person. He looked toward the table and watched. The pitcher rose and poured water into a glass. The outline of a slim young woman appeared, her light-colored hair dancing in the sun. Jonna felt his face warm and quickly closed his open mouth.

She smiled at his unspoken compliment. "Can you see me now?"

Jonna nodded but temporarily lost his voice.

She winked at him. "I wanted to meet you before my mother did.

Please don't tell."

He cleared his throat. "I—no."

Her musical voice caught him off guard. There was a hint of familiarity to it, like a song he knew but could not remember. The water well from when he was a boy came to mind. Could it be?

"You have come to save our people?" She brought the water to him, and their fingers touched as the glass exchanged hands. A tingle went up his arm.

"When word came that a hero had been found, rumors flew throughout the city. No one guessed it was not an elf." She sat down, motioning him to do the same. "Oh—" She blushed. "You must think me terribly rude. My name is Elfleda, Princess of the Woodland Forest."

Still gaining his composure, he took a breath and focused. "I—I was given to understand you did not like that title." Uh-oh, what had he just said? He remembered the pixies' warning.

"The pixies make too much of many things." Elfleda musically laughed, sending tingles up his spine. She looked at him curiously, each word she spoke going through him. "There are some secrets better left unsaid, even for them."

Oh, my lord, this could not be happening. No wonder the elvish people fell in love with their queen. But there was something else also. Recognition?

She abruptly became shy. "Did the pixies mention anything else?" Elfleda glanced away as if expecting to hear something—something she was not sure he knew.

He thought back. "I heard your dad wasn't too happy, either." *Was that a look of relief on her face?*

She smiled, tossing her hair, and tiny magic glitters flew off in all directions. "That's just my father." She waved his statement away. "Though I will admit my choice did anger him."

"So you do not wish to be queen?"

A mischievous twinkle hit her eyes. "We shall see. It might even depend on your choices today."

Surprise crossed his face. "My choices? Why?"

She paused, listening.

He tried but heard nothing. These elves certainly had good ears.

"Someone's coming. I must go." She faded from view, her voice trailing off like soft, musical bells.

31

Sir Verity walked in. "The queen is ready. We need—" He blinked at Jonna. "Why is your face so red?"

"Face red?" *Oh, my!*

Sir Verity looked around the room. His eyes narrowed, but he remained silent. "I see," the elf finally said. He checked each corner suspiciously and then turned away. "Come, Queen Freya awaits."

Jonna already knew Verity's thoughts without anything being said. No one could meet the queen or her daughter and not show the signs. Jonna placed the full glass of water on the table beside the pitcher. He had even forgotten to drink.

He followed the elf down the hallway to a circular chamber. A lemniscate inlaid in gold decorated the center of the floor. Around the sides of the room were exhibitions of artifacts, documents, armor, and weapons. A display to the right caught Jonna's eye.

"The queen will be but a moment." Sir Verity waited, head lowered. He elbowed Jonna, nudging him to follow his lead.

They stood before the huge doors of the throne room. As the light glittered from the carvings, Jonna could see the elves' history presented in a pattern around the room. However, no matter how hard he tried to keep his eyes averted, Jonna felt compelled to move toward a particular display he had seen, despite Verity's warning.

"Verity," Jonna whispered, trying to keep his voice low. Something about this place made him whisper, although he did not know why. He pointed toward the display. "What's that?"

Sir Verity glanced in Jonna's direction, catching the view of a sword thicker at the tip than the handle. "The Rune Blade of Knowledge," the elf answered, a curious look crossing his face. "Why do you ask?"

Just hearing that the sword had a name should have been enough to discourage Jonna. It did make him swallow, wondering what was going on, but he continued despite this. "Remember you said I would know?"

Sir Verity paused and turned very slowly to gawk at him.

Jonna might as well continue. He had gone this far. "That's the one," he finished, then saw Verity's expression and knew something was wrong. Somehow, some way, he had just violated a multitude of rules.

Sir Verity held very still. All expression left his face. Unexpectedly, he spoke. "If you can take it from the case, the blade is yours."

There was nothing ominous in that, right? "Uh, okay."

Sir Verity stood there, watching, waiting for Jonna to move. "Well?"

Though it still pulled at him, Jonna was not sure he wanted to try. "Should we wait for the queen first?"

"You're stalling." The elf's eyes narrowed. "If you are the one, take it."

The phrasing of the words caught Jonna's attention. Not *if it is the one*, but *if you are the one*. He turned to look at the weapon. It gleamed with light bouncing in ways metal should not reflect. It spoke to a part of him he could not even comprehend. As he first saw Sir Verity standing by the tree, so the impression was no less real.

Time seemed to hold still, though he knew he moved. In a blink, he was there, standing before the display, ready to lift the blade from its resting place. With a hand that felt unreal, he reached forward and grasped its handle. The moment he touched it, the hilt changed, fitting his palm and adjusting to his grip.

The Rune Blade glowed, pulsing with a life of its own. Jonna turned to face Sir Verity and found the room full of elves all bowing before him. At that moment, the doors to the great throne room opened, and in walked the queen.

"Jonna McCambel." The queen's voice flowed out across the chamber. The musical tone sounded much like her daughter's, but firmer, more elegant, and more controlled. "Come forth."

The elves parted, opening a path to Queen Freya. At the same time, they turned and faced the queen.

Sir Verity waited, watching as Jonna approached. Was that amazement on the elf's face? Jonna believed it was.

"Place the Rune Blade on the pedestal," Sir Verity whispered, motioning with his eyes.

Jonna watched as the whole room glowed. The closer Jonna came, the more the pedestal matched the light of the sword.

The queen spoke again. "Jonna McCambel."

Jonna's gaze fell on Queen Freya. Trapped by her soft blue eyes, he could not turn away.

"Our kingdom is in dire need of a hero, one who will not run from the challenge he must face. The tasks you will undertake will not be easy, nor are you guaranteed success. Will you accept this challenge?"

The sword called him to action. Pictures flashed through Jonna's mind, and as they did, his life before the cabin felt more like a dream. Only one thing stopped him: Stephanie. Stephanie, his wife. She waited for him, now, at the cabin. Maybe she was reading a book, or maybe she was preparing for the night's fire. Was this fair to her? Did he have the right to risk his life?

This place felt real. He thought back to the story he had started to tell Stephanie in the cabin bedroom. The face in the water had happened, but he had never seen it again—until today. It was the face of Queen Freya.

Sir Verity cleared his throat, bringing Jonna from his thoughts. The queen's question demanded an answer spoken aloud to all in the room.

Bob slid up behind Jonna's right ear. "What are you waiting for? Do it! Say it!"

Jonna opened his mouth and tried to speak the words, but his voice would not come.

Sadly, Queen Freya shook her head. "Very well, you are not ready." Her voice, though musical, held an icy touch. Jonna could feel it in the air around them. Her disappointment made his stomach sick. He blurted out, "It's not that I don't want to. My wife—"

With a smile, Queen Freya gave a single nod, pushing the sadness away. As she turned back toward the throne room, the glow that lit the chamber faded. With it, the pulsing of the sword diminished until only the light of day reflected from its blade.

Jonna turned to Sir Verity, pleading for him to understand. "I can't take the chance."

Sir Verity stated without emotion, "I will take you back." Though he did not say it, disappointment laced his every word.

Jonna sighed. Did no one understand? Did they not see what he could lose? Real or not, how could he take the chance? Doubt stabbed at his conscience.

Bob fumed, "How could you not?"

Had Bob read his mind?

The pixie pushed. "How could you not say yes? Yes! That's all it took, one little word!"

Steeling himself against the onslaught of his own mind, Jonna held to his decision. "Bob, I can't take the chance."

Bob bellowed in Jonna's ear, "You're afraid!"

"Of course I'm afraid. What man wouldn't be? Risk my life for a world that is not even real, or at least doesn't exist in my own? How could Stephanie accept that?"

"Stephanie," Bob stated with defiance, "would have told you to do

34

it!"

"Oh, would she?" This conversation was getting under Jonna's skin. "I think I know her better than you do."

"Do you?" A mischievous look crossed the pixie's face. "You humans are all alike: afraid of risk, and afraid of a challenge. Let's just sit back in the status quo—"

Jonna's face flushed crimson. "I think that's enough. Maybe it's time you left."

"Maybe it is," Bob roared back. "Go, have your boring life. Forget the fact that an elvish kingdom will be destroyed. Goodbye, Jonna McCambel!" Bob grabbed Jonna's ear and pinched.

"Ouch! You little—" Jonna slapped near his own ear but only succeeded in hitting himself. He turned, checking the area around him. Everyone had left except two: Elfleda and Sir Verity. He swallowed. For the princess to be disappointed would be more than he could bear, although why, he did not know.

She stood by a side door. Jonna was certain she had been there the entire time. The sickness in his stomach grew. Despite the sad smile on her face, she approached. It would have been easier had she just gone away.

Elfleda glided, her long elven gown flowing behind her, until she stood on his left side facing the Rune Blade.

He barely got the words out. "You heard."

Elfleda nodded. The sadness did not go away. "You did the right thing," she said more to herself than to him. "Just as I did the right thing in refusing to be the next queen."

At least someone was on his side. Then the last part of the sentence hit him. "Why don't you want to be queen?"

"You saw my mother. I could never be all that she is, nor would I want to excel her. She is the Queen of the Woodland Elves. There can be no other. Besides—" She smiled. "I am in love with someone else who is not prepared to live here."

Jonna's heart fell at the words *in love*. Now he was being silly. He was married to Stephanie. For all the glitz and glimmer of the elves, Stephanie was real. Right? He shook his head. Determining reality had become difficult.

"But when the queen dies—" he continued, hoping his own voice would give him respite from the war in his mind.

"Elves do not die," Elfleda stated as if he should know better. "At least, not by natural causes. There is no reason for me to be queen. And you, Jonna—" She turned to face him. "You truly love Stephanie that much?" Twinkles danced in her eyes.

Jonna nodded.

"It is an interesting thing, love," the princess stated. "It can turn lambs into heroes, and heroes into lambs. Go. Enjoy your life with Stephanie. Love is the most powerful magic of all."

Footsteps approached behind them. By the sound of the echo, Jonna knew Sir Verity drew near.

The male elf nodded with respect toward the princess and then turned to face Jonna.

Jonna sighed. "Is it time?"

Sir Verity gave a single nod. "Excuse us, Princess."

"I should have said yes," Jonna said abruptly. Both Elfleda and Sir Verity stopped.

"No," Sir Verity countered. "You are not ready. You said this yourself."

"But your people." Jonna's stomach was churning worse by the moment.

Calm finality focused Sir Verity's words. "Things will happen as they should. If we are to leave this place, leave we shall."

"Leave?"

"We do not die as humans. We simply fade."

The doom of the statement came out in Jonna's words. "All of you would leave?"

Sir Verity nodded, and Elfleda agreed. The male elf continued, "To prevent war, our kingdom here will disappear. The land will be left to the humans."

"Without a fight? Why?"

"It is the choice of our queen."

"You cannot do that." Jonna looked at the walls around him. "This place, all its wonders—you can't let it go away." He reached out and gripped the Rune Blade. "I'll do it."

"No." Sir Verity shook his head sadly. "It is too late."

36

CHAPTER 5
THE LAST OF THE ELVES

Jonna waited, expecting the Rune Blade to pulse to life, determined to see the light shine bright in its reflection, but nothing happened.

Elfleda placed her hand on Jonna's, forcing him to lay the blade back on the pedestal. "No, Jonna, your decision was final. You cannot go back."

"I can." His eyes darted from Elfleda to Sir Verity. "I can!" But the protest weakened. The elven faces said it all. Reluctantly, he released the Rune Blade and turned away. "It is too late, isn't?"

Neither Sir Verity nor Elfleda answered.

"I've let everyone down."

"No," Elfleda encouraged. "You have a vacation, and a cabin, and a wonderful life. Your years will be long, and—" She looked up as if seeing something. "I see the possibility of children. You will be happy." She put her hand on his arm. "And you will believe this was all a dream."

A warm wind stirred outside the building, but Jonna felt a cold breeze inside his heart. The weather in the forest was changing. The leaves would soon drop as fall arrived.

Sir Verity cleared his throat. "We need to leave. Remember the time?"

Jonna nodded, but his head drooped as he followed. How could he be so stupid? If Stephanie knew, she would think him a coward. No, he was not a coward. He was practical, level-headed, and had a family to consider. These pixies and elves showed up in his life and tried to mess it all up. How dare they! Who did they think they were?

They passed out of the palace, across the winding branches that supported the city paths, and descended in the basket held secure by spider silk. None of the elves turned out to see him go. Not even the elves that disliked him watched him leave. The two walked away in silence.

As the path before them opened, Jonna's eyes narrowed. He studied Sir Verity. The elf appeared so poised, always acting so special. Where was his family? Could he so easily risk losing it all? Forget them. Forget them all!

They reached the gate in the cabin fence. Jonna barely remembered getting there. The wagon, the axe, the splitter, and the wood waited for him as promised.

Sir Verity watched his face sadly. "It's all here. Good luck, Jonna McCambel. May Mother Earth bless you." The elf stepped back and faded from sight.

Jonna roughly pushed the gate open and stepped past with the wagon in tow behind him. A shiver went through him as if he were passing into something cold. The gate slammed shut.

Gray clouds had overtaken the sky. The dark, heavy bottoms gave the promise of rain.

The elves had done a wonderful job. All the logs had been cut the same length. Jonna placed the wood under the outside shelter, picked up an armful, and carried it through the back door.

"You're back!" Stephanie's voice leaped to life. She danced from the living room into the kitchen, threw her arms around him, and kissed him. "I'm glad you're back!"

Jonna forced laughter into his voice. "Me too, silly. But let me put down the wood."

She noticed the difference in his tone and followed him into the living room. "Jonna, is something wrong?"

He gave a lame smile. "Why do you say that?" Three of the logs he put in the fireplace. The other two he sat to the side.

"Your voice. Your expression. You act like the world fell apart. Did I do something wrong?"

Jonna closed his eyes momentarily. *Okay stupid, straighten up. You're going to bring her spirits down, too.* "No, not at all." Jonna forced a smile on his face, trying to figure out how to explain and not seem crazy. "I just had a hard time in the forest. The wood was…difficult…to find, and cutting it seemed impossible."

"Aw, I'm sorry to make you work so hard. Let me make it up to you." She started to unbutton his shirt. His hands came up and caught both of hers.

"No, no. Remember what you said before the shower? That's dessert." He laughed. However, his lack of enthusiasm concerned him. For the first time, he actually did not want to do that now.

"I know," she agreed, smiling whimsically. "We'll see how long dinner really lasts." Stephanie winked, sniffing the air. "Smell that?"

The whiff made his mouth water. "That smells good. What is it?"

"No, you don't." She stopped him from going back into the

kitchen. "If you want more wood, you'll have to bring it through the front door. This is a surprise." She spun around and went back to the stove.

Jonna sighed. Who needed elves with a wife like that? To the right of the fireplace sat a utility closet. Opening it, he looked around. Inside he saw a box of matches along with rolled-up newspapers.

Pulling them out, he turned to the hearth and stuffed the paper under the logs, then struck the first match. The head of the match flared, caught the edge of the paper, and curled it as it burned. Something about it reminded him of the pixie soap bubble.

Stop it, he reminded himself. *It is over. There are no pixies. There never were any pixies.* His hand bumped against his pocket, and he remembered the three twigs Snovipa had given him. He pulled them out and started to toss them into the fire.

"Jonna," Stephanie called. "Can you help me a moment?"

He teased, "You mean I can come into the kitchen?"

"Yessss," she played. "But only if I blindfold you."

Jonna laid the twigs beside the extra logs. If nothing else, the sticks would make good kindling. "That sounds fun. I take it there's a surprise in store?" He got up, following the sound of her voice.

"Just come here, silly."

Rounding the corner, he spotted the kitchen table.

She caught his look, warning him with her eyes not to do anything other than what she asked. "Help me bring this to the living room, and no tasting the food."

"It wasn't the food I wanted to taste." He reached over and nibbled her ear.

"I see." For a moment she let him, but when he started kissing her neck, she stopped him. "Here." She handed him the tray. "Living room. Now. You had your chance."

"Okay." He pretended to be sullen but couldn't help a smile. He placed the plates and bowls on the coffee table, hiding the tray behind the sofa. Stephanie brought the drinks.

Jonna gazed up at the ceiling and tried to get into the romantic mood. "The lights." He dashed to the front door, flipped the off switch, and returned quickly.

Firelight danced around the room, giving it a reddish-yellow glow. He reached over and touched Stephanie's cheek. She turned to look at him.

Jonna spoke with all his heart. "You know I love you."

She nodded slowly. "I know you do. I love you, too." She smiled, her eyes twinkling in the firelight. "Even at the expense of the elves."

Jonna blinked. His heart skipped a beat. He heard the words, saw her lips move, but the last statement was not her voice.

"Stephanie?" Jonna pulled back, still looking at his wife's face.

"Yes, Jonna?"

Stephanie's body answered, but the voice—

"What's wrong, love?"

Jonna moved back toward the fireplace. "Who are you?" His mind whirled with no place to land. He bumped into the wall and stopped.

"What do you mean? I am your wife. Are you all right?"

"No." He swallowed. "You are not Stephanie. What did you do with my wife?"

Stephanie smiled. "Maybe we should head back to the city tonight."

"No."

"You're acting *irrational*." She stressed the last word.

"No!"

"Jonna," the strange voice said. "Look at yourself. You don't even know what's real."

Jonna sat down by the fireplace, his right hand landing on the three twigs by the logs. He closed his eyes and then opened them quickly. "Say that again?"

"You don't even know what is real." Disbelief showed on her face. "How can you know what is imaginary?" Her eyes dared him to ask more.

His low voice became a whisper. "How would you know that?" All his senses tingled, saw, read, and deciphered the little things that did not fit.

Stephanie's face lost the smile as her lips pulled into a thin, hard line. "Have it your way." Her face changed. "We could have been happy together."

"You are not my wife."

"No," a different female voice answered. "I am not." Stephanie became a dark-headed woman who stood to her feet, her countenance showing what was in her heart. "Did you really think we would let you save the woodland elves?"

He stared. "How do you know about the elves?" This made no sense.

The woman ignored the question. "You've betrayed your own kind. You don't deserve to be human."

A tiny knock sounded at the door. The dark-headed woman's eyes narrowed.

"They can't save you, you know. You betrayed them and your wife."

"What?" How did he betray Stephanie? Fireflies danced at the window, and for a moment Jonna thought he saw Dorothy pushing at the glass. "What do you want?"

The dark-headed woman laughed. "You, of course." She raised her hand, flipping it palm side up in his direction. "Nostrum Contorium."

Light built at the edge of her fingers as energy pulled from the surrounding walls. Jonna could see Queen Dorothy staring, her face jammed against the window, eyes wide, screaming and shouting in his direction. As the energy reached its peak, the dark-headed woman smiled maliciously.

"Goodbye, Jonna." She gave a single nod. "I'll make this as painless as possible." As the energy lanced out, Jonna threw up his left forearm. His right palm inadvertently landed upon the twigs. He grabbed them, trying to keep from tumbling backwards.

The room exploded with light so bright he dared not open his eyes. Someone screamed, but in what direction he could not tell. As the brightness faded, the firelight returned, and Jonna looked around. The dark-headed woman was gone.

"Stephanie!" Jonna leaped to his feet and ran through the cabin. He threw open the bedroom door but found no one in there or the shower. His feet thudded on the wooden stairs as he raced to the kitchen, only to find no one. He hastily swept through the guest room. *Where was she?*

Now standing by the front door, he looked to the right and saw Dorothy, face still plastered against the window, begging to be let in. Unlocking the door, he threw it open wide.

"They took her! They took Stephanie!" Jonna breathed hard, forcing out the words. Dorothy flew in, took him by the arm, and sat him down on the sofa. A firefly turned on the lights.

"Jonna, I think it's time you know the truth." She looked to the fireflies and demanded, "Go. Keep watch."

Jonna sat up straighter. He had never seen Dorothy act this way. Good. He was serious, too. "I'm listening."

Dorothy gritted her tiny teeth but nodded. "The problem is—I don't know how to begin."

There was no time for games. She needed to know that right up front. His voice firmed even more. "How about the beginning?"

"That, unfortunately, would take too long." She sighed uncomfortably. "And we don't have the time."

Jumping right to it, he demanded, "Who has Stephanie?"

"That's part of the problem." The pixie shifted position on the coffee table. "We don't know."

His nostrils flared. "Did the elves take her? If they did this just to make me fight—"

"No, no, no," Dorothy cut him off. "It's not that simple!"

"How is it not that simple? Somebody took my wife. Somebody tried to kill me—" His anger forced away all words, his body shook, and his fist clenched. This was no way to find his wife. He had to get control.

Jonna breathed slowly, in through his nose and out through his mouth, struggling to slow down the thumping in his chest. With the calm came reason, and with the reason came another question. "Why didn't I die?"

"Check your right hand."

Jonna raised his right hand and saw that he was still holding the twigs his palm had landed on. "The twigs?"

She nodded.

"How?"

"Snovipa gave you protection from her own tree." Dorothy pointed toward the forest. "There is no stronger defense against dark magic, save one other."

"Dark magic? Dark magic kidnapped Stephanie?" Jonna shook his head. "We are off the subject. How do I find Stephanie?"

"You don't," Dorothy said, but something in her voice said that was not entirely right. She shook her head. "It's so complicated. Oh, I told her not to do it!" The pixie seemed to be talking to herself.

"Told whom not to do what?" Jonna growled. "Who did you tell?" He heard the frustration in his own voice rise. "What are you talking about?"

"Oooo." Dorothy gritted her teeth tighter, but then her eyes lit up. "Find Princess Elfleda. She will find your Stephanie." Dorothy looked out the door, worry lines showing on her face. "But you must move quickly!"

42

Jonna looked out at the forest. The sun had set, and the clouds hid the moon. In the distance, he could hear thunder. "I'll need a flashlight." He started to rise.

"Wait." Dorothy motioned to one of the fireflies guarding the entrance to the house. It buzzed over, making lazy circles in front of Jonna. "Hold still," she cautioned, and tapped her wand twice over its tiny head. The firefly grew in brightness, casting light all around the room.

"There," Dorothy proudly announced. "Your flashlight." She laughed. "And he doesn't need batteries."

CHAPTER 6
THREE LITTLE WORDS

"Thank you, Dorothy."

Jonna placed the twigs safely in his pocket and headed out the door. The firefly stayed to his right. He reached the fence, threw the gate back, and stepped through.

The change felt strange. There was something about this place. This place of elves and pixies, this place outside the cabin fence—it belonged, and yet it was not part of his existence. It was like stepping into a different world, one hidden and normally out of reach.

Jonna headed down the trail, noting wagon tracks. Hoofmarks stood out as well: some coming, and some going. By the way the marks shifted, this had happened multiple times.

Turning a corner, he came to Snovipa's tree. She was nowhere to be seen. Could she be asleep? Though he did not want to wake her, he could not remember the way to the elvish city. He whispered, "Snovipa?"

"Jonna." Snovipa's voice sounded sleepy. "What are you doing out here so late?" A dark-skinned hand appeared from the side of her tree, followed by a head tilted sideways. Her voice held a playful note. "Shouldn't you be with your wife right now?"

"Something terrible has happened." Jonna could hardly get the words out of his mouth. "Someone's taken Stephanie."

"Oh, my!" Snovipa slipped quickly from the tree and moved closer to him. "Are you all right? How can I help?"

"I need to find the elvish city."

She looked around, listening to the wind in the trees. "Good, we're alone." Snovipa looked at Jonna very seriously. "Only the elves know the way to the city. Only they can find the path."

"But I know it's here," Jonna pleaded. "Sir Verity took me up just a little way and turned to the right. The path appeared before us."

"The path opens only for the elves." Snovipa shook her head. "Even my magic cannot bring it back."

"Then what can I do?"

She took a deep breath, the wind playing with her long, dark, woodsy-scented hair, and then nodded. "Got it. Down the trail to the left is a small cottage. When humans come by, I hear them speak of many things, and one of them mentioned a mage, a friend to the elves. Maybe he can tell you the way."

Jonna took her hands, kissing her on the cheek. Her cheeks turned a darker brown. "Thank you, Snovipa. You are the best!"

She blushed further as he finished the words, watching as he turned to go. The firefly hurried to catch up, doing its best to stay on his right.

"Farewell, Jonna McCambel. The woods go with thee." Snovipa pulled back into her tree.

The mage's cottage was not as far as Jonna thought. Either that or he made good time. Not even a flashlight could have brightened the path like that firefly's glow. The insect drove back the darkness.

"There." Jonna pointed. "You think that's it?"

The firefly buzzed several sounds. Crazy as it seemed, Jonna was starting to understand them. "Yeah, I know. Be careful."

The light in the cottage flickered. Smoke issued from the stone chimney, though that was the only part of the cottage that was stone. Everything else was wood, and the home had a straw roof. Jonna reached the one crooked door, hesitated, and raised his fist to knock.

A loud voice boomed, "If you're gonna do that, you might as well knock the door off the hinges. It is not locked. Just open it!"

Jonna looked at the firefly. It whispered a few buzzes.

"Well," the voice inside said in agitation. "Don't make me have to get up!"

Jonna pulled the door handle, which was nothing more than a piece of rope secured through a hole. The bright orange glow of a raging fire broke the darkness, temporarily blinding him. He blinked, stepping into the cottage. The musky smell of things left too long unclean and the bubbling of liquid in a cauldron assaulted his nose. Jonna sneezed.

The mage waved his hand. "Ambrocate!"

Jonna blinked. "Ambro what?"

"I said ambrocate. Ambrocate. Are you hard of hearing?"

Jonna laughed, extending his hand. "I'm Jonna McCambel."

The mage pointed his staff in Jonna's direction. "Don't you be friendly to me! I was not born yesterday! State your business or be gone!" He looked Jonna in the eye.

"Okay." Jonna studied the wrinkled man's face. "I need to find a way to the elf—"

"Ha! No you don't!"

Jonna narrowed his eyes. "Yes I do, and you really should let me finish."

"My house, my rules, young one, or do you intend to attack an old man, hmm?" The wizened old mage poked his staff in Jonna's direction again.

Jonna took a step back. "N-No." He shook his head, not sure how the conversation had turned sour. "I mean, it is rude to—"

"It's a rude world, sonny, and no one gives a care. Don't you know that by now? Everybody just wants what they want. Take, for instance, this last young lad who left the woodland elves to die."

For the first time, the mage noticed the firefly, not an easy feat in the bright room. He looked back to Jonna, a funny look on his face. "You did know about that, didn't you?"

He answered cautiously, "I may have heard something, but there's a little more to the story than that."

"Oh really?" the mage mocked. "How 'bout you tell me then, Mr. Sage. As a matter of fact, why don't you sit over here when you do it?" The mage smacked a chair that was within range of his staff.

Jonna jumped at the sound. "Maybe I ought to stand."

"Have it your way." The mage stared at him. "Well?"

The firefly buzzed something in Jonna's ear. He nodded.

Jonna began. "I heard the young man was concerned for his wife, who didn't believe in pixies or elves."

"Not believe in pixies?" The mage laughed with all his might, tightly closing his eyes. He finally opened them and looked at Jonna. "Not believe in elves?" A roar of laughter filled the cottage again. After a couple minutes, the mage settled down, wiping the tears from his eyes. "You must be an entertainer. I haven't laughed that good in years."

"But it's true." Jonna tried to press the point without being too abrupt.

The mage huffed. "And I suppose he was afraid to lose her as well?"

Jonna nodded slowly.

"And when he got home, he found she was gone?"

Jonna nodded even more slowly.

The laughter dropped out of the mage's voice. "And now he's trying to find her." The mage stared him in the eyes.

Jonna stood there, looking back at the mage, not quite sure what to think.

"Not as old as I seem, am I?" the mage said more quietly. He touched his temple. "I've been around. You must be Jonna."

"I—I am, sir."

The mage smiled. "That's better. According to Dorothy, you have quite a mouth."

"You know Dorothy?"

"Of course I know Dorothy. We have a cup of hot chocolate every other Sunday."

Something about that did not sound right. How could Dorothy have told him anything?

"But this is Friday."

"Really?" The mage smiled slightly. "What does today have to do with Dorothy's conversation with me?"

"In order for her to have told you last Sunday—"

The mage cut him off. "Can they not divine the future in your world?"

"I—I don't know, sir."

"Then maybe that's part of the problem, hmm? No wonder you don't know what to do."

Jonna looked at him, trying to decide what to say. "So you knew I would be here tonight?"

"Nope, it was the firefly that gave you away."

"Firefly?"

"Yes, firefly. Don't you think I know a pixie guard when I see one?"

"You're a guard?" Jonna turned to look at the firefly, which buzzed something back. "He's a guard in training," Jonna countered, turning toward the mage. "And proud of it."

The mage laughed, and suddenly, so did Jonna.

"It is good to meet you, sir." Jonna's voice grew serious. "Snovipa told me—"

"Who?"

"Snovipa, a wood—"

The mage held up his hand. "I don't mess with wood sprites. They're a little too possessive."

"I wasn't saying—" Jonna stopped and stared at him. "You like to pretend you're hard of hearing."

The mage smiled. "Do I? How about we get to the point? You need to get to the elf city, and I need you to get there."

Eyes widening, Jonna continued to stare at the mage. "You do?"

"How else are you going to save the elves?"

Jonna's tone held a warning. "I need to save my wife." For the first time, the mage appeared to listen.

"Jonna," the mage said quietly. "By saving the woodland elves, you will save your wife."

A half-skeptical look crossed Jonna's face. "I will?" *Did he promise?*

"Yes, but there's something you have to do first." The mage reached toward a small jar and opened the lid, pulling out an amulet that was missing a stone in its center. He handed the amulet to Jonna.

"What is this?" Jonna held it in his hand, looking back at the mage.

"Find the stone for the center, and it will guide you to the elves." The mage tapped his staff on the ground three times, listened, and frowned. "I think we are going to have visitors."

Jonna started to drop the amulet into his pocket.

"No, no. Around the neck." He watched Jonna do as he was instructed. "Good. Now, before they get here, you need to remember three things. I want you to say them with me: Unum."

"Unum."

"Clastor." The mage paused, waiting.

Wondering where this was going, Jonna mimicked, "Clastor."

Satisfied, the mage continued. "Fillum."

"Fillum."

"Now say it again, seven times fast."

"Unum." Jonna thought. "Clastor." He thought again. "Fillum."

"Faster." The mage put his hand to his ear. "They're coming."

"Unum, Clastor, Fillum."

"Faster."

"Unum-Clastor-Fillum."

"Good." The mage nodded. "Faster."

"Unum-Clastor-Fillum." Something was happening to Jonna. His skin was becoming transparent.

"Don't stop," the mage warned. "Keep going!" His eyes went to the door of the cottage.

"Unum-Clastor-Fillum. Unum-Clastor-Fillum."

"Good, now listen. You are now invisible, and this cottage is about to be vandalized in ways I've never experienced. No matter what you see, no matter what you hear, do not speak. If you do, they will see you. Do you understand?"

Jonna nodded.

"Good. Now, when this is over, head to the north. Do not worry about a path. There you will find a small stream. Follow against the

49

current until you come to a large cave. Once there, you will find the stone you seek inside."

Jonna started to ask a question but stopped, remembering the mage's order not to speak. If he was invisible, how could the mage tell what he was doing?

The mage turned to the firefly. "Hide, young one, or you won't make full guard!" The firefly disappeared just as running horses heeled to a stop outside the cottage.

"Knock, knock," someone outside called, kicking in the door. It bounced across the room and struck the wall.

The mage continued to sit in his chair. "Can I help you fellows?"

"We're looking for a human who betrayed his own kind." The lead man's eyes narrowed. "Have you seen him?"

The mage shot back, "Does it look like I've seen him? I'm an old man. I don't dabble in foolishness."

The intruder laughed. "That's what I told 'em, right, boys?" Chuckling came from behind the leader.

"But Charles here"—the man reached back, pulling Charles roughly by the shoulder—"said you were lying."

Charles looked from the mage to his boss. "I did?"

"Yes, you did." The boss nodded, turning to fully face the mage. His voice became deadly. "You've been called a liar, mage. What say you?"

The mage just sat there and smiled. "Do you get all your women that way, or do you have to chain them down?"

"Shut up." The lead man stepped forward, striking the table in the middle of the room. It cracked in half.

Jonna moved a little to the right as the man kicked the table leg, making it fall.

"When we're through with you, you'll be begging to die."

"I think not." The mage raised his staff and struck the bottom on the ground. The ground shook. Things on the shelves fell. Even the men had a hard time standing. "I think your attitude needs a little adjustment. Calipso Mostratum." The mage's words boomed around the room. The sound of his voice erupted against the men. An unseen force picked them up, held them briefly in the air, and tossed them out the door.

The mage dove for the floor and whispered, "Get down."

Jonna ducked. Something hit the outside of the cottage, ripping at the roof and walls. Boards jerked off. Roofing material flew into the air. The mage crawled for cover. Pieces of furniture rose from the ground and jerked backwards through the walls.

Jonna continued to jump back and forth, dodging the shifting debris, yet unaffected by the pull himself. It made no sense. How could he be affected by one and not the other? He considered dashing out of the hut but refused to leave the mage.

The warning the old man had given him went through his mind. *Do not speak.* He moved closer to the mage.

Raising his voice over the wind, the mage growled, "What are you doing?"

Jonna nodded toward the roof.

"I'll be all right. Just go!"

Jonna shook his head.

"Leave me be!" The mage attempted to pull away just as a cottage beam fell. It caught him, pinning him to the ground. "Leave," the mage demanded.

Jonna went to the beam and tried to lift it, but it was too heavy. Only leverage could make it move. He picked up one of the broken table legs, made a fulcrum, and lifted the beam off the old man.

"Fine. Now go!" But the mage's eyes showed appreciation.

Instead of leaving, Jonna chanted, "Unum-Clastor-Fillum." At the first sound, he faded into sight. "Unum-Clastor-Fillum."

"No, no, no," the mage said in exasperation. "There's not enough time to complete the spell again. Run!"

"Shut up," Jonna stuck in quickly, rather enjoying it. "Unum-Clastor-Fillum. Unum-Clastor-Fillum. Unum-Clastor-Fillum." The entire roof ripped off, torn away by the unseen force. The walls rent backwards one by one, showing a horde of black-capped, pointed-hat mages. They all wore masks, with their attention directed at Jonna and the owner of the hut. "Unum-Clastor-Fillum."

"No," one of the black-capped mages shouted, reaching a hand toward them. He wore a pendant bearing the mark of a skull. "Stop them!"

Jonna placed a hand on the old mage's arm. With finality, he said the phrase the seventh time. "Unum-Clastor-Fillum!"

CHAPTER 7
A MAGE IN TRAINING

Fire bolts shot from the circle of dark mages, striking over and over at the spot where Jonna and the older mage had been. The ground burned. The wood around it caught fire. Enraged, the dark mage with the skull pendant raised his hands, and a huge ball of flame crashed into the center of the cottage. Flames leaped around them like wisps of wind brushing the skin, but they did not burn. It was the last thing Jonna saw as those attacking them faded from view.

Jonna tried to see, but there was only darkness. "What happened? Mage, are you there?"

"Call me Väinämö."

The older mage was somewhere to his left. "What happened? Why is it so dark?"

"How should I know?" The mage chuckled. "That spell was meant for one, not two."

That distracted Jonna from the darkness. "There are singular and plural spells?"

"Of course, just like there are singular and plural words." The mage looked toward Jonna's voice. "You don't know much about magic, do you?"

"Not at all." Jonna shook his head. "Where I come from, there is no magic."

"There's magic." Väinämö smiled. He raised his left hand, rubbed two fingers together, and said, "Erebos illumini." The top of his staff glowed to life. "There. That's better." He could see Jonna now. "Just because you don't know something doesn't mean it can't exist."

Jonna's eyes went wide as he thought back. "The firefly! Did he make it?"

"I would suspect he is already talking to Dorothy." Väinämö studied Jonna thoughtfully. "He listened and got out, unlike someone I know."

"I couldn't leave you there."

Väinämö paused, pursing his lips. "I suppose you couldn't. Perhaps that's why Dorothy chose you."

"The pixie chose me?" Jonna's eyes narrowed. "That's what Sir Verity said. I'd like to know why."

"Well—" The mage cleared his throat and became careful with his words. "Maybe I should say—" He paused. "No, no, she chose you all right, but it was a long time ago. Of course, there were other factors involved too—" He stroked his beard. "But that's not my place to say."

Squinting, Jonna stared at him. "Does everyone here speak in riddles?"

"Only when we want to." Väinämö gazed past Jonna as if studying something in the darkness. "I think we can go back now."

"Won't those, whatever they are, still be there?"

"You mean the Dark Mages?" Väinämö scratched his chin. "Dark Mages are only truly dangerous in groups. Their power is weaker alone, all except, perhaps, the first." Väinämö hesitated as his gaze turned to Jonna. "But back to the point. I don't think they'll be there because—" He looked Jonna in the eye. "They get really nervous about hanging around when they've just been outsmarted." The mage winked and grinned at him. "Ready to go back?"

"If we don't know where we are, how can we get back?"

"Grab my staff, and chant again."

Jonna looked warily at the staff glowing in the darkness. He remembered the thump Väinämö had given that chair. "You're sure?"

Väinämö nodded. "I'm sure. It won't bite."

"I've heard that before." Jonna reached out, touched the staff, and chanted the phrase seven times.

The darkness vanished as the world faded into view. Both he and the mage stood in the cottage. Well, sort of. Not much was left.

Väinämö kicked one of the scraps still burning and sighed. "I needed to fix it up anyway." He spotted a trail of hoofprints leading away from the clearing. "Do you remember the directions I gave?"

"Yes, sir, er, Väinämö." The light of early dawn streamed through the trees. How long were they away? At the cabin, it had been late evening.

"Good. Begin." Väinämö started to fade from sight.

"But where are you going?"

"I have other things to attend to." He waved a hand in Jonna's direction. "Go. Shoo."

Jonna took a few tentative steps toward the woods and then looked back at Väinämö's waning form.

"Shoo! Your way lies different from mine." The mage's words trailed off as he vanished.

54

Jonna stood a moment, hesitating at the debris. What type of people were he dealing with? Though he asked the question, the answer really did not matter. Whoever they were, they had Stephanie, and he would follow them to the ends of the earth. He dove into the foliage.

A short time later, he found the stream, just where Väinämö had said. A cool breeze swept through the trees, intertwining with the branches. He thought of Snovipa enjoying the leaves as they floated down toward the ground. She relished and was part of nature. Yet the elves weren't trying to enlist her help. Why had they chosen him even before Stephanie had been kidnapped?

He looked down into the gentle stream, remembering something like this from before. When he was a boy, out on the farm, he had found an old well and seen a face in the water.

No, he wasn't crazy, but no one would believe him. It was not his face in the reflection or a distortion by the wind. The image of a woman had formed. She had long, light hair, blue eyes, and had smiled back. Later, even his best friend had laughed, saying, "If you don't stop talking about it, everyone will think you're nuts."

His friend was right. Jonna stopped talking about it. He even stopped going back to the old well. Eventually, he pushed the event from his mind. Not until he met Stephanie in college did the memory slip into obscurity.

Why did he think of that now? He did not know it at the time, but now he knew whose face it was: Queen Freya's. When she walked into that elvish chamber, the memory had come flooding back.

Jonna turned to the right, heading along the bank. The water gurgled, speaking in whispers, running in the opposite direction. What did it say? Something about a cave.

It bubbled, "On the right side, in a hole by the wall, the Jewel of Wisdom you will find. Place it in the holder bare. See the city of your mind."

Jonna listened. The short song repeated over and over again. The mage said magic was everywhere, even when you did not expect it. "Why would the stream help me?" Jonna thought aloud. "Why can I hear it speak?"

"I can answer that." A small man stepped out from the edge of the trees, dipping his cane into the water. "Did that change the song for ya, now?"

Jonna jumped. The man seemed to have come from nowhere. "And you are?"

"O'Conner McBear, at 'ur service." He tipped his hat toward Jonna. "I see the mage gave ya the medallion." He nodded enthusiastically. "Fine piece of work it is, if I say so myself."

Touching the medallion around his neck, Jonna held it up. "You know what this is?"

"Gave it to 'em from me own pot-o-gold." McBear nodded, leaning toward Jonna. "A gift we don't often do."

"Pot-of-gold? You're a leprechaun?"

"Bingo. Give the man a cigar." He reached into a coat pocket, pulled out a cigar, and offered it to Jonna.

Jonna shook his head.

"No matter." He stuck it back in, and it disappeared. "Just more for the future. I take it you seek the stone for the medallion?"

"Why, yes." Behind the leprechaun, Jonna could hear more movement in the bushes. "If you know what this medallion is, perhaps you could help me find the stone."

"Why would I do that?" O'Conner made a funny face. "When I just want my medallion back."

Jonna pulled the medallion to his chest. "I thought you gave it to the mage?"

"Duress, duress." A chant came through the trees. All along the bank other leprechauns appeared, forming a line by the stream.

"You see—" O'Conner tilted his head. "No leprechaun freely gives anything from his pot-of-gold. Väinämö caught me one summer morn and forced me to show him my pot. It was either give him the medallion, or he'd take the whole kettle." The leprechaun extended his hand. "Now, I want it back."

"No." Jonna stepped away, closer to the stream and further from the little man. "I need this to find the elvish city."

"Come now, laddie." O'Conner sighed. "Give me the pendant, and I'll take ya to the city. Leprechaun's oath." He held up two crossed fingers and gave a big, wide grin.

"Only the elves can find the city." Jonna stepped back again, his foot finding a tree trunk across the stream. He stepped up, getting his balance. If nothing else, he could cross to the other side.

"Then why do ya need the medallion?" McBear countered through gritted teeth. "It's not that hard." He advanced toward the tree trunk.

"Or would you rather fight for it?" The leprechaun waved his cane in front of him.

It looked so funny, Jonna stifled a laugh. "You can't be serious?"

"Oh, but I am." O'Conner leaped forward as Jonna backed up once more. He somersaulted over Jonna's head and landed behind him on the trunk.

Jonna spun around. "I really don't want to hurt you."

O'Conner swung at Jonna's knees. Jonna jumped and then ducked as the leprechaun's cane just missed connecting with his head.

"For having no weapon, you do well," McBear admired. "How about this one?"

The leprechaun lunged, somehow slipped through Jonna's guard, and jabbed him in the stomach. The blow forced Jonna to bend forward and brought the medallion within the little man's grasp. Jonna jerked back, knocked the leprechaun's hand away, and lost his balance. He frantically reached out, grabbing for anything, and found O'Conner's cane.

A look of surprise showed on McBear's face right before they tumbled from the trunk and hit the water. Down Jonna dropped. As the current caught his body, he knew it was taking him in the wrong direction.

No! He tried to turn around. The mud on the bottom squished through his fingers, and his hands slipped off the rocks at the stream's sides. He shoved against the bottom, stirring soil to muddy the clear water. His body rose enough to hit the surface, allowing him to gasp for air before bobbing down again as the current grabbed hold once more.

I am going to drown. Statements of fact were something Jonna knew well. His practical side always kept him out of trouble—until this moment.

There was nothing practical about this strange world, and now he was going to die. Pictures flashed through his mind: the cabin, Stephanie, Sir Verity, Stephanie, the elvish city, Stephanie, Freya, Elfleda, Väinämö, Stephanie . . . His mind began to fade.

Though he struggled to reach air again, something held him down. The surface appeared as shiny mirrors somewhere above his head. He looked down at his ankles. Wisps of white wrapped around them, pulling him further down the stream. The stream was alive? His eyes widened as he tried to focus.

O'Conner was not doing much better. Just to Jonna's right, the leprechaun struggled with the same strange wisps. No matter how much the leprechaun thrashed, he could not break free.

I wonder . . . Jonna mumbled the chant Väinämö had given him, reached a hand out, and grabbed O'Conner. The leprechaun's eyes darted toward Jonna, but the small man was too busy fighting the wisps to shake off Jonna's grip.

One, two, three, four, five, six—six times. At the seventh chant, he shouted underwater, "Unum-Clastor-Fillum!" Bubbles swirled out. Water sucked in. The view changed.

He landed on an unleveled floor, his chest heaving as he spewed water into the darkness. "O'Conner," he coughed, "you okay?"

McBear's response did not sound pleasant. He, too, coughed up water. "That I am," he said at last, looking around. "But where are we?"

"I don't know." Jonna tried to peer across the darkness but saw nothing. "It was the only thing I knew to do."

"Well, laddie." O'Conner tapped the floor around him with his cane. It sounded solid. "It seems ya saved ar' lives."

Jonna frowned. "If I take us back, we'll be right back in the stream. We have to find another way."

"Then it's time for me to do the helping." O'Conner tapped his cane three times. A rainbow appeared, spreading colors in all directions. He reached out his hand to Jonna. "There's no place I can be without a way to me pot-o-gold." He laughed. "Grab on."

Jonna no sooner caught O'Conner's hand than he found himself flying through the air. Distance did not seem to matter. The darkness gave way to trees and sky. The scenery around him blurred. In less than a moment, he stood beside a huge cauldron filled with gold, not to mention sparkling jewelry and gemstones.

O'Conner sighed, gazing at his cauldron, and then grinned at Jonna. "Home at last." He motioned to the pot. His eyes grew round, the grin dropped, and he looked suspiciously at Jonna. "I've been tricked again!"

Jonna looked at the pot-of-gold, remembering the stories he'd read about myths and magic while growing up. "No." He waved the leprechaun's implications away. "I helped you, and you helped me. Call it even."

"Call it—" A bewildered look crossed the leprechaun's face. "You can't do that!"

"And why not?" Jonna looked around him. O'Conner set a nice home.

"It's improper, that's why. What type of leprechaun would I be if I did not live up to me promise?"

"You never promised me anything." Jonna shook his head. "And I never wanted your gold."

"Never wanted the gold? I cannot believe me ears! A human not wanting a leprechaun's gold?" O'Conner held his chest. "There's never been such a thing!"

"Just let me keep the medallion."

O'Conner stopped. "So that's 'ur angle." He closed one eye and stared at the medallion around Jonna's neck. "It's really to go to the elvish city?"

Jonna nodded.

The leprechaun exhaled slowly. "Why do ya want to go there?"

"I have to find a way to save the elves. They know the secret to saving my wife."

O'Conner tapped his toe, and his face contorted as he thought. "Oh, very well. Ya can keep the medallion, but if I find out ya're lying—"

"I'm not," Jonna assured. He crossed his heart.

O'Conner pulled back. "Enough! Don't play with religious symbols here!" He looked around as if expecting something to happen and prepared to guard his pot-of-gold. When nothing did, the leprechaun relaxed. Turning back to Jonna, he pointed the cane. "Back to the stream. Back to the water. Place this human on his right path."

The scene faded. A moment later, Jonna dropped, landing on the right bank of the small stream. It happened so fast, it took a moment to catch his breath. A glance around showed the leprechauns were gone, leaving no footprints. Picking himself up, he noticed that his clothes had dried. How had that happened? Had it happened on the flight to the pot-of-gold? He shook his head. At least he would not be trudging in wet clothes.

"It's time to find that stone," he said aloud, remembering what Väinämö had told him about the cave.

"Yessss, it isssss," something hissed from the foliage behind him.

CHAPTER 8
ASK THE NEIGHBOR

"Who is it this time?" Jonna turned around to look. "I'm getting really tired of playing games."

Something stirred in the foliage as he stood waiting.

"Why don't you show yourself?"

"Cccccertainly," it hissed again, sliding out between the roots.

"You're a snake." Jonna stated the obvious.

"Thank you. I like living up to my reputation."

Jonna thought about that one. "No, I mean you're a talking snake."

"It takessssss all kindssssss." The snake slithered around Jonna, checked the water, and swerved slowly about to face him. "The water nymphsssss like to play tricksssssss, even on usssss snakesssss."

Jonna thought back. "You mean the strange white wisps that wrap around your legs and pull you down the stream?"

The snake nodded. "Exxxxactly. Why do you think it'ssssss sssssso hard to come up for air?"

"Hmm, it was curious." If there were tree sprites, why not water nymphs too? Jonna nodded, but this line of thought was getting him off track. "Why do you want to help me?"

"I can go where you can't," the snake offered. "I can move in the dark without having light."

"And why would you do this?"

"It issss in both our bessssst interesssssst." The snake adjusted position, looking toward the cave. "Sssssshall we?"

Jonna always considered himself a fast walker, but even he felt a little winded trying to keep up with the snake. The cave, which fed the stream, came into view. Its entrance was large enough for Jonna to enter upright. He stopped a little ways from the mouth. "What assurance do I have that you will give the stone to me?" If he was going on alone, it had to be now.

"Assssssssssuranccccce?" The snake stuck out its forked tongue. "Why would you doubt me?"

"For one thing"—Jonna looked him in the eye—"I've only known you a short time, and for another, you're a snake."

"Sssssso, you judge all reptilessssss by their ssssskin?"

Jonna did not expect that, and it made him wonder how smart this snake really was. "Well, no, but then I don't normally talk with reptiles."

"I sssssssssee. Well, if you don't want my help, I cccccccertainly undersssssssstand." The snake headed off into the forest.

Jonna watched him disappear around a rock and whispered to himself, "Maybe I was wrong?"

"What wasssss that?" Startling Jonna, the snake stuck his head out from a rock ten feet over.

"I said—" Something about this did not feel right. "Thank you for your offer, but I think I really should do this alone."

The snake bobbed its head up and down. "Asssss you wissssssh." It seemed to smile as it slithered over a larger rock. "Sssssshould you need my help in the future, just call out. I live along thissssssss ssssssssstream."

Even though the snake had left, Jonna did not feel much better—if the reptile was, in fact, gone. No matter, he had to find that jewel. He stepped toward the cave entrance, traveled around the rocks, and slammed into something solid.

Pulling back, he blinked, trying to clear his head. What was that? Reaching forward, his hand encountered an invisible wall securing the entrance to the cave. Using crossing stones to hop to the other side, he discovered the wall stretched all the way across, as high as he could feel. How was he going to get in?

He looked to the stream. A portion of it came from the cave mouth. However, the memory of the white wisps wrapping around his ankles stopped him from trying to swim under the barrier. No thank you.

On one side of the cave, close to the edge, he spotted a rock with a flat side. Jonna read the words carved into it. "He who wishes to cross must not be seen."

"Be seen by whom?" he thought aloud. He looked about to see if anyone else was watching. If so, they were staying well hidden, including the snake. Thinking back, he mumbled the spell Väinämö had given him.

His skin went transparent, as did everything attached. He stepped up to the invisible wall, stuck a hand forward, and smashed it.

Dang! He pulled back, shaking his hand to distract from the pain. After making sure nothing was broken, he looked back at the words. Maybe he had read them wrong. No, they were the same, but obviously there was some secondary meaning, or else he would have passed through. What was he trying not to be seen by? Perhaps that was the real answer to the question.

"Had enough?"

Jonna stepped back from the barrier, looking for the voice.

"Yeah, we know you're there. Just because you disappeared doesn't mean you've left. Right, Wilbur?"

"He's right, you know." Wilbur elbowed his friend. "Me and Wallace know all the tricks."

Jonna followed the voices. Two chipmunks sat on a ledge just to the right of the cave. They were looking in the wrong direction. Actually, it was not so much in the wrong direction than at something else.

Within their sight was a small tree worm inching its way up a branch. Whenever they stopped talking, it walked.

"We're gonna tell." Wallace picked up an acorn and cracked it. "Some bird's gonna have a real nice lunch."

The inchworm stopped, looked both ways, but saw no birds. It called out, exasperated, "If you two keep chattering, you'll get me eaten!"

"That's the idea." Wilbur laughed. "You have no business in our part of the forest."

"This is as much my part of the forest as yours," the worm growled. "If you don't like it, stick an acorn up your—"

"Now, now," Wallace cautioned. "No reason to be nasty. Besides, don't you realize with just a couple of jumps, we could squash you?" He showed his big feet. "You wouldn't want that, would you?"

"I'm tougher than I look." The worm made a face, lifted himself up, and stood tall. "Do it!"

"Have it your way." Wallace leaped over a branch, jumped off a rock, and dropped to hit the worm's twig.

The worm ducked, anticipating the strike, and tried to move to the side. Jonna, still invisible and having stepped up behind the worm, batted Wallace out of the air. The chipmunk flew backwards.

"Ay, caramba!" Wallace bounced off two flat stones and fell next to Wilbur, his eyes bulging. "Sheesh, what did I hit?"

"I can't believe it." Wilbur rubbed his eyes. "Did he really hit you?"

The worm peeked above the branch.

"No way." Wilbur stood up, stepping back for a good run-jump. "I'll get him."

"You go, Wilbur!" Wallace rubbed a spot near his tail. "Just watch out for his—"

Wilbur launched into the air, almost reached the branch, and shot back with a double twist flip, landing on top of Wallace. Both chipmunks looked at each other with bulging eyes.

The worm moved to the top of the twig and raised the front part of its body. "Care to try again, boys?"

Wallace's and Wilbur's eyes grew even larger. Without another word, they scampered off into the forest.

"Thanks." The worm looked directly at Jonna.

Jonna smiled. "You can see me?" Immediately, he became visible.

"Of course." The worm chuckled. "I'm an insect. We use different senses than most mammals. Although, when you first approached, I was a little wary. But as soon as you batted that first chipmunk—" The insect laughed. "I can still see the expression on his face."

"Glad to be of service." Jonna nodded. "Well, I've got a cave to get into." He turned to walk away.

"You're trying to get into a cave?" The worm turned in the cave's direction. "Which direction is it? Move that branch so I can take a better look."

Jonna pulled the branch back, giving the insect a side view.

"Oh, that cave." The worm nodded. "That's a beauty, that one."

"What do you mean?"

"Not very many know the secret of how to get in."

Jonna eyed the worm. "Do you know?"

"Sure, but before I tell you, you need to know why it's protected."

That made sense. There had to be a reason. "Say on."

"Many years ago, a very bad mage came to this forest. He was not bad at first, or at least he did not act so. However, he was after something of great value. He vowed to stop at nothing to get what he wanted. In order to keep him from finding what he sought, a series of caves were set up with spells as guards. The spell not only protected the entrance but also caused the item he sought to move once a day from cave to cave. There was a pattern to the move, you see. Got it?"

The insect waited for a response. Though the point to this story was eluding Jonna, he nodded anyway.

"One day, the mage figured out the pattern, but he was faced with a dilemma. In order to pass the protective barrier, he could not be seen. In order to do that, he was told he had to become something else.

64

Without thinking, he used his magic to change himself into a snake, and immediately gained access to the cave. No sooner did he enter the cave than he tried to change back, but it was too late. His informant had not bothered to tell him about the second part of the spell. Its magic would trap him in the form he took until the day his power was broken. The words inscribed beside this cave are a memento to that great event."

"So—" Jonna considered. "Why is the shield still in place? If the mage was stopped and turned into a snake—" He thought back to the snake that offered to help him. Surely it couldn't be the same one, could it?

"Why take it down?" The worm shook his head. "What good is a memento without some evidence of why it's there?"

"O-kay." Jonna looked puzzled. "I suppose there could be a rationale to that. So, you are saying I can't get into the cave because I can't turn into a snake, and even if I did, it wouldn't help me?"

The worm chuckled. "Not at all. Had the mage bothered to check his sources, he would have known there was a better way. And since you've been so helpful—" The worm looked around as its antennae shifted directions. "Come closer, and listen very carefully."

Jonna moved his head nearer.

"Okay, there are a few things you'll need. First, you'll need a bucket of sap."

Frowning, Jonna repeated, "Sap?"

The worm angled his head. "You want to get in, don't you?"

He nodded. "What else?"

"You might also want some spare clothes. And leaves. Lots and lots of leaves."

It seemed a little strange, but what didn't in this world? Jonna tried to make sense of the combination. "Are we making something? Sap, clothes, and leaves?"

"You'll wear the clothes. You'll apply the sap to the clothes. You'll apply the leaves to the sap. Just get them. You'll see." The worm smiled knowingly.

Jonna looked around the area. Sap from the trees was not a problem. These particular ones seemed to be oozing with it. And leaves were scattered everywhere. However, this still left one issue: the clothes. "Any suggestion on where to get the clothes?"

"Hmm, I think there is a farm just beyond the cave up the hill. You can take some from them."

"I can't steal clothes." Jonna stood taller. "What type of a person do you think I am?"

The inchworm volunteered, "In a hurry? Of course, you could always go back home, come back, find the cave, put on the clothes—"

"Fine," Jonna grunted. "I see your point." He could always strip and then apply the sap with the leaves directly to his skin. Something about that seemed wrong, though, not to mention—his eyes darted to the stream where he would have to wash it all off. No, absolutely not.

Jonna looked at the hill above the cave. Climbing it should not be too difficult, and maybe he could barter for the clothes. He checked his pockets, but he had neglected to bring anything extra from the cabin. His only hope was that they would take pity. Taking hold of the cave wall, he started up the side, gripping small trees to pull himself up.

It was not bad going, but the climb took longer than he first thought it would. At the crown of the hill, he gazed down. The place where the inchworm hid looked even tinier from this perspective. Falling off would not be wise.

Certain it would be better not to be seen, he used the mage's spell to hide. Twigs broke and the occasional leaf crunched, but they were the only evidence of his passing.

From what he could see, the farm had a small barn with one horse, two cows, and a brood of chickens. All were fenced and locked up. To the left of the barn was a well of water with a roof. The main house stood on the other side of the well.

The chickens squawked louder the closer he came. Could they sense him like the worm did? A small child rushed out of the house, spurred on by a female voice behind him. Jonna jumped back and avoided the boy's path. After seeing no reason for the chickens to be squawking, the boy put his arms over the lower part of the fence and stared into nowhere. Jonna recognized that look. The young child was daydreaming.

After a moment, the boy climbed the fence, trying to stand on top. Using the post, he balanced, and then took a few tentative steps. He teetered. His back foot moved out too quickly to balance him. He fell toward some metal tools.

Jonna rushed forward, sliding to make it beneath the boy. With arms extended, he stopped almost perfectly in position. The boy dropped into his arms, but one of the child's thrashing limbs knocked off a handheld rack. The tool struck the ground, bounced, and landed on the bottom edge of a shovel that leaned against the fence. The shovel flipped sideways, banging into Jonna's knee.

"Ouch!" Jonna faded into view, still holding the child. He swallowed as the boy's eyes grew wide. "Are you all right?" Jonna put the boy on the ground, standing him up.

The boy backed up a few steps. "Who are you?" His feet were poised to run.

"I'm Jonna." He smiled, extending his hand. "And you are?"

The boy looked from Jonna to where he would have fallen, his chest still heaving from fright. "Why did you catch me?"

"Why wouldn't I?" Jonna countered, withdrawing his hand. "You were going to fall."

"Pa says we get what we deserve." The boy looked back at the metal tools. "But that sure would've hurt."

"Then why did you do it?"

"I didn't think I would fall." The boy raised his chin. "But I did, didn't I?" He frowned.

Jonna nodded.

The boy made a decision. "Thanks."

Jonna relaxed.

"I don't know why you did it, but you did help me. My name's Phillip."

"Good to meet you, Phillip." Jonna looked around. "Say, by some chance, you wouldn't happen to have any old clothes no one wants, would you?"

Phillip threw him a curious glance. "You've got clothes. What do you need more for?"

"I have to do something very dirty, and I don't want to mess these up."

"Pa has some in the closet in the house." The boy stopped. "But I'm not so sure he'd let you use them."

"That's too bad." Jonna frowned. "Well, I guess I need to be going. It was good to meet you." He turned, heading back toward the forest. He would have to find another way.

"Wait!" Phillip came running up beside him. "If I do help you, I need you to do me a favor."

67

Jonna stopped and looked down at Phillip. "How can I help?"

"You have to help Mom and me get away."

That was an unusual request. "Get away? Get away from what?"

The boy nodded. "We want to leave Pa."

The door to the house opened a crack, and a female voice called out, "Phillip, get in here. You haven't finished with your chores."

"Aw, Mom." The boy looked from Jonna back to the house.

She opened the door halfway and then saw Jonna. Eyes wide, she panicked. "Phillip, get in here right now!"

The boy sighed, turned, and walked toward the house. Jonna followed, but not too fast. He did not want to alarm her.

She eyed Jonna suspiciously. "Who are you, and what do you want?"

"I was looking for some clothes, ma'am."

"You want a boy's clothes?"

Phillip answered, exasperated, "No, Mom. That's silly. He needs clothes like Pa's."

"What do you want clothes for? Do you know what farm this is?"

Jonna shook his head. "No, ma'am."

"This ain't no place for a human being. Pa will most likely kill you, do you understand?" She snatched Phillip inside. "Leave!" The woman slammed the door.

Go or stay? There was something in the way the woman spoke, something that did not seem right. Jonna wasn't completely sure, but it sounded like the woman feared her own husband. Maybe he ought to try again? Jonna knocked on the door.

The woman snarled from the inside, "Don't you know what *go away* means?"

"Ma'am, I don't know what's wrong—"

"You bet you don't." The door swung open. "Five times the village has sent people to help us. Five times they've had nothing but dead to carry back, and you're only one man. Leave before it's too late!" The door slammed again.

"But Mom," Phillip called from inside the house. "You don't understand. He's magic!"

"Magic my foot," the woman called out. "Go to your room. Now! Be grateful Pa'll just beat you for not finishing your chores."

The ground shook, almost knocking Jonna off his feet. It felt like someone stomping as they walked, but that was impossible. The door opened just a peek, and the woman looked out. Her eyes went wide with fright. "You're still here?"

"Yes, ma'am. Something is shaking—"

"He's coming! How stupid are you?" She jerked him inside, closing the door. "You're going to have to hide. After he drinks his milk, he'll go fast to sleep. Then, we'll sneak you out."

"Why are you so afraid of him? Maybe I could—"

The woman cut him off sharply. "You're not listening. There is no explaining. He does not care. If you're found, you're dead." She listened to the stomps and pushed him toward a spare bedroom. "In here, and be quiet."

After looking around the sparse room, Jonna knew only one way to hide, so he mumbled the mage's spell.

The stomping stopped. The front door flew back, slamming into the wall. The floorboards creaked as Pa walked into the main room, sniffing the air.

"Woman," Pa said gruffly. "I smell an odor."

"Of course you do, my dear," the woman said sweetly. "I've been cleaning today."

Pa snorted. "Not that kind." His eyes narrowed at her. "Strange humans have been here, but not from the village."

Whoever Pa was, he had an amazing nose. Jonna listened as well as he could, but it was not enough. Adjusting his stance, he found a crack in the wall to see through, and there was Pa's huge physique. While the bottom half was human, the top half was bull. Was Jonna looking at a minotaur?

The minotaur sniffed the air.

"Pa, there's no one here." The woman reached over to a bucket and poured out some milk. "Why don't you just drink this?"

The minotaur roared, knocking the cup from her hand. She ducked, expecting another blow to follow, but he moved toward the spare bedroom instead. "He's here." He sniffed again. "Had I found him outside, it would have been quicker. Now, I'll savor the moment." Opening the bedroom door, he passed through but saw nothing.

Pa snorted again, moving about the room. As the minotaur approached, Jonna backed up and managed to stay just out of the way. Jonna reached the door, stepped into the main room, and moved toward the far wall. As Pa came out he sniffed again, this time in obvious confusion.

69

"Are you certain you smell something?" The woman cringed, having found the courage to approach him again. He looked at her with suspicious eyes.

"You know the bargain," the minotaur growled. "You and your son protected, your husband kept alive, and no humans."

The woman nodded. "And I have kept my word."

"Good." The minotaur growled again, slightly softer. "Make sure it stays that way. Now comb my mane and find me some milk."

The woman scurried over, found the wooden cup, and poured more milk. From a drawer near the table, she withdrew a brush.

Jonna caught sight of Phillip peeking out one of the side doors.

"Boy," the minotaur yelled.

Phillip opened the door slowly.

"Do you like being beat? Get my firewood."

Phillip hurried to the front door with Jonna trailing behind. He followed the boy outside to a spot beside the barn.

"Phillip—" Jonna appeared, and the boy jumped. "What happened to your dad?"

"It was long ago, and I was too young to remember. Mom says one day the minotaur came and announced this was his farm, and she was his wife. In order to keep Dad safe, she had to obey. He then took Dad away to some cave."

"Did she say what cave?" If the worm was right, and humans could not enter the cave he knew of, it would be the perfect place for the minotaur to keep the boy's father.

Phillip shook his head.

"Is it near?"

"I think so." He looked in the direction of the chickens. "Each morning Pa goes out that direction, taking food and drink Mom has prepared. That's all I know."

"I've seen only one cave that direction." Jonna formulated a plan as he spoke. "It is the same cave I need to enter, but to do that I need clothes." He looked into the boy's eyes. "I don't know what has happened in the past, but if you get me these clothes, I will rescue you and your mom. What do you say? Are you willing to take a chance?"

The boy studied Jonna's face. "I believe you. I'll do it."

"Good. Can you find an excuse to come back out here?"

The boy nodded. "It'll take at least two or three trips to get the wood."

"Good, just do what you normally do."

The boy hefted the first load of logs and carried them toward the house. Jonna said his spell, hurried to catch up, and kept pace behind him.

As soon as they stepped inside, the door closed, and the minotaur sniffed. He looked in the boy's direction, saw nothing, and then relaxed. Phillip dropped the logs next to the fire and hurried to get a second load. His mother, still tense, brushed the minotaur's mane, being careful not to pull his hair.

As the minotaur's eyes slowly closed, Jonna moved up beside the woman. Becoming visible, he whispered, "Where is the closet?"

The woman almost released the brush as she turned frightened eyes toward the minotaur. The creature started to snore, so she forced herself to relax, mouthing back with no sound, "First bedroom, right side." The brush never stopped stroking the minotaur's mane. Hesitating, she continued, "What are you doing?"

"I'm finding a way to rescue you, Phillip, and your husband."

The brush in her hand shook, but she stilled it. After another moment of hesitation, she whispered, "Okay."

"Thank you."

Jonna moved into the first bedroom, found the closet, and went through the clothes. Most were too big, but at last he found something. Leaving the closet ajar, he moved back into the main living area. After a moment, Phillip came in carrying a load of wood.

"I think that's enough," the woman said quietly, watching the boy struggle to add one more piece. "You know how he gets about too little or too much."

"Just one more," Phillip pleaded. "I want to do a good job." He darted his eyes toward Jonna, who was stepping from Pa's room, but the woman didn't turn.

"I said—"

Jonna needed to talk with the boy one more time, and inside the house was not the place to do it. "Please," Jonna whispered beside her, "let the boy go." He tried to make the words short and quick. Who knew what might make the minotaur wake?

"Go ahead." She focused back on brushing the minotaur's mane, watching the creature's face intently. For the moment, he was still unmoving. The boy opened the exterior door, allowing Jonna to pass through. Until both were by the woodpile, neither said a word.

"Thank you, Phillip. And don't worry, I'll find out about your father."

Excitement filled the boy's voice. "Let me go with you."

"No, you must stay here or you'll draw suspicion." Jonna pointed toward the door. "We don't want him waking up too quickly." Phillip glanced toward the house. The look in his eyes said there was going to be trouble, but he would try to obey.

"All right," Phillip answered. He walked slowly toward the house.

Jonna hurried past the farm. Spotting a trail, he followed it to the right and off the crown of the hill. A well-worn, crooked path seemed the only obvious choice for the minotaur. Had Jonna searched the base of the hill instead of climbing up the side, he would have stumbled upon it.

As the path ended, it descended toward the bottom, becoming less obvious and leading to the stream. When he reached the woods beside the cave entrance, Jonna changed his clothes.

"I see you found clothes," the worm said in a very sleepy voice. He had just finished off an entire leaf, and his stomach looked quite full.

"Yes." Jonna finished donning the clothes. He hid his own in a ball beside the base of a tree and presented his new attire to the worm. "Better?" He took some leaves, dabbed them with sap, and started applying them to the clothes.

"I'm not the one putting on leaves with sap." The inchworm chuckled.

Jonna tried several ways, but ultimately, he coated the leaves in the sticky substance and stuck them to the clothes without any real pattern. In the end, he looked like a tall pile of leaves. "Okay, now what?"

"Just walk into the cave."

"What?" Jonna gawked. "It's that simple?"

"It's that simple."

He turned toward the cave, stepped from the thicket of trees, and pushed his hand forward, expecting to hit a solid surface. His hand passed through.

"Camouflage," he said aloud, finding no sign of the invisible wall as he stepped into the coolness of the cave. "The barrier thinks that I'm a pile of leaves." His voice echoed as his eyes adjusted, and he listened for movement. Satisfied that nothing else stirred, he continued into the dimness.

A man's voice cracked from somewhere out of sight, "Who's

there?"

CHAPTER 9
BOB THE PIXIE

"I'm looking for a man." Jonna hunted to find the voice's location. "Whose son's name is Phillip."

"You know Phillip?" Relief flooded the man's voice. "By the gods, how can this be?"

"It's not by any god," Jonna answered. "But by one man helping another. Can I ask your name?"

"Thomas," Phillip's father called out. "To see another human face! I've been here for nine years!"

Jonna moved toward the back of the cave. Thomas sat shackled to a cave wall lit by torches.

"Is the minotaur gone? Is my family safe?"

"One thing at a time." Jonna found a key on the other side of the room. "This can't be for the shackles. Why would the minotaur be this lax?"

"He has my family and knows I could not escape, nor could anyone get in." Thomas paused, staring at Jonna's strange attire. "It was the minotaur's way of taunting me, leaving the key in plain sight."

Jonna released the shackles. As they fell to the floor, the man watched in disbelief. The ground shook. The stomping returned.

"Stay here," Jonna warned. "When you hear no more noise, you can go to your wife and son."

Thomas's eyes grew larger as he rubbed the calluses around his wrists and ankles. "What are you going to do?"

"I'm going to get rid of your minotaur," Jonna promised. "But first, I have to make sure your family is safe."

The stomping became louder, and the bellow of a bull called out. Jonna rushed to the front of the cave, passing through the barrier. Phillip came running down the hill, tripped, fell, and rolled to the bottom.

Jonna helped dust him off. "What happened?"

"I—" Fear leapt into Phillip's eyes. "I made the minotaur chase me."

"You what?"

"I wanted to help you. I wanted him to leave my mom alone."

The bull roared again. Small stones rolled down the side of the hill, shaken loose as the minotaur stomped closer.

"Okay, Phillip, do exactly, exactly, what I tell you. Do you understand?"

Phillip nodded, eyes wide, and glanced back at the minotaur bearing down upon them.

"Turn around, face the minotaur, and hold onto me with all your might. Whatever you do, whatever happens, do not let go. Understand?"

The boy nodded again.

Jonna chanted, "Unum-Clastor-Fillum."

The boy squeezed his hand, fidgeting as the creature rushed closer. "What are we doing?"

Glancing toward the boy, Jonna shifted back toward the minotaur. "Shh. Stand your ground." But Jonna was anything but calm. His heart beat rapidly. The plan in his mind was the only thing he could come up with as this situation was thrust upon him.

"Unum-Clastor-Fillum, Unum-Clastor-Fillum, Unum-Clastor-Fillum." *Oh joy, the minotaur was almost there.* "Unum-Clastor-Fillum."

The spell had to be timed just right. *Slow down, breathe deeply, and prepare for it.* "Unum-Clastor-Fillum." *Plan the words. Don't say the last one until he hits.* With blood pounding in his ears, he focused on the minotaur bearing down upon them.

"Unum-Clastor-Fil—"

The minotaur collided with them, almost knocking Jonna's breath out of him.

He gasped the final sound. "—lummm."

Jonna and Phillip shot back, but not into the place they knew. The trees were gone. Darkness covered everything. They hit the ground and rolled as Phillip lost his grip. The darkness echoed with a roar of anger. The minotaur, finding himself not where he had been, was as blind as they.

"Phill—"

The minotaur roared again, drowning out the last part of Phillip's name.

"Jonna?" the boy called somewhere to his left.

"Phillip, follow my voice, quickly!"

"Humans!" The minotaur roared in the darkness. "What is this trick? How have you blinded my eyes?"

"Quickly," Jonna called again. He could hear Phillip's footsteps coming in his direction. "That's it, follow my voice!"

The minotaur's words came closer. "Humans, do you think blindness can hide you forever? Do you not remember that I can smell?" The minotaur hissed, successfully drowning out Jonna's voice.

"Phillip!" Jonna knew the boy was close, but where was he?

"I'm here! I'm stuck!"

"Stuck?" Jonna tried to find him, groping around in the darkness.

There was something to his right. Something larger than it should—

Jonna jumped back, smelling the minotaur as it slammed a fist beside him.

"I may not have your nose," Jonna taunted. "But I can't miss your scent."

The creature roared, striking out in both directions. Jonna jumped back, bumping into the boy.

"Phillip?"

"Jonna?"

"What are you stuck—" Jonna felt a sticky, strand-like substance. If he did not press too hard, he could pull away, but if he did— Jonna mumbled the magic spell, holding onto Phillip.

"What is it?" Phillip felt around on the sticky thread.

"Don't," Jonna cautioned, still mumbling the words.

The strands had started to vibrate as if something moved in their direction. A twittering sounded in the distance like chelicerae clicking together. How big the spiders were in this darkness, Jonna could only guess. However, based upon the strand size, it was even money as to whether the minotaur could survive. That was one contest he would rather not wait around to see.

The minotaur gloated, "You cannot hide. Now I have both of you!" As Jonna finished the final phrase, the creature lunged, and Jonna jerked Phillip to the side.

They bumped harshly, hitting the ground outside the cave, blinded by the sudden light. Phillip had his forearm up over his face, but the minotaur was gone.

Thomas, legs shaking, walked out through the hidden barrier. He raised his left hand over his eyes, giving them time to adjust. After a moment, he looked down at the young boy sitting beside Jonna. "Phillip? Phillip, is that you?" He squinted.

"Dad!" Phillip leaped to his feet, releasing Jonna's hold. He grabbed his father around the waist, hugging him tight.

"Whoa." The man patted his son on the back. "Not quite so tight."

"Thomas?" a female voice called from up the path. "Thomas, you're free!" She hurried down the path, crying as she reached him at the bottom.

Getting up, Jonna did not bother to try and dust himself off. After all, he was still wearing the clothes, sap, and leaves. In spite of his mess, he smiled at the family. Not wanting to disturb them, he slipped through the cave barrier.

What had the waters said about the location of the stone? "On the right side, in a hole by the wall, the Jewel of Wisdom you will find. Place it in the holder bare. See the city of your mind."

Jonna looked around for the stone, searching the right side of the cave. The outside light was not nearly good enough to see with. He went to the back of the cave, pulled out a torch, and started inspecting the wall.

There were many holes and nothing to distinguish one from another. He moved back and forth, over and over, working his way into the darker reaches.

He mumbled to himself, "On the right side, on the right side . . ." Jonna felt tired, hungry, and exhausted. The thought of finding Thomas and asking for a bit of food crossed his mind, but he dismissed it. For the first time, Thomas had his family back, and the minotaur was gone. Let them be alone.

He went back to the section where Thomas had been shackled and looked over the contents. There was a large chest in the right corner with a lock in place. Was it possible the minotaur had found the gem and placed it in the box? Why a locked chest, unless it contained something of value? He took the key that opened the shackles and tried it on the box. No good.

He looked around for a large stone, something he could strike against the lock. In the end, he placed one of the shackles catty-corner on the padlock, raised a rock of sufficient size, and broke the catch on the shank.

The hinges squealed as he raised the lid. It had been a long time since this chest had been opened. Staring down into the chest, he raised the torch over the top. Strangely, the light showed nothing but darkness no matter how close he placed the torch. On top of that, if he pushed the torch beneath the rim, the light vanished completely. As far as he could tell, it was like looking into a deep hole.

Okay, so much for the trouble. Jonna started to close it and then thought better. He reached in a hand, swept it around, and felt—something. Pulling his hand out, he peered into the abyss. It still looked like a black hole—nothing, nada, not a thing—but something was definitely in there. Sticking his right hand in again, his fingers found a bag.

The bag faded into view as he pulled it from the chest. The old cloth was nearly threadbare, yet it still contained something. He untied the drawstring and widened the top. A light glimmered from within, showing a ruby red gem. He hefted the jewel and thought about what the water had said.

"On the right side, in a hole by the wall, the Jewel of Wisdom you will find. Place it in the holder bare. See the city of your mind."

The chest was on the right side of the room. It appeared empty, just like a hole, yet contained a gem. The Jewel of Wisdom?

He took the amulet from around his neck, checked the size, and placed the jewel in the holder. The moment the jewel touched the holder, it began to glow. The holder's short metal prongs bent of their own accord, grabbing the jewel and holding it in place.

It was time. Dropping the amulet around his neck, he closed his eyes and thought of the elvish city. Tiny prickles danced across his skin. Energy flowed around his body. *My clothes*, he suddenly thought, but it was too late. They were still in a ball, rolled up by the base of the tree.

"Don't we smell good," Bob exclaimed on his shoulder. Jonna opened his eyes. He stood in the middle of the elvish citadel, where he last saw Queen Freya. Bob was at his ear.

"Told ya you'd be back!"

Jonna scowled at him. "You did not!"

"Did too!"

"Did—" What was he doing arguing with a pixie? Jonna, refusing to be drawn into the pixie's game any longer, cautioned him, "If you expect to stay, you better not pinch my ear again!"

Bob chuckled. "Like you could do anything about it."

The exchange helped to lighten his mood, though he would make good on his threat. "Try me."

As their voices echoed in the silent corridors, Jonna became aware of the chill in the room. His voice grew serious. "What's going on, Bob?" Even as he asked the question, the answer floated within his mind.

Bob's voice lost its fun. "They're moving out: wives and little ones,

79

leaving. The males are preparing for war."

"No." A cold feeling went through Jonna. He looked to the pedestal but saw the sword gone. "Where did they take it?"

"What?"

"The Rune Blade of Knowledge."

"I don't know. I'm just here to supervise."

Jonna turned to glare at him. "Bob, if you want me to help, you have to tell me where it is!"

Bob walked back and forth, mumbling to himself on Jonna's shoulder.

"Bob, you do want to help me?"

"But I promised," the pixie pleaded. The look in his eye told Jonna to guess.

Jonna ignored the invite. "Promised who?"

Bob bounced back and forth again. "I can't tell you!"

"Bob!"

"All right, all right, stop shouting!"

"I wouldn't have to, if you would tell me what I wanted to know."

Bob sighed. "It starts with an E."

Jonna glared at him, but it was obvious he would get no more information until he played along. He thought of the first E name that came to mind. "Elfleda?"

Bob nodded but would not say it. "When you left, she took the sword and hid it. She said—" He sighed again. "That way you would not come back and endanger yourself."

Jonna frowned as he looked around the room. "Why would she do that? And how did she know I'd be back?" He stopped, shaking his head. "Can you find it?"

"Hmm?"

"Bob, no more games!"

"But I can't!" Bob changed locations, hovering in the air in front of Jonna.

"Yes, you can. Tell me, where did she take the sword?"

Bob swallowed. "You're not going to like this, and I really shouldn't tell you."

"Did you ever think she told you on purpose?" Jonna looked him in the eyes.

"Huh?"

"Did she have to tell you where she took it?"

"Well, no."

"Then she was leaving me a message, knowing I would be back." The smell of the sap wrinkled his noise. "Sap and all." His frown deepened.

Bob held still, thinking as the wind blew into the citadel. The breeze sang a low, moaning song. Finally, the pixie nodded. "You might be right."

"I am right. Tell me."

"She went to the Dark Mages. She went to make a deal."

"She did what?" Jonna remembered the mages who tore Väinämö's cottage apart. "You mean the humans? The evil mages?"

Bob nodded, moving back to Jonna's shoulder.

Jonna's voice hardened. "How do I find them?"

Bob shook his head back and forth. "You don't want to. Not even a pixie can fight their magic alone!"

"And you think Elfleda can? Hmm, what sort of pixie helper are you?" Jonna turned his head to glare at Bob, a feat in itself given where the pixie stood.

"I don't know!"

Jonna's voice was harsh. "And that answers which question?"

Bob ducked his head. "That wasn't very nice."

He was right. Jonna had let the situation get to him. Taking it out on Bob was not acceptable. The emotion of it drained from Jonna as he realized the root of his anger. "I'm sorry, Bob. The fact is, whoever these Dark Mages are, they appear to have kidnapped Stephanie. On top of that, now I find out Elfleda is in trouble, and she is the one hope I had of finding my wife."

Jonna sat down on the floor, head forward, listening to the wailing wind, which echoed his feeling of hopelessness. It flowed through him, trying to steal the flame of his will buried at the core of his soul. No, he would not give up!

"Where are they, Bob? No playing around." His voice held urgency. "The balance of this world is at stake, and so is my heart. Do you want to save it?"

Bob looked offended. "Of course, how could you say that? We pixies are allies with the elves!"

"Good. Get ready to show me how to get there."

Jonna stood up, glancing at the other items still sitting around the elvish chamber. He needed a change of clothes, and his own were too far away.

Unfortunately, there was nothing like clothes within this chamber. So he moved to a connecting hall and pressed against two closed doors. The unlocked doors swung back, revealing a rather large room. The king's crest glowed on the ceiling, creating a type of hologram. Did he dare? What elvish taboo had he broken now?

Jonna went to the closet, finding several types of armor and clothing. The armor was not like the heavy mail used by the knights of his world, but more like the thin leather of archers or woodsmen, yet made of cloth resembling spun gold. He pulled one out, rubbing the soft, pliable material between his fingers. Though a little on the large side, the armor was good enough for the moment.

There was no one to ask permission and very little time. The elves had given him the Rune Blade. Surely clothing to aid him would not be a problem, would it?

Dropping the leaf-sap clothing to the floor, he donned the shirt, pants, and belt. Just as the sword had once conformed to his hand, the strange clothing now did the same.

He liked the belt with its small pockets around the outside edge. It would make carrying things very easy. As he connected the belt, it too conformed perfectly.

"Amazing," Bob said, echoing Jonna's own thoughts.

He looked at Bob. "Hold it, why is this amazing to you?"

"Humans cannot wear elvish clothing or armor," the pixie stated flatly. "At least, I've never heard of any."

"Humans normally can't hold elvish swords either," Jonna responded. "And yet, I can." But it did make Jonna wonder what was going on.

"Good point."

An elf walked in behind them and said in alarm, "What do you think you're doing?"

Jonna turned around. The elf quickly bowed. "I'm sorry, Your Majesty." His head stayed down and would not rise.

Jonna was stunned. "What did you say?"

"I'm sorry, Your Majesty." The elf glanced up, his eyes going wide. "You're not the king!"

"No, but I needed some clothes, and—"

"You're human!" The elf backed up. "This is not possible!"

That irritated Jonna. "Everyone keeps telling me that. What is so blasted wrong?"

The queen's musical voice came out of nowhere as she glided into the room. "I shall tell you, Jonna McCambel." She turned to the elf. "Leave us." The elf backed up, closing the doors behind him.

"Jonna—" Her voice was kind but very sad. "I sorrowed the day you came to our kingdom, yet knew it was meant to be."

"Why?"

"Our world is changing. No longer are we the carriers of only good magic. Evil has come into our ranks. Elves fight elves, something unheard of in the past. No longer are we the Protectors of the Forest, as there are those of us who destroy it. This change did not come by you alone, but with others. You are the final one."

That sounded ominous. "What do you want from me?"

"Within your hand is the ability to heal the elven-kind or destroy our people forever. When you could not raise the sword as defender for the elves, Elfleda, my daughter, chose to make a bargain with the Dark Mages. It was her hope to save those whom she loved. Unfortunately, she, too, has failed. They have broken their promise. They took your wife."

A shiver went up Jonna's spine as terror tore through his heart. "Have they hurt her?"

CHAPTER 10
THE SIGHT

"Nay." Queen Freya shook her head. "But her fate is tied to that of Elfleda."

"Then you know where to find her?"

The queen nodded. "As I also know the trials you will face and cannot tell." She frowned, and the whole room felt like doom. The light dimmed, and the blowing wind paused. How could one person's emotions so change the weather? The chill cut into his soul.

"Because—" Jonna hesitated, fighting back against the assault. "If you tell me, it might change the decisions I must make in order to find her." As his final words fell, the silence thickened.

The queen nodded. The light dimly brightened as the wind blew once more.

His body tensed, and his voice hardened despite the calmness brought on by the queen. "Where can I find these Dark Mages?" He was sure she would not answer the direct question, but it was his right to try.

"I will send you to the beginning. From there, you must find your way. But be cautious, Jonna, the Dark Mages are not to be taken lightly."

He stood taller. "I am ready." In the dimness around him, the thin armor began to glow.

The queen gave a single nod. "This time you are. I can see it in your eyes." A slight smile lit her face, and the light level in the room rose again. "There is hope, Jonna. There is hope in you. Find the Rune Blade of Knowledge. Use it to open the door to freedom."

He looked into the queen's eyes, seeing, feeling the emotions that she broadcast. "I will."

"Bob," the queen said quietly. "You are his guard, his companion, and his friend. Do you understand?"

Bob bowed his head. "Yes, my queen."

"Good." She smiled. The chamber reflected the glow. "Find my daughter. Locate your wife. Save the kingdom." She looked Jonna in the eye. "Delvium Adventi. Let your journey begin."

"Goodbye—" Jonna stood outside the cave of Thomas and the minotaur once more.

"Changed your threads?" the inchworm admired. "Wow, you look like an elf!"

Jonna spotted his rolled-up clothes, still untouched. He flipped them over, dug into one of the pockets, and pulled out the three twigs and pocketknife. These he safely tucked away in one of the pockets on his belt. The billfold and keys he left in his other clothes.

He looked around, not speaking to anyone in particular. "What do I do with the clothes?" He needed something to carry them in.

Bob moved forward, pulled out a pinch of pixie dust from his bag, and raised it up. "I can take care of that." He turned around three times, and stomped a foot on Jonna's shoulder, slinging the dust toward the clothes. Sparkles descended toward the ground.

"Hey!"

"Sorry about that. Can't help the spell, though." The clothes faded away before their eyes.

"What did you do?"

Bob winked. "They're in storage, so to speak. If we need them, we can get them."

"Thanks." Jonna looked around at the trees. "Now what?"

Bob placed his palm on his head, humming.

After a moment, Jonna squinted at him and asked, "What are you doing?"

The pixie opened one eye. "Thinking, of course."

"That's thinking?" Jonna rolled his eyes.

"Beats the way humans do it, especially males, when they think with their—"

"That's enough. Not all males act that way."

"Oh, yeah?" Bob challenged. "Let's list a few examples."

"Let's not." Jonna turned toward the cave, spotting the hidden path that led to the top of the mountain. "Maybe Thomas will know where to look." He started up the trail.

"Hey," Bob called, bouncing up and down as Jonna walked. "Shouldn't we talk about this first?"

Jonna turned to the right, following the path. "Why?"

"Well, the queen did say I was responsible for you. So we really should discuss—"

"Are you going to tell me where the Dark Mages are?" Jonna slowed his stride but did not stop.

"Well, no—"

"Are you going to tell me where my wife and Elfleda are?"

Bob grumbled, "You know I can't do that!"

Jonna's stride picked up again. "So, what is there to talk about?"

Bob opened his mouth only to close it again. He gave a funny grin. "I guess you're right. Lead on, oh wise one. Although, technically, I am the elder . . ."

Up the trail, around the hill, and along the side of the barn, the corral finally came into view. The horse and two cows watched as they approached. The chickens did their normal squawk.

Bob stiffened. "Oh, my." Glitters appeared above him as he turned invisible. "We don't have to talk to them, do we?"

"Why Bob, you aren't afraid of chickens, are you?"

Bob's eyes were wide. "Only when they peck me."

Jonna laughed, that is, until he saw the front door of the house. It had been smashed in.

"Thomas?" Jonna hurried to the door, stepped over the busted boards, and dodged the broken table. "Phillip?"

"Janice?" Bob called, looking around from Jonna's shoulder.

"Who's Janice?" Jonna went room to room, moving with caution.

"His wife, of course."

"I didn't know that."

Bob snickered. "Of course you didn't. You're only human."

"Thanks for reminding me." Jonna came back to the front room. "Who could have done this?"

"I think that's pretty clear." Bob pointed out the shattered furniture. A blunt instrument had destroyed it.

"Humans," Jonna agreed. "And they used maces. The Dark Mages?" Stepping outside, he peered at the ground, studying the footprints left behind. "Most of them were on horses with a few on foot. They lead off down that trail."

"That goes to the village," Bob added, his eyes wide. "They don't believe in magic there."

That was hard to fathom. "You mean someone in this world doesn't believe in magic?"

Bob nodded. "That's why they sent so many to help kill the minotaur. It went against their belief. Funny thing was when the survivors returned to the village, *if* they returned, they disappeared when they told what they saw."

"That doesn't seem fair." Jonna thought of Thomas's family dealing with that now. "But I've met the same type of people myself. If something doesn't fit, they destroy it." He looked at Bob but listened to a strange sound in the distance. "We've got to help them."

Bob squinted. "I thought you'd say that. Well, what are we waiting for?"

Jonna pointed toward the forest. "Did you hear that?"

"Hear what?"

He moved closer to the broken door, his eyes scanning the trees. "There were several popping sounds, like soda cans being opened."

Bob scratched his head. "What's a soda can?"

Absentmindedly, Jonna said, "You know, a soda can. It's a small cylindrical tube with a flat top and bottom. On the top, there is a small tab you pull to release the—" He stared at Bob. "You don't have a clue what I'm talking about, do you?"

The pixie shook his head, eyebrows raised high.

Jonna huffed. "Don't look at me like I'm crazy."

Bob shrugged with a grin. "I didn't say anything."

"Oh, be quiet. Just because you've never seen something doesn't mean—" Now he sounded like Väinämö, though it really did not seem to matter. The popping had stopped anyway. "I guess we ought to go."

"Didn't I say that already?" Bob rolled his eyes, turned around to face Jonna as he flew backwards, and hovered under the porch. "Well, what are you waiting for? Hear another *pop* or something?"

Jonna froze, staring as a dark mage walked toward the well. A skull medallion hung on his chest. Could the pop have been made by the mages? So far, no one had seen Bob or him. Jonna whispered, "Bob, keep your voice down."

Without paying attention, Bob answered in his normal tone, "What did you say?"

It happened in slow motion. At Bob's words, the mage started to turn, while at the same time Jonna started to point. Bob's head followed Jonna's finger, and Jonna leaped to the right just inside the door.

A flash of bright light lit the sky. A thump sounded on the porch. Jonna peeked through a crack in the broken door. The mage was heading toward the house.

"Looking for me?" Bob appeared on Jonna's shoulder.

Jonna jumped. "I thought he got you."

"Not me." Bob smiled triumphantly. "I'm smarter than I look, you know." He stopped and thought about his own statement.

Jonna didn't comment but kept his eyes on the approaching mage. "Dark mage at eleven o'clock."

"What's an ol' clock?"

"No time to explain. He's heading for the door. Any ideas? How dangerous are they?" The Dark Mages had certainly torn Väinämö's hut apart, but then he remembered what Väinämö had said. As individuals, they were not as strong. But how strong was strong?

The room did not offer much in the way of weapons: the busted door, broken furniture, and scraps of wood. He shifted through the debris and found a snapped-off table leg. That might give him an edge on his opponent.

Bob unsuccessfully tried to whisper, "You're going to use that?"

Jonna put a finger to his lips and spoke quietly. "You have a better idea?"

"There is always pixie magic."

Jonna looked at him. "Well, do something, pixie."

"Let me think." Bob pondered the ceiling.

"If you hum again, I'll swat you myself."

"Hey there, that's sort of rude!" However, the pixie did not hum.

The wooden porch squeaked. The dark mage came closer. There was no place to hide.

Jonna nodded at Bob. "Don't let him catch you. I'll be back."

"Where are you going?" Bob's eyes darted in all directions. "What do you want me to do?"

"Shh." Jonna mumbled the words of the invisibility spell and faded from view.

"Jonna!"

The dark mage stepped through the doorframe. "Meddling little pixie!" He raised his hand in Bob's direction. "*Nostrum Contor*—"

Jonna slammed the table leg into the dark mage's midriff, buckling him over. He dropped the leg and, in quick succession, struck a right sword hand to the dark mage's throat, followed by a heel palm to the chest. The dark mage flew back, tumbling out the door. He landed with a loud crash that echoed from the porch.

"Come on!" Jonna leaped out the door, becoming visible once more. He headed toward the woods on his right and ducked out of view. There had been several pops, and the dark mages could be anywhere. For all he knew, taking out one dark mage could alert the others.

Dark shapes hurried toward the house as both he and Bob slipped further into the forest. It did not make sense. If a village that did not believe in magic kept trying to kill the minotaur, why would mages show up here? Could they be searching for him?

Jonna and Bob moved deeper into the forest. Avoiding the thicker brush, they cut back, moving closer to the road. To stray too far without directions would not be wise.

Jonna took a deep breath as they walked, almost yawning. He was in need of food and rest. He glanced toward Bob. "You're being unusually quiet."

Bob's face turned red. "You shh'd me."

"Oh, come on, Bob. I was trying to save your life."

The pixie gave a questioning grunt. "You were?" His coloring toned down to pink. "Really?"

"Why do you think I went invisible to begin with? If I wanted to leave, I could have walked away."

For a moment, there was silence. "I never thought of that. You really do care?"

Jonna grinned. "Of course I care. You help me. I help you. Besides, where else am I going to get such a good guide?" Maybe he stretched on that one, but Bob did have his uses.

Bob's eyes lit up. "True." He squared his shoulders, straightening his back. "Not just any pixie would risk their neck to help a human."

That almost sounded prejudiced. Jonna laughed. "What do you mean?"

Bob closed his mouth, swallowed, and spoke more slowly. "I-er-mean, pixies and humans don't get along so good these days."

"Then why help me with the duel?"

They reached the trail to the village. No one was in sight. Surely the dark mages would not follow them here, even if they knew where he and Bob had gone.

"It's—" Bob paused, and though Jonna could not hear it, he imagined Bob humming in his head. "Complicated."

"You mean, you can't say."

"Nope."

"Or won't say?"

"That too."

"Whatever happened to cooperation? I did just save your life, you

90

know."

Bob stood firm. "I was assigned by the queen."

"You came to our cabin long before the queen sent you."

Bob clicked his tongue. "I was assigned by Queen Dorothy?"

Now he was grabbing for justification. "What are you hiding?"

Growing more stubborn, Bob looked the other way. "It's not my place to say."

Jonna sighed. "This is one of those, 'I can't tell you directly' things, right?"

"It's worse than that." Bob's eyes opened wide. "I can't tell you at all."

"Tell me what?"

"Can't tell you that—" Bob stopped and shook his finger at Jonna. "No, you don't! You're not tricking me. I'm supposed to be the trickster, you know. I'm the pixie."

"If you say so."

"I am!"

A sign appeared, sure to catch the attention of any traveler. It said, "Warning: NO Magic Allowed!"

"I thought you said they did not believe in magic?"

"They don't."

The duo passed the sign. Another fifty feet or so, just around a bend, another sign appeared. It said, "If you're a mage, turn back."

Jonna studied the new sign. "It sounds like they know magic exists. They just don't want to admit it."

"Sounds like you." Bob threw his hand up, stifling a laugh.

"Thanks, smart aleck."

"No problem." Bob hummed.

"Maybe you ought to hide yourself," Jonna suggested. "No magic probably means there is no such thing as pixies."

From a pouch, Bob pulled out pixie dust, waved his hand, and disappeared in a sparkle of stars. "Good idea." At least he was sounding like himself again.

At the next bend, just past a gate, two men stepped out, both shouting at once, "Halt!"

Jonna continued as if to walk past, slowing only a little.

"Halt, I say," both shouted again. One brought a halberd even with Jonna's chest.

Looking from one to the other, Jonna shook his head. "Who's

talking?"

"Me, idiot," the one to his left responded. "The one with the halberd pointed at your heart!"

"I could have sworn you both sounded the same."

The guard on the right stepped forward. "We don't sound the same."

"Well—" The other guard thought. "We sort of do when we yell out halt."

"Do not." The right guard turned to face the left. "That's insulting. I didn't take this job to be insulted."

The left guard inhaled. "What do you mean? I'm the one who should be insulted. You think it's an insult to sound like me?"

"No, you idiot." The right one moved closer, getting in the left guard's face. In the process, the left guard lowered the halberd. "You sound like me!"

"Do not!"

"Do too!"

Jonna glanced at Bob, walked to the right of the two guards, and passed through the gate. The dirt path turned to stone—cobblestone, to be exact. They walked over a small bridge that carried them over a moat and into the village walls.

"This looks more like a large city." Jonna spotted the main street. Food vendors stood on every side, selling all sorts of merchandise.

"Buy a slave?" A shifty-eyed merchant drew their attention. Jonna caught sight of a cage full of girls sitting in very skimpy clothes. "All the benefits of home, and none of the hassles. Guaranteed not to cut your throat while you sleep."

What a guarantee!

"Apples, apples." Another vendor thrust his hand briefly in front of them before jerking it back. "Get your delicious red apples here!"

A chicken squawked, and Bob moved from Jonna's right shoulder to his left.

Jonna chuckled. "Feel better?"

Bob shook his head, eyes wide open. "You just stay between us."

An older man on the side of the road caught Jonna's attention. "Can I interest m'lord in a drink?"

"No, thank you." Jonna looked around. "But I could use some information." The man threw a look at the other vendors. "Whatever your business, it can't be done here. Buy the drink, and we can talk."

After a pause, Jonna nodded and followed the man into the badly lit tavern. What few seats still worked sat up near a large table and counter.

"George," the old man called. "I've got a customer."

"Oh, really?" George appeared from nowhere, moved to the counter, and poured a drink. "Three pence." He looked at Jonna expectantly.

Jonna paused. "I don't—"

Bob whispered, "Check your belt pouch."

Jonna reached inside and felt some coins. He pulled out three and handed them to George.

"You're a good man." George nodded. "For a second, I thought you were going to say you didn't have any."

Jonna laughed nervously and watched as the drink slid toward him. What would have happened if the money had not been there? In the dim shadows, he could see outlines of other people, some in groups, some not, all indistinct. He redirected the drink toward the old man. "It's yours."

"Much obliged." The old man picked it up, took a sip, and put it down. "You said you were looking for information?"

Jonna nodded, spotting more shadows elsewhere in the room. However, the light was so dim he could barely make them out.

"I'm looking for a family." Jonna glanced from the old man to George and back again. "A man, his wife, and son, brought in just today."

"They bring lots of families here." The old man paused, took another sip, and continued. "Every day." His expression said this might require more money.

"Would it help if I told you their names?" Jonna reached in his pocket and placed a few more coins on the counter. Bob was providing the money, but how, Jonna could not fathom.

The old man shook his head. "It wouldn't do any good. They just take them down into the Chamber of Truth."

"Chamber of Truth?"

The old man nodded, and his voice went very low. "That's where those who believe in magic go." He looked around, checking to see if anyone else heard.

"And you don't?"

The old man shook his head vigorously. "And you'd best not be

93

talking about it either," he warned. "You're a good chap. Talk about magic will get ya dead."

"This family was really unique." Jonna tried again. "They were held hostage by a minotaur."

The old man began, "You mean Thom—"

George's hand covered the old man's mouth. "Are you trying to get us into the Chamber, too?" George looked around. "We haven't seen anything. Maybe you should take the rest of your money and leave."

Something stirred in the darker areas of the building. Shapes of all sizes moved in their direction.

"Uh, Jonna," Bob whispered. "I think we need to go."

"Who was that?" The old man turned, studying the area around Jonna. "You talk to the spirits?" His eyes opened wide as he leaned back.

George pushed the money away. "Mister, if you don't leave right now, you'll be hurting when you do."

Jonna stood up, reached into his pocket, and cast two more pence on the counter. "Thanks for your help." He nodded to the old man and George and then moved toward the door.

A shadow with a brutish voice stepped in front of him. "Where do you think you're going?"

"I was just leaving."

The man did not budge. "You think so?"

"Calander," George ordered. "Let him go. He's leaving."

"He talked about magic." Calander raised his voice so all could hear. "We all know the penalty for talking about magic." The murmuring in the crowd continued to grow.

"No, I didn't," Jonna assured. "I was just asking about a family brought into town. The old man said he hadn't seen them."

"He said Thomas," someone in the dark called. "Everyone knows what happened to Thomas."

"Shh." George raised his voice. "You want the guards to show up? Sit down! Shut up!"

"He said magic!" Calander raised his voice another notch. "We got to take him in." He grabbed Jonna by the front of his shirt.

"Wrong move, Sherlock." Jonna reached over, pinned Calander's hand with his left, and hyper-extended the man's elbow with his right.

Calander jumped, cringing in pain. He watched as Jonna brought his right arm over the top of the man's arm, knocked the man's arm down, and sword-handed the man's throat. Stepping in, Jonna right elbowed-left palmed the man's head, hooked him under the nose with a right crane hand, and tossed him to the side. Calander ran into a pole, knocking himself out. The unconscious man hit the ground. Jonna turned to face the dark room. "Next?"

The room went silent.

Bob's eyes went wide. "I didn't know you could fight."

"Four years of martial arts," Jonna whispered, keeping his eyes on the dark room. "Well, any other takers?" The crowd backed up, finding their seats.

A man dressed in a guard's uniform walked in and looked down at Calander. "What's going on here?" Both George and the old man waited to see what Jonna would do next.

"I think my friend—" Jonna reached down, hoisted Calander up, and sat him on a chair. "Has had a little too much to drink." *Sheesh, he was heavy!*

"Looks like he did." The guard looked from Calander to Jonna. "You're new around here?"

"I'm just visiting."

"Visiting who?" The guard studied Jonna's clothes, unable to place them.

"The village." Jonna smiled. "I've been abroad for a while."

"I see." The guard's eyes narrowed. He nodded toward Jonna. "Mind your manners."

Jonna gave him a nod. "Yes, sir."

The guard walked to the counter where George waited and ordered up a drink. Jonna walked out.

Bob exhaled. "That was close. I thought we were caught for sure!"

"He was just doing his job." Jonna ignored a merchant trying to get in his face. "Keeping the peace."

"If you say so, but if one of those people in the bar speaks out—"

"Stop!" The guard from the bar came running out. He motioned to several others standing around. "Stop him. He's a magic zealot!"

Bob's eyes widened. "You're a what?"

"Hold on!" Jonna skated around a vendor's tent, ducked through the back flap, and slid under a table. On the other side, he turned to the left, choosing a passage between two buildings.

"Where are we going?" Bob watched him navigate.

Jonna was amazed they had not hit a dead end. "I have no clue."

He breathed quickly. Ducking to the side of a pillar, Jonna crossed through an archway and found himself on another street.

Leaning up against an old stucco building, Jonna took a breath. "I don't think this is going to work very well." He watched other people moving from vendor to vendor. "We are already criminals."

Bob chuckled. "I think we were the moment we walked around the guards."

"You've got a point." Jonna listened for their pursuers. "They're serious about not using the word 'magic' around here."

A quiet female voice whispered behind them, "What did you say?"

Jonna turned and saw a young girl rocking back and forth in a small chair. In spite of the chaos behind them, the child's presence made him relax.

"What's your name?" Jonna smiled. "I didn't know anyone was here."

The child pointed at the pixie. "Who's that?"

"Bob—" Jonna threw a glance in the pixie's direction. "She can see you?"

"Huh?" Bob checked, but he was still invisible. "Can she?"

"Of course I can, silly." The little girl giggled. "I have The Sight."

Jonna frowned. "The what?"

"The Sight." She turned back to Jonna. "You do, too, at least when you want to."

"I do?" A curious thought crossed Jonna's mind. "The Sight is magic?"

"Shh." She put her finger to her mouth and nodded. "We aren't supposed to use that word here. Bad things will happen."

"I see." Jonna nodded. "So we call it The Sight instead?"

"Mom says we aren't supposed to tell anyone, but when I saw the little man on your shoulder, I knew you were one of us."

Bob shook his head. "I can't believe she saw me. That was my best invisibility spell! What am I going to do?"

Jonna laughed. "Practice more?"

"Okay, wise guy." However, Bob did crack a smile.

Jonna turned back to the girl. "Can I ask your name?"

"Elpis," the little girl announced proudly. "And may I ask yours?"

"Jonna." He smiled. "And this is Bob."

"Good to meet you both." Elpis giggled again.

The noise in the streets warned him the guards were coming. "Uh,

Elpis, you wouldn't have a place we could hide a moment, would you?"

She nodded, pointing to a bush just around the corner. It did not look like much.

"Don't worry." She seemed to read his thoughts. "They won't see you."

They could hear the lead guard pushing through each vendor. "Get out of the way! He's here some place!"

"Go," Bob urged as Jonna hurried toward the bush. Once they were safely behind it, the guards came into view.

They looked directly at Jonna but did not see him. They turned toward the little girl. The harshness of the lead guard's voice was disturbing. "Young lady, have you seen a stranger coming this way?"

"See what I can do." The little girl ignored his question. "I can rock real fast!" Elpis speeded up her rocking. "Want to play dolls?"

"No, I don't want to play dolls. Have you seen—" The guard looked at the little girl's face. "Come on." He abruptly turned around. "This is a waste of time." The troop of guards moved back to the street, the idea of hunting down the stranger apparently forgotten.

Jonna stared. "What did you do?" He moved from around the bush and squatted beside the little girl.

CHAPTER 11
WHAT'S IN A NAME

Elpis gave a large smile. "I let them see what was in my mind. I pretended you were not here, and that they weren't chasing anyone on this street."

"You made them forget." Jonna looked more closely at the little girl. "Do your parents know what you can do?"

The little girl nodded.

"Where are they?"

"Mom is—" She thought a moment. "Mom is here," she finished. "Dad has gone away." She went back to rocking slowly, watching the people as they moved past.

Something was not right. "Elpis, where is your mom?"

A small tear formed in one eye. Elpis wiped it away. "She is here."

Jonna began to suspect something. "Elpis, can you show me your mom?"

The little girl looked up, large puppy-dog tears dropping from her eyes. She nodded and moved to an entrance just around the bush.

They approached a small door barely large enough for Jonna to squeeze through. The dust was heavy on the furniture, and as he pressed into the room, his presence alone caused it to fly into the air. Bob coughed.

"Here." Elpis stopped beside a grave, chin down, in one corner of the room. There was no headstone.

It seemed like an odd place for grave to Jonna. "Your mom is dead?"

Elpis nodded and then forced her sad voice away. "But she's always here with me."

That was sort of obvious. He shook his head. "Why was she buried her?"

"It was the only way to keep them from burning her body."

This story was getting stranger by the moment. "Did your dad go away after your mom died?"

On the surface, the room gave very few clues as to what had taken place there. Jonna spotted several dust-covered books. He moved over to them.

Elpis shook her head. "It was me and Mom for a very long time."

Bob gawked at her. "How are you surviving? Without parents to help—"

A voice outside called, "Elpis! Doggone you, child, always running off! Where are you?"

"Wait here." The child's eyes went wide. She hurried out the small door.

"There you are! I told you not to run off. Now, go take this to Mr. Furgonson . . ."

Jonna picked up one of the books, moving back the cover. A dust cloud puffed into the air. Bob whisked it away.

"The Year of Stagnus," Jonna read, and then stopped. "Someone smudged the date." He skipped forward, noticing some of the details. "This diary was written by a woman's hand." Jonna glanced down at the grave. After a moment, he turned back to the book, beginning to read again. "They took him yesterday without a word or reason. It did not make sense. We never showed anyone what we could do. It was like someone was betraying our people one by one."

"Is that possible?" Jonna turned to Bob.

Bob nodded. "It would take a mage to find a mage, and they would have to know approximately where they were located."

Jonna skipped forward in the book, skimming the details of how hard life had become. Without her husband to help, they gradually lost their status and wealth. He turned another page.

". . . This is not a normal sickness, but so far, Elpis has shown no signs. Many of the older Sighters are dying, leaving the kids to go untrained. I have taught Elpis all I can, but her mind is so young, I cannot be sure she will remember the teachings . . ."

He skipped again and stopped on another page. This time the penmanship lost its form.

". . . I tried to tell Elpis I was dying, but she could not understand. The few friends we have left have agreed to try to watch over her, but I fear they, too, will suffer the same fate. With no other family, what will happen to Elpis, I cannot tell."

"It just stops." Jonna flipped to the next page. "No more entries. No more notes."

Bob looked from the book to the grave. "I think we know what happened."

"I'm back," Elpis announced happily. "And look what they gave me. Food!" She handed the apple to Jonna.

"Elpis." Jonna smiled appreciatively, and though his stomach grumbled, he shook his head. "I cannot take your food."

"But I have more!" She went to a small drawer, pulling it out. Assorted fruits and a small portion of cooked meat lay in wraps of cloth. "Each day they give me a little for helping."

Jonna shook his head. "Does no one take you into their home?"

"I am at home." Elpis looked surprised. "Mom is here."

"Yes." Jonna nodded sadly. "Your mom is here. Don't you get lonely?"

"When I do, I think of all the wonderful things we did, and all the loneliness goes away." She smiled, though something about the smile said it did not always work.

"Elpis, you need a home. Bob?"

Bob jumped. "I'm a pixie, remember, not a human." He looked at the little girl. "But I suppose we could work out something. I—"

"You want me to come to your home?" She looked straight at Jonna.

It felt like a knife stabbed through his heart, and suddenly Stephanie came to mind. "I would love for you to come to my home." It was hard to control his emotions. "But I have a problem. Some very mean people have taken my wife, and now I have to find her."

"I can help you!" The innocent, pleading look struck at Jonna.

He tried to think of an easy way to explain this. "I know you would, but these people are very mean. They might hurt you, and I wouldn't want that to happen."

Elpis looked down and sighed. "I can't come with you."

Jonna's heart stung like someone had just slapped it. "No, but—" What could he say? What could he do? To raise this little girl's hopes and then break them would be unbearable. And what if she had relatives somewhere who just hadn't been found? The diary said there were none, but what of the father? He could still be out there, somewhere.

He reached down and raised her chin, looking into her eyes. "If you will stay safe, here, where I can find you, I will be back. I promise." Jonna heard his own words and felt them come from his very soul. No matter what happened, no matter how things turned out, he would be back. "Then we can figure out what to do. Do you believe me?"

Elpis nodded, abruptly lunging forward to hug him. He found himself hugging her back, tears trying to form in his eyes. All she wanted was a place to belong. How could he blame her?

He removed her hands gently, holding Elpis at arm's length. Tears ran down her cheeks. Wiping them from the corners, he smiled. "There now, that's a big girl." Elpis smiled back. "Stephanie will be glad to meet you."

"Stephanie is your wife?" The little girl's eyes were bright.

"Yes, she's—"

Elpis suddenly shook her head, looking up at the ceiling. "You must find Elfleda first." She looked back at Jonna. "Elfleda will guide you to your wife."

Jonna moved back a little, looking at the child. "How do you know that?"

"I just know." Elpis looked at Jonna, suddenly afraid. "Did I say something wrong?"

"No, no, not at all." He smiled once more and thought about the sections he had read from the book. "Did your mom teach you how to do that?"

She nodded.

Bob moved to stand on Jonna's left shoulder. "Just like the diary said. Don't you think we need to go?"

"You're right." Jonna moved toward the door. Stepping through, he turned back to see Elpis's face. "Remember what I said."

She waved goodbye excitedly. "I will!"

Jonna stepped around the corner, bumping into a guard.

The guard stood back, sneering. "And who do we have here?" He looked for any weapons Jonna might be carrying.

"I'm sorry."

"You should be! Don't you know assaulting a guard is punishable by death?"

"I wasn't assaulting. I just didn't see you there."

The guard's eyes narrowed. He studied Jonna's clothes. "Those are pretty fancy for a common man."

"They were given to me." Jonna looked him in the eye. "A gift from the queen."

The guard's eyes grew large. He stepped back and saluted. "I am so sorry, sir. I should have recognized you right from the beginning." The guard lowered his eyes. "Please, forgive me."

Jonna glanced at Bob with a bewildered look. "Of course."

Bob just shrugged and whispered, "Ask him where the palace is, while you're at it."

"I seem to be disoriented." Jonna raised his chin. "Can you direct me to the palace?"

"Yes, sir!" The guard gave brief directions. "If you're done with me, sir, I'd like to return to my duties." He fidgeted, waiting for Jonna's response.

Jonna nodded.

The guard hurried off.

Turning toward his left, Jonna glanced at Bob and noticed his own reflection in the glass. He jumped.

"Who is that?" Jonna reached up and touched his cheek, watching his hand do the same to the strange face. Behind him, he heard a giggle. "Elpis, what did you do?"

"I made him see the prince." She giggled again.

"And me, too." Jonna peered closer, studying his face. "Elpis, does this trick work on everyone?"

"If they come close." She sat back down in her rocking chair. "Someone far away will not see it."

"So it has a range," Jonna thought aloud. "It's a mental illusion."

Bob whispered again, "We could always take her with us."

Jonna frowned, ignoring the comment. "Bob, having me ask directions to the palace was a good idea." He did not bother to say his last suggestion was not. "If we are going to find out where Thomas went, I think we need to visit the palace."

"Me too?" Elpis looked up with big, round, hopeful eyes.

"She's got a point," Bob pushed. "She's the one who controls the illusion. Without her—"

"But she's safe here," Jonna countered. "Out there, we don't know what will happen."

"Please," she begged, looking up. "I'll be good!"

The words twisted his heart. Bob was right. She would be an advantage, but the last thing he wanted to do was exploit a little girl or put her in danger. Then again, she was in danger just being in this city. If the guards captured people for only talking about magic, what would they do to her if she was discovered?

Jonna shook his head. "I know you will." He squatted down beside her. Logically, it made sense, and yet, logically, it did not. Still, it would be easier than trying to find her when this was over, wherever his journey took him. "If I give you an order, you will obey?"

Elpis nodded vigorously.

Even Bob begged, "Oh, come on, between us both, I'm sure we can keep her safe."

Jonna closed his eyes. "Oh, all right."

Elpis's eyes brightened, and her smile melted away all his other resistance. She looked toward the street, losing focus. "Guards coming this way." Her focus came back.

Jonna nodded. "That means we better go."

The trio turned and moved through the vendors into the street's main traffic as the guards approached from across the way. The city guards bullied their way through, pushing and shoving, demanding the vendors to move. Elpis stayed by Jonna's right side, keeping out of the main thoroughfare. All of this was very familiar to her. She reached up, grabbing hold of Jonna's fingers.

Jonna took her hand, his heart going out to her. She was so young and alone. If only he and Stephanie could—what would Stephanie say? For that matter, how would she react when this was all over? A creeping fear challenged his mind, demanding that he know the answer. What was happening to Stephanie now? What was happening to Elfleda?

"You there," one of the guards called out. The guard stood on the street corner, watching as the people went by.

Jonna turned, looking in his direction. "Yes?"

"Not you," the guard growled. "The man behind you."

"Me?" The voice came from a fruit vendor. Jonna stood in front of the man's booth.

The guard growled again, his hand tapping on his weapon, "Give that man with the fancy clothes an apple and have him bring it to me."

The fruit vendor stated through gritted teeth, "Would you like an apple?"

Jonna did not say a word, merely giving the vendor a questioning look.

"You would? Fine. Take this one." The vendor raised Jonna's hand, forcing him to take it. "Bloody guards," the man mumbled under his breath. "Think they own the whole town."

"You there—" The guard looked straight at Jonna. "Bring it to me."

"Watch him." The fruit vendor's voice was low. "Most are just looking for a reason to take someone in."

Jonna nodded and headed across the street. Several small groups caught the guard's attention, but he said nothing to them. Obviously, they had nothing he wanted to steal, right?

Jonna stepped up, drawing the guard's attention. "Is this what you wanted?"

"It took you long enough." The guard's eyes went back to a particular group, eyeing their merchandise. Finally, he turned back toward Jonna. "Maybe I ought to run you—" In a sudden fit of panic, the guard bowed. "Excuse me, sir. I am so sorry." Fear shot across his face. "I—I don't—I don't normally do this."

It had to be Elpis, so Jonna played along. "Don't let it happen again," Jonna stressed, forcing the guard to take the apple. "Consider this your last."

"Yes, sir!" The guard hurried away, retaking his post.

Jonna looked back at Elpis and could not help but smile. "You did it again."

She nodded. "If I hadn't, he was going to take you to jail, claiming that you stole the apple."

For a kid, she really knew how to read people. That was exactly Jonna's impression of the guard.

The fruit vendor motioned him over, laughing up a storm. "I've never seen a guard do that," he bellowed. "That was worth the price of an apple. As a matter of fact, why don't you both accept a gift?" He handed one to Jonna and another to Elpis, patting her on the head. Elpis made a funny face.

Jonna bowed slightly. "Thank you. I'm glad we could amuse."

"You sure did." The vendor continued to smile. "We'll be talking about that for a very long time. What I don't get, though, is how you did it." He looked puzzled. "I was sure that guard would haul you off."

Elpis pulled at the base of Jonna's shirt. "The palace." She pointed off to the right.

"Thank you!" Jonna gave the vendor a final nod and headed where Elpis indicated. He tasted the apple. It was good. Before he knew it, he finished it all—waste not, want not. A few minutes later, the palace came into view.

It was not much, not in the way of fairytales. However, there the palace was, taller than the other buildings, protected by a wall and a gate. At one time, ornate decorations were carved into its battlements. Now, through time and neglect, they were either gone or falling apart.

"You would think it would be in better shape." Jonna remembered the elvish city: the glimmering light, the bright reflections, and a people standing in awe of their queen. This palace had none of that. It was like a worn-down rock sitting in a puddle of grime and dirt.

"A palace measures the heart of the ruler," Bob said as if quoting from something he had read. He shook his head slowly. "That heart is measured in darkness now."

Jonna frowned. "The city ruler still lives here?" Their group moved forward, forgetting what was behind them, amazed at the deterioration. In spite of the building's poor standing, multiple guards stood outside the gate's entrance.

"Halt," the one closest called out. "In the name of the City of Diggory."

Jonna acted surprised. "And not in the name of the king?"

"What century are you from?" the guard asked. "The city has absolute rule!"

"Through the king and queen," Jonna added, making a guess based upon the previous guard's responses. He looked from one guard to the other.

"What's it to you?" A second guard turned to face him. "Are you his—" The guard stepped backwards. Elpis had done her magic again. "Sir—" The guard kneeled, hitting the other guard to do the same. "My apologies. I didn't know you were back."

"Well, I am." Jonna glared at them all. "I hope I won't need to report this?"

"No, sir!" The guard kept his head low. "Go on through, sir."

"Thank you." Jonna walked through the gate, turned a corner, and passed into a small garden. He was not even sure what king and queen the guards were talking about. That sort of information would certainly be handy if he was going to carry this charade much further.

Lifting himself from his thoughts, he realized there was a scenery change. It was the first relatively large green area he had seen in the city. Everything else was buildings and streets.

"A pixie's haven!" Bob looked around at the trees. "I was starting to get agoraphobic!"

"Too many people, eh?" Jonna blinked. "If you know that word, why don't you know what a soda can is?"

"I do read," Bob huffed. "Just not human stuff." He paused. "Well, not usually human stuff. But I have a few friends and when we get together we talk about all kinds of things." The pixie nodded proudly.

Jonna spotted a large fountain at the same time Elpis did. Her eyes lit up.

"Can we?" She was ready to run to it.

"Back to the point." Bob stuck his tongue out at Jonna. "I define it as too many of the wrong kind of people—not enough nature."

"Should I remind you two we are in hostile territory? Just because we walked past the guards does not mean it is a walk in the park. Doesn't it seem strange there are no more guards?"

The water leaped from the top of the fountain, falling on a series of brightly colored plateaus. It ran in all directions, finally coming to rest in a basin at the bottom.

Jonna looked for any sign of human life. "Be cautious." He took Elpis's hand and walked to the fountain. The sun caught in the tiny water drops, casting a rainbow of colors.

"Wow." Elpis took in every drop that fell. "It's beautiful!"

Jonna nodded. "It is." However, he kept watch. They were in. Now what?

Bob folded his arms. "I've seen better." He turned away, refusing to admire it.

"Where?" Jonna laughed.

"The elvish city, of course," he answered matter-of-factly, as if Jonna should have already known this tidbit of information. "And since we are on the topic, shouldn't we be finding out where we need to go next? Hmm?"

"He's right." Jonna looked at Elpis. "We need to find Thomas. I have to find the Dark Mages."

"Dark Mages?" Terror danced across Elpis's face. "No, they are evil!"

"They are evil," Jonna agreed. "But they also have my wife."

"Jonna McCambel," a soft female voice said. He followed the voice and saw the fountain.

"Yes?" Although surprised that the fountain seemed to be speaking to him, he was starting to expect the unusual.

The water seemed to whisper, "Help me."

There, just to the side of the fountain, standing in the flow of water as it poured from the last basin, was a water sprite. The falling liquid helped to conceal her near-transparent body.

Jonna turned. "How do you know me?"

"A mutual friend. I heard rumor of your coming."

Bob scratched his head. "Who knew we were coming here? I thought water sprites only existed near natural water deposits." He crossed his arms and then pointed a finger at the creature. "And I see no spring. How do we know you're telling the truth?"

"Look for yourself." The sprite waved toward the feed for the fountain. "Through leverage and motion, they lift the water to the top, letting it flow down, hiding the spring and water source."

Elpis stepped forward. "Why are you crying?"

The little girl's eyes were as sharp as an eagle's. However, it took Jonna a moment to see what she was talking about. Elpis was right: the water creature was crying, though it was hard to see through the mist and water falling into the pool.

The water sprite turned toward Elpis. "It has been a long time since I have been free."

Jonna moved around the fountain. "What's holding you here?"

"It is a magical filter." The sprite followed Jonna. "Placed there by a dark mage. It was designed to trap and contain me."

Jonna peered into the water but could not see anything. "How can we help?"

"Remove the filter, and I can go free."

"That sounds simple enough." Jonna contemplated her request and then shook his head. "Too simple, if you ask me." He studied the sprite. "You are telling the truth?"

She nodded.

"And there's nothing else?"

The sprite thought. "The filter chants words, though only a mage can hear them."

"What are the words?"

"I do not know. I am not a mage."

"No, that's right." Jonna touched the water beside him and considered the sprite's words. He remembered what Sir Verity had said about Snovipa—by knowing her name, she no longer had power over him. Did that apply to all sprites? If he knew this sprite's name, could he safely help her? "What is your name?"

"Will you not help me?" The water sprite stepped closer to Jonna, her water-blue eyes sparkling in the sunlight. "It will only take a moment."

Something played in the air around them, a flowing of sound and musical notes produced from the fountain itself. Elpis yawned, still gazing at the sprite's beauty.

Bob stretched. "I think I'm getting tired." He, too, yawned.

"What is your name?" Jonna held his ground, though the effects of the music hit him also. "If you want me to help, then speak."

CHAPTER 12
LILITH OF DIGGORY

The water sprite reached out, touching Jonna's hand. She followed his arm up to his shoulder, reached his neck, went across his cheek, and finally stopped under his chin. In spite of what he saw, her caress was soft.

"Come." She took his hands, leading him into the water. "I must do as my master bids." Yet at the same time, Jonna saw the battle within her as tears flowed from her eyes. This water sprite was under a spell and could not leave until it was broken.

"Tell me your name," Jonna whispered, pleading. "And I will do all I can to help you." From the corner of his eye, he saw Elpis sleeping beside the fountain. Bob had begun to snore, right beside his ear—that was annoying.

"I—can't." The water sprite shook. The conflict showed in her eyes. "If I do—"

"I can escape, but I won't," Jonna promised. "I will fulfill my oath to help you."

Her expression softened, hope against hope. "You would do this for me?"

Jonna nodded. "Yes."

"Naida Perdita," she whispered very quietly, gently releasing her hold on Jonna's hands.

"Thank you, Naida." He smiled. "Thank you for trusting me." He looked down at the pond. By the water sprite's power, he stood upon the surface. "Who is the mage that traps you?"

"His name is Lilith Magnus, controller of the city."

"I thought magic was outlawed here?"

She nodded. "It is, for all except him." Naida looked up at the palace with disdain. "It is cruel what he did to me. It is cruel what he's done to this city."

What Dorothy said about Snovipa came rolling back. If her magic of the forest was that great, could Lilith be using Naida's magic to increase his own? "That explains how he found the others who did magic." Since everyone else had fallen asleep, none of the group heard him. Jonna looked toward Elpis, concerned.

"He comes," she said softly. "He knows I have captured someone."

Jonna nodded. "But not three. Hide the young girl and the pixie. Protect them. Leave me for the mage to find." As Jonna lay down beside the bank, still suspended above the water, the bodies of Elpis and Bob faded from view. Seconds later, two large doors in the side of the palace flew open.

Lilith strolled to the fountain's edge, turning to the water sprite. "What have we here? Another poor mage caught unexpected?" He grinned. "A pity none of them are very bright."

A young woman came up beside him. "Father, what is it? Oh my!"

"Don't let it bother you, Serena." Lilith narrowed his eyes, scanning around the fountain before turning to his aide. "Find the guards, and have him taken forth."

"No." Serena's voice softened. "Father." She touched Lilith's arm. "There is something about him. He is different from the others."

"Hmm?" Lilith took a closer look. "There is something. I believe you're right. On second thought—" He turned to the aide again. "Take him to a guest chamber, and make sure he is well cared for. He will dine with us this evening."

"Yes, m'lord."

The aide twirled a finger in the air. Four servants materialized from within the palace doors. They hoisted up Jonna and carried him, not too ceremoniously, toward the palace doors. Jonna dared a peek toward the fountain and saw that Naida had kept her word. Elpis and Bob could not be seen, not that Bob was visible anyway.

The palace floor was white stone. The stairs were decorated with rugs showing an emblem of the city. At the top of the stairs, he was taken down a hall with portraits of other city rulers. Three doors down, the servants opened a smaller door and tossed him onto a bed.

"He'll have a nice headache when he wakes up," one of the servants snickered. "That water sprite gets them every time."

"What do you think Master Lilith will do with him?"

Before Jonna could hear the answer, the servants passed out the door, closing it behind them. Jonna sat up, went to the door, and listened. The hall was quiet.

The good thing was the water sprite trusted him. Apparently, she had never done that before, or perhaps no one had ever asked.

He stepped to a window, noted the balcony, and looked out. The fountain was not too far from his location. Opening French-style doors to the outside, he stepped up to the balcony's railing.

From here, he could see over the walls and down a few streets into the city. It was still packed with vendors as people went about their business, never knowing what was happening just a few hundred feet away. Though he did not know all about magic here, he suspected the water sprite was how Lilith captured all the mages one by one. Yet, the fact that Elpis was still living in the city said his magic was neither infallible nor all-powerful. No magic. Jonna laughed. It was just a ruse to limit Lilith's contenders.

The doorknob to his room turned. Jonna stepped back inside and closed the balcony doors.

"Up so soon?" a woman called. A smile lit her face as she extended her hand. "I'm Serena Magnus."

Jonna caught the hand, held it, and kissed it. "It is a pleasure to meet you, m'lady."

She blushed, letting her hand linger a moment, and then pulled it back. "Yet a gentleman does not come in a lady's court uninvited. Do you often enter a palace in such a fashion?"

"Ah, but the guards invited me in."

"We shall see. And you are, sir?"

"Jonna McCambel."

"Really?" Her eyes lit up, dancing in the light. "I've heard rumors, but of course, information from the outside world is limited. My father is very protective about what we know and what is published."

"So he's a dictator?"

Serena studied him. "You say that as if it were bad."

"Where I come from, it is. It normally results in an abuse of power and a loss of free will, no matter how well the intentions." The statement came out before Jonna thought through it, and he wondered if it was too much. He had not had time to figure out how she might react.

She contemplated his words. "The city has been preserved due to his diligence."

So her first reaction was to think and her second to justify? That was intriguing. At least she considered his words. "Your city cannot breathe. It is like a body preserved in a coffin. There is no life."

She frowned momentarily. "You disagree with my father?"

Uh-oh, maybe he had overstepped, but there was no time to be coy. Jonna studied Serena's expression. His words seemed to spark excitement in her. "I do. Does that make me a villain?" He could see it in her eyes. She liked that he was willing to speak his mind. Could it be that she, herself, desired to exercise her own freedom?

She avoided his direct question. "Your mannerism, the challenge in your eyes, evaluates, and then you make your own judgment." She acted like a kid who had just learned a secret. "Something I admire," she finished somewhat wishfully. Stephanie would have scratched her eyes out.

Jonna caught the hint in her voice. "And something your father does not?"

She turned away, a moment later glancing back over her shoulder. "Maybe." Her smile did not wane. "But there is something different about you, Jonna. If it had not been so, you would have already been with the others."

"Others?" Now they were getting somewhere.

"Those who oppose my father." Her face filled with consternation. "Step carefully, and he may count you as his own. He looks for those who know their own mind and lend it to his cause." Serena walked slowly to the door, trying to catch his attention. "Would you like a tour of the palace?" she asked, not turning to face him. "I would be glad to show it to you."

Jonna nodded. "I would, m'lady."

The glitter in her eye was back again as she turned around. "Well then." She held out her arm, waiting.

Jonna moved closer and accepted. They passed into the hall. "You have many rooms." His eyes swept slowly from side to side.

"This is the guest floor." She nodded toward the hallway. "We don't have many guests anymore. That all ended when Father declared martial law." She pointed to a painting.

He followed where she pointed—the artist was very good. Picking back up where the conversation had stopped, he asked, "Why did he do that?" The duo made their way to a smaller set of stairs with no handrail. Slowly, they worked their way down. Serena seemed in no hurry at all.

"There was an uprising." She thought back. "But why, I don't remember. I was very young. Most of the mages were killed or taken prisoner."

"Just the mages?"

"They were the ones who revolted. It was then that Father placed a ban on magic throughout the city. I'm not even sure if anyone knows how to do magic now."

She certainly did not know how resilient people could be. "And you?" Jonna asked with curiosity.

"Oh, I know a few tricks." She dismissed the thought with her hand. "But nothing of any consequence. I have no desire to spend the time." Her words did not fit her personality. She came across as a person who knew her own mind, though maybe not enough to cross her father. The fact that he was walking with her, and not already cast with the others, argued the evidence.

"Your father must be a great man." He noted the change of decorations on the wall. They were more foreboding here and less trite. The two passed into a large room with scrolls of all sorts stacked on shelves. A few books and maps were also thrown in.

"The library." She dropped her arm, allowing him to release her. Turning around in a slight dance, she curtsied and laughed. "Do you dance, Jonna?"

"I have." He looked around the room. "But I don't think this is the proper place."

"I agree." She walked back and took his arm again. "The grand hall would be much better." They strolled out into a hallway and passed a door that was bolted shut. Unlike the others along the way, this one was plain and larger.

"What's that?"

"You don't want to go there." She shook her head in warning. "Nothing good happens through there."

They continued down the hall until he could hear birds chirping. She pulled him toward the sound. "Here is where I want to go."

Removing a bolt, she pulled the door open, revealing a large room with a type of wire mesh ceiling. The clear blue sky showed through where the shadows did not obstruct. Small spots jumped from branch to branch. The chirping was much louder here.

Jonna stepped in and was met by a flock of birds taking off from the top of a tree. A small stream ran through the room with a stone path following beside it like a guide.

Serena sighed. "This is my favorite room." She released his arm and walked around on the green grass. She picked a spot and seated herself, patting the grass beside her.

Jonna moved toward her and sat down so he could face her. "M'lady, does it not bother you the way in which your father rules this city?"

"Why do you ask?"

She either truly did not understand or had chosen not to. "It is the cruelness by which he keeps magic from the city. Not only that, but he searches the countryside looking for others. If they are connected to magic, he brings them here."

"He is only protecting his people." She looked toward the flowing stream. "How else could he have kept order all these years?" She glanced back at Jonna. "But I'm tired of this topic. I don't want to talk about such things anymore." A mischievous twinkle crossed her face. "Jonna, are you married?"

"Yes, m'lady. I have been for three years." Maybe this would put a stop to the foolishness. Then again, maybe he should have lied. How was she going to react?

Serena looked down and then up at the air as if listening to someone. "No." She turned toward Jonna. "Not like you think."

Did she have The Sight, too? "What are you talking about?" Jonna sat back, still looking at her. "Is my wife okay?" The fear he had pushed down tried to pull itself back up.

That funny look crossed her face again, and she gave a small laugh. "You really don't know?"

"Don't know what?" He smiled, fighting to keep the concern from showing.

"About your wife." She stood to her feet. "I want to walk, and maybe, if you're good, I'll tell you."

Jonna stood, too. "Tell me what?" Was she playing with him? Of course she was, and somehow she knew the subject of his wife kept him on edge. It was hard to relax when he knew she was in danger, though he tried to pretend otherwise.

"My father built this many years ago, before my mother died. He used to come here to meditate, before the rebellion in the city. Now, I am not sure he remembers it still exists."

"He built it for your mother." The knowledge just popped into Jonna's mind.

Serena's head turned toward him. "So you do know magic?"

"Me?" He shook his head. "No, no, I am no mage. I'm just a normal person trying to find my way through this magic land."

"You don't lie very well," she said coyly. "I think you're doing more than trying to find your way. I think you are looking for someone."

116

"Well—" *What do I say?* "I am looking for some friends."

Serena frowned, suddenly nodding. "That's true, and yet I sense there is something else."

"Serena?" Both turned around and looked behind them. "Your father needs to speak to you." The guard glared at Jonna and then turned abruptly, leaving the garden.

"Ignore him." Serena laughed, seeing the expression on Jonna's face. "His name is Ajax. He's been asking for my hand in marriage, but Father won't allow it." She giggled and headed for the door. "I'll be right back." She disappeared through the entrance.

"Bob," Jonna called out, but tried to keep it down. "Bob, where are you?" Where was that little pixie? Surely Naida would have woken him up by now.

Maybe he should turn invisible, go out to the fountain, and try to get some more information to help the water sprite? He shook his head. That would be stupid. The moment he talked, he would become visible. The moment he became visible, he could be seen.

Serena strolled back into the garden, swung around a tree, and smiled at Jonna. "Did you miss me? Father thinks I need to watch you closely." She laughed, her eyes saying more.

"I've been good," he assured. "I even stayed right here."

"Don't be too good." She giggled. "That might be boring." She grabbed his arm and started to walk. "But I'm glad you did not try to escape. If you had, the guards would have stepped in." She motioned to the door, where a halberd was just barely visible. "Aren't you glad you didn't try it?"

"Of course," Jonna agreed. But he was still thinking, *Bob, where are you?*

They came to a small pond with a waterfall in the center. "Your craftsmen must have been very good." Jonna studied the design. The use of curves gave a relaxing feel.

"This," she stated proudly, "was not made by men at all. Father caught a water sprite. This is made by magic."

"Your father made this by magic?" Okay, so he was playing a little dumb.

Serena sat down on a bench, guiding Jonna beside her. "No." She shook her head. "The water sprite made this for my father."

He looked from one end of the fountain to the other. "I don't see a water sprite."

117

"You won't, either." Serena pointed to the center of the fountain. "After she did this, he cast a spell on the metal mesh that controls the water flow to the front fountain. When the sprite touched it, trying to leave, she became bound."

"Why doesn't he release the sprite?"

"Why would he? She is bound to his service forever, and a sprite on your side is powerful magic."

"So he feeds off her magic—" Jonna put it together for her to hear her own words. "And that makes him stronger." He was right. That was how Lilith curbed the rebellion in the city.

Serena nodded and then stopped, thinking about what she had said. She looked at Jonna. "I shouldn't have said that."

"No, you shouldn't." Jonna shook his head in amusement. "But that's okay." He smiled.

"Good." She closed her eyes and leaned against his shoulder. "It is pleasant here, is it not?"

If this had been time with Stephanie, he would have agreed, but now— "This is a nice place. Peaceful when the world is in chaos."

Serena looked up at the tone of his words. "What do you mean?"

"Don't you find it hard to relax, knowing that there are others suffering somewhere below in the city?"

"I—" Her expression darkened. "I guess I never thought of that."

"Most people don't consider what goes on outside their circle." Jonna pointed to the waterfall. "What was created here is beautiful, but at what price? How much suffering does the water sprite do, knowing she can never be free?"

Serena sat up. "She is a water sprite. She doesn't—"

Jonna cut in. "You're just like her, you know." He was determined not to let her explain it away. "You, too, are a prisoner—a prisoner of your father."

"I am not a prisoner." She turned to look at him sharply. "I come and go—"

Jonna shook his head. "You come and go with a guard's escort," he countered. "You answer to Lilith's every call. If he told you to take a knife and have the guards thrust me through, you would do it."

"I—" She shifted further away, thinking over the words. "I don't want to talk anymore." She stood up and turned toward the door. "If you try to escape, the guards will kill you."

Jonna sadly shook his head. "Given a word from Lilith, they'll kill you, too."

She paused, walked to the door, and disappeared, not looking back. The door slammed behind her. A moment later, it opened, and in walked Ajax. The guard's voice was gruff. "You, up!"

Jonna stood, his eyes going from the halberd pointed at him to the face of the man holding it.

"I ought to run you through! I don't know what you said—" He stopped, eyes narrowing. "Or did—" He aimed the halberd at Jonna's midsection. "But I don't like it."

Jonna answered politely, "I did nothing she didn't need." And then, a thought occurred to him. If he provoked this guard enough, it might just get her father's attention. It was time to make sure Ajax got the wrong impression. A wisp of a smile dropped onto his face. "You're a man. You know how that works."

Ajax's face turned blood red, and his grip tightened on the halberd. "You touched her?" He rushed forward, an insane look in his eyes. Stabbing the air where Jonna had been, he sliced down and tried to catch him with the point. "You son-of-a—"

Jonna jumped, landed on the pole of the halberd, and drove it to the ground. The halberd's shaft flexed, ripping from Ajax's hands and jerking him forward into the kick Jonna prepared. Ajax bent over as Jonna slammed a forearm across the back of his neck. Without pause, Jonna elbowed the man's spine. Ajax hit the ground, temporarily unable to move.

"Halt!"

Jonna backed up as three guards entered, followed by Master Magnus.

Clap, clap, clap. "Very impressive, Jonna McCambel."

Jonna bowed. "How is it everyone knows my name, and I have yet to learn theirs?"

The mage chuckled. "Are you a mage or a warrior?"

"Neither." Jonna shook his head. "Only a man."

"A man, yes." The mage gave a slight frown. "But 'only' may not apply." He looked Jonna in the eyes. "You've upset my daughter, and I would like to know what you said."

"She didn't tell you?" That was interesting. Had Serena really listened?

"No." The frown deepened. The look on Lilith's face showed this was unusual. "Then again, you are different from the others."

119

"There have been others?" Jonna filed that away.

"Oh, yes. Many suitors have tried to find their way into this palace, but only a few have made it." He looked down at Ajax. "I knew his jealousy would be the death of him." There was something final in the man's words.

"He's not dead." Jonna looked curiously at Lilith. "Yet you used the past tense."

Lilith's tone became hard as he turned to the other guards. "Not yet. You two, take him down."

Ajax's eyes went wide as they dragged him to his feet. "No, please no!"

Lilith spoke coldly. "I have no use for a guard who cannot control his emotions. You know that."

"No," Ajax hollered out as two guards dragged him through the door and his voice trailed away. "I am a loyal servant!"

"Now then—" Lilith turned back to Jonna. "Let us behave as civilized men."

"I'm not sure that applies."

"Come now, Mr. McCambel. We do what we must to protect those we love. What one man calls ruthlessness, another calls loyalty."

Jonna gave a single nod. "If that's all it took, you'd be right, but knowing we answer to others always makes a difference."

Lilith's voice became stone-cold again, pleasantries aside. "In the City of Diggory, there is no higher power, but I do not think this is the place to discuss it." He dropped his serious expression and smiled, giving a single nod. "Tonight at dinner, perhaps?"

Jonna nodded back.

"Logan—" He turned to the nearest guard. "You have assumed Ajax's position. You will be Jonna's companion until dinner. Serena is occupied."

"Yes, sir." Logan turned and raised his halberd in Jonna's direction. "It's going to be a long wait."

"Logan," Lilith chided, still walking toward the door of the garden. "He is a guest—at least for the moment. He is free to look around."

"Yes, sir." Logan lowered his weapon and stood to attention.

"Do you often act in such a disciplined manner?" Jonna looked toward Logan. "Or is it just for show?"

"No," the guard growled, eyes narrowed. "Normally, he lets us run your type through."

"My type? You mean free men and women?" Jonna laughed. "Come on, companion. I'm free to look around." He walked toward the garden door, passing into the hall. As he turned the corner, a maid bumped into him.

"Excuse me, m'lord." She backed away quickly, terror in her eyes, and expected to be chastised.

"Pardon?" Never had Jonna seen a human act so scared.

"I—I said, excuse me, m'lord." She looked at the floor and waited.

"It was an accident. You've done nothing wrong." He waved the maid's accident away.

The maid looked up slowly, eyes wide. "Thank you, m'lord." She curtsied quickly and hurried off.

Bob suddenly whispered in Jonna's ear, "What's wrong with her?"

"Where were you?" Jonna mumbled, trying to keep his voice low.

"Asleep." Bob sounded disgusted. "I've never been caught by a water sprite before!"

"First time for everything." Jonna glanced back. Logan had a curious eye on him.

Bob chuckled. "He thinks you're talking to yourself."

"I know. Is Elpis all right?"

Bob nodded. "The water sprite is taking care of her, and she seems to be enjoying herself."

"Good." Jonna took a deep breath, and a thought crossed his mind. "Bob, I know how to free the sprite."

Bob did not like that one bit. "Why would you want to do that? Turnabout is fair play!"

Jonna rolled his eyes at the pixie. "How would you like to be a prisoner?"

"Yeah, but she—"

"Is being forced to do things against her will."

"You've got a point." Bob looked back at the guard, who could not see him. He stuck out his tongue. "Stupid humans."

Jonna warned, "Watch your mouth."

"Oh yeah, well, present company excluded."

"Thanks. There is another reason why we need to help the sprite. It appears she gives the mage power."

"But that's—he can't—that's slavery!" Bob looked indignant. "What do we need to do?"

"The magician uses a—" Jonna stopped whispering and said loudly,

121

"Hello, Serena." He nodded politely.

Bob gave a slight whistle. "What a looker!"

Serena was still upset. "Jonna, we need to talk." She took him by the arm and led him down the corridor. They came to a room with tall oak doors, the symbol of Diggory carved into them. As they stepped in, Logan tried to follow, but Serena gave a sharp order. "Wait outside."

"But m'lady, your father gave strict orders."

She spoke with such venom that Logan stepped back. "I am my father's daughter. When he is not present, my word is law. Do you understand?"

"Yes, m'lady."

"Then wait out in the hall," she snapped.

"Yes, m'lady." Logan moved further back, pulling the door closed behind him.

Serena turned to Jonna. Her eyes were puffy and red. "What you said—"

"Was the truth," Jonna put in, keeping hold of her gaze. "You do not have to believe it." He moved her toward an ornately covered bench, and both sat down.

She turned away from him, speaking as if she were someone else. "I see it more every day: the feeling in the air and the loss of hope in the city. Until now, I could always deny it." She turned back, chin dropping. "But not anymore. When I left you, I went to see my father, but for the first time, I was afraid to tell him what happened. I was afraid to tell him my thoughts."

"Because you know what he'll do. Daughter or not, if you stand against him, he will kill you."

Tears formed in her eyes. "I don't believe that."

Jonna said kindly, "I believe you do. I know it hurts to see it."

"No." She wiped her tears and looked up at him. "I think this is a trick. My father would never hurt me."

CHAPTER 13
CHERNOBOG COMETH

Jonna just looked at her, watching the internal battle go back and forth. "You have magic," he said at last. "Use it to see."

"No."

"Are you afraid of the truth? Are you so concerned for your own safety that your people do not matter?"

Serena stood up, glaring at him. "I care about our people!"

"Then do something about it," Jonna countered. "Save them. Help them. Don't oppress them." He stood up, taking her hands. "You're a beautiful woman. You have a good heart. But the shadow of your father is evil. He cares only about power."

Serena paused as if hearing something very far away. She looked up and then brought her gaze back to Jonna. "I wish—" She stopped. "Jonna, there is something you should know about your wife."

Jonna watched her. "I'm listening."

The door to the room opened, and Logan looked in. He frowned, seeing their hands touching. "M'lady, it is time."

Serena gazed into Jonna's eyes and smiled. "I'll be back. There's more that needs to be said."

Jonna nodded, releasing her hands. He followed her to the door. As she passed through, the door slammed, and a lock dropped into place. So much for his freedom.

"Bob?"

"I'm still here."

"What's she talking about? If she can see it, surely you know what is going on."

Bob looked away, studying one of the walls. "What do you mean?"

"You know what I mean. My wife. Has something happened to her?"

Silence. It was amazing how silent Bob could be.

"Bob?"

"Er—How should I know?" The pixie cleared his throat. "I haven't seen her since the cabin."

Jonna's voice held a warning. "Bob?"

"There are some things better left unsaid." Bob closed his eyes. "A pixie's right, you know."

Jonna's tone was grave. "Bob, this is my wife. If something is about to happen to her, I need to know." He stopped and for a moment caught an inkling of something that didn't make sense before it faded. "You know where she is, and what's going on, don't you?"

"Mmm—Not exactly."

"But you do know enough! Forget this whole, 'too much information messes up my choices' bit. Why didn't you tell me this before?" Jonna could feel his frustration building. He was losing both perspective and reasoning, and for Serena to be this close to telling him the truth . . .

Bob shrugged apologetically, giving a half-frown. "It's not my place."

"What do you mean? What are you hiding from me?" This was not making sense.

The pixie shrugged again. "I'm sorry, Jonna. It's not my place." He refused to turn around and look Jonna in the eye.

Jonna felt the anger swell. His voice rose. "Whose place is it then?"

Bob held his ears, a grimace on his face. After a moment, it vanished, and his eyes darted to Jonna. "Elfleda." Bob nodded rigorously, lowering his hands. "She is the one who has to tell. You will only believe it from her."

Jonna's heart fell. The dread he had pushed away came rolling through his mind. *What if—no, it was not possible. They would not have hurt her!*

Bob shook his head but refused to say anything else.

Was the headshake from the pixie saying she wasn't hurt? The pixie did not seem to know what a straight answer was.

Jonna looked up. "Why are you doing this to me?" Frustration hit him from every side. Maybe a higher power knew what was going on.

"Who?" Bob looked up, trying to see what Jonna was looking at, but no matter how hard he tried, he could not figure out who Jonna was talking to. "Is this some sort of mage thing?"

Jonna turned to Bob. "I wish. You know I will find out."

Bob nodded. "You will."

"I mean it!"

The pixie nodded again, still not taking the hint. "I know you do."

Jonna looked him square in the eyes. "You're not going to tell me, are you?"

Bob cringed and slowly shook his head. "I'm sorry." He stared at the ground. "I cannot tell you."

"Arrrgh!" Jonna sat down and closed his eyes. "All right, no more questions."

Bob's face brightened. "Good. Now, how do we need to help the sprite?"

Jonna took a deep breath, letting it out slowly. "We have to remove a filter that allows the water to pass through. Once removed, the water sprite can leave. But there's a catch."

"There's always a catch." Bob grinned. "We pixies wrote the book on catches."

Jonna ignored him. "Whoever touches the filter becomes bound."

"You mean they can't leave?"

Jonna nodded. "That's what happened to the sprite when she tried to leave. I suspect the same thing will happen to anyone else, and I assume whoever is bound cannot destroy the filter themselves."

Bob closed his eyes. "Then it will take at least two: one to get the mesh, and the other to destroy it."

"Sounds like it to me." Jonna glanced at the door, hearing footsteps.

The door opened, and Logan walked in. He looked around suspiciously. "I see you're still talking to yourself."

Jonna nodded. "You should try it sometime. It's good for the soul."

Logan snickered, standing straight, chest out in Jonna's direction. "If you don't shut up, you'll be talking only with the spirits." His grin widened as he gave a mocking invitation. "Master Magnus says dinner is ready. You can come out of your room now."

"Thanks." Jonna gave a slight nod. As he approached, his eyes caught Logan's, and he continued. "You saw what happened to Ajax, right?"

The guard nodded.

Jonna smiled and kept the eye lock. "Well, I won't be that easy next time."

Logan took a step back. "I have a weapon."

"So did Ajax." Jonna laughed. "And you know where that got him."

Logan's grip tightened on the halberd's shaft. His voice became grave. "No funny business." He shook his weapon in Jonna's direction.

"Then you better show me to the dining room."

The guard increased his pace. They headed for the exit and turned down a second hallway. A series of doors appeared. After opening a middle one, they walked through.

"Right on time." Lilith sat at the end of a very long table. He motioned toward a spot at the middle, his words laced with sarcasm. "Is that too far?"

Jonna accepted the imbedded challenge. "If you want to have a conversation, we really should sit closer."

"Oh, very well." Lilith waved his hand. A man entered and directed Jonna to a seat closer to Lilith. "And instruct Serena she can sit over here." Lilith motioned to a spot nearer his end, on the opposite side from Jonna.

Around the room were many pictures of both men and women, all in various parts of the city, interwoven into the tapestries. Most of the early tapestries depicted happier times. However, those closer to the present showed fewer people and more objects, until the last showed only the palace itself.

Serena entered. Lilith and Jonna stood simultaneously. She came around the table in a beautiful evening dress. As the butler seated her, her eyes twinkled in the firelight. "Gentlemen," she said very softly.

Lilith nodded grudging approval in Jonna's direction. "I see they teach *some* manners where you come from." He sat down, pleased with himself. The first attack had begun.

"Upon occasion." Jonna took his seat as the main dishes came out. "Although, I have found the customs here somewhat *different*." Parry with a slight counter strike.

"Yes." Lilith picked up his fork, tasting one of the dishes. "*Different* as in your heritage. That means, the place you are from." He chewed for a moment. "*You* are different somehow. When I gaze to see the details, a fog hangs over the past."

Serena looked disapproving. "Father."

"Serena does not like me to pry." Lilith took another bite. "But the fact is, when it comes to you—" He looked in Jonna's direction. "There is nothing to see." The words held a slap.

Jonna was nonchalant, easily fending off the blow. "And that disturbs you how?"

Lilith smiled. "But of course. To know one's enemy, you must always find out his secrets." It was a blatant stab for the heart, and straight to the point. The mage had finally established which side they both stood on.

Serena's face bordered on anger. "Father!"

126

Lilith looked unabashed. "Pardon me. My daughter reminds me of the improperness of this line of thought, especially while dining." He looked toward Jonna, showing his teeth in a smile. "The truly puzzling issue is not so much who you are, but why you are here." He sipped his wine. "There is something about you. You come in elvish armor, yet you are not elvish. You battle with a guard, yet do not kill, in spite of the fact that he would have gladly killed you. You speak other ways." He glanced toward his daughter. "And have no concept of true power. Without power, there is no way to control one's destiny."

"Power is fleeting." Jonna smiled. "And fame flies away. Only things of the heart survive."

"So it is said." Lilith sat back, thinking. "Yet, here I am, the ruler of the City of Diggory. I am the great and mighty Magnus with whom no one can contend. I have ruled this city for fifty years, and see no reason why I can't continue." He stared straight at Jonna, challenging him. "Who can stand against my might?" The "you?" was all too obvious.

"So oppression, murder, the killing of innocents and all those who have magic, is justified to you?"

Serena looked from her father to Jonna. Her face turned redder.

"If it takes that to maintain status quo, by all means." Lilith smiled. "Surely, you see that order must be maintained."

Jonna shook his head. "Your very own people will not bear this. Despite your attempt to destroy any magic competitor, the people will revolt. You cannot stop them."

Lilith narrowed his eyes. "I have quelled their rebellion before. To do so again would be child's play."

"You underestimate the human spirit."

"Bah." Lilith waved a hand in Jonna's direction. "You are a dreamer. You would give all this wealth"—he did a broad sweep of the room with his right hand—"simply to waste it on human lives. They know nothing. If I gave them help, they would simply stick their hand out for more. Why not let them battle it out? Let them destroy those who cannot help themselves. By doing so, they make themselves stronger. Life must be fought for every single day."

"While you are here—" Jonna's voice held pity. "Safe, sitting in luxury."

Serena looked uncomfortable.

Lilith's eyes bore into Jonna. "Those who can, take."

"No." Jonna shook his head as if explaining to a little child. "Those who can, help."

"You are a fool." Lilith stood up. "You pretend to bring hope when there is none. You try to disrupt a system that is already working." The man tightened his fists. "Why," he boomed, "have you come here, Jonna McCambel?"

Jonna smiled, his voice remaining calm. "I have come to help, and help I shall."

"Guards, take him!"

"Father, no!" Serena leaned toward Lilith.

Her father glared at her. "Has your allegiance changed daughter? Sit back or I may deal with you the same!"

Serena jerked back, stunned by her father's words. "You wouldn't!"

His pupils seemed to darken in the light. "I have done worse." He paused, a faraway look crossing his face. "Now stay out of this." He turned toward the doors. "Guards!"

The doors to the room flew open. From all directions, his men filed in, Logan coming up beside Lilith.

Lilith turned to Logan. "Serena has told me of our friend's interest in the locked door. I think it's time we showed it to him."

"No." Serena's eyes grew wide. "You promised!"

Lilith ignored her, turning to Jonna. "Farewell, Jonna McCambel." He sat down to finish his meal.

Logan moved up beside Jonna. His voice quivered slightly. "Time's up. You can either make this easy or hard—your choice."

"I'll make it easy." Jonna stood up, bowing to Lilith and then to Serena. "If you'll excuse me."

Lilith gave a slight smirk, but his eyes watched his daughter. "By all means."

Serena sat perfectly still, her eyes on Jonna and Logan. Logan motioned for Jonna to rise, staying with the overall presentation, but there was definite relief in the guard's voice. "This way, m'lord."

The guards behind them parted, creating a path that led to the nearest door. As they reached it, Jonna glanced back. Serena had already left the room. Lilith was frowning. Lost in his own thoughts, Jonna's walk to the locked hallway door seemed short.

"Open it," Logan commanded those with him. Two guards moved forward, unlocking the mechanism that kept it secure. "Throw him in."

They caught Jonna's arms and legs, lifted him up, and tossed him through the doorway. He landed unceremoniously on a rough stone floor. Beside him was a flight of stairs that went down into the darkness. He looked back at the guards curiously. Standing up, he dusted off his pants. "Is that it?"

"'Is that it,' he says." Logan looked back at the other guards, laughing. "Try to walk toward us. We won't stop you." Jonna looked at the doorway, seeing nothing unusual. He stepped forward and cautiously held out a hand. The air in front was solid. His hand could not pass through. It reminded him of the invisible cave barrier.

"Lilith's magic." Logan's eyes sparkled. "Once you go in, you can't come out. We could even leave the door wide-open if we wanted, but Serena was afraid someone might accidentally walk in. Lilith permitted the locked door for his daughter's sake, although, I recall, the thought of an accidental walk-in actually amused him." Logan looked back at Jonna and grinned. "So long." They slammed the door and dropped the locks into place. Jonna's only source of light was a sliver at the door's base.

"Bob, you still there?"

"Of course I'm here. Did you think I fell off or something?"

"Well—"

"A fine thanks I get for sticking around."

"Bob, I need you to go find Elpis. I need you two to remove the filter."

"Me?"

"Well, it's obvious I can't get out, but maybe you can."

"I don't know." Bob looked at the door. "I don't know what magic this is, and I get a funny feeling we are not even in the palace."

Jonna studied the doorframe. It looked like the palace wall. "What do you mean?"

"It's not human magic. For all we know, the doorway could be a portal to another location."

"One way?" Jonna nodded slowly. It made sense. Since Lilith was drawing on the sprite's magic, it was the sprite creating the one-way portal. "I suspect it is held in place by the water sprite." Was the cave barrier done the same way? Jonna looked at the dim stairway going down. "If we release her, his control of her powers will wane."

Bob stood up and squared his shoulders. "Okay, let me try." He pulled a pinch of pixie dust from his pouch, measuring it carefully. "This is going to take some strong magic." Tossing the dust at the barrier, he leaned toward the door with his eyes closed, and—

"Bob?"

Bob opened one eye and looked over at Jonna. "Yes?"

"Nothing's happening."

"I know. I'm still trying!"

"Come on." Jonna turned toward the stairs.

The pixie looked indignant. "You don't want me to finish?"

"I think if you stood there all year long it wouldn't work."

"A lot of faith *you* have in me." Bob folded his arms, held them a second, and then dropped them. "But I think you're right. If it was going to happen, I would already be gone."

Jonna nodded. "Unfortunately, I agree. Wherever we are, our only choice is down."

There were no lights. Jonna placed a hand on the left wall to follow it, feeling for each step. After about five minutes, he wiped the sweat from his brow. "You couldn't make a light or something, could you?"

"A light?"

"Yeah, something we could see with." Jonna motioned toward the darkness. "It is dark, you know."

"Sure!"

"Sure? Why didn't you say so before?"

"You didn't ask."

"Pixies!" Jonna's voice was a little irate. "Do you think I like stumbling around in the dark?"

"Well, you weren't exactly stumbling."

"Bob? The light?"

"Oh, yeah. Here." Bob did something Jonna could not see, stomping a foot on his shoulder. Glitters of light descended over Jonna's head.

"Ouch! Do you always have to do that?"

"Shh." Bob held his hand in front of them. The glitters swirled around Jonna until finally reaching the floor. He dropped his hand abruptly to his side. "There," he whispered. "See it?"

Jonna tried to focus, but there was nothing to see. "Are you trying to be smart?"

"No, no, look!"

Jonna squinted as faint lines as the shape of the stairs began to appear. "This is a light?"

"It's better." Bob danced on his shoulder. "You see, with a traditional light, you can only see a certain distance from you. But—"

He motioned all around them. "With this type of light, you can see everywhere! All you do is focus on what you want."

"Bob, if I can't see what I need to focus on—" The scenery in front of Jonna changed. He saw the stairs, the walls, and if he squinted just a little more, he could see behind the walls. "I think you just gave me X-ray vision."

"X-ray? What's that?"

"It's—" Jonna tried to think. "It's a form of magic used in my world to see through objects."

"Hmm." Bob looked around. "Never heard of that. We pixies use it to see in the dark."

"I thought you used fireflies?"

"Only the females." Bob shook his head. "They like the entourage."

"I see."

Jonna moved down the stairs a little unsteadily. This type of sight took practice, but he was getting used to it. It was like putting on glasses for the first time and having to adjust to the distortion. At the bottom, they could hear the sound of chains, metal grinding against metal, and human voices crying out. In the dim glow they emerged in, his eyes reverted to seeing normal light.

He looked out through an archway and caught sight of a medium-sized, single-horned man. The man's skin held a red tint. His voice cracked as he said, "Greetings!" There was a note of laughter hidden beneath the words. "Welcome to my domain!"

"And who are you?"

"Why sir, did they not introduce you to my name before coming down?" He shook his head. "It is a shame how little respect I get."

"You live beneath the palace?"

The red-skinned man grinned. "Not exactly. To be precise, no. Welcome to Chernobog, my home, and now yours. I am Azazel, controller of this domain. Can I ask your specialty?"

Jonna frowned. "Specialty?"

"What do you do?"

"Well, I'm a—"

Bob whispered in his ear, "Hero."

"Hero." Jonna stopped and looked at the pixie. "Bob!"

"And I see there are two of you." Azazel's smile broadened as he took note of the pixie for the first time. "This is unique. We've never had a pixie before! It is normally so boring, human after human, all doing the same thing." The man's eyes widened in delight. "But you, a hero, and with a pixie? Ha! We have the perfect thing!"

"Bob, what did you just do?"

Azazel laughed. "This way, please."

Taking a side door, they emerged into a large arena. In the center of the arena were three women, each chained to a post. Azazel handed him an axe. "Now, here's the objective: you have to get to the girls and free them."

Jonna looked at the axe, and then at Azazel. "You want me to go to the center of the arena and let the girls loose?" He paused. "That's it?"

"It's what a hero does, doesn't he?"

"Well, I'm not—it can't be that simple."

Azazel wrinkled his nose. "I may have left out a few small details, but those are the essentials." His eyes brightened. "Ready?"

"No, I'm not ready. I'd like to hear the other—"

A burning arrow shot up over the arena, and Azazel waved them forward. "Go, there's not much time!"

"Go," Bob yelled excitedly. "Go!"

Jonna sprinted toward the center. A roar went up from the crowd all around him.

"Uh, Jonna?" Bob held onto his collar to keep from falling off.

Kicking the word out between breaths, Jonna answered, "Yes?" While he was used to physical activity, it had been a while since he had done an all-out sprint.

"Duck!"

A huge claw swooped out of nowhere, catching at the spot Jonna had been. Another claw grabbed at his right side. There was barely any time to look. No sooner did he turn than another claw tried to catch him. "What is that?"

"Uh." Bob tried to get a better view. "I don't know. I can't see them. They just swoop down and immediately disappear."

The word "them" seemed very ominous to Jonna. He eyed the first girl chained to a pillar. He was approaching her position fast. "The center is getting closer, but what is an axe going to do against metal chains?"

Bob ducked, even though a claw missed them by a foot. "Just try it!"

A blast of wind beat down upon them, and Jonna caught sight of huge wings flapping above their heads. The ominous shapes danced on the fringes of his thoughts, but the moment he turned to look, they disappeared into the shadows. The smell of putrid breath met his nose. He knew without turning that some huge mouth waited—waited for them to trip or fall.

He reached the first pillar and immediately checked the girl. Her eyes were closed; she was apparently unconscious. He swung the axe up over his head and sliced down, striking the metal surface. A metallic spark shot up, and then the chain snapped smoothly in two. "That's some sharpening!"

A roar went through the crowd. Jonna turned, dodged, and a claw smashed into the pillar. Whatever the claw-creature was, it screamed as it left.

Bob yelled, "Next!" He pointed at the girl to their right. Jonna bent down to check the first girl's pulse. "We need to get this one to safety."

The pixie screamed, "Duck!"

The sound of flapping wings forced Jonna to dive over the girl's body before rolling back to his feet. He returned, checking to make sure all was clear, and then pulled the girl into the safety of the center pillars.

The pixie wiped sweat from his brow. "What are you doing?"

"I can't just leave her in the open."

Bob's voice rose an octave. "I don't think there's time."

Jonna saw the claw coming. He swung the axe, slicing off a part of it. The creature screamed out in pain and swept away before Jonna could give it a second blow. Moving to the next girl, he cut the chain and pulled her into the center as well.

Bob looked in all directions. "One more to go!"

The calls of the claw-creatures became distant. The remnants of their voices echoed away.

"I think they're planning something big."

Silence. All the wings stopped flapping, and even the crowd held completely still.

Slowly, Bob said, "I don't like this."

Jonna hit the chain binding the third girl, slicing it clean, and then brought her quickly inside the pillar area. A roar went up from the crowd. Drums started beating. As the drums echoed around the room, the tempo built, accelerating the longer they played.

Bob pointed up. "Look at that!"

Flying objects with beaks and claws poured down from all directions. They swooped among the spectators, jerked them out of their seats, and carried them off into the darker reaches above the arena.

Azazel walked up, clapping furiously. A smile lit his face. "Very good! Very impressive!"

Jonna could not take his eyes off the carnage. "What—what happened?"

It did not make sense. If he and Bob were the center of the attack, why attack those watching? Even though the terror among the stands had died down, he could still see the horror and mutilation.

"You won, of course."

Turning in a circle, Jonna gazed at the massacre around him. "But, the people in the arena?"

"Oh, those—" Azazel shook his head. "Never mind them. The fact is you won. You saved the three women. You should be proud!"

"No, this is wrong. This is all wrong. Doing something right should not cause something wrong."

Jonna looked back to the stands. The crowd had dispersed, although a few stragglers were still running for cover.

"No." He looked harshly at Azazel. "I won't let you do it."

CHAPTER 14
AZAZEL'S ANGER

Bob jumped up and down, trying to make sure Jonna was awake. "Did you say something?"

Jonna opened his eyes. His head hurt. Reaching up, he felt a sore spot. "What happened?"

The pixie frowned. "When they threw you in the jail cell, you hit your head. For a while, I thought you would not wake, and then you mumbled."

The stone floor under him felt cold. He rubbed his eyes. *When had this happened?* "How long have I been here?"

"Since they tossed you in." Bob's frown deepened. "Don't you remember?"

Jonna got up, went to the wooden door, and pushed on it. "It's locked from the outside."

Bob nodded. "Azazel was very concerned that you not be allowed to walk around free and brought you to the jail at the center of town. He didn't like the way you reacted when you won the match."

It was something Jonna could not remember. "What did I do?"

"You almost succeeded in killing him."

"Then it wasn't a dream?" Jonna felt his head again. "What and where is Chernobog?"

Bob shrugged. "There are rumors. That's all I know."

"So what are the—" He looked at Bob and saw his expression. "Fine, forget I asked. You would think you really wanted to help."

"But I do," the pixie stated sincerely. "I just can't!"

"It's the whole *interfering with destiny spiel* again?"

The pixie nodded apologetically. "I do what I can."

Jonna sighed, taking in his surroundings. The room was eight by ten with only one door. "Any suggestions?"

"The guards did say dinner was to arrive later. Apparently, you merit a special meal."

Jonna grimaced. "No telling what that will be. What was this *hero* occupation you told me to say, anyway?"

Bob smiled proudly. "It was the first thing off the top of my head."

"The first—are you crazy?"

"Well, if I am, you more than me." Bob looked offended. "You're the one going to fight in the duel."

"Ah, that's right, the duel. It was the mysterious duel that started this whole mess." Jonna sat down on a bench, looking at the door. His thoughts drifted to Stephanie, the strange woman who had pretended to be her, and Elfleda, but he always came back to Stephanie. When was he going to find her? It certainly would not happen with him in jail.

Jonna went to the door and studied the lock. There had to be a bolt or bar holding the outside. "Bob, what type of mechanism holds the door shut?"

"Mechanism?"

"The lock, is it a bolt or a bar?"

"Bolt," Bob thought back. "I think. It's about the middle of the door."

"Good." Jonna pulled out his pocketknife, opening out the blade.

The pixie watched with interest. "I've never seen a dagger do that. The blade is so small." He reached out to touch it.

"Watch the blade," Jonna cautioned. "It's sharp. And it's not called a dagger. It's called a pocketknife." He ran the blade down the seam of the door and found the bolt. Working the blade back and forth, little by little, he slid the bolt back. "Good thing they're not more sophisticated." With a final slip, the bolt moved back far enough, and he pushed the door out.

Torchlight glowed around the wide room, illuminating the tables and chairs. Cell doors were lined along all four walls, with a narrower hallway leading down a darkened corridor.

"No guards?" Jonna walked toward the small corridor. He could see an exit in the dim light. All the cell doors around him contained small, square windows with bars.

A female voice came from the right side of the room, echoing from a cell. "Thank you, sir."

He turned at the voice, caught sight of one of the women he had rescued at the arena, and then moved to the barred window of her cell. "Are you all right?" Her door was bolted, but there was no lock. Pulling the bolt back, he let the door fall open. "You're free. Go."

The woman shook her head. "You don't understand. Where would I go?"

"What do you mean?"

"We are here, forever, locked in this city."

"That, I doubt." Jonna's face said what his words could not. "If I can leave, you can leave."

She turned away, tears coming to her eyes. "No."

"She's lost hope." Bob's own eyes shone with tears.

"Lost hope?" Jonna remembered coming close to that himself when he'd sat on the floor of the elvish palace. Moving into the cell, he took her by the hand. "What is your name?"

The woman's voice shook. "Deela."

"Deela, look at me." Jonna gently turned her head. "There is always hope. We will find a way to leave."

"Is that so?" Azazel walked in behind him. "I see cell doors do not hold you."

Jonna released Deela and faced Azazel. "I want to go home, and so do all these others."

"This is your home." Azazel smiled. "You must accept that."

"No, I don't." Jonna took a step forward. Azazel backed up.

"Now, now." The red-skinned man raised a hand as if to ward Jonna off. "You saw what happened the last time."

"And I say again, I want to go home, now."

Bob tugged Jonna's ear. "Uh, Jonna, perhaps it would be wiser to—"

"There is no way home." Azazel looked Jonna in the eye and sneered. "Don't you understand? It's a one-way, last-stop, never-come-back trip. That is our arrangement."

Bob spoke up, suddenly curious. "Arrangement with whom?"

That surprised Jonna. So even Bob didn't know?

"The Dark Mages Consortium, of course." Azazel grinned. "So you see, you really have no choice. Anyone here stays, and despite your success in the arena, you can't break the combined magic of all the Dark Mages."

"Maybe not." Jonna reached over and took Deela's hand, standing her up. "But we don't have to sit in jail." He turned to Deela. "Are the others in here?"

Deela shook her head. "I don't know."

"How quaint." Azazel gave a small, gleeful jump. "That's it. This will be the best entertainment yet. Give them hope, Jonna. Build them up so I can dash it from them!" He skipped around the room. "This is going to be better than eve—" Azazel fell down, hitting the floor.

Thomas materialized from the shadows behind him. He held a

wooden club. "I've had enough of his prancing around." He looked to Jonna. "Do you really think there is a way out?"

Jonna nodded. "If they can send us here, there has to be a way back. Besides, I am sure they communicate with Azazel somehow, and I can't imagine them not checking up on him. How else could they make sure he keeps his part of the bargain?"

Thomas nodded.

A familiar voice called out, "Jonna?"

"Phillip?" Jonna grinned. "Good to see you!"

The young boy beamed. "I'll never forget how we got that minotaur!"

Jonna laughed, and then thought about the spell that the old mage had given him. No. If he used it to try to leave, the spell would only bring him back, and this time there was no leprechaun to help him escape it. He looked down at Azazel. "Let's lock him in."

They left Azazel lying in a cell. They bolted the door with a little extra contraption Jonna added so the bolt could not be eased free. When they stepped from the jail, they saw the street was crowded with people.

"I'll be back." Deela squeezed his hand and disappeared into the crowd.

Thomas looked to Jonna. "Word of what you did in the arena has already spread."

Jonna's face fell. "I'm really sorry. I didn't know what he planned for the people watching."

"No." Thomas shook his head, completely discounting the event. "It wasn't that. It was the fact that you actually attacked Azazel that started the talk. No one has ever done that before."

Bob smirked. "And you don't even remember."

Jonna shook his head. "I don't."

"Don't what?" Thomas looked at Jonna curiously.

Jonna chuckled. "Believe it or not, I don't remember attacking him."

"Well, you did." Thomas nodded. "All three girls testified to it, as did some of the spectators watching from a distance. The spectators were hiding, of course. For the first time, you gave them hope."

"No wonder he locked me up."

Thomas nodded again. "That's why I came to find you. You've given hope to the people who are trapped here."

The crowds of people were increasing, spilling from the side alleys into the street. There were so many, only their heads could be seen. Jonna wrinkled his brow. "What do they want me to do?"

"Save them, of course," Thomas stated as if it were obvious. "Just as you helped me and my family with the minotaur, they want to be rescued from this place."

Deela came up behind him, leading another woman. "Jonna, this is Artemis."

"A pleasure to meet you, m'lord." Artemis curtsied. "When we return to my homeland, my family will reward you."

"I am not looking for a reward." Jonna paused, caught by the woman's eyes. "But you are welcome." Concern crept over Jonna. They were starting to get sandwiched in. "Thomas?" It took a moment to spot him in the crowd.

"I'm here." The man's voice rose to be heard over the crowd's voices.

Jonna raised his too. "Where is the main citadel?" He thought about the word he used and then changed it. "I mean, where does Azazel normally stay?"

"Close to here in the center of town." Thomas pointed, but it was impossible to see. "Azazel normally makes it a point of pride to show newcomers around the city." The crowd became louder than before.

"We need to get there."

Thomas nodded and spoke to Phillip. "Stay close," he warned. "Where's your mother?"

Phillip shrugged. Thomas turned to Jonna, almost yelling to be heard. "I have to find my wife. Phillip will lead you to Azazel's lair." Thomas turned toward Phillip. "Meet back at the house."

The boy looked excited. "Yes, sir!"

Jonna focused on Phillip. "Thank you." He motioned in the direction Thomas had pointed. "Lead the way."

Phillip slipped through the crowd with Jonna trailing behind.

"That's him," someone to Jonna's right called out. The crowd shifted, hands grabbed for Jonna, caught him, and pulled him in the wrong direction.

The crowd began to chant, "Jonna, Jonna!"

He tried to pull free, but there were too many hands. "No!"

They hoisted him in the air. A moment later, he was being carried on top of their hands, passed along like a log trapped in a river current.

Phillip was gone, lost in the sea of people, and Jonna had no idea which way to go—not that he could reach the ground anyway.

"Bob!"

"What do you want me to do? I'm caught too, you know!"

"Please, everyone," Jonna attempted. But no one could hear him over the chant, and he had no idea where he was being carried. The crowd worked with a mind of their own. They passed him several blocks, finally letting him down on a dais in the center of a large square.

"Speech," the crowd bellowed. "Speech!"

Jonna stared at the sea of people, his heart going out to them, but at the same time, he was afraid. Any crowd caught up like this could very easily turn into a mob, and in a way, they already had. If they wanted him to lead them, then Jonna had to take control.

He held up his hands, waiting for silence to fall. As more of the people saw him, their voices dropped away. The city became silent.

"You who live in Chernobog, whoever you are, wherever you came from, I know your greatest desire. I know you want to return to your own lands." A feeling of expectancy came from all directions. It was in the faces of all the people, who trusted him to show them how to go home.

"I, too, wish to return home. I am not a mage. I am nothing more or less than a man, just like you. If we band together, if we stand strong, we can, and will, go home."

The crowd roared. The sound shook the dais. When the noise dropped again, Jonna continued.

"For the moment, though, I need you to all be vigilant. Watch for Azazel's minions. Watch for his treachery. Just as he turned the flying creatures upon you in the arena, he looks for a way to dash your hope. Do not let him. Stand in your belief. If we can do that, we have already won."

The roar came up again, shaking the dais. As the voices died away, the shaking should have stopped, but it lasted a little longer. Jonna frowned. Something else was happening.

"How many sections are in this city?" He turned back to the crowd.

"Ten," someone hollered out.

"I need ten volunteers who are good sprinters. The rest need to return to their homes. When the way has been found, the runners will call you. Until then, you should prepare yourselves."

A surge of people pressed toward the dais, and Jonna numbered them off. "Those of you who are numbered, come with me." Jonna glanced around. "I need a guide to Azazel's lair."

"I'm here!" Phillip, almost out of breath, wormed his way through the crowd.

"Phillip!"

The boy grinned. "I saw them grab you, so I followed."

The dais shook. Jonna looked around as it hit again. "Do you have earthquakes here?"

"Earthquakes?" No one recognized the name.

"Times when the ground shakes?" Still no recognition.

A roar, a scream, broke through the city, sending shivers up Jonna's spine. All eyes turned in the direction of the sound, which came from the jail.

"Bob," Jonna said without taking his eyes off the spot. "I don't like this."

"Me neither." The pixie stared in the jail's direction as well. Something slammed inside the building. Huge pieces of stone shot up. The ground quivered, and loose stones clattered to the street.

Jonna left the dais, climbed onto a wagon, and used a series of barrels to get to the nearest roof. As he reached the top, the rest of the jail collapsed, revealing Azazel's head.

Bob's eyes opened wide. "Boy, did he grow!" He whistled. "I'd say he's at least twenty times your size."

Jonna watched Azazel as he turned around. "And he doesn't look happy."

"Jonna McCambel," Azazel boomed across the city. He spotted Jonna standing on the roof and smiled. "It's my turn now!"

The people panicked, trying to run in all directions at once. This was exactly what Jonna had been afraid of—mass hysteria.

"How did he do that?" Jonna was unable to stop the panic. The best he could do was draw Azazel away. He stared at Azazel, making a decision.

Bob shook his head. "He's a demon. Who knows what powers he has?"

"Demon?" Jonna glanced at Bob. "You let me attack a demon?"

"You would have done it anyway."

Jonna threw Azazel a look. "You're probably right."

Azazel reached down, pulled apart the jail wall, and pushed the rubble into the street. Picking up one of the pieces, he tossed it in

Jonna's direction.

"Get down!" Jonna leaped off the building into the wagon, not necessarily the best move, but easier than hitting the street. Parts and pieces of the building shattered as the missile slammed into the roof.

"Sheesh, time to go!" He jumped off the wagon, racing down the street. Phillip ran behind him, but Jonna warned him back. "Now may not be the best time. You'll be safer the further you are from me."

"But what if you need a guide?"

He answered between breaths. "Phillip, I need you safe. Your dad would never forgive me if you got hurt."

The boy's shoulders slumped. "Are you sure?"

Laughing, Jonna shook his head. He remembered being a young boy himself. "I'm sure. Go!"

Turning toward a series of stairs, Jonna rushed to the top of a house. From this vantage point, he could see Azazel moving in the wrong direction rather than chasing him. He could hear screams coming from the people Azazel carelessly stepped, shoved, knocked around, and squashed.

Jonna searched the city with his eyes. "I can't let this go on." From this position, he could see how it was laid out. Behind him was the city wall. It ran along a chasm all the way around the city. Over the wall, past the chasm, was a desert as far as the eye could see.

"No wonder people want to leave." Bob shivered. "No trees or grass anywhere."

"Not to mention they were forced to come." Jonna glanced at Bob. "However, there are people who like places like this."

"Well, that can't be good! They must be out of their minds."

Jonna chuckled, and let it drop. He caught sight of Azazel. "Ready?"

"Ready for what?"

"We need to get his attention."

Bob looked at Jonna as if he were crazy. "We just got out of his attention. Can't someone else play for a while?"

"You're the one who told me I was a hero."

"Yeah," the pixie agreed. "But don't let it go to your head."

Jonna reached the bottom of the stairs. *Good, Phillip was nowhere around.* They moved from building to building, following the trail of debris that Azazel left. Rounding a corner, they ran into his leg.

"There you are!" Azazel reached down and tried to catch hold of Jonna to haul him up.

Jonna sidestepped. In Azazel's present form, his motor skills were clumsy. "You've got to be faster than that," he taunted. Avoiding a second grab, Jonna picked up a three rocks and chunked two at the demon.

"So you want to play that way?" Azazel picked up a table-sized rock and tossed it in Jonna's direction.

Jonna leaped, dodging to the left, but the explosion of debris knocked him off his feet.

Azazel laughed. "Want to try again?" He picked up another huge rock.

Jonna gritted his teeth. "Sure, my turn." The third rock he had picked up flicked out, following a tight curve. It went between Azazel's extended hands, passed into his mouth, and slammed into the back of his throat.

Azazel's face went red. He gagged and coughed as tears came to his eyes. The projectile spewed out of the demon's mouth as he gasped for breath. The rock in demon's hands crashed down in front of him. He glared at Jonna, eyes red, and roared.

Bob screamed, "Run!" It deafened Jonna's ear.

"I can hear you," Jonna called back, turning heel and sprinting down a side street. The ground shook as Azazel stomped, chasing Jonna as best he could while maneuvering around the houses. Anything not nailed down jumped, including Jonna. With each step, Jonna found it harder to stay on his feet.

"The wall." Bob pointed to a narrow set of stairs. "Go there!"

Jonna turned, taking the steps three at a time, leaping the last few. The stomping stopped. He turned back to get his bearings and saw Azazel. For a moment, he must have lost Jonna, but now his gaze bore upon him.

Azazel took a deep breath, his face and ears turning bright red. He started to run, building speeding, and headed straight for Jonna.

"Uh, Jonna." Bob shifted nervously. "Don't you think we ought to run again?"

Jonna continued to stare at Azazel as the wall itself began to shake. "Not yet." A hundred feet and closing, seventy-five, fifty, twenty-five . . .

"Jonna!"

"Now, we run." Jonna leaped, jumping to reach a tower set upon the wall.

Azazel roared when he saw Jonna changing direction but was unable to stop his momentum. He slammed into the wall, knocking it off the foundation, off the edge, and down into the chasm surrounding the city. His eyes went wide. He clawed for the remaining portion, trying to find something to grab. Stone by stone the tower came apart, unable to support the demon's weight, with stone chunks falling into the abyss.

The tower support beams collapsed around them. The floor split as the tower was pulled closer toward the chasm.

"If I go," Azazel boomed, grabbing hold of a window in the tower wall, "so do you!" He ripped the final support from the structure, reached a hand over the wall, and crumpled the window arch.

The demon fell along with the tower and part of the wall. Jonna was caught in the midst of the tumbling stones falling with the debris. The wall opened up behind him. He could see what was left of the supports to his right. They were still standing, but the distance was too far to jump.

"Leap," Bob cried out. "Leap now!"

"I can't make it!"

The pixie growled, "Just do as I say! Leap in the name of all that's good!"

Jonna grunted as he pushed off. The stones beneath him collapsed. He reached out, trying to grasp the edge of the nearest standing wall, but his fingers fell short.

He watched the wall pull away as a calmness settled over him. "And now, I fall."

Jonna knew what was going to happen next. The chasm below laughed at him. As he turned in the air, a rope slapped him in the face. He grabbed it, felt himself swing wide, and slammed into the other part of the wall.

"Hold on." Phillip peered over the edge. When the boy saw Jonna had the rope, he cried out, "Pull!"

CHAPTER 15
A CITY WITH DESIGNS

The rope heaved upward, Jonna clinging, digging his fingers into the twine that gave it strength.

Phillip called, "Pull!"

Jonna watched as the journey upward continued. Phillip's face came closer.

"Pull!"

Hands grabbed hold of Jonna. They hauled him up the remaining few inches. When the hands let go, his body rolled over. Jonna lay there breathing in gulps of air.

"Bob?"

Bob wiped sweat from his own forehead, exhaling. "Yes, Jonna?"

Jonna took a deep breath and then exhaled. "You do know pixies can fly?"

Bob nodded. "I know."

"But you stayed. Why?"

"I told you I was here to help."

Jonna closed his eyes a moment. As he rested on his back, the strained muscles in his body burned. "I think I need a good night's rest." He sniffed. "And a bath, too."

Bob stifled a snicker. "Yep, you stink." Both began to laugh.

Thomas moved past the others, sitting down beside Bob and Jonna. "Jonna, you okay?"

Jonna opened his eyes and moved to a sitting position. He could feel every muscle. "A little sore, but still alive." He extended his hand. "Thanks."

"You're welcome." Thomas smiled, shaking his hand and patting him on the back. "Glad you made it." They both stood up.

"And you." Jonna spied Phillip standing a little way off. "Come here."

Phillip came forward, a wide grin on his face.

Jonna gave him a hug. "You were great!"

Phillip beamed.

Looking back down the wall, Jonna saw people beginning to gather. "Thomas, you think I could find a place to rest before we head to Azazel's lair?"

"Sure." Thomas turned to the others. "Okay, everyone, the party's over."

A cheer came up as Jonna crawled down the tumbled stones. The burning had let up, though his muscles still ached.

"Follow me," Thomas guided. "We've a place down here."

He was led to a small two-story house a few blocks down.

"Janice thought you might need a rest."

They showed Jonna a building at the back of the house, and to Jonna's surprise, the smell of hot water met his nose. "A bathhouse, here?"

"This prison city is larger than the populace that lives here. New comers are cordially invited to pick where they want to live. It's not like the farm, but—"

Jonna chuckled. "No apologies. This is exactly what I need."

"My wife prepared this while we were at the wall. She insisted, almost like she knew." Thomas opened the door, let Jonna pass through, and then closed it behind him. A table held a small assortment of things to eat. The moment he saw it, his stomach went into overdrive.

Without a pause, he gobbled down a few of the fruits, and then tasted the bread and meats. It was not so bad for a prison city.

When he'd had enough, the sore muscles returned. Sitting his drink down, he remembered the smell of the hot water and the promise of a bath beyond the next door. It would be nice to relax.

Steam wisped out as he opened the door. The smell of the hot water cleared his head. He anticipated the heat soothing his muscles. Passing through the door, he went to the shallow end of the pool, dropped his clothes by the edge, and slid in.

"This is nice." He moved back, floating in the water. "Bob?" A good five minutes went by, and Jonna relaxed, finding some soap and a scrub cloth. *Where was that pixie? Probably still eating. Wait a minute, what did pixies eat?*

His face stung. Apparently, he had managed a few scratches from the falling debris. He was lucky it was no worse.

The cleanup was quick. After that, he soaked. The heat did wonders for his muscles, but the pixie had yet to answer. "Bob?"

When no one responded, Jonna closed his eyes. He was too tired to go look around. "I guess he gave me the time off."

A female voice answered, "Somebody did."

146

Jonna sat up, looking around. He moved back over to his clothes, reached for them, and found them gone.

Artemis stepped from a side area, naked, and moved into the water. "I told you my family would reward you. Your clothes were taken to be cleaned."

"Uh—" Jonna moved back toward the stone steps, thought better of it, and went deeper into the water.

"You have saved our lives twice now." Artemis smiled, moving toward him. "For that, I am your slave."

"I really don't need a slave." Jonna scooted further away, bumping into the edge of the pool.

"A wife then? A lover?"

"I have a wife." Jonna grabbed onto the words. "She is my lover."

"Hmm." Artemis almost purred, playing in the water with her hands. "Do you not find me attractive?"

"I—you're very attractive." Jonna spotted a towel beside the pool. He grabbed it, putting it around himself as he stepped out. "But I am very taken."

Jonna slipped into the other room and placed his back against the wall. Whatever happened now, he was sure there would be trouble. He meant no disrespect, but you do not go walking up on someone and making that kind of offer.

"Bravo, lad." Bob appeared, coming to stand on his shoulder. "You did well against the sirens."

"Sirens?"

"A figure of speech." Bob scratched his head. "But I can't remember where it came from."

"It was one, and she was not hard to resist." He sighed. "Well, maybe a little."

Bob shook his head. "Did you not find her attractive?"

"Bob, what type of person do you think I am? Of course I found her attractive. But the fact is I am married, and happily so."

"Yeah, there's that." Bob frowned, that something-else-not-said on his mind.

"Okay, spill it." Jonna closed his eyes. "What's on your mind?"

The pixie remained silent a little too long.

"It's about Stephanie again, isn't it?"

The pixie nodded. "Yes and no."

"Is Stephanie okay?"

The look on Jonna's face made Bob cringe. "Yes." The pixie paused. "And no."

"Which is it?" Jonna growled. "You, Dorothy, all of you, always hinting about something I don't understand! Isn't there enough drama going on here without me having to deal with this?" He looked away from Bob, spotting the window. There was no glass, only an old wooden shutter. If Artemis had gotten in, who else might be listening? He lowered his voice. "Sorry for yelling." Jonna laid his head back against the wall.

Bob's focus stayed on a small speck in the floor as he listened to Jonna's words. Twice he started to say something but each time stopped.

"Jonna, it will be okay." However, it was not Bob who spoke. It was Artemis.

Jonna's eyes went wide. "I—"

She smiled at him, now fully clothed, and placed his elvish clothing beside him. "I didn't understand before, but I do now. Your wife has been taken, and you fight to free her."

"Yes." He nodded. "I meant no insult."

She nodded. "You are loyal and true, even better than I thought you to be. I am a little saddened to see you not available." She winked. "But I am honored that you are who you are. If you have a need, you know to ask." She bowed slightly and then moved backwards, disappearing out the door.

"Holy cow!" Bob tumbled back, sitting down on Jonna's shoulder. "Wow, talk about luck!"

"What do you mean?"

"Don't know who Artemis is?"

Jonna shook his head. His whole body was playing out, and the guessing games were not keeping him awake.

"You don't know? Don't know!" Bob slapped his own forehead, grunted at the slap, and blinked heavy eyes. "Just the daughter of King Dagda, second ruler of the North West Kingdom."

"North West Kingdom?" Jonna found it hard to say the words as his eyes tried to close.

"Aye, I have relatives there." Bob's eyes twinkled just as he closed them and yawned. "And she just told you to ask what you will."

"What?"

"You really don't know?" Bob shook his head. "Silly humans don't

148

even know their own kind."

"Bob." Jonna leaned his head toward him. "You know I'm not from here."

"Oh yeah." The pixie gave a small chuckle and a yawned longer. "I keep forgetting that."

Jonna mimicked the yawn, fighting to keep his eyes open. Bed or no bed, his body was about to give out. "Bob, do you think—"

Bob began to snore.

Jonna's own eyes were just as heavy, so heavy he could hardly see the floor. The wisp of a delicious perfume caught his nose, but he could not open his eyes to see who it belonged to. After all, it had been some time since he had slept. His days and nights between the cabin and here were all messed up. Talk about jet lag. He wondered why that was so. Perhaps, if he rested only for a moment—

He stretched, feeling refreshed, and pulled the covers around him. Covers? His eyes snapped open, and he found himself lying in bed with the smell of perfume in the air. It was the same scent he had detected before falling asleep.

A young woman approached, bowing before him. "Did you sleep well? I've made you a delicious sweet tea."

Jonna accepted the cup, shifted to a sitting position, and tried to figure out where he was. She spotted his confusion.

"You are in my home. I am one of the women you rescued from the pillars, Almundena. Thomas was good enough to help me bring you here. We thought you would be more comfortable." A bit of laughter crossed her face. "Apparently, you fell asleep in the bathhouse."

Jonna's face went red. He had been tired but had not realized how much. "It's a pleasure to meet you." He nodded, tasting the tea. "This is very good."

"I had hoped you would like it." Almundena sat down on the bed beside him, frowning as she studied his face. "I have some ointments that may help." Rising, she left the room.

He looked into the mirror beside the bed. The minor scratches, and one small cut, were the main troubles. Nothing serious, but they did need attending. Almundena returned with a small vial, dabbing it on a cloth. She gently rubbed it over his face and neck. It stung yet soothed at the same time.

149

When he looked in the mirror again, the abrasions were gone. "How did you do that?"

She laughed. "I'm a mage, servant to a great lord in the city of Varona. I traveled to Diggory to do my lord's bidding. When I arrived at the gates, I was taken prisoner and brought here."

"They never said why?"

Almundena shook her head. "Nor did they tell me to leave."

"They must have thought you a threat." Jonna looked at the girl, her dark hair dropping past her shoulders. It reached the small of her back. "I take it your lord and Lilith were not on good terms?"

"Actually, no." She laughed. "You are very perceptive."

He laughed with her. "I've been told that a time or two."

It was strange how comfortable he felt. It was as if they were old friends. Something about her reminded him of—he shook his head.

"Something troubles you?" She studied his face.

"No, not really. I—" Almundena looked up, as if seeing something else.

The Sight. Jonna recognized the reaction more easily. "What do you see?"

"I see a kingdom at war," she said in a faraway voice. "A princess that offers herself, and—" She stopped and then turned back to Jonna, a look of concern on her face.

"And?"

Almundena forced the concern away, replacing it with a smile. "It is enough. You need to get ready." She stood up, going to the door. "Your clothes are at the foot of the bed. When you are finished dressing, we can leave." Almundena stepped into the other room.

"We're going somewhere?" Jonna slipped out of the covers and donned his clothes. They smelled clean, and for the first time, he realized his hair was washed. He finished slipping on his shirt and headed in the direction Almundena had gone. "Did somebody wash my hair?"

"You were really out." Almundena gave a slight smile. "And apparently, you left the pool a little early." She winked.

Jonna blushed. "I guess I did."

"You're an unusual man, Jonna," she said thoughtfully. "I see things in the future, things you will not expect but have ample strength to deal with." She looked to the front door. "And now, I need an escort."

"To where?"

"To the celebration of the fallen Lord Azazel." She took Jonna's arm. "I suspect there are many who want to thank you."

"Maybe I should go check out his lair." Going to this celebration was not his idea of fun. He would prefer to continue his search.

She shook her head. "The people need you right now. You've given hope to the city. Seeing you tonight will help make it grow, and the more it grows, the stronger the bond. When the time comes, they will obey you."

Okay, this was getting just a little out of hand. "Almundena, I don't want people to obey me. I want to find my wife."

"Exactly." She smiled. "That is why you are the best candidate. The others will abuse their power."

Jonna sighed. "There are others? Someone is already trying to gain control?"

"In the absence of authority, all people seek a leader, even if it is they themselves. You have captured their hearts. Show them you will stand by them, and they will follow you anywhere."

"Guide them to a place of safety." Jonna found himself looking up at nothing in particular. Just as he had received knowledge in the garden, so he saw it now.

There was a sparkle in Almundena's eyes. Did she know what had just happened?

They stepped out into the street. People moved in from other areas, flowing toward a central square. The closer they came, the louder the music. Young and old played and danced, clapping as they moved about. Young children dashed from place to place, weaving through the crowd.

"Ah, there you are." Thomas came forward, excusing himself from a group. "I see you brought our sleeping hero." He grinned at Jonna. "I take it you are well rested?"

Jonna nodded. "Thank you. I didn't realize how tired I was."

"Jonna!" Deela came from nowhere, giving him a hug. Her eyes were bright. She was enjoying the music and song.

Another woman approached, and Almundena gave a single cultured nod. "Artemis."

"Almundena." Artemis smiled, returning the nod. "I see you brought our hero with you."

Almundena smiled back. "He has been safe and untouched."

Both women laughed, but Jonna caught an unspoken edge.

Thomas whispered in his ear, "They are slightly competitive. It is a female thing. Think nothing of it."

That brought to mind an interesting question for Jonna. "How did the three of them get chained to the pillars?"

"Deela was chosen by Azazel. The other two volunteered."

Jonna's eyes grew round. "Why?"

"He was going to sacrifice someone. In a place like this, what choice did they have?"

"They both care for the people." Jonna's heart went out to those around him, despite the fact he would rather be somewhere else. "They needed hope."

Thomas nodded. "When the two stood up and volunteered, it annoyed Azazel greatly. He wanted to make an example of them, to show everyone their foolishness. Then, you showed up."

A feeling of déjà vu went through Jonna, and he realized he had seen this before. What did that mean? Was it The Sight or silly superstition? Did he really have The Sight? Moreover, if he did, why couldn't he find his wife?

Janice came up and took Thomas's arm. "I want to dance. Azazel is dead, and we are free! Well—" She looked at Jonna, hope in her eyes. "We will be free!" She reached over, kissed Jonna on the cheek, and then spun away, dragging Thomas with her.

Almundena whispered in Jonna's ear, "Amalric is coming. He's pompous enough to think he should be in charge."

Jonna turned, watching the man approach. Upon seeing Jonna, Amalric changed from smiling and greeting people to adopting a very formal, businesslike stance.

He congratulated Jonna. "You have done wonders for *our* city. A superb battle of wits you did with Azazel."

Jonna blinked. The word "our" was just a little too prominent in the sentence. "Why, thank you." He nodded acceptance, slowly.

"Battle of wits?" Someone came up behind Jonna, slapping him on the back. "He single-handedly took him down!" The person slapped Jonna again, looking toward Amalric. "And where were you, o' boisterous one?"

Amalric's face kept composure, but the tips of his ears turned red. "This is not about who did what." He redirected the comment. "But about how we all pull together for the future."

"That is true." Artemis nodded, slipping seamlessly into the conversation.

Encouraged, Amalric continued. "We need a leader, not a warrior. There are a few of us here who would humbly take that position." He bowed. "Yours truly, for one."

Artemis nodded, but Jonna could see the steel glint in her eye.

Another man stepped up, having spotted the group talking. "I think you're right."

"Gerontius." Almundena nodded to the newcomer. "Have you met Jonna?"

"Only from afar." The look in Gerontius's eyes said even more. It would not bother him if Jonna went so far away, he never came back. "I think we do need a political leader."

"So you think the threat is over?" Deela stepped from behind Jonna.

"Most certainly," Gerontius continued. "Azazel is dead. The city can rule itself now."

Almundena's face turned hard. "We don't want to rule ourselves. We want to go home." She motioned to those around. "This festival is a celebration of that fact alone. No one *wants* to stay." She bore into Gerontius's eyes.

"Excuse me." Amalric stepped forward, turning the spotlight on himself. "Before we go making promises we cannot keep"—he frowned at Jonna and then smiled at the others—"shouldn't we see if we can go home?"

"There is a way," Jonna declared, his faith standing forth. It was a shield against their words, and it spread to those who listened.

"That's a matter of opinion, not fact," Gerontius tried to counter, yet he could not win. Not here and not now. "But this discussion is for another time and place."

There was something funny about that statement, and Jonna remembered when Lilith had spoken with him in the garden. Was Gerontius trying to hint at something, a hint directed at Jonna?

"An evil heart," Almundena said quietly to Jonna. "There are some who came to this place who truly belong. Gerontius ingrained himself well with Azazel. You might call him his shadow."

"Dance with me." Deela grabbed Jonna's hand, pulling him into the circle of people, twirling around and around. He did, though his thoughts kept going to somewhere else.

Deela moved close as the dance called for it. "Thank you, Jonna.

You have saved a part of me I thought lost."

"I'm glad you're happy." A smile crossed his face. He spotted Gerontius in the crowd. The man had not taken his eyes off Jonna since they met.

"May I step in?" A young man moved up, offering his hand to Deela. She looked at Jonna for agreement.

"Of course." Jonna bowed and stepped away, reaching the outer ring of people. Where were the others? Artemis was talking with a group to his left. Almundena could not be seen.

Drinks shifted through the crowd. The celebration started to grow. Food piled on the tables as more people arrived.

Jonna spotted Phillip sitting on a bench and eating some treats. "May I join you?"

The boy's eyes lit up. "Sure, want some?"

Jonna waved it away. "But thank you." He looked around at the festival, yet his thoughts would not rest. "Do you think you can show me Azazel's lair? You can come back when we're done."

A look of excitement crossed the boy's face. "Sure!" He put down the food. "I'm ready!"

"So am I." Gerontius came up beside them. "And I think we need to go this way." There was something in his pocket. Something pointed. A wand? He had only seen Queen Dorothy with one. They did not have guns here, did they? Gerontius nodded toward the alley. "Be my guest."

"Phillip, go find your father." Jonna nodded toward the party. "We'll go to Azazel's later."

"But I want to—"

Jonna shook his head. "I'll be back, and then we can go."

Gerontius waited until the boy was out of hearing. "You want to go home? I can show you."

"You can?"

The man nodded. "But we don't have very much time." He headed for a side alley, looking back. "Are you coming?"

Jonna nodded, following him into the darkness, though he felt like someone was behind them. To his amazement, as the light from the celebration faded, the X-ray vision Bob had given him kicked in. It was nice to know he still had it, but no matter how many times he glanced back, he still saw no one else.

A candle waited at the end of the alley, and the X-ray vision disappeared. Gerontius picked up the candlestick and turned into a small building. The room was bare with only odds and ends for furniture.

"Several years ago," Gerontius began, "I overheard Azazel talking about how he communicated with the Dark Mages Consortium." Gerontius stopped, throwing a glance at Jonna. He was obviously trying to judge Jonna's interest and to know how much to reveal.

They left the room, moved down a small hall, and turned to the right. The second room they entered contained old tables and chairs. Gerontius checked each table, found what he was looking for, and slid one of the tables back. As he did, a spot on the wall opened, revealing stairs that led down. "This way."

Jonna hesitated. Not only did he feel like they were being followed, but Gerontius was also dragging out the explanation of what was ahead.

His guide stepped onto the stairs and then glanced back. "Are you coming?"

The truth was in Gerontius's eyes. The man was planning something. Yet if there was any chance of escaping, Jonna had to follow up on every single lead. He nodded slowly. "Show me the way."

CHAPTER 16
CRY FOUL

Jonna moved to catch up. "You seem to know quite a few secrets." He stepped behind Gerontius, following the lone candle light.

"If you listen, you can hear lots of things." Gerontius glanced back. They reached the bottom of the stairs and walked down a long hall with extinguished torches. Multiple doors, all shut, stood to their sides. Only their footsteps echoed down the empty corridor as Gerontius lit the torches one by one.

"I first came to this prison city in search of my father," Gerontius confided. "I found him, not realizing there was no way to leave. After a while, I learned to adapt, and won the trust of Azazel."

"So he told you how to get out?"

"No." The man shook his head. "He would never tell me, and I would never ask. I worked as his liaison, finding ways to help the people when I could, lessening the burdens he placed upon them when I dared. It worked. Over time he seemed to become more—human. At least, until you showed up." Gerontius slowed down, focusing on the words as he spoke them. "You brought out the worst in him. In a matter of moments, he reverted to the being I first knew many years ago. I tried to reason with him when he threw you into jail, but he would not listen. It was then I knew that things were going to change."

They reached a small door. Gerontius swung it back, motioning for Jonna to go ahead. Something stirred behind them, but the man paid no attention, caught up in his own story.

"They did change," he continued. "Azazel is dead."

"You sound almost sorry." Jonna listened closely to the man. "You are free now. You can go home."

Gerontius's voice turned angry. "This is my home. All that I knew, all that was in the outside world, is gone forever. Why should I want to leave?"

Jonna looked him in the eye. "I do not share your feelings. I have a wife waiting somewhere beyond the border of this realm, and I must find her."

A smile crept upon the man's face. "I believe you, and so I give this gift. Go ahead. Step into the room."

Jonna paused. The man was telling the truth, and yet, there was something about his words. . .

Gerontius sneered. "If you don't want to know what's in there, we can go back."

"So, if I don't go in?"

"You'll never find your way home." A faraway look crossed the man's face. "It's your choice: now or never."

Jonna looked at the pointed object still in Gerontius's pocket. "I don't really have a choice, do I?"

The man smiled. "No, but I thought I'd give it a try." He pulled the wand out of his pocket. "Get in."

Jonna stepped into the circular room. In the center was a dais containing a large red gem. Gerontius placed the candle on a table. "This is the key to Azazel's communication with the Consortium. This is the way out."

"What do I do?"

"Walk to the pad and speak the words, 'Baqir Janus Tillo Cassius.'"

Jonna walked around the room, putting the dais between him and Gerontius. "So you found out despite Azazel not telling you? When I do, what happens?"

"You go home," the man stated without emotion. "And the city will live on."

Shaking his head, Jonna frowned at him. "They will know what happened. They will know you did something."

"They will suspect." Gerontius put his hand on a lever beside the door they came through. "After you're gone, I will bury this room."

"A kill switch?"

The man nodded. "It was designed by Azazel himself should something ever happen."

Jonna said quietly, "You've become just like him, and you want to take his place." The words drifted across the room to Gerontius.

The man flinched as if jabbed by something sharp.

Jonna pressed again. "You've become just like Azazel. You want to rule this city."

"No," the man denied. "I will help this city. We will grow and prosper!"

"By keeping people against their will? When they find out what you've done"—Jonna shook his head—"your fate will be worse than Azazel's."

"It will be too late. They will have adapted to their new life. Don't you know the old saying, time heals all wounds?"

"But it can't bring back the dead." Jonna's words fell like stone, crashing to the ground.

"You're the guilty one," the man challenged. "You killed Azazel!" The wand in his hand circled twice. "Perun!" Lightning shot from the end of the wand, lashing out at Jonna.

Jonna ducked behind the dais, feeling the heat as it surged overhead. "You're not doing a very good job of avenging your friend."

"He was not—" The man's eyes bulged, and his face turned red. "You dare put me on the side of the enemy?"

Jonna called from behind the dais, "You defend his name. You avenge his death. What do you think?"

The man shifted, moving around the dais, looking for a spot to get a clear shot at Jonna. "You speak the words of trickery and deceit," he growled. "I'm rescinding my offer. I will enjoy watching you die!" He struck again. The lightning scorched the floor.

Jonna checked the room for something, anything he could use as a weapon. There was a chair in the far corner, a small writing table, a few stones, dust on the floor, and the kill switch on the wall. He stayed low, judging the distance, keeping out of sight. Without a weapon, it was much harder to attack. He had to get closer.

Jonna continued to goad the man. "And when you have kids, what will you tell them? I killed innocent people in the name of justice? I killed a man who was willing to help save you from being locked here forever? What blood is on your hands? What decisions did you make in the name of Azazel?"

"No!" Gerontius lunged forward. "I did what I had to do. I saved the people!"

"You chose who would die, didn't you?" Jonna continued to taunt him. "You picked those who Azazel would abuse and torture. You enjoyed how it made you feel. You enjoyed that feeling of power, and now it's all gone."

Rage took Gerontius, and he leaped onto the dais. "NO, I was his right-hand man!" His eyes suddenly went large. "I was his—" He spun, trying to find Jonna. Gerontius's narrowing, knowing stare came back. He screamed, firing the wand in all directions. The smell of charred wood and stone filled the room. "You are the villain! You killed Azazel!"

Bob was on Jonna's shoulder again. "He's lost it!"

Jonna ducked as bolts went in all directions. "When did you get back?"

The pixie shook his head. "Leave you alone and look what you do."

"Bob, there's no time for that!"

Even Bob jumped as energy crackled overhead.

With pursed lips, Jonna focused on Gerontius. "Ready?"

"What are you going to do?"

"When he gets close to this side, I'm going to take his wand."

The pixie grabbed onto Jonna's collar. "Are you crazy? You'll get us both killed!"

"What do you mean both of us?" Jonna countered. "You can fly right out."

Bob growled, standing his ground. "I told you, I'm here to help!"

"Then help." Jonna reached over the stand, caught Gerontius's feet, and jerked them out from under him. The man fell backwards, striking the dais, gasping for air. At the same time, the wand flew up, arced to the ground, and skated across the floor. Jonna reached over and picked up the red gem.

Gerontius screamed, "You can't do that!"

Jonna looked down at him. "I can. I will. These people will have a choice to leave." He walked toward the door.

The man rolled over, reached the wand, and aimed it in Jonna's direction. "No—you—don't," he challenged. "PERUN!"

Lightning arced out as Jonna ducked. Most passed over his head, striking the kill switch on the wall, but a wisp caught Jonna, knocking him out the door. His body tingled all over. His lungs refused to breathe. Gradually, the pain subsided. It was a good thing most had missed!

The walls shook as cracks formed. Huge stones began to fall, striking both in and out of the room.

Bob dodged back and forth. "Get up!" Moving as fast as he could, the pixie diverted stones that fell too close to Jonna. "We've got to get out of here!"

Jonna rolled over, realizing he had dropped the red gem. Using his hands, he searched the immediate debris. "It's gone! Where is it?"

Both hunted around before spotting it near the door. A pile of stones had already made it hard to get through.

Bob leaped forward. "I'll get it!"

For the first time, Jonna saw Bob really fly, zooming through the falling debris, racing to the corner. Bob picked up the gem, turning around with a smile. "See? I got it!"

"Bob!"

A stone dropped, slammed down, and sprayed fragments in all directions. Bob was knocked backwards. Though he still managed to keep the gem, he was not acting coherent.

Jonna shifted past the barrage and reached the area beside the door. "Bob, snap out of it!"

Gerontius's hand appeared through the door. "No, you don't!" He grabbed Jonna.

Jonna leaned to the right, avoiding a stone that slammed into the floor. Hooking Gerontius's arm, he hyper-extended the elbow, popping the man's shoulder out of socket. Gerontius screamed, going limp as the ceiling continued to shake.

Jonna called out without turning around, "Bob!"

"I'm okay." The pixie staggered to his feet. He shook his head slowly. "What did I miss?"

"We've an additional complication." Jonna picked up Gerontius's limp body. "Now we have three to get out."

"I thought he tried to kill you?" The pixie's amazement turned to disgust.

Jonna nodded. "But he's still alive. I can't leave him to die."

"But we won't be if we take him with us!"

"You go ahead." Jonna waved him on. "And remember the phrase, 'Baqir Janus Tillo Cassius.'"

"Baqir Janus Tillo Cassius," Bob repeated. "What's that for?"

"It's the spell that opens the gateway. Go. You have to get the gem out."

"But—"

"Go!"

Bob took off, moving through the stones as fast as he could. Jonna shifted Gerontius's weight, took a deep breath, and started forward. A shadow stepped from a nearby room. He leaped back as a halberd arced toward him, still fighting to keep his grasp on Gerontius.

Ajax stepped forward. His eyes burned with hatred.

Jonna exhaled. "Not you too."

"You cost me everything!" Ajax lunged forward, ignoring the stones that fell. Bits shot in all directions. The halberd sliced toward Jonna.

Jonna sidestepped, but with Gerontius's weight, his speed was hampered. The blade narrowly missed. "You do know we're in mortal danger?"

Ajax swung the weapon, this time side to side, knocking ceiling stones to the left and right. "You're going to know what mortality really means!" He lunged, but a stone deflected the blade. As the stone hit the ground, it burst apart.

Jonna worked his way backwards, using the falling stones as a distraction, and placed Gerontius up against the hall wall. The falling stones clattered together, joining the accumulation on the floor.

The hall shook, and he knew it was just a matter of time. "If you really want to leave this city, I can get you back." He moved away from Gerontius, guiding Ajax a safe distance from the man just in case a swing went wild.

Ajax hesitated. "You can't do it. No one can."

Jonna stared at him. "You're wrong. That's Lilith talking. I just sent a red gem outside this building. With the right words, it can take you home."

The halberd slashed again, making a distinctive metal ting, as Jonna shifted out of the way. "You're lying," Ajax said. "You're just saying that to save yourself!" Stones crashed behind them, but Ajax ignored them all.

Avoiding another crashing stone, Jonna spun to the right as the halberd came down again, sounding louder than it should. He glanced up and saw the ceiling above Ajax shift. Jonna dove to the side.

The move surprised Ajax, but he was too angry to reason it out. "Where are your fancy moves now, Jonna?" He raised the halberd as something cracked above him. Ajax looked up.

With a mid-waist tackle, Jonna knocked Ajax from under the falling ceiling. The halberd flew from his hands. They hit the ground and rolled, a thunderous crash sealing off the hall behind them. Bob materialized through the dust, dragging Gerontius's body.

Jonna chuckled, tasting sweat as it ran down his face. "I thought you wanted to leave him for dead?"

The pixie huffed. "If he's important to you—" Sweat poured off his brow. "Then he's important to me."

"What a good pixie you are."

Bob stuck his tongue out, but by the reddening of his cheeks, Jonna knew he liked the compliment. Jonna looked down at Ajax. The ex-guard was out cold. He slapped the guard's face.

Ajax's eyes fluttered open, and he gave Jonna a bewildered look. "What did you do?"

"I just saved your life," Jonna growled. "Despite you trying to kill me again. So, before I let you up, let's get a few facts straight." Another stone crashed somewhere behind them. "I'm on a quest to find my wife, not marry Serena. Got that?"

A strange look crossed Ajax's face. "You're not?"

"No, but it is up to you to woo the girl you want. She is not some kind of gift or prize. Do you understand?"

Ajax nodded, still mulling over the words. A contortion of emotions raced across his face.

"So, I'm going to let you up." Though the shifting of the stones had slowed, they were beginning to pick up again. "And you need to get out of here." Jonna rolled over, ignoring Ajax. He made his way to Gerontius and then hefted him onto his shoulder.

Ajax just stared after him. The ex-guard finally stood to his feet. "Why?"

Why? That was a good question, but Jonna already knew the answer. "Because I value human life. Because I feel everyone deserves a chance." He paused for effect. "If they'll take it. I've given you yours."

A stone dropped. The hallway was still falling apart. Ajax gave a quick nod and hurried toward the exit.

Bob huffed, standing on the shoulder that Gerontius was not on. "You would have thought he would be a little more grateful!"

"He's got a lot to think about." Jonna dodged several stones and began making his way down the hall. "You might want to follow him to make sure he gets out okay."

The pixie squinted at Jonna. "And what about you?"

"I'll be fine." Jonna laughed, though he sounded more encouraging than he felt. He was tired. "Besides, you're fast. Look how quickly you came back to help Gerontius." He gave the pixie a half-smile.

"I'll be right back," Bob warned, rushing after Ajax.

Despite the lull in the falling stones, the collapse of the hallway made up for lost time. Jonna dodged as stone pieces crashed down beside him. He was almost there. He could see the foot of the stairs. His legs buckled as something hit from above with a glancing blow.

Gerontius gasped. Jonna stood up, staggering, his eyes focused on the stairs leading up. With his free hand, he wiped the sweat from his brow, wanting nothing more than a moment's rest.

The foot of the stairs came up fast, but the last strike had taken a lot out of him. At the base of the stairs, he was forced to sit Gerontius down, doing his best to keep him close by the wall.

The stone had hit them both, but apparently, Gerontius's body absorbed most of the impact. He was bleeding from the mouth and nose. Several ribs were broken.

Jonna swallowed, looking up the stairs. There was nothing to be done until Gerontius was outside. Taking a last deep breath, he reached down to pick the man up.

With the air barely coming from Gerontius's lips, the man whispered in a hoarse voice, "Jonna."

"Gerontius?" He looked quickly at the man's face.

The man gasped out, "Jonna—I'm—dying. There is no more reason to risk your life."

Jonna did not know what to say.

"You tried to help me, even though I would have destroyed you." Taking a breath, Gerontius coughed raggedly. "Funny how a little thing like death will make a man reevaluate."

"Especially one's own." Jonna watched him. "What do you want me to do?"

"Leave me, and return to the surface. Give the people a choice." Gerontius gasped again, reaching up, but his pointing finger did not quite extend. "I only ask one thing."

The shaking walls had reached the point of collapse, but Jonna still listened. "What's that?"

"Go easy when you tell them about me. Don't let them know what I became."

Jonna nodded. Gerontius took a few more breaths, paused, and stopped. Laying him back on the steps, he closed the man's eyes.

The stairs shifted, bringing Jonna back to reality. He raced up, jumping debris, fighting his way through the distorted maze. At the top of the stairs, the ceiling rumbled. He dove forward, rolling into the room with the secret passage just as the archway leading down collapsed. The dust settled. He stood up, dusting himself off.

"Well I'll be." Bob flew into the front of the building, followed by others. "You did make it out!" Thomas held the red gem. Phillip trailed behind. And Ajax? He was nowhere to be seen.

"When I heard Gerontius had led you away—" Thomas stopped, looking at the debris. "That must have been some collapse." He gazed at the building around them, noting the cracks. "What happened?"

"We've found the way home." Jonna gave a tired smile. "But I think I'll need some of Almundena's magic salve." He chuckled, looking at the abrasions on his hands, feeling those on his neck and arms.

"And Gerontius?"

Jonna shook his head. "He didn't make it, but he was a big help in finding the stone." Bob grunted but said nothing.

With relief, Thomas handed the red gem back. "I thought he wanted to kill you."

Jonna looked at Bob. He knew the pixie itched to say something but held his tongue. "In the end, his heart was in the right place."

With a single nod, Thomas let it go.

"Let's go find the others." Jonna turned to face the door. "Now, we can celebrate."

Word had already spread. As they stepped into the dark alley, candles showed in all directions. With the orange glow reflecting from faces full of expectancy, Jonna contemplated the red gem in his hands.

He had never tested this gem, and only had Gerontius's word that it worked. Would using it outside the dais make a difference? Where would they appear? Would they be safe? His only assurances were Gerontius's last words. Could he trust what the man said?

The light from the square was bright compared to the candlelight. Artemis was still there. Almundena had returned. Janice stood by a group of people whose conversation stopped at Jonna's entry.

Amalric came toward him. "What have you done?" He looked from the red gem to Jonna's face.

Was that a hint of recognition? "With Gerontius's help—" Jonna raised the gem up so all could see. "We have found the way home!"

Amalric backed up. He pulled at the collar around his neck, looking wide-eyed at the crowd. "What are you doing? Are you crazy? You can't bring that out here!" Amalric leaped at Jonna, trying to knock the gem from his hands.

"Amalric, what are you doing?" Thomas and several others grabbed him from behind, hauling him backwards. "What's gotten into you?"

"The gem—" He pointed, eyes wide, lips quivering. "He has the gem!"

"Of course I have the gem." Jonna stepped toward him. "I also know the spell."

Amalric started to laugh almost maniacal, shaking his head. "You'll destroy us all! That gem cannot be used as a gateway. It is red, not blue."

"What are you talking about?"

"Amalric—" Almundena stepped up, looking into his eyes. "Are you so desperate to keep us here that you would lie about the stone?"

Fear crept across Amalric's face.

"Look at him!" Almundena turned to all those around. "See the man who would lead and keep you here, locked away from the true world. Is that what you want? To be slaves to Azazel's henchman? To raise your children in a city at the end of time?"

Jonna watched as Almundena spoke, hearing the words, seeing the faces. Something had been going on while he was down there fighting.

"I call for a vote. Let the roar of your voices determine your decision. Do we stay here and listen to Amalric?" She cupped a hand to one ear, waiting for a response.

The crowd was silent, all eyes watching Almundena.

"Or do we travel home under Jonna?"

A roar went up. It started in the square and increased as word spread. When the noise from the street echoed away, she turned to Jonna. "It is all yours, m'lord." Almundena bowed slightly, showing a smile.

"You're all fools!" Amalric shouted out. "If you use that stone, you will all die!"

"Bob," Jonna said quietly as murmurs came from all directions. "Is what he says true?"

"I've never heard of the color of a stone being a problem," Bob thought aloud. "It is normally the enchantment that makes the difference. But then again, I've never been here."

"Thomas—" Jonna caught him by the shoulder. "Right or wrong, we can't take the chance in this city."

Thomas nodded, his face appearing very grave.

"I need volunteers." Jonna's voice rose. "I want ten good fighters and any weapons they might have. Where is a good place to test this stone?"

"The desert," Phillip suggested. "Just to the west of town."

Thomas nodded. "Phillip's right. That would be the safest place."

Amalric tried to shake free of the hands.

"Lock him up." Jonna's face was grim. "Show me to the desert."

166

CHAPTER 17
AN HEIR OF HELP

Their eyes took in the desert. They stood on the far side of the chasm, outside of the city. Very little wind blew, the sand on the flat plains having rested for a very long time.

Jonna and a small troop of people made their way to a flat, open spot. Azazel never forbade the people to leave the city, but why would they? With nothing but sand in sight, there was no place to go.

"Every place is somewhere." Jonna stared at the sand around them. "You just have to know what's around it." However, that was for another time. Right now, the stone was their best shot at going home.

He put the stone in the center of the open area. There had been no markings on the dais to indicate how the stone should be laid. Unfortunately, their only consultant was now buried beneath the city.

"Wait." Almundena came forward, picking the gem up and placing it on a small pedestal. She looked to Jonna. "It is tradition."

Jonna nodded and turned toward the group. "I want only ten. If we are successful, we will return. If we are not, I want you to destroy the stone." He looked at Artemis as he spoke the last sentence. She nodded.

He studied the crowd who had followed him outside of the city. "Who will go with me?"

Thomas stepped forward.

"No." Janice took his arm. "I lost you once. I swore I would not again."

Jonna saw Thomas's determination yet heard his wife's pleas. "No, Thomas." Jonna shook his head. "I need you to be a leader here."

Phillip peered out of the crowd and then wormed his way between his parents.

Thomas hesitated but reluctantly nodded. "As you wish." He stepped back, making the hole larger so Phillip could watch more easily.

Nine stepped forward, each having shown their willingness to follow Jonna as runners to alert the rest of the city.

"And I too." Almundena stepped up. "Fighters aside, you will need a mage. Who will watch out for the evil spells?" She smiled, taking her place.

"Me," Phillip shouted, but the adults paid no attention.

Jonna stared at the stone. His only experience with doing magic was what Väinämö had taught him. Even Gerontius had not mentioned how many times the spell should be said. Was it only him, or did others have to say spells seven times as well? Would one time be enough? What if he could not make it work at all?

"Stay back." Jonna motioned to those outside the circle and then began to chant the words. "Baqir Janus Tillo Cassius!" The red gem picked up a glimmer of light. That was enough for Jonna.

"Baqir Janus Tillo Cassius. Baqir Janus Tillo Cassius." The gem glowed. He wondered if the others thought he was crazy, but no one seemed to mind that he was saying the spell over and over. "Baqir Janus Tillo Cassius. Baqir Janus Tillo Cassius. Baqir Janus Tillo Cassius."

A field of red erupted from the gem, spreading out in all directions. It enveloped the small group of ten, creating a sphere of glowing magenta.

"Phillip, no!" Janice reached out to catch her son, but it was too late. He leaped forward into the sphere, grabbing hold of Jonna.

"Baqir Janus Tillo Cassius!"

"What the—" Lilith leaped to his feet, his study suddenly filled with people. "What is the meaning of this?" Then he saw Jonna, and his mouth dropped.

"Yes." Jonna smiled. "I'm back."

Lilith's face grew red. "Guard—"

Jethro, one of Jonna's group, knocked Lilith off his feet. Lilith fell backwards, hit the wall, and slipped slowly to the floor.

Jonna turned to Phillip.

Phillip's eyes were wide. "I know, but I had to come!"

"This is not the place to discuss it." Jonna looked stern. "Almundena, can you protect him?"

Almundena nodded.

There was a knock at the door. "Father." Serena knocked again. "Are you all right?"

Jonna moved to the door and opened it a crack.

Serena's face lit up. "Jonna!" She rushed in, putting her arms around him. "You're back!"

Almundena cleared her throat, ready to cast a spell. "I assume this is your wife?"

168

"Er—No." Jonna brought Serena's arms from around him. "Let me introduce Lilith's daughter."

"I see." Almundena raised her hands to chant.

"No!" Jonna put himself between her and Serena. "She's okay, really." He turned back to Serena. "You see these people?"

Serena nodded slowly, looking at the weapons they carried. "Remember that choice we talked about? Now is the time to decide."

Serena's eyes moved around the group, stopping on Almundena. Her expression narrowed. "Who's she?"

"A friend." Jonna drew her gaze. "And someone who can help you."

Lilith groaned, stirring on the floor.

She looked at Jonna, disbelieving. "Did you hurt him?"

"He'll be fine, but we have to release the water sprite before he comes around."

Almundena waved in Lilith's direction. "Hectora." The stirring stopped. She turned back to Jonna. "He's a dark mage and strong. The spell will not last long."

Jonna looked into Serena's face. "Serena, will you help us?"

Serena nodded, closing her eyes. "It will mean the end of the City of Diggory."

"No." Jonna raised her chin, and she opened her eyes. "It will be the beginning of a better Diggory."

She reached up, put her hand on his, and held it a moment. Her faith was in him, and for the first time, Jonna could feel the weight of that responsibility. Serena turned around, leading him out the door. "This way."

Down the hall and through the courtyard, they found the fountain as Jonna had left it. The water sprite could not be seen.

"Naida," Jonna called out. "Show yourself."

From the center of the fountain, the water sprite came. Her long hair flowed back and forth as if deep in the depths of a lake. "I am here, Jonna McCambel." Naida waved her hand.

"These are my friends, and we have come to help you."

"Jonna!" Elpis appeared, running toward him. "You're back!"

"I see Naida took good care of you."

"We had such fun. None of the guards could see us." Her eyes were bright until she caught sight of the others. "Who are they?"

"They are going to help the city. They are going to make your people free. But first, we need to free the water sprite."

Elpis looked away, The Sight catching her attention. "They're coming," she whispered, glancing back at the group. It was not necessary to explain who *they* were.

"Guard the fountain," Jonna called out. "Phillip and Elpis, stay with Almundena." He looked to Naida, taking Serena's hand. "Show us the filter."

The world changed, and Jonna found himself under the surface of the water. Serena floated beside him, her hair waving like the sea. Instead of drowning, as they obviously should, both were able to breathe.

The water sprite nodded, answering their unspoken question. "As long as you stay within my magic, you will be able to breathe."

Naida caught hold of them, guiding them down. As they went deeper into the pool, around a small pocket, they came into the center of the fountain. The light of the sun danced, spilling vibrant colors in all directions. Rainbows struck the surface above, disappearing in explosions of color.

"It's beautiful," Serena said, seeing the smile on Naida's face. Although she could not miss the longing in the water sprite's eyes. The water sprite wanted to be free.

"It is my home for the moment," she said sadly. "Will you not release me now?"

Serena nodded. "Too long you have been tied to my father." She looked down at the base of the pool. There, against the wall, was the filter of magic. Though it pulsed with a life of its own, it was alien to the beauty that surrounded it.

Serena swam down, pushing against the current. It was here the water connected to the natural spring under the palace. Through a series of channels, this water took care of the wells in the city. The closer she went to the filter, the louder it sang its magic song.

"Children come and children go, like water they do always flow. I keep contained a child here. She is my guest. She's everywhere."

"What is that?" Jonna looked to Naida, and then he remembered. It was the chant that only a mage could hear, but that did not make sense. He was not a mage, at least not like any other he had met.

The filter continued, "To hold her in this place of mine, my function determined by magic design. A warning to all who would take me away, only those of a family, one mind can betray." The chanting stopped, and the filter took on a personality of its own. "Who approaches?" Though it appeared to have no eyes, the filter searched about as if sensing their locality.

"It is I, Serena Magnus, daughter of Lilith Magnus, the magician who placed you." Serena floated before the filter, watching to see how it would react.

"Hmm." The filter slowed the water current, observing her struggle against the flow. As it returned the current to normal speed, it asked, "And why do you approach?"

"It is time to let the water sprite go." Serena moved her hands, fighting harder to stay in place.

"Oh really? Your father approves?"

"I am his daughter. My command is not to be questioned!"

"Very well." The filter sounded skeptical. "If you truly are Lilith's daughter, what is the word of release?" The filter waited for an answer. If it could have tapped its foot, it would have.

"Father uses many words." She tried to redirect. "How can I give the right word without knowing the proper context?"

The filter paused, thinking over her statement. A burst of current surged against her. She struggled against it, barely maintaining her position. "I wasn't made yesterday, girl," it scoffed at her. "That you should already know."

The filter went silent a moment. Just when they thought it had decided to ignore them, it spoke again. "But I am bored, so perhaps I will play your game. But be warned, to answer wrong will cost your life."

Jonna shook his head and whispered close to her ear, "Serena, we can find another way."

"No," she said quietly. Her voice rose in volume. "I accept your challenge."

The filter vibrated in excitement. "Very well, here is a riddle. What is known, but not known. Seen but not seen. Never controlled, and always flowing. Imperfect, it continues to move forward. In it are lost and found both hopes and dreams." The filter peered at her. "Well?"

Serena glanced toward Jonna, who shifted closer.

"And who is this?" For the first time, the filter acknowledged him.

"I am Jonna."

"You are not permitted to answer the question, Jonna. I will only accept the answer from the daughter."

"I understand."

"Well?" the filter nudged. "Have I won already?"

Serena hesitated. "How many times may I guess?"

The filter snapped, "Is that your answer?"

"No."

"Answer the riddle."

"But there are so many replies that could fit."

The filter's flow took on a low vibrational growl. "There is but one answer. Do you know it or not?"

A bewildered look crossed her face. Panic took her eyes. "I—"

"I is not the answer. Tell me, girl."

Her eyes narrowed. "I am thinking."

"You are stalling." The current whipped at her. "How slowly shall I have you die?" Levity entered its voice. "It is just a matter of time."

"Time?" She blinked, glancing at Jonna. "My answer is—" Her eyes grew large. "The future." Serena focused on Jonna. "That's what you have been telling me all along. I can make a better future."

Jonna nodded. "For all your people."

A vibration rippled through the water, and the water sprite's eyes went wide. "I'm free," she exclaimed, doing a smooth flip. "The bind is broken!"

Serena reached down and picked up the filter, removing it from the hole it covered. "It's done."

"No!" Jonna remembered the story of how the sprite became ensnared. Serena had done the very same thing.

She froze, a hollow expression coming over her face. Her clothes, which had been dry before, were now soaked. She was no longer protected by the sprite's magic. She was going to drown.

Jonna threw a look at Naida. "Help her!"

"She is bound." Naida moved beside them. "Just as I was bound to the filter through magic. She, too, is now trapped."

"She can't breathe!" Jonna grabbed Serena by the hand, pulling her toward the surface. He looked at Naida, who followed beside them. "Help me!"

"I cannot." She shook her head. "If I touch her, I will be trapped once more, and Lilith will regain his power."

Jonna fought to swim upward quickly, but the pool was deeper than it appeared. He had to do something or Serena would drown. He took a deep breath and moved closer to her. Holding her nose, he pressed his lips to hers and exhaled.

She blinked as oxygen filled her lungs. He released, took another deep breath, and then gave her whatever he siphoned from the water sprite's spell. Her body relaxed, and she helped him swim. As they reached the surface, Jonna pulled his arm from around Serena, helping her to the side of the fountain.

"Thank you." She coughed, pulling herself up.

Naida came up behind them. "I am sorry I could not help."

Jonna gave a reassuring smile. "But you did. By giving me the ability to breathe, I was able to give air to Serena."

He turned to Lilith's daughter. "Lay the filter down." Jonna refrained from touching it himself. He picked up a large rock by the edge of the fountain and slammed it down on top. Was this the right thing to do? It was only a guess.

Serena gasped and exhaled as the filter's hold died away.

"It is done." He looked to Serena and Naida. "Now, you are both free."

Naida nodded. "Thank you." Her gaze took in all of them. "I shall never forget this kindness." The water sprite disappeared into the depths.

A halberd sliced through the air, cutting the ground near Jonna. He reached up onto the bank, grabbed the pole, and jerked the guard into the fountain. Climbing up, he saw what was left of the battle.

Guards lay still in various places. Most of Jonna's troop could not be seen.

Almundena came up behind them, both children staying close, sweat showing on her forehead. "We've chased them back. I think they've become soft in our absence." She smiled. "I see you were successful?"

Jonna's clothes were still dry as he pulled himself out of the water. It was a last gift from Naida's spell. Serena was not so lucky.

"The sprite is freed." Serena nodded gravely. "It is time to face my father." She stood up and frowned, her clothes plastered to her. "Perhaps I should change."

"There is no time," Elpis said, looking up at the adults. "I saw a room filled with all sorts of things, and several gems there too."

"His laboratory!" Serena rushed toward the palace.

Jonna and the others hurried to catch her. "Wait!" he called.

Serena entered at the nearest palace door and moved quickly toward an area Jonna had not seen. Several rooms down, she pushed open an entryway and then moved to the nearest wall.

Without hesitation, she said, "Baqirum." The wall in the small study glowed, shifting as reality changed. An arch formed, leading into a darkened tunnel. "This way!"

As the last person stepped through, the archway closed behind them. Immediately, Jonna's eyes adjusted, seeing through the darkness.

"I forgot a candle!" Serena turned back, running into Jonna. "Excuse me." She backed up. "I didn't realize—"

"I can see," Jonna stated, having already located each person. "Is it straight down this hallway?"

She nodded.

"Good. Everyone hold hands. I'll lead."

Serena's voice held surprise. "You can see?"

"A little gift a pixie gave me." Jonna chuckled. "Come on."

Serena reached back, feeling for the person behind her as Jonna stepped in front of the group. Her fingers found a smaller set—Elpis's hand.

Jonna studied the human chain. Elpis held Almundena's, who held Phillip's. Jonna grabbed Serena's, leading the way.

Based upon what Jonna saw, this was not really a hall at all, but some type of magic. It appeared liquid, rather than solid, moving back and forth, expanding like a pumping heart. Finally, they reached another wall.

"Baqirum!" Serena said, and the wall parted. An arch formed again, granting passage into a large room. Within the one room were several smaller ones leading off through their own archways.

"That's far enough." Lilith's voice hardened as he spoke the words. "And you, also, my daughter?"

"Father!" Serena moved toward him. "This must stop."

"This can never stop." Lilith raised a green gem and released it, allowing it to float in the air. He glared at Jonna. "Did you really think all my magic was water sprite-driven?" He laughed, glancing toward Serena, and then turned with narrowed eyes to look at Jonna. "I was a dark mage long before I captured her."

"I have no doubt." Jonna met the man's eyes. "The sprite's release was not intended to destroy you. It was simply to right a wrong."

"Don't you realize what you have done?" Lilith turned his back to them, moving toward a second counter. "You have destroyed this city.

174

Diggory will fall to the forces outside."

"Diggory will not fall." Serena shook her head. "It will grow. It will learn. The people will be happy."

Lilith's eyebrows rose. "They will never be happy. What foolishness this stranger so quickly taught you!" He turned around, holding a large black pearl. His voice mocked her as his eyes glinted in the light. "Shall I show you the future?"

"Father, no!"

Lilith glowered at Jonna, a strange smirk on his face as the dark pearl rose into the air. When he pulled his hand down, like the gem, it too stayed suspended. "Do you recognize this pattern, Jonna? You of the far-off land?"

"I do." Almundena stepped to the front. "And I cannot let you do this!"

"Mage of Lord Honorius of the city of Varona." Lilith paused and then smiled. "Almundena, I believe."

"Then you knew who I was?" Almundena's expression changed to a hard line.

Lilith laughed. "But of course, my dear. Why else would I have you immediately thrown in?"

"Father!"

"And you." Lilith's eyes darted back to his daughter. "So ungrateful, putting yourself morally above what I have done, just like your mother." Lilith raised a third gem the color of sky blue into the air. "It was my way that gave you the life you have."

"Lilith." Almundena stepped toward him. "You must stop this. If you do this, you will destroy your own city!"

"The city is already destroyed." Bitterness swept his features. For the first time, he noticed Elpis and Phillip. "I would rather it go away than these children have to bear it."

The kids! Jonna glanced back, spotting them both.

Almundena raised her hands. "I'm warning you."

A smile showed on Lilith's lips. "Go ahead. Stop me if you can."

Focusing on the dark mage, Almundena said, "Stamato Zaman." A flash of bright light flew from Almundena's hands, lashing against an unseen sphere. It lit up the sphere's form with an electrical discharge. She stared in disbelief. "He's called for the Protection!" Almundena backed up, her eyes very wide. She took both Phillip and Elpis by the arm, drawing them to her.

175

"You see, time's up." Lilith waved his hands, whispering an unheard spell.

Jonna's head darted toward Almundena and Serena. "What is the Protection?"

"It is demon magic." Serena's face fell. "And can only be called upon once. When it is over, the mage and all within the sphere's fiery influence lose their lives."

"No." Jonna rushed forward, heading toward Lilith.

"Jonna, stop!"

He collided with the invisible sphere. A shock rippled through his body, not unlike a high voltage wire. It knocked him backwards, throwing him against the wall.

Jonna groaned, trying to focus his blurry eyes. The group hurried to his side.

"There is no way in." Serena touched his face. "It is over."

"There has to be something we can do." He groaned, bracing himself as he stood. *If physical force could not penetrate the shield, some form of magic must!* He remembered the twigs in his pocket, reached in, and took hold.

Bob appeared back on his shoulder. "Jonna, what are you planning?"

Jonna growled, "Where have you been?"

"Doing—" The pixie paused. "Things."

"Fine, don't tell me."

"But I just did!" Bob looked around the room and noted Jonna holding the twigs. "Tell me you're not going to do what I think you're going to do."

"What choice do I have?" Jonna walked toward the sphere again. However, Bob hung back.

"There's no way to tell what will happen," the pixie called out. "You might make things worse!"

"They can't get any worse," Jonna countered. "And I won't let this city die."

The others, except Elpis, were just staring at him. To them, this was a one-sided conversation. That realization popped into Jonna's brain. "Bob, will you please show them that I'm not crazy."

"Oh, very well." Bob appeared, floating in the air. "We might not be here much longer anyway!" He scooted back to Jonna's shoulder.

"A pixie!" Phillip's eyes went to Jonna. "I didn't know you knew pixies?"

Elpis giggled. "Of course, silly!"

Jonna touched the sphere.

CHAPTER 18
THE HEART OF FOREST LOST

The world stopped for everyone but Jonna. In slow motion, Jonna watched Lilith turn toward him, the chant he had been saying interrupted by Jonna's expression. Stepping through the protection of the sphere, Jonna reached up with his left hand and knocked the blue gem toward the ground. Before Lilith could take a step, Jonna reached the black pearl and watched it also crash to the floor.

"Noooooooooooo!" Lilith's words dragged out like a record player on slow speed. He tried to grab Jonna, but Jonna slipped easily by. Moving at a faster speed, Jonna reached up and knocked the green gem down. It burst into a million shards.

The ground shook. The laboratory walls swayed back and forth. Jonna glanced back toward his group. Serena had opened the passage in the wall. In slow motion, they were escaping the room one by one.

Jonna moved to the wall of the sphere and pressed through to the other side. He caught up with the others and waited for the last person to pass into the arch.

The sphere collapsed slowly. Lilith's eyes met Jonna's, burning with hate, as the dark mage raised his hand. He tried to chant a final spell, but it was too late. The sphere came in around him and then exploded.

Jonna could see the explosion expanding in tiny intervals, circling out across the room. His friends would never make it since they moved at the same speed as Lilith. He went up behind the last one and pushed. At the first touch, a wave of disorientation swept through him. With each person he helped through the gateway, the disorientation grew. His change in momentum, his reality working against theirs, resulted in him facing the explosion of the sphere. It was too late to get away. The explosion caught him.

Light and sound, darkness and light, all of it was gone. He was senseless. He could not touch or feel. There was no sight or smell. The world that he knew vanished.

Was he lying down or standing up? Which direction was up? He thought he moved his arm, but was unable to tell if he really had one. The twigs— was he still holding onto them?

Images danced before eyes that could not see. Visions of his past, places, and people came from all directions. *Release the twigs*, he told himself, the knowledge jumping into his mind. He thought the action and found himself back in the room, lying on a blackened floor.

The air stank. Everything around him was charred. Lilith was nowhere to be seen.

Jonna stood up and found that he was still in one piece. He watched his fingers wiggle just to be sure. Sense deprivation was a strange thing to go through.

The others! Scooping up the fallen twigs, he turned toward the wall. Like an echo coming from far away, he heard the spell that opened it.

"Jonna!" Serena jumped forward, squeezing him tight. "We thought—" She looked at the room, smelled the stench, and started to gag.

"Those were my thoughts exactly." Jonna walked her into the archway as she stared back at the remains of the room.

"I don't see my father. It is as if he never existed." She turned her head into his shoulder. The tears began to flow.

Jonna held her, not quite sure what to do. Almundena and the children came up next to them.

Elpis touched her hand. "It'll be all right," the little girl assured her. "My father went away, too."

Serena heard the words and looked down at Elpis. Through tears, she asked, "What happened to your father, child?"

"He was taken away by the guards," Elpis stated matter-of-factly. "He never came home."

Somehow, Elpis's words helped to quench Serena's tears.

"You are right." Serena fought to smile at the girl through her own pain and wiped away the tears. "It will be better now." She looked around at the tunnel. "But we need to get out of here first."

As they reached the end of the magic hall, Serena spoke the word of opening. They stepped into the room that began the magic tunnel. Noise erupted from the hall outside, and a group of guards hurried through the doorway. One of them slammed the door shut while the others looked for something to block it.

"M'lady—" The nearest guard caught sight of her, paying no attention to the others. "Rebels have taken the palace. Our forces are scattered."

"Lilith is dead." She hid her emotion. "There is no need to continue fighting."

"Lilith is—"

"Pass the word." Her eyes swept across all the guards in the room. "Lilith Magnus is no more."

Something hit the door from the outside. It bowed but held. The guard raised a horn to his lips, blowing with all his might.

Both Phillip and Elpis covered their ears before it started. The adults were a little slower. As the horn played the notes of surrender, the attack on the door fell off.

Jonna turned to Serena. "We have a large group of people who are trapped in another land. It is time to give them their exodus."

Serena nodded. "They will be welcomed back. All who wish to stay in Diggory may remain."

Jonna paused. "Serena, your father was a dark mage, isn't that correct?"

Serena sighed but nodded. "More than I knew." She looked away for a moment. "I wish I could undo all the evil he caused."

Jonna shook his head. "We can't go back, but you can go forward. I have a request."

She looked at him, her eyes focused on his. "Ask, and it is yours."

The emotion in her response caught Jonna off guard, and he felt slightly embarrassed. He had never had someone trust him that completely. It was normally, "No, let me hear it first," or "We will see, maybe." Sheesh, the responsibility he felt was like a two-ton rock. "I—" He thought about how to phrase it. "You know that my wife was taken. I know that you know more."

She started to speak, but he held his hand up to stop her.

"I don't want to know what you know, but in my effort to find her I have to find the Dark Mages. They hold the key to saving my wife."

Serena frowned. "Jonna." She paused. "Jonna, your wife—" She saw the expression on his face, the hope in his eyes, and changed her words. "Your wife is lucky to have you." She smiled. "Very well, there is something you must see."

She led them to a room filled with books, and though bookshelves were on every side, they were not in the main library. This room had only books on magic.

"My father studied many things but never anything as much as magic."

Jonna nodded. "To him, magic was power to control his destiny."

"I have no doubt." She went to a bookcase, searched the titles, and pulled a manuscript from the shelf. "This contains the information you seek."

Jonna placed it on the table, opening its cover.

"By the light of the full moon," he began to read, "within the heart of Forest Lost, the mages of the dark begin their ritual of hate and sin." He looked up at the others. Elpis's eyes were wide. Phillip's were curious.

"That's a bad book." Elpis shook her head. "You should throw it away."

Almundena nodded. "She's right. The dark arts are best forgotten."

"I need to know where to find them." He shifted his gaze toward Almundena. "Do they have a fort? Do they have a castle? Surely there is some place they all meet? See here?" He pointed at a place in the book. "It says Forest Lost."

"No one knows where they meet." Almundena shook her head, avoiding his eyes. "Only those of the inner circle know. You would need a spell of transportation or something of the sort."

He turned back to the book and scanned the next few pages. There were more of the rhyming verses, more of the hidden half-clues, half-spoken.

Almundena stepped forward, putting her hand over the open book. "Do you not see what they do? They get your attention through some action, such as kidnapping your wife, they draw you into finding them, and then, when you cannot get away, they capture you forever." She pulled the book from his fingers, closing it.

"You act as if you speak from experience." Jonna caught an emotion hidden below her exterior.

"I once knew a man who thought as you." Almundena's seriousness caught him off guard. "He, too, sought to go into the Dark Mages' lair." She looked away. "And he never did return."

"A relative?"

Her shoulders slumped. "My brother." Her eyes caught his. "You would be better leaving them alone."

"She's right," Serena added. "Whatever they've done, it can't be undone. Remember my father's actions if you don't believe it."

In disbelief, Jonna looked from Serena to Almundena. "Do you know what you're saying? You're telling me to forget the fact that they've taken my wife. Just leave, and don't turn back?" With his eyes, he took them all in. "I will not let them win!"

"There is a dark side to us all," Almundena said thoughtfully. "They will play upon this: your fear, your hate, your revenge. What you begin to do as good may turn to aid their evil cause."

"And so the Queen of the Elves warned me, but even she would not tell me of those future events." He picked up the book. "I have to make up my own mind, and until I have something else to go on, this is my only lead." Jonna looked to Serena, pushing aside his thoughts, bringing back his smile. "Thank you. Will you come with us to Chernobog?"

Serena shook her head. "Not at this time, but maybe in the future. At present, I have a city to help." She led them out of the room, back into the main hallway.

"I want to go!" Elpis grabbed Jonna's hand as they headed down the hall. "Let me go, please!" The doorway leading to Chernobog appeared just ahead.

Would the door still work? With the water sprite free, and Lilith gone, what magic would be left to bind it? He thought back to the pixie sight Bob gave to him. He thought back to the barrier that guarded the minotaur's cave. Though he did not understand many of the principles of magic, it seemed to him spells did not stop simply because the person that cast them was gone. *Was that rule number one in the magic handbook?*

"Yes." Phillip gazed up at Jonna. "Can she come with us?"

With Azazel gone, the threat should be at a minimum, right? Jonna felt a nagging doubt in the back of his mind, but in worst case, he could leave her in the hands of Thomas and his wife. "Of course." Jonna looked for Almundena as they reached the wooden doorway. "Are we ready?"

She nodded.

Jonna grabbed the door, swung it back, and stepped through. There was nothing to stop him. However, when he pressed his hand to reenter the palace, the barrier was firmly in place. Yes, he may have discovered a rule of magic. Magic may indeed persist unless it was removed. Turning toward the stairs, they joined hands and started down.

He could hear the others behind him, finding the next step as best they could. The stairs were still unlighted. Were it not for his pixie sight, he would have had trouble himself. As they reached the bottom arch, a strange smell caught their nose. It was smoke. Something burned.

It was then he saw them—huge, black, billowing clouds coming from the direction of the city. A feeling of hysteria drifted on the wind as groups of people ran in different directions, sometimes colliding but usually with a near miss.

"Phillip—" Urgency filled Jonna's voice. "We need to find your dad."

The boy nodded and took the lead, guiding them through the back alleys when the streets were blocked. With the fire consuming a large part of the city, groups of people appeared everywhere. If they were not hauling water buckets, they were carrying ladders and shovels.

"Jonna!" Thomas saw him from a distance and waved to get his attention. "You're back!" He wiped sweat from his face. Black soot adorned him.

Jonna nodded. "We can all go back. The palace is secure. What happened here?"

"Good, because after this fire, I don't think there will be much left!" Someone handed him another bucket, and he passed it down the line.

"What caused the fire?"

"No one knows." Thomas passed another bucket. "There was some commotion about trying to break into Azazel's lair. The next thing we knew, homes were going up in flames."

"Phillip?"

The boy turned and looked at Jonna.

"Can you guide me to Azazel's lair?"

"This way." He started to run, leading them down a series of zigzagged passageways. They slipped through the square where the people had celebrated the day before and moved past the building where Jonna extracted the red gemstone. A little further up and to the right, they found the steps of a cave opening.

"It really is a lair." Jonna went up to the door. When he pushed it, the door swung back. Someone had broken in. Ornate tables were smashed, chairs with gold engravings had been busted, and the contents of bookshelves had been pulled to the floor. Yet something in Jonna's mind told him they had not found the room's secrets.

It did not make sense. Azazel had a one-room cave dwelling? Here was a huge city with multistory dwellings, and Azazel stayed in here? In this place? In one room? No way.

Jonna checked the walls, looking for something, anything that might show a secret room. The book he carried kept getting in the way, so he laid it down on one of the few pieces of furniture still intact.

"What's that?" Bob pointed to a small cubbyhole in the right corner.

"Ah, so now you're back?" Jonna felt around and saw what the pixie was talking about.

Bob snorted. "Who said I ever left?"

"Well, when you disappear for hours at a time—"

"I did not disappear. Can't a pixie have a little quiet time once in a while?"

Jonna grinned. A series of small engravings were cut into this spot on the wall. If viewed from the right angle, it looked like the mold of a skull.

Almundena moved up behind him. "I have seen that symbol."

"Me too." Jonna remembered the mages who destroyed Väinämö's hut. "Was Azazel part of the inner circle?"

"'Was' being the operative word," Bob added.

"Then he must have a way to Forest Lost." Jonna's words dropped off. For the first time, he felt like he was getting close.

"No, Jonna," Almundena pleaded. "You do not want to go there."

"I know what you said," he assured. "But I will not turn to dark magic. I want to save my wife." Couldn't anyone understand that? There was no way he was going to stop.

"There's more," Almundena suddenly blurted out, turning away, forcing back the tears.

Everyone shifted to look at her. The room became silent.

"What more?" Jonna forgot the ire that filled him. Then, it hit him. "Something else happened about your brother?"

Almundena nodded. Her voice became low. "It was why my brother went there to begin with." In spite of the softness, her voice echoed around the room. "You see." She turned to face Jonna, moving her shirt over to reveal a mark just above the breast bone. "My brother went there to set me free."

There, on her right side, was the mark of a skull. Everyone in the room stepped back, looking at her in a different light.

Only Jonna stood where he was. "You were one of them?" He focused on her face. For the first time, he realized how little he knew of these people. It was all happening too fast, too quick. How could he tell the good from the bad?

Almundena nodded, noting the change in the others, noting that Jonna did not pull away. "I was brought there as a servant girl and quickly moved up through the ranks. It was a better life than at home, where my parents struggled to bring in enough to eat." She sighed. "I didn't know any better. Magic was a thing of amazement. No one realized—" She held her breath a moment. "No one realized the true nature of what they taught us until it was too late."

She met Jonna's gaze. "Like a creature of the night, it sneaks up on you, eating away your soul. Until one day, you look around, and you can no longer tell the difference between good and evil."

Phillip began, "How did your—"

Almundena hurried on. "My brother came to save me. I would not listen. When I would not leave, he offered to buy me away. They laughed at him. When that didn't work, he challenged their authority."

Elpis's eyes went wide. "They killed him?"

"I don't know. Days went by, and I asked. However, they never gave an answer. When I graduated into the inner circle, they took us all out into the forest. We surrounded a small family hut."

"And then destroyed it." Jonna remembered how Väinämö's cottage was torn apart.

Almundena squeezed her eyes shut, remembering the scene. "With the family in it. For the first time, I realized how evil they really were. The family had done nothing wrong. It was simply a demonstration of power."

She went silent a moment and then continued. "I fled and found myself in the city of Verona. There, Lord Honorius took me in. In spite of my past, he taught me the way of good magic. He sent me as an ambassador to Lilith. I was to try and reason with his madness."

Things were falling into place for Jonna. "That was why you recognized the sphere. That was why you insisted I not read the book."

"I am sorry." She clenched her fist. "I truly want you to find your wife, but I fear the cost will be too great. And—" She could not go on.

His voice remained firm. "Will you help me get in?"

"No." She shook her head, making up her mind. "Not unless I come with you."

Bob yelled from Jonna's shoulder, and Jonna flinched. "Nope. No way. Absolutely not!"

"Remember my ear!" Jonna turned his head to look at him. "And why not?"

"Why not? Did you hear what she just said? She was part of the inner circle! She's as addicted to dark magic as a water sprite is to water!"

186

"You heard what she said. She's through with all that."

"Through like a drunk who goes back to the bar!"

"Bob." Jonna had never heard the pixie talk this way before. "Mind your manners. We have kids in the room!"

"Er." Bob blushed and mumbled, "Sorry about the expression."

Elpis giggled. It was funny to hear a human chastise a pixie.

"Besides—" Bob's cheeks turned redder. "Who's going to take care of the kids?"

"You trust her to take care of the kids but not to go with us? Do I hear something funny in that?" Jonna pushed aside some rubble.

"Well—"

"Well's right." He turned to Almundena. "I would be honored to have you along." He poked Bob. "And he would too."

"Hey! Just because I pinched your ear—"

Almundena could not help but smile. "Thank you." Her voice became solemn. "I will prove my worth."

"You already have." Jonna turned back to the skull in the wall. "Now, how do we open this?"

Almundena went to the closet, moved the clothes around, and came out with a pendant. "I think this is what you're looking for." She handed it to Jonna, who ran his finger over the face.

"Do all inner circle mages wear this?"

She nodded. "Usually. With every group that goes out, there is always one from the inner circle. The inner circle's presence is twofold: to make sure that the job is done right, and to make sure that no one escapes."

"Escapes?"

"Just as I did." She moved her hair out of her eyes. "There is dissension within their ranks. There are those of us who know the difference between right and wrong, regardless of the training."

Jonna was thoughtful as he studied the skull. "Which may play to our own purpose."

He placed the pendant on the wall and pressed it into the depression. The wall to his right became transparent, showing another room.

"Phillip, you and Elpis go find your dad." He turned to look at the boy. "Promise me." Jonna was not about to have the boy leap along again.

Phillip frowned but nodded. "I promise. Come on, Elpis."

Jonna motioned to the transparent wall. "Almundena, after you."

CHAPTER 19
THE ART OF DALLIANCE

They stepped through, finding a huge room on the other side.

"You must be guests of Azazel." One of the menservants came up and bowed, noting the pendant in Jonna's hand. The servant's skin was extremely pale. "Our master has not yet returned, but you may wait here if you'd like."

Jonna looked to Almundena. Almundena looked at him.

"We would be honored." Almundena spoke first. "But we have business with the inner circle. Might we use the communicator?"

"The master does not normally let others into his private chambers." A frown crossed the servant's face.

Was it that strange of a request? Had they overstepped already?

"Perhaps you should wait until Azazel returns."

"I understand." Almundena bowed slightly to him.

The man returned the bow, motioning toward a series of pillows stacked in a corner with two small tables. "You may wait here." He led them to the spot. "Someone will be out with refreshments soon."

"Thank you."

They sat down, sinking into the pillows that swallowed them on every side. The servant disappeared through another door.

"Azazel doesn't believe in chairs, does he?" Almundena shifted, trying to get comfortable.

A frown passed over Jonna's face. "Azazel is dead. I think we're going to have a very long wait."

In the reflection of a mirror, one of the female servants caught Jonna's eye. She kept peeking around a corner, looking at Almundena and Jonna, whispering to someone not seen. "What do you think they're saying?"

Almundena tried to read her lips, but the shadows made it difficult. "I think they're wondering why their master has been gone for so long. And why two strangers showed up without any advance warning."

Jonna smiled, hearing someone coming.

"Refreshments while you wait." The servant handed them each a glass, bowed, and disappeared. The liquid looked greenish, with just a hint of brown.

"Not very appetizing." Jonna made a face. "What is it?"

Almundena sniffed. "Avocado, cinnamon, a hint of chopped up carrots, and—" She sniffed again. "A slight amount of grape juice."

"You could tell all that?" Now it really turned Jonna's stomach.

"When you've worked with potions for as long as I have, it becomes second nature."

Jonna stared at the swirls in the top. "Is it safe?"

Almundena looked around.

Jonna threw her a glance and watched at his drink again. It still looked no better. "The drink?"

She laughed. "That's a relative term," she finished. "But yes, it should be digestible. Besides, we don't want to offend our host."

"Our host is dead, and this doesn't look much better."

"Not that host, our host." She nodded to the others passing into a side hall. "With the Dark Mages, it is considered a privilege to be presented with the family's special drink. Complimenting the servants on how well they made that drink will earn their favor."

"So I have to drink it?"

Almundena nodded. "But it's up to you. It might help throw off suspicion of why we are here."

Was that a smirk he saw on her face?

She tried her own. "Not bad. They did a good job."

"You like this stuff?"

She laughed at him again. "Not exactly *like*, but you do sort of get used to it."

Jonna breathed out, put the cup to his mouth, and drank. He stopped a gag, swallowed hard, and felt it hit his stomach. He said between gritted teeth, "This isn't good."

Almundena laughed some more, chuckling at his facial expression. "I reacted the same way the first time I tried it, but you might as well get used to it. Once we get to Forest Lost, you'll probably be faced with more."

"I'd rather go in fighting." He placed the cup on a small table beside them.

"They're coming," she whispered, hearing their footsteps first. She leaned closer to him and teased, "Finish up."

Jonna heard the approach, picked up the cup, and swallowed the rest of the drink. He hoped his face did not turn green.

"Did you enjoy your beverage?" The servant looked toward them, but Almundena caught his eye, giving Jonna a chance to pull himself together.

"It was delicious." She kept the man's attention. "A servant in Forest Lost could have done no better."

The servant beamed. "Thank you, m'lady. That is good to hear." He turned toward Jonna. "Would you like another?"

Jonna's first reaction was to lose his stomach, but he managed to control himself and maintain a smile. "I'm good. Thank you."

"I think we would prefer to wait for dinner." Almundena caught the servant's attention again. "But thank you for the offer."

"As you wish." The servant started to leave.

Jonna sat the mostly empty cup down. "Would you happen to know when Azazel will arrive?"

The servant stopped and turned back to face them, slightly embarrassed. "There may be a slight delay."

Almundena smiled at him. "Delay?"

"Yes, m'lady. It seems our master has not answered our call."

"I take it this is unusual?"

The servant nodded. "He does stay away for days at a time, but always answers if we try to reach him." The servant looked around and whispered, "I probably shouldn't tell you, but it has the staff a little worried."

Almundena frowned, nodding thoughtfully. "I should say. Do you think someone should go look for him?"

Jonna threw a glance at Almundena. She ignored him.

"Oh no." The servant shook his head. "We are forbidden to leave this place. To do so would merit death."

"So you have always been here?" Jonna looked at the servant more closely. That could explain their unusually pale skin. They were never let out of the estate.

The servant nodded. "Ever since we came from Forest Lost." Someone called behind the man, and he bowed. "Excuse me, I need to get back to my duties."

Both Jonna and Almundena nodded. The servant turned away. When he was out of hearing, Almundena whispered to Jonna, "If they have never left this place, there has to be a portal inside of this building, if nothing else but for the transport of goods."

"Good thinking." Jonna looked both directions, but saw no one else. "So how do we find this portal?"

"It is probably very close to the communicator. We get there, and

191

we find the portal."

Jonna agreed. "But first we have to leave this spot."

"I think I know a way we can do that." Almundena looked at him. "Kiss me."

Jonna's eyes went wide. "What?"

"Kiss me," she said again, motioning with her eyes toward a female servant who entered the room. Jonna reached over to kiss her cheek. At the last moment, she put her arms around him and kissed him firmly on the lips, holding tight.

There was a change in the sound of the approaching footsteps.

"Uh, excuse me," the servant said quietly, her voice saying she hated to intrude but had to. "While our master has nothing against this type of action, he does prefer it to be in private. Might I suggest a room?" She looked from Almundena to Jonna.

Jonna's face turned a little red.

Almundena released her hold on him and smiled. "What did you have in mind?"

~

The door closed behind them with a distinctive wooden thud.

"She thinks I started it!" Jonna looked at Almundena, who laughed quietly.

"It normally is the male."

"This male is married." He caught her eye.

She turned to look around the room, ignoring his implication. "You wanted to find a more discreet place. What could be more discreet than this?"

The room was gorgeous. The lack of furniture in the main room was all forgotten here. There were two dressers, his and hers, a side area for bathing, two armoires, and a bed with a canopy decorated with carved pictures.

"Besides, it wasn't that unpleasant, was it?" She glanced back at him, daring him to contradict.

Jonna paused. There was no good answer to that question. "That's not the point. If we are going to work together on this, you can't do that again."

She laughed lightly. "Unless absolutely necessary. They think we are a couple now. To continue to keep suspicion down, we have to act like it."

He sighed, taking in the items in the room, and went to the door. It would not budge. "I think someone suspects something. We appear to be locked in." Turning around, he looked back at Almundena. "How long do you think they'll keep us here?"

"Till at least dinner. If Azazel doesn't show up by then, protocols become a little iffy."

Frowning, Jonna finished her thought. "Their nervousness will grow. What happens if they think he's not coming back?"

"They will report to Forest Lost." Almundena's face went solemn. "An investigation will ensue."

Jonna frowned. "And the gig will be up."

"Gig?" She made a funny face. "Are you hunting frogs?"

"It's an expression. It means they'll find out about us."

Almundena agreed, sitting down on the bed, offhandedly running her hand over the silky bedspread. "Now what?"

He looked from her to the bed. "Certainly not that."

"What type of girl do you think I am?" She abruptly stood up to face him. "I think I'm offended!"

His mouth dropped. "I didn't mean—"

"You men are all alike. One little kiss, and you think—"

"That's enough." Jonna glanced at his shoulder. "Bob, tell her."

Bob looked whimsical. "I don't know. It was an interesting kiss."

Jonna glared at him. "Whose side are you on?"

"Thank you, Bob." Almundena calmed down. "It is nice to be appreciated."

He beamed. "You're welcome."

"Will you two stop that?"

Bob looked around and whistled. "Stop what?"

Jonna laughed nervously. "Fine, the joke's on me. How about something serious?" He went to study the door. "Can't you use some sort of pixie dust to open the lock or something?"

"Me?" Almundena looked surprised. "I'm not a pixie. I'm a woman."

"Hence his problem." Bob shook his head. "He just can't tell up from down."

Jonna was determined to get them back on track. "Come on, guys, fun is fun, but we need to get out of here. Somewhere out there, my wife is in trouble." He studied the door, trying to understand how it was held. "Hold it." He looked around the room at the candles. "Kill all the lights."

Almundena looked at him funny. "What do you have in mind?"

"I can see through things in the dark. I can look through the door and see the mechanism."

"Maybe," Bob cautioned. "But remember, there is a lot of light outside this door. It might not work."

"It's worth a try."

"That's right," Almundena remembered. "You did lead us down Lilith's magic hall without an additional light source. Curious—"

He preempted her next question. "It was a pixie gift."

"It was a Bob gift," the pixie corrected. "And of course, I am a pixie."

"Someone help with the lights, please?" Jonna used a small snuffer at the front of the room. Almundena worked on those at the back. Bob caught the ones on the sides. When they were all out, Jonna's eyes adjusted.

"Wow." He looked around the room. It was the first time he could really experiment with the magic. "Give me a second. I have to adjust the focus again." He caught sight of the dresser, moved around the walls of the room, and saw Almundena. Oops, not there. The night sight could be a little too revealing, if he was not careful.

He turned his head toward the door and focused on the center part. The outer glow vanished, layer by layer.

Jonna passed through the wood until he saw the other side. For a moment, he was blinded, but his vision gradually adjusted to the volume of light. It was not a lock at all but a bar. The bar slid from the wall, keeping the door from pushing out. There was a catch holding the bar in place.

"Maybe the frame," Jonna thought aloud. He could hear someone moving up beside him. Glancing back, he caught sight of Almundena, and turned back to the door, refocusing. "If I can get part of the frame loose, we might be able to stick something through to move the bar back."

"Your knife again?" the pixie announced, back on his shoulder. "You used it in the jail cell."

"I don't know. It might not be long enough."

"How about this?" Almundena reached up her right leg and pulled out a blade. "No woman should be without one." She smiled innocently.

"That might work." He used the tip to work part of the doorjamb loose. Her blade was thicker than his knife, and it pushed it apart with relative ease. Looking through the small open area, he could just see the bar on the other side in ordinary light, but it was easier to use the pixie sight. This way, he could see everything at once. He decided to work on the underside so that his knife marks would be less likely to show on the wood.

As he slid the knife through the slit, the tip of the blade found the bar, catching it enough to inch it back. However, it took time. It had only been pushed back a few inches when a servant came their way.

"Incoming," he whispered, unsure of how much could be heard outside the room. "Bob, the candles!"

Bob zipped from place to place, lighting the candles as quickly as he could with tiny pixie dust glitters. Jonna pulled the knife, pushing the doorjamb back. The servant slid the bar out from in front of the door and knocked.

"Yes?" Almundena took the knife back, slipping it into the sheath on her leg. She grabbed Jonna by the hand, pulled him toward the bed, and sat down at the end. "Hold me," she demanded in a whisper.

Jonna put his arms around her. The door opened.

The servant, seeing the position they were in, turned to face the other way. "The master has not yet arrived, but we will set dinner shortly."

"Take your time," Almundena purred. "We've plenty to keep us busy."

"Thank you, m'lady." The servant closed the door.

Jonna was impressed, releasing his hold. "You're very good at this."

"Oh, am I?" She winked. "I was taught the art of deception extremely well at Forest Lost. I suppose it does have its uses."

Jonna remembered what she had said about the Dark Mages. "That's right." He also remembered the woman who had pretended to be his wife at the cabin. Had she been a dark mage, too?

"What's wrong, Jonna?"

His eyes held sadness. "Right after they took my wife, I didn't know it yet, but they left an imposter." The entire event flashed through his mind. "She was very good, too."

Almundena's voice softened. "I see." She reached over and touched his hand, her voice very serious. "But you discovered who she was, right?"

"Yes, but for a brief time, she fooled me."

"Jonna," Almundena said quietly. "True love sees through even the most powerful magic, and that is what drives you to find your wife." She smiled. "It is refreshing to see. That is why they could not fool you—your heart knew the truth." She looked away, seeing something not in the room. "I can tell you this." She spoke with no expression. "You will find her."

"There is something foreboding in the way you say that."

Almundena paused, thinking, and cautioned, "Perhaps what you are hearing is in your own thoughts, not the words. I wish only to encourage."

A servant knocked at the door. "Dinner is ready, m'lord and lady."

Coming back to Jonna's shoulder, Bob whispered, "Dinner!" He leaned out toward Almundena. "Are we ready?"

"Bob," Jonna started. Almundena joined in, speaking the next words at the same time. "You know you can't—" They stopped and looked at each other, then laughed.

"They won't see me." Bob smirked. "Besides, pixies can have a lot of fun during dinner." He frowned, looking at them both. "Did you two—you sure did!"

"I guess we're on the same wavelength." Jonna stood up, turned around, and lifted Almundena's hand. Her body followed suit. "It is time to pretend. After you." He motioned toward the door.

"Thank you, m'lord." She stepped forward, taking his arm. The door opened.

"This way." The servant gave a whimsical smile as the couple passed in front of him.

Almundena whispered in a giggle to Jonna, "I know what's going through his mind."

They passed several other servants along the way, each smiling in their direction—real smiles, not fake. It seemed the couple had caused quite a commotion. As they reached the entryway to the dining room, a female servant curtsied and opened the door. There was something about the look in the servant's eyes, something a little too frisky. . .

"I think she's interested in you." Almundena poked Jonna with a whisper.

Jonna had not missed the signals. "But I'm with you," he whispered back, suppressing a laugh. "At least for the moment."

"Ah, so sad. Tossed aside." Almundena twirled around, catching his arm.

"We're making quite a spectacle," Jonna noted as she came back close to him again.

"Now that's the point, isn't it? Distraction?" She gave a small laugh as the servant showed them to their seats. When the servant tried to place them on opposite sides of the long table, Almundena stopped him. "We prefer to sit side by side. Isn't that right, love?"

Okay, Jonna had done many things, but this was the first time some other woman, not his wife, called him love. It threw him.

"Of course." He smiled, trying to take it in stride. He liked Almundena, he really did, but this was definitely easier for her than him. As the servant went to draw her chair, Jonna waved him away, pulled it out for her, and took his own.

The smell of special delicacies wafted up from the table. Oysters, clams, curry chicken, sushi with wasabi, crepes with caviar, and spices mixed with ginseng and yohimbine were placed at strategic points. The main courses consisted of curry chicken and spiced meats. A bowl of incense, patchouli, added to the aroma. Drinks were placed before them.

As Jonna sipped his, he was startled at the taste. "There's vanilla in this." Surprise filled his face.

"What did you call it?" Almundena tried hers. "Oh, I see." She blushed. "You mean vainilla?"

"I've never heard it called that." Jonna looked curious. "It sounds Spanish."

"What is Spanish?" Almundena turned, looking at him through soft, strange eyes. Well, maybe not strange, but they were different. He had never seen her look that way before. She was playing her role extremely well.

The serving butler came to the table. "M'lady." He bowed, placing on her plate a sample of each item. Turning to Jonna, he did the same.

Jonna tried the sushi, dipping it into a small bowl of wasabi. "Horseradish?" He reached for his drink, the spice breaking him into a sweat. In the meantime, his heart seemed to be beating faster, and when he thought of Almundena—

Jonna scolded himself. This was becoming harder than when Artemis showed up at the pool. Sheesh, that thought didn't help! A glance at Almundena told him the same thing was happening to her. And, to add insult to injury, as they finished the meal, coco desserts were brought out.

He was not thinking straight. Something was messing with his brain. Could food have this sort of effect on people? He caught sight of Almundena from the corner of his eye. She was just looking at him, smiling. Oh my word, what had they been exposed to?

"Jonna," Bob whispered on his shoulder. "Get a hold of yourself, man!"

Jonna mumbled out of the side of his mouth, "What's going on, Bob? Did they poison us?"

The pixie laughed. "Nope, but it's the oldest trick in the book. My people call it the Art of Dalliance."

"Art of Dalliance?" Jonna's brain couldn't focus. All he wanted to do was— "I've never heard of it." He shook his head, trying to clear it, but his thoughts kept going back to Almundena, and hers were obviously toward him.

Bob spoke very near his ear. "Jonna, look at me!"

"Ouch!" Jonna glanced toward him.

"You're under the influence of almost every type of aphrodisiac known to pixies, and I can sense there's magic mixed in. Although—" He checked the table. "They may be missing a few dishes." He began to count on his fingers, reached ten, and threw his hands up, shaking his head. "It doesn't matter. The point is—"

Jonna glanced toward Almundena. Their eyes met.

"Jonna!" Bob pinched his ear.

CHAPTER 20
TWO FOR THE PRICE OF ONE

"Da-gum-u," Jonna growled. "What do you want?"

"Your attention, please!"

Jonna swung his head back to stare at the pixie. He was tingling all over, his heart rate was up, and now Jonna was beginning to sweat. Almundena found his fingers. He held perfectly still, fighting to control the emotions.

"Focus," Bob demanded. "They saw you two and believed you to be in love. They prepared this dinner to help you further along that road."

Jonna tried to turn away, but Bob pinched him again. "Don't you turn away from me!" Just for good measure, he pinched Jonna's ear a third time. "Didn't you hear what I said? There's magic involved here, too!"

"Will you stop that!" Jonna's comment was a little too loud, catching the attention of others in the room.

Almundena looked hurt. "You mean me?"

"No, no," Jonna backpedaled. "Not you. I was talking to—"

What was he doing? Was he going nuts? He kept trying to focus on the words Bob spoke, but it was like listening through a dream. His reality kept going to Almundena.

Bob growled. It was obvious he could not get their attention. Maybe it was time for a little pixie dust.

Ordinarily, Bob rarely used the stuff. He liked spells better, but something had to be done, and nobody was listening. He reached into his pouch.

"I don't think so." A man picked Bob up and held him by the back of the shirt.

The pixie's gaze darted back toward a tall man with a black beard. The man wore a grayish cloak.

"Let me introduce myself." The man grinned. "I'm Azazel Sampo Elam, dark mage, and you appear to be my guest." He pulled a small box from his coat pocket.

"Let me go!" Bob tossed the pixie dust, but the change in elevation shifted his throw, and the majority of it hit the table.

Azazel dropped Bob inside the box, closing the lid. "You missed.

What a nice surprise to show the Consortium."

He looked at Jonna and Almundena, smiling. "Take the two love birds back to their room. We'll deal with them in the morning."

It took four servants to help them to their feet, guiding them quietly from the table. In spite of this, their hands found each other, tingling as they touched. From the corner of his eye, Jonna caught a glance of the dark mage, the skull medallion impossible to miss. However, the man could not hold his attention. All Jonna wanted to do was look into Almundena's eyes. Yet, the more he did, the more his resistance gave way to things he ought not to think.

The hall around him was a blur. He could no longer focus. Was Almundena having this same trouble? He had never been this out of control in his entire life.

A door appeared directly in front of them. The servants pushed it open and took them inside. It was their previous room: the room they had tried to escape. As the door closed behind them, they stood together in the dark, their hands still clasped. Jonna was sweating profusely and found it hard to breathe.

"What did they give us?" The longer he stood, the dizzier he became. No, not dizzy, disoriented and confused, or was it . . . The last thing he saw was Almundena's face, her outline, and her arms wrapping around his own. She glowed like an angel in the pixie sight.

~

Jonna sat up, sweat pouring from him. He saw images in his mind, terrifying pictures of things that either had happened or would. Lying back on the bed, he realized it was a dream. As he turned to his side, he found his arm dropping over smooth, soft skin. He snuggled in, smelling a delicious fragrance, and held her tight.

"Her!" Jonna's eyes went wide, and he froze. He was in bed with someone other than Stephanie. "Oh god, what did I do?"

Jonna tried to think back. He remembered going to dinner, the food, the aroma, the—his eyes went wide—the attraction.

There was something else, something Bob had been trying to say, but the next thing he knew, he and Almundena were back in their room. Past that point, he did not remember, or was it more that he did not want to remember?

Guilt? Fear? Had he betrayed his wife?

"Jonna," Almundena called in a sleep-filled voice.

He tensed. "Uh, yes?"

She smiled up at him with soft, pleasant eyes when she saw the expression on his face. "Are you all right?"

"I—I hope so." He blushed. "I didn't do any—I am so sorry." He blushed again.

"Sorry for what?" She sat up, keeping the covers around her. Her eyes were silently laughing.

"This isn't funny."

"Isn't it?" She smiled, still struggling to hold it in.

"No! I behaved badly. I—"

"You did nothing," she assured, reaching over and kissing him on the cheek.

"I didn't?" Jonna sighed, relieved, but a odd thought crossed his mind. "What stopped me?"

"You men are all alike." She chuckled. "First, you're glad you did nothing wrong, and then you wonder why you didn't. It was Bob, Jonna. He tossed some pixie dust, which saved us both."

"The aphrodisiacs." Jonna suddenly remembered all the stimuli around them. The smells, the drink, the food—

"It was the magic." Almundena caught his thoughts. "The rest was topping on the cake. It started the thoughts—" Her cheeks turned a little red. She looked down, fighting a smile. "For both of us. Apparently, we are both guests of the notorious Azazel Sampo Elam himself."

"But Azazel is dead."

"Quite right you are." Azazel's voice came from around the room. "My guests, that is. Pardon me for starting to eavesdrop, but I did hear you say Azazel was dead?" A floating face faded into view, its lips matching the voice as it spoke.

"At least, the other one is dead," Jonna said into the room at large. "I understand you are another."

"Not another, the," Azazel answered with pep. "Welcome to my humble abode. That moron demon I used was just a pawn. I was rather impressed by his dispatching."

Jonna looked at Almundena, but spoke to Azazel. "If you knew about his dispatching, why didn't you know he was dead?"

"I'm not all-knowing, you know. I can't see everything."

"But you saw some of it?"

"Unfortunately, my location for watching was somewhat blocked, so I couldn't be sure. And once those imbeciles broke into his cave, the spells of seeing were distorted." He huffed. "Never trust a demon to do a dark mage's job."

"Then you know about the city?"

"Of course, why do you think the fire started?"

Almundena tilted her head. "You set the fire?"

"Certainly." Azazel's face shifted, floating higher. He studied the room. "And I see you two made it quite a night." He grinned. "A pity I was too busy to watch."

Jonna spotted their clothes cast this way and that—all around the room. He gave Almundena a glance, and she smiled back, snuggling in beside him.

She spoke pleasantly. "We appreciate the privacy."

"I thought you might." Azazel nodded. "However, if you would be so kind, breakfast will be served shortly, and we have much to discuss." The face disappeared.

Jonna looked around the room for any sign Azazel was still there and whispered, "You think he's still listening?"

She leaned closer to him, whispering back, "He could be, but probably not."

He cleared his throat and questioned in a normal tone, "Do you know this person?"

"I know of him," she agreed. "But I've never met him. He stayed away from Forest Lost, which is probably why he volunteered to be here."

"Volunteered? What an odd choice."

"Rumor said he never cared to have too many dark mages around. He likened it to having a bunch of sharks in a small, contained area."

"I thought dark mages worked together?" This was a new piece to the puzzle.

"When they have to." She rolled her eyes. "But there are always those who don't like to play. Now, would you be a gentleman, and hand me my clothes? Or, should I get them myself?" She started to throw back the covers.

"No, no." Jonna held up a hand. "I would be honored." He looked at her and smiled, feeling genuine affection. "Almundena, I—"

"I know." She grinned. "I like you, too. However, I can respect that you're married."

"Thank you." He picked up some of the clothes flung around the room and brought them back. "But how in the world did the clothes get scattered around like this, if we did nothing?"

"Do you really want to know?"

He handed her the clothes. "On second thought, no, not really."

"Thank you. Now turn around." She twirled her finger.

This time he laughed. "Of course, m'lady." Jonna slipped into his own clothes, facing the door.

"Done," she called as he finished pulling on his shirt. "Now we are respectable."

He turned around, realizing in the back of his mind that something was missing. He checked both shoulders. "Where's Bob?"

"You don't know?" Almundena thought back. "No, of course you don't. I was the one facing him." She frowned, trying to remember, and a look of fear formed on her face. "Azazel has him."

Jonna reached the door just as a servant knocked and pulled it open. Apparently, they had not been locked in this time.

"Breakfast, m'lord, is this way."

Almundena came from behind, and they walked arm in arm, following the servant. There was a tingling when they touched, both remembering what they had felt the night before. With this sort of reaction, could they really be sure nothing had happened? To Jonna, Almundena seemed convinced, but for the first time, both purposely released, stepping into the dining room.

"And the love birds return." Azazel motioned to the seats at the table. "Please."

"How kind." Almundena waited as Jonna pulled out her chair. Her head turned, her long hair flowing slightly to the right.

"How lovely." Jonna spoke before he could stop himself. Was this still an act?

"I see your night did not stop your passion." Azazel grinned. "That's good, for passion is what you need to survive." His tone moved from playful to a twinge of seriousness.

Both looked at the food before them. Jonna studied the drink but refused to taste it.

Azazel laughed. "No, no. No such magic this morning. I need you both sharp." He caught their eyes. "I only ask that you hear me out." As a show of good faith, he tried his drink first.

Almundena followed suit.

Jonna tasted his after the other two. There was a genuine friendliness about their host, not like Lilith. He was, for the most part, acting very un-dark mage like. "Say on."

Azazel gave a nod and began. "I had a falling out, so to speak, with my brothers in the craft." He motioned to the room around them. "And hence, my present surroundings. For years I have kept silent, watching the Chernobog beyond these walls. I have waited for a time when someone would come who was strong enough to take on Forest Lost."

The words fell across the table. Almundena looked surprised. "You're a dissenter." She studied Azazel's features. "Then the stories told were true?"

"To every legend, there is a splinter of truth." He shook his head. "No, I would never go against the Consortium by myself. I would have no way to win." He leaned forward. "You see, all our magic would simply cancel each other out. It was so designed by the first dark mage to ensure no one would try."

"But another." Azazel looked to Jonna. "One not of this land, who fought with magic other than our own." He smiled. "You might defeat the Consortium, just as you bested Azazel the demon. Passion." He looked them both in the eyes. "Do you have the passion?"

"I have the drive." Jonna stared. "If I don't do it, I will die trying."

"Then you will die." Azazel sat back, eyes narrowed at Jonna. "You must either do or don't. Otherwise, you're wasting my time." Azazel's voice became hard. "I think we need to up the stakes, so here's the deal. You invade and destroy the Consortium. In return, I'll spare what's left of the people in the city." He looked at them both. "Is that a deal? Will you *try*?"

"If you thought we would fail," Jonna countered, "you would have already tried to destroy us yourself."

"Who says I didn't?" Azazel laughed. "The moment you entered this prison city, you belonged to me." He picked up his drink, sipping it again. "Delicious." He smiled.

"You did well against my demon," Azazel continued. "What will it be, Jonna?" He moved closer to them. "Will you take the challenge and go against a dark foe, or will you suffer the same fate as the city?" He stood up from his chair. "It's your choice."

"Where's Bob?" Jonna stared at him, watching a smile creep up Azazel's face.

"You mean the pixie?" Azazel tapped his pocket. "He's safe."

Jonna stood to his feet. "I want him back."

"Interesting. Are you willing to risk your chance at the Dark Mages? Are you willing to sacrifice an entire city simply to free one pixie?"

"I'm willing to risk my life for a friend." With eyes narrowed at the mage, Jonna held out his hand. "Bob, please."

The mage chuckled. "I like the way you play." Then, he frowned. "Just remember who has your back." Azazel pulled the box from his pocket, handing it over to Jonna.

"Now, with that settled—" He sat down, motioning Jonna to do the same. "What questions do you have for me?"

"There is a sword that was stolen from the elves." Jonna opened the small box anxiously. Bob stuck his head out, red-faced, and Jonna relaxed. "I want it back."

"Done. Seek a man called Matthias Omid at Donovan's. If anyone knows, he will. Tell him my name."

Glancing from Azazel to Almundena, Jonna saw she already knew his thoughts.

She nodded at Jonna. "I know the place."

Bob leaped out of his box, turned in the air, and waved both fists in Azazel's direction. "You—"

"Calm down, Bob." Jonna put his hand up.

"Calm down? Calm down, he says!" Bob spit at the box. "Let him pick you up and lock you away overnight in a magic box!" Bob reached for the pixie dust.

"Is that a challenge, little pixie?" Azazel laid a wand on the table. "Quickest draw." He grinned. "Ready?"

"Bob, please." Almundena's voice cut through the air, catching their attention.

Bob shook with anger. "Oh," he growled. "All right, but this isn't finished!"

"Agreed." Azazel's eyes narrowed. "When the mission is done, you can take a shot if you wish."

"Done!" Bob pulled his hand from his pocket and turned to Jonna. "And there you are, consorting with the enemy. I'm ashamed of you!"

"He made an offer, and we accepted," Jonna said calmly. "We are allies of a sort, at least for the moment."

"Hmm." Bob did not like it. "We'll see!"

"And?" Azazel ignored Bob, turning back to Jonna. "Anything else?"

"Give us passage to Forest Lost."

"Done. This way, lord and lady." Azazel clapped his hands, bringing a servant to him. "Lead these two to my chambers and return."

The servant hurried forward, leading the way. It was a short trip. Down the hall, through the main room, turn left, and there it was. Had they been given time to roam, they could have found it themselves. As they entered Azazel's chambers, the disarray was obvious.

"He isn't much of an alchemist." Almundena studied the vials and jars scattered about. "But he does try."

"I think his skills are in other things." Jonna felt nervous. It was one thing to risk his own life, but knowing that everyone else's was in the balance— "What happened to him?"

"I know rumors only." Almundena moved past one of the tables. "When he came to Forest Lost, even when I was there, it was very seldom." She went to a small side room and studied the placement of the candles. "This is where he talks to them." She pointed. "And over there is the portal to Forest Lost."

"So it is a real place?"

"A code word." She nodded. "But real."

"Shall we, then?" He stepped into the smaller room, moving to where she indicated.

"Grab my hand." She moved beside him. "And I'll speak the words, Faunus Perditus."

He took her hand, holding tight. Was she trembling, or was that an effect of the night before, too?

"Faunus Perditus."

The air in front of them changed shape, looking like a concave lens. They could see people wearing grayish cloaks walking around. Their hoods were down, and Jonna could see a lake behind them. He stepped forward, pulling Almundena with him.

"Wow." He stopped short right before stepping into the water. What looked like a lake was really a bay leading off into a sea. "Where are we?" He walked away from the water's edge, following the shore. There were trees everywhere. The moss on the trees helped him realize the direction. A large path headed toward what he suspected was north.

Almundena thought it an odd question. "Forest Lost, of course."

"I mean, what are the—" He stopped to think. How do you explain longitude and latitude in a world that had not developed it? "If you had to get here by land, how would you do it?"

She thought but shook her head. "I don't know. I don't remember anyone doing that."

Something sounded to their left.

"Down, gray cloaks are coming." Almundena pulled him behind a group of trees on a steep embankment. Their feet slipped, and both went sliding to the ground, rolling over each other. When they stopped, both held their breath. In the distance, they could hear a group of people talking, moving closer and then further away.

They exhaled, and Jonna realized he was staring down into Almundena's face. Their eyes locked. With his body lying on top of hers, he could hear each breath she took, feel the warmth that radiated from her skin, and his memory of the night before—

He rolled to the right to lie beside her, getting hold of himself. Slowing his heart, he forced himself to focus. If it was the last thing he did, he would make Azazel pay for this.

"Gone, I think," he finally managed in a voice that broke. Sitting up, he cleared his throat. "Are you okay?"

Almundena lay there a moment, her cheeks slightly red. "I think so." She started to look at him but then gazed out at the water instead. Her face reddened some more. "Truly, I didn't expect a fall like that." Forcing herself to turn toward him, she continued. "I think we better stand." Jonna nodded quickly, stood to his feet, and helped her up.

Standing was definitely better. Focusing his thoughts, he asked, "Where do we find this Matthias Omid?"

A wind stirred the waters of the bay, creating miniature white-topped waves. The water calmed Jonna, much like the water on the Washington coast. They made their way to the top of the hill.

"The city is protected." Almundena checked to make sure no one else approached. "By three gates. Matthias should be toward the third. We are starting at the first."

Jonna looked from the sea to the land. Not far up the shore was a broad set of stairs, leading up into white rock cliffs. "That way?"

"That way."

The sun glistened. The stairs reflected the sunlight as they approached. Thunder sounded from far away to the east, but the clouds were not showing in the sky just yet.

Almundena shivered. "It looks like a storm tonight."

"How appropriate." Jonna gave a slight smile. "I came to this land with a storm."

A curious look crossed Almundena's face. "Really?"

Jonna nodded and then laughed. "And I thought it was going to be an ordinary vacation."

"Vacation?" The word was new to Almundena.

"In my world," he began, "when a person is tired of being somewhere for too long, they travel to another place for a short time and then return home. It gives them a chance to do something different. It is resting from what you do all the time."

She listened. "And you took this vacation with your wife?"

"I did." Jonna bit his lip. "Though, if I had to do it over, I'm not so sure I would."

Almundena shook her head. "There are no accidents, Jonna. You could not have avoided this event, even if you had not taken your vacation, just as we could not have avoided each other." Her eyes caught his.

There was a connection between them, and they both knew it. Was it lingering magic, or had something unexpected happened? In any case, it was something both refused to explore.

She dropped the subject entirely. "When we get to the city, we'll need to find cloaks." She stopped to think. "I wonder. It should still be there."

"What should?"

"My home." Almundena glanced at him. "They don't know I ran away. Unless someone suspected, my home would still be here. The good thing is—" Almundena's eyes brightened. "There are enough people in the inner circle that no one knows them all. That might play to our advantage."

"Or disadvantage." Bob was pessimistic. "If we do run into someone who knows you—"

"It's possible." Almundena looked thoughtful. "But since many of us are sent undercover, they may think I am just getting back. Besides, only someone in charge of security would even know I ran away. It's not something they like to advertise."

The main gate had two tall doors that stretched up and attached to the rock walls. Skulls were carved into each door's center, inlaid with gold and glistening as the light of the sun bounced from them.

A mechanism for locking the doors stood to one side, but it had not been used for a very long time. Debris had accumulated where the doors would track to close.

Jonna checked the small watchtowers on either side of the entry. "There are no guards?"

"Looks are deceiving." She motioned to the runes carved into the walls. "Our sentries are magic. Although we do occasionally have lookouts, it is not necessary."

"You just said *our*," Bob pointed out, looking around at the runes.

"A habit." Almundena's eyes narrowed at his words. "Nothing more intended."

The pixie did not sound convinced. "Hmm."

"You're just hurting from being thrown in a box," Jonna countered. "We've had this discussion. Almundena is not a dark mage."

They passed from the gate into residential housing. People came and went, moving up multi-storied buildings on exterior stairs.

"If you were tossed in a box, you'd be upset too." The pixie turned around, looking the other way. "Fine, I'll just sit here and be quiet."

Jonna added, "And invisible."

"Oh, alright." Bob huffed and disappeared.

"My home was there." Almundena pointed to the top of a three-story building. A small stairway led to the front door, and not many people were walking around.

"How do you know it's still safe?" They worked their way up the stairs, seeing only an occasional gray cloak moving down the street. "And why aren't we hiding?"

"We are in the city now." Almundena reached the top of the stairs and waved her hand over the door. "Ne Hectora."

Something changed. Jonna could feel it in the air but saw nothing.

"There." She opened the door, stepping in. "This used to be my home-sweet-home."

The room was clean, with not a speck of dust. "How did you do that? I saw no lock." Jonna noted the furniture in the front room. He touched the sofa. "Nice."

"It is a magical lock. If you know a person's magic signature, it is easier to open." She looked around, thinking back. "Had it not been for my brother, I would never have known the danger I was in. It was he who began to open my eyes."

"Do you think the people who live here know the danger they are in?"

Almundena shrugged. "Perhaps. Perhaps not. People tend to stay with what they know. They are more afraid of change than a lie." She looked toward the bedroom. "Let me find those robes."

Jonna drifted around the room, stopping at a bookshelf. He found a hand-drawn picture of Almundena's mother and father but could not read the artist's name.

"That was done a long time ago." She walked up behind him, holding two robes and an amulet. "By a friend."

"More than a friend." He noted the "love" closing down toward the bottom and remembered the story she had told about her family. "How did he know what your family looked like?"

"Through a dream." She placed the amulet around her neck. "At least, that's what he said, but I haven't thought of it in a very long time." She looked back at the picture. "Maybe it wasn't a dream after all. For all I know, he could have been there when I was sold."

"What's that?" Jonna nodded toward the amulet.

"A symbol of my status. I'm required to wear it in the city. Once a person reaches a certain level of training, it is a mandate." She pointed to a second drawing. "The dream also said I would be reunited with my family, but to this day, I have never found them again."

"And the friend?"

"He was here when I left. I'm sure he found someone else."

The door opened behind them, and a man stared in shock. "Almundena, you're back."

CHAPTER 21
A CHANGE IN AGES

The man looked from Almundena to Jonna. A frown darkened his face. "I'm sorry. I did not know you had company. I saw the door open and thought—"

She interrupted with a smile. "I'm back—for a while. Anos, this is Jonna. Jonna, Anos."

"Good to meet you." Jonna extended his hand, which Anos reluctantly took.

The man's eyes went to the gray cloak on Jonna's arm. "A new member? When were you recruited?" However, his interest was not in Jonna. He turned back to Almundena. "Where have you been?"

"Undercover," she stated matter-of-factly. "For a very long time. I have come back only briefly before going out again."

"I see." Something in his voice said, *I do not believe you, but I'll let it slide for the moment.*

"Jonna was just admiring your handiwork."

"That was a long time ago," Anos said stiffly. "Things change." He glanced from Jonna back to Almundena. "Apparently." Anos's gaze bore into her eyes, the unspoken question on his lips: *What happened to you?*

"They certainly do." She dodged the question, looking hurt. "What's going on?"

"I just thought—" He stepped back toward the door. "I need to think." His eyes leaped to Jonna. "I'll find you later." With the same quickness by which Anos had appeared, he was gone.

"Anos!" Almundena moved to the front door, but the man was nowhere to be seen. She turned back to Jonna. "We can't stay here long. He knows something is wrong."

"I would agree." He nodded slowly, but his curiosity was piqued. "Did you dump him?"

"What?"

"Leave without telling him."

She turned away, directing her eyes around the room, and then sighed. "I didn't tell anyone. I couldn't." She leaned back against the wall.

"That explains why he's upset." His eyes went to the door as he pulled on the cloak.

She fought back the tears in her eyes. "What would you have done?"

"The same." He smiled, raising her chin and looking into her face. "It's okay, but we do need to be going." He gently wiped the tears from her cheeks.

Almundena nodded absently and picked up her cloak. Dropping it over her head, she moved to the door. The way was clear. As the door swung shut behind them, she turned and said, "Hectora." The light distorted for a moment, and Jonna heard a slight click.

"That's a handy spell. I'll have to remember that."

"You couldn't use it." She shook her head. "The use of dark magic is bound upon a person at a young age. Without the binding, the spells are worthless."

"Are you sure?"

Bob, who had been silent until now, chipped in, "Beats me."

"I wasn't asking you." He glanced at the pixie and then looked back at Almundena. It was the first time she mentioned some sort of binding. "What did they do?"

They reached the bottom of the stairs.

"It was a ceremony. Only the elder mage knows the ritual. That is why it is so important that we be taught young."

"Like indoctrination." He watched as other gray cloaks passed them. No one paid them any attention. "Almundena, if they have to initiate you into the cult, what else could they have done?"

Her innocent eyes looked up at him. "What do you mean?"

"I mean, if in order to use dark magic, you have to be initiated, it's possible they implanted some sort of control."

She shook her head, frowning. "I have never heard of such a thing, and I was close enough to some of the elders to know." Thinking, she glanced at him before looking back at the street. "That's not possible."

They were entering the central part of the city. The crowd on the street grew dense. If Jonna did not know he was in Forest Lost, he would have thought it was any other medieval city.

"It would explain why a mage like Azazel would not challenge them directly. If he could exert that kind of power, and they could exert that kind of power, they would cancel each other out. Perhaps it even stops them from fighting each other."

"Once a dark mage—" Bob snuck into the conversation.

"Always a dark mage," Almundena finished, turning toward Jonna.

"But that is not true. I am not a dark mage!" She moved in front of him, stopping their walk, stressing the meaning of her words.

One of the street vendors turned toward them, catching part of her last phrase. She smiled, took Jonna's arm, and moved past.

"Not in your heart." Jonna nodded to those who looked their way. "Not in your soul. However, you may still be controlled."

"No." She looked past the next few vendors, putting a smile on her face, and caught sight of the place called Donovan's. "There." She pointed. "That is where he is supposed to be."

A moment later, Jonna pushed back the curtain that served as an exterior door and stepped into the gloomy light. A clerk with a black, neck-length beard sat at a dusty counter. A registry lay next to him. The top of a bag was visible to the man's right, suspended off the desk's edge. "Can I help you folks?"

He sounded friendly, but his face said he did not like to be disturbed. The clerk laid down the scroll he was reading and stared at them both.

"We are looking for a man called Matthias."

"What's it to me?" The look on the man's face said I-don't-give-a-care. "Do you want a room or not?"

"Two rooms, please. I'm Jonna." Jonna stepped forward, extending his hand.

The clerk eyed it. "That's no good here. We only take money."

"But I didn't mean—" The look on the clerk's face stopped him. Jonna reached into his belt pouch and felt two coins. Bob was on his toes. He placed the coins on the counter.

The clerk picked both up, placed one between his teeth, and bit. "Looks good to me." His smile was more like a sneer. "Enjoy your stay." He dropped the coins into the bag beside him.

Eyeing Jonna and Almundena, he reached under the counter and pulled out two dark metal keys, holding them up so all could see. "The rooms are upstairs on the left: seven and nine. Two keys go to you. Two keys come back. Got it?"

Jonna nodded, accepting the keys, and turned toward the stairs.

"Good." The clerk frowned at Almundena. "Nothing underage. I don't like dealing with mage security." The man lifted the scroll and resumed his reading.

Jonna started to turn back as the meaning of the words hit him. "Nothing underage!"

Almundena laughed, caught his arm, and pulled him toward the stairs.

He glared at her, but her smile cut through the anger, washing it away. "Why are you laughing? He was trying to imply—"

"He gave me a compliment." She released his arm, taking the stairs two at a time. Jonna paused, shook his head, and followed.

The stairs went up to a flat area, turned to the right, and then went up again. As he reached the flat area, he called, "How old are you, anyway?"

"Wouldn't you like to know." She disappeared around the corner.

He took the stairs two at a time and caught up to her. She stood before a door with the number seven on it. After trying both keys, the second one fit. "Room seven." He held up the key. "Bob, hold this." The key disappeared from Jonna's fingertips.

"What do you want me to do with it?" The pixie studied its shape. "Nothing important here, except maybe it is laced with magic."

"Let me see that." Almundena took it from him. "It is. I didn't know they had started doing this. What better way to make sure only the original key works."

"Just keep it." Jonna went to the second room marked with a nine. He tried the lock, watched it open, looked around, and locked it back, giving Bob the key. "Do you think this place is very busy?"

"By the stack of coins at the counter—" The pixie shook his head. "I think he just barely gets by."

"Good." Jonna moved to room number eleven, tested the knob, and found it locked. "Bob, can you get this open?"

"Me?" the pixie exclaimed in a shocked voice. "You want me to aid in breaking and entering?" He gasped. "What type of pixie do you think I am?"

"A trickster?"

Bob grinned. "There is that. But truly, for me to enter a locked room, I must be invited. An open window or door will do. I've even skated in by only as much as a crack."

Jonna pointed. A gap existed between the bottom of the door and the floor.

"Gotcha." Bob winked. He leaped off Jonna's shoulder and plummeted downward. Right before he hit, he vanished in a sparkle of pixie dust, which a gust of wind sucked under the door.

The handle jiggled. The lock clicked. The door swung back. Jonna stepped into a dusty room. "Better than the ground." He frowned and then moved to one of the windows in the far wall.

The window showed another building only three feet away. For escape purposes, that seemed bad, but it would have to do. The plus was they had a great view of the street.

"Now what?" Almundena looked around at the room. "There certainly is not much to do around here."

"We were told to find Matthias, so I guess we need to get started."

Almundena shrugged. She went to the door, pulled it back, and jumped. There was the clerk, and he was not happy.

"Don't like the rooms?" He shoved the door inward. Almundena stepped further from him. "Magic has a lot of uses, including knowing when the keys aren't used."

"I don't trust the rooms." Jonna caught his eye.

The clerk moved toward a desk chair and sat down, his back to the wall. "What do you want with Matthias?" He rocked back and forth in his chair.

For a proprietor who had just found two people taking the wrong room, he did not seem *that* upset. Jonna kept his eyes on him.

"It is our business."

"Okay, play it your way." The clerk withdrew a wand, letting it lie in one hand. "I'll say it again, what do you want with Matthias? And if I don't get an answer, there is always mage security." He stared at Almundena. "Don't I know you?"

She shook her head.

"Hmm, I never forget a face. Give me time." He turned back to Jonna. "Don't make me have to ask three times." He pointed the wand, toying with it.

Jonna reached into his belt pouch and felt the twigs while continuing to maintain eye contact. He taunted, "Give it your best shot."

"Jonna, what are you doing?" Almundena stepped in front, placing herself between the two.

"It seems your lady friend doesn't want you hurt." The clerk grinned. "You must be some"—he paused for effect—"performer."

"That's enough," Jonna warned, pulling his hand from his pouch and pointing at the clerk. The seriousness in his voice was unmistakable. "I want to know where we can find Matthias Omid, and I want to know now."

The clerk raised the wand at both of them, chuckling. "You've got gall—"

The wand shot out of his hand, bounced off a wall, and landed in a corner. Rather than being surprised, the clerk looked amused. In the brief distraction, Jonna jumped forward, slammed into an unseen surface, and fell back onto the bed. He looked up at the clerk, wide-eyed, and then slowly got to his feet.

"You've got a lot of nerve." The clerk chuckled. "But no magic sense. Don't you know about personal firewalls?"

"Personal firewalls?" Jonna frowned. "Where are we, a technology seminar?"

The man narrowed his eyes at him. "A what?"

Jonna waved it away. Explaining technology might take a while.

Almundena turned to look at the clerk. "A personal firewall is a shield only a dark mage elder can raise. You must be Matthias."

"Might be." He chuckled again. "Might not." His face went serious. "What do you want?"

"We were sent by Azazel Elam." At the mention of Azazel's name, Jonna saw a flicker of recognition in the clerk's face.

The clerk put his hand to his beard. "It's been a long time." He looked at the two cautiously. "Azazel and I were partners once." Throwing a glance toward the corner, he added, "Tell that pixie friend of yours to retrieve my wand."

"He saw me?" Bob looked disgusted. "How did he do that?"

The clerk grunted. "You fly too slow."

"I—I do not fly slow!"

"No?" The man looked at him doubtfully before turning back to Jonna.

Bob brought his wand back but held it just out of reach. The pixie wrinkled his nose at the man in dislike.

The clerk continued, "This has all been very entertaining, and I don't get much of that around here, but what do you want from me?"

Jonna nodded. "Then you are Matthias?"

"If it takes that to get you to tell me, sure."

"I'm looking for two things: the Rune Blade of Knowledge, and my wife."

"Wife, uh?" The clerk looked at Almundena, raising an eyebrow. "Why do you need a wife?"

Ignoring the comment, Jonna continued, "Do you know where they are?"

When no answer came, Jonna looked at Bob. "Bob, I bet without his wand, your pixie dust would be quite effective."

Bob started to reach into his pouch. "What a wonderful idea."

"Hold it." The clerk held up his hand. "I'll cut out the wisecracks."

"Thanks, now, about the Rune Blade?"

Matthias leaned back in his chair. "Do you believe in prophecies?"

"What prophecy?" Almundena stepped forward. "I've never heard of—"

"Of course you haven't." The man grinned. "Only a few of the elders know. Even old Azazel did not have a clue. That's why the inner circle drove him off. There were too many things adding up too quickly."

"Azazel was driven off?" Jonna thought back. "He did say—"

"Oh yes, driven right out of Forest Lost. Then he struck a bargain with the elders to watch Chernobog, a prison of a sort. It was a good deal for all involved: Dark Mages could start controlling the outsider cities, Azazel got a life of luxury, and dissenters were sent where they weren't any threat."

Jonna caught his eye. "What about the prophecy?"

Matthias stood up, checked the shutters, and closed the door. Taking the chair again, he resumed. "It tells of a Change in Ages," he said cryptically. "Of a pivotal point in our future when the balance of power can be swayed. The elders have been preparing for this for quite some time. If the tale is true"—he winked at them both—"and I don't doubt that it is, this rune thing of yours should be in the Well of Tears." He looked at Jonna and chuckled. "The prophecy doesn't mention a wife."

"What of the elvish princess Elfleda?"

Matthias raised an eyebrow. "Didn't know about that, but if power's involved, I'm sure she'd be connected." He thought, glancing down. "If she were here, they'd have to keep her locked up. It'd take a group of dark mages to do that." He looked up with an idea. "The Consortium's main building, where the strongest magic is weaved, is called Berk Hecktor." He watched Almundena in expectation. Her eyes went wide.

"No, Jonna." She turned toward him. "You cannot go there!"

"And why not?"

"Listen to her, laddie," Matthias agreed. "Not even a dark mage dares go there uninvited."

"Why?"

A funny look crossed Almundena's face. "I—I don't know, but whatever is there, it is dreadful!" Her eyes pleaded as she moved toward him. "Stop the quest."

"What's gotten into you?" Jonna held her back, studying her demeanor. The eyes were no longer Almundena's.

"Do not go!" She bordered on panic. "If you do, there will be no return."

"Bob?"

"It's an enchantment." The pixie took a closer look, checking Almundena's pupils. "A prearranged spell, designed to be invoked at—"

"The mention of a certain word." Jonna stepped back, looking from Almundena to Matthias.

Matthias chuckled again. "I knew I had seen her before. She's a Sarka."

Jonna's eyebrows narrowed. "A Sarka?"

Matthias nodded. "Every so often, the elders create a Sarka. A Sarka is someone controlled by the use of a spell, but only under a certain circumstance. They must have suspected this girl would run. Something must have happened in her past."

Jonna nodded slowly. "It had to be her brother when he came to take her away. So the dark mages did this to her?"

"It's a common practice." Matthias nodded. "And part of their training. I would not doubt that all of us have something like that hidden. Why do you think Azazel didn't come himself?"

"We've got to help her."

"Leave her alone." Matthias seemed unconcerned. "She'll come out of it in a few moments."

He was right. A few minutes later, Almundena looked around. "What's going on?" She found herself standing by the bed.

"You're a Sarka." Jonna observed the change in her pupils. "You've been programmed to protect the inner circle."

"Jonna—" She shook her head in disbelief. "We've already had this discussion." She glanced at Matthias, who nodded.

"I'm sorry, girl, but he's right."

Almundena swung back to face Jonna, her eyebrows raised. "You believe him?"

"Both Bob and I saw it. You kicked into defensive mode when the—" Jonna paused. "The BH word was mentioned."

"You mean—" She looked at her hands in disbelief. The memory of what had happened came rolling back. "Why?" Her eyes showed fear as she remembered. "My brother—" Almundena's head dropped. "I remember. It was right after he disappeared." She looked up at them both. "They said it would help me find him."

Matthias stepped in. "More than likely, it led you further from him. I remember the commotion your brother's presence caused. Of course, that was still when I was privy to the inner workings of the council. Since then—" He shrugged.

"Then my brother could be in—in BH?" Now, she was afraid to say it.

A tingle went up Jonna's spine, and he watched as the hairs on his arms stood up. "Something's going on."

Bob tilted his head, listening. "Yep. And coming this way."

A moment later, there was a commotion in the street. Matthias moved to the window, opening one shutter. People stepped aside, forming a clear path toward his inn.

"Mage security." The clerk turned to catch their eyes. "I think someone turned you in."

Almundena moved beside Matthias, trying to see. Guiding a security patrol was Anos.

"I can't believe it." She glanced toward Jonna. "Anos turned me in."

"You mean Anos the Alexius?" Matthias laughed. "You make strange friends for a dissenter."

"I didn't know he was promoted."

Matthias nodded. "Just after you disappeared."

Almundena grabbed Jonna's hand. "Come on, we have to get out of here."

"Hey." Matthias came up behind them. "You can't go that way. They are too close."

Jonna stopped her, turning around. "Will you help us?"

"You think I want them tearing my place apart after discovering you were here?" He led them to a corner at the turn in the stairs and pointed. "Hide here."

Jonna looked at him as if he were crazy. "You want us to stand in the corner?"

Matthias grinned. "Wand, please."

Bob appeared and handed the tool to him. "You'd make a good bellboy. Need a job?"

Jonna laughed. "Unfortunately, he has one."

"Hey," the pixie retorted. "What's so unfortunate about my job?"

Matthias tapped an area of the wall with his wand. The wood became transparent, revealing a hole they could climb into. "Is that better?"

It would be small, dark, and very cramped, but two could fit.

Jonna nodded at Almundena. "If you're game, I am, unless you know a better choice?"

She shrugged and crawled into the cubbyhole. Jonna followed. It *was* a tight fit.

After testing several positions, Jonna found his back to the wall with her back pressed into his chest. Her head was slightly below his, and he could smell—it was the same fragrance that he smelled upon waking that morning. Jonna felt heat rising in his cheeks.

Matthias looked inside. "It was designed for one but will have to do—" His voice trailed off as he squinted, noticing their red faces. "Are you two okay?"

With Jonna's voice higher than normal and Almundena's almost a squeak, they both answered in unison, "Perfectly."

Bob laughed, floating in the empty space neither of the two could use. "I've got plenty of room."

Matthias shook his head, tapped the wall with his wand, and everything went dark.

With the light cut off, their sense of touch immediately increased. He could feel the presence of Almundena's body vividly, too close for comfort. As his pixie sight kicked in, he turned his head. Almundena's hair pressed into his face. He smelled the fragrance and immediately turned away.

Attempting to ignore the emotions brought on by the night before, he focused on their cubbyhole. He could see the cubed walls that made up their hiding place, along with the glow of Almundena and his own body that showed up like lanterns in a cave, only with different degrees of brightness. It was the alien feel of the view that helped to distract him.

Almundena tried to steady her voice. "Uh, I—" Her breath was labored, and he could tell she was trying to get her own emotions under control.

Suddenly, she dropped her head, shook it, and began to laugh. "In all my life, I have never been in a situation like this."

He knew exactly what she was referring to, and it had nothing to do with the cubbyhole. Well, almost nothing. It was all about the night before. Her laughter got worse. "If you weren't already married, I would swear the Fates were telling me that I was supposed to marry you right now."

The laughter was contagious. Jonna found himself laughing, too. As the laughter broke the stress, both relaxed. Almundena settled back. "Thank you for understanding."

"I should thank you." Jonna felt the tension ebb away, despite the security mages just outside the building. "You are an incredible woman, unlike any I've ever met."

"Well, thank you." Her smile brightened.

Jonna thought a moment. "Except maybe my wife."

Almundena gave a wide smile. "I wouldn't have it any other way. If I were your wife, I'd want to be number one, too."

The more they talked, the more comfortable both became, despite being in the cubbyhole hiding from the Dark Mages. Almundena told him about the place she grew up, about the dark castle spire that loomed many miles away but always caught the light in a spectacular display at sunrise. She told him about the unicorn she saw as a child, and the valley that they, she and her brother, were warned never to enter. "The valley was called Conria, and the castle was called Cyneduban."

Though Jonna could not see her eyes as she talked, the light around the front of her face brightened in the pixie sight. It was not until she finished that the light dimmed.

"But what about you?" Her face glowed again. Though she tried to glance in his direction, the space was too cramped.

He felt her hair move across his skin and looked at her glowing image. "I've never met a unicorn," he joked.

When she remained silent, waiting, he went on, telling her of the face in the water when he was just a boy, how everyone thought he was nuts, and finally ending with meeting Sir Verity.

"So, here I am." He shrugged. "There is nothing mystical or magical about it."

She gave a knowing laugh. "There is always magic and mystery, even when we don't recognize it."

Jonna chuckled. "A mage I know said the same thing." He shifted thoughts, the levity dropping away. "Maybe we should check on Matthias."

"Can you?"

Jonna nodded. "If I just focus—"

His voice trailed off as he looked at the wall by the stairs, adjusted the light, and passed through to the registration counter. It was a strange sight, more like viewing a negative than seeing a picture. He spotted Matthias and watched the man's lips move. With no way to hear, his only choice was to lip read, relaying it like a narrator for Almundena to hear. The clerk prepared a spell.

~

Abruptly, the exterior curtain walls parted, and Matthias looked up. "What can I do for you boys?"

"We're looking for a woman and a man." Anos stepped forward, presenting some type of scroll. "They're intruders wearing gray cloaks."

Matthias, not even bothering to look at the scroll, turned away, picked up something else, and began to read silently. When Anos did not take the hint, he spoke. "None of my business."

Anos's next words came out with venom. "They were *seen* coming in here." His tone promised more if the clerk did not cooperate.

Matthias looked up. "I don't care if they are enemy number one. It's none of my business either way." He turned back to what he was reading.

Anos half-shouted, "They *are* enemy number one, you fool." He reached forward and tried to grab Matthias's shirt. Matthias dodged away, and both their firewalls came up, knocking them back at the same time.

Anos got up from the floor. "Do you always keep your firewall at hand?" His eyes narrowed.

CHAPTER 22
SARKA

"Have you seen this part of the city?" Matthias rolled his eyes. "Why don't you thugs clean it up?"

Anos growled. "Watch him. Check upstairs."

Two of the guards went up. The other two stayed down. A moment later, they came back, shaking their heads. "No one's there."

"If I find you've helped them—"

Matthias looked up, cutting Anos off. "Watch who you're dealing with, boy." The deadly tone in Matthias's voice physically pushed Anos back.

Anos's eyes widened.

"I was there when they brought you in." The clerk's voice remained stone-cold. "I can help them take you out."

The security mage shot him a look of hate but did not approach again. "How low have the mighty fallen. Your previous status with the council of elders won't save you now, friends or no friends." Anos spun toward the others. "Continue the search." Both Anos and the guards left Donovan's.

~

"They're gone," Jonna finished the tale. He glanced toward Almundena and adjusted his focus to inside their hiding place.

The stairs creaked, the noise stopped, and something tapped on the outside wall. As the wood became transparent, it finally vanished.

"They—" But the looks on their faces told Matthias they already knew what had taken place. "Interesting."

They untangled, crawling out in reverse order, and then stretched as Matthias went downstairs to get something behind his counter. He pulled out a piece of parchment, along with an inkwell, and began to draw. They met him at the desk.

"You are here." Matthias put an X on the map. "And this is how you get to the Well of Tears." After a few moments, he rolled up the scroll and handed the map to Jonna. "There's not much time. When they see your trail really does stop here, they will be back."

Almundena kissed Matthias's cheek while Bob laid both keys on the counter. "Thank you."

Matthias's face reddened. "Now why did you have to do that? Go, both of you. Remember the trail behind the building. It will take you to the correct street."

Jonna and Almundena headed toward the back door.

"Follow the directions," Matthias warned, and watched as the door closed behind them. "To the letter."

The door shut, and they stood in a deserted alley. It occurred to Jonna that Bob had been very quiet. "Bob, are you still there?"

There was a noticeable pause before the pixie answered, somewhat agitated. "I'm here."

"You were silent for the most part in the cubbyhole."

The agitation was still very plain. "I was."

"Then what's going on? Why were you so quiet? And why are you so agitated?"

There was a commotion from the street, but they could not see what was going on. Almundena gave him a worried look. "Jonna, we really don't have time—"

Bob cut in with a mock high-pitched voice, "Jonna, we really don't have time—"

"Bob?" Jonna was shocked. "What's got into you? You can't be jealous."

"Jealous? Me? Ha!" The pixie laughed. "But you really should keep your mouth shut."

"Bob!" Almundena glared at him. "What did we do this time? All we did was talk."

"You—" Bob huffed and closed his mouth. "And you—" He pinched Jonna on the ear.

"Hey, that's enough," Jonna warned. "Either tell us what is wrong or get over it."

Bob looked up and closed his eyes. If Jonna did not know better, he would have sworn the pixie was praying for strength. "It's too late anyway. Just forget it."

Jonna's agitation flared. "Forget what? You bring up this world-ending implication, imply Almundena and I did something wrong, and then say drop it?" A funny thought hit Jonna. "Are pixies bipolar? Could it have something to do with too much pixie dust?"

"Pixie dust?" Bob's eyes widened as he thought, and then he quickly shook his head. "You're just trying to confuse me. No, of course not, and what's bipolar?"

"Boys." Almundena tried to be patient, despite the fact they needed to go faster. "We really need to move."

Jonna continued, though he edged away from the back way of the inn. "It's when a person can go from one emotion to another with little or no reason." He eyed Bob. "Perhaps you should see a psychiatrist."

"A psy-what?"

Almundena frowned. "Jonna, I don't know what you're talking about either."

Jonna winked at her with the eye Bob could not see. "Are you better now?" he said to Bob.

The pixie exhaled. "Yeah, I'm good."

"Do you want to tell me what's going on?"

Bob shrugged. "Maybe later." He looked over at Almundena. "Er, sorry."

"Apology accepted." She nodded. "Now, can we get out of here?"

Three paths led off. Bob pointed at one between the buildings. "That way."

"I see you studied the map." Jonna held the parchment up, verifying the right direction.

"But of course." Bob folded his arms. "What type of a pixie would I be not studying a map?"

Almundena chipped in, "A lost one?"

"Ha, ha, very funny." He paused. "Actually, that was pretty good. I'll have to remember that."

They stepped into the next street and merged with the crowd. It was elbow-to-elbow, pushing and bumping, trying to keep each other close.

Jonna did not like it. "Are the streets normally this crowded? This is worse than Diggory."

"No." Almundena looked around. "There must be something special going on."

That strange tingling went through Jonna again, and he remembered what happened at Donovan's. "Over here." He pulled Almundena into a small, unoccupied vendor tent and moved them back into a darkened corner.

The crowded street parted, creating a pathway just like the first time, and here came Anos. There was something about his face. Determination? Yes. Anger? Yes. However, Jonna could also see fear. If they had only been able to ask a few more questions about the prophecy, maybe it would have given Jonna a clue.

Mage security stopped almost in front of the tent. Anos turned. Jonna could have sworn the security mage looked right at them.

"Donovan's was clean," a guard reported to Anos. "No sign of the two when we spot-checked again, but the owner was just as hostile."

"I'll deal with Matthias through the council," Anos said darkly. "Time grows short." He looked around at all the people. "How can we do a proper search with all these people in the streets? Get them off!"

"But sir." One of the guards stepped forward. "It is the Aatto of Ptah. Even the council cannot interfere."

Anos spun around, trying to see through the crowd. "Bah!"

"He's right," Almundena whispered. "Once a year the people of this city celebrate when the first dark mage came to power. It brought prosperity to this place, and a thriving city grew. I didn't realize it was that time."

"And?" Jonna glanced at her, though his eyes returned to the group outside the tent. The name, Aatto of Ptah, had no meaning for him. As the wind stirred, a flap on the back of the tent flipped open. Maybe they ought to slip out?

"You don't understand," she continued. "The council cannot interfere. Without this celebration, the dark mage power cannot be renewed."

Now that had Jonna's attention. "They would lose their magic?"

"Basically." She continued to watch the front of the tent. "Only minor spells can be done without this annual event."

"Like the spells you've performed so far?"

She shook her head. "Less than that."

Two of the guards backed into the tent, making a place for Anos to come in out of the sun. Fortunately, they were not very close, and the tent was large.

Bob pulled Jonna's ear and whispered, "Time to go."

"I agree, Bob." Jonna moved the flap back, checking the area behind it, and thought over what Almundena had said. A narrow trail led behind the tents. Without warning, he grabbed Almundena's hand and pulled her through. He whispered, moving as fast as he could without running, "I think we now know another piece of the prophecy."

A cool breeze whipped through the open flap, catching a guard's attention. He stepped to the back and caught sight of them leaving. "Halt!"

Jonna cringed as Bob hollered out, "Run!"

Anos followed, spotting their backsides as they raced away. "After them, you fools!"

Bob kept watch from behind. "Faster, they're trying to follow!"

Almundena spoke between breaths, continuing the conversation Jonna began. "What piece of the prophecy is that?"

"Isn't it obvious? We're here on the exact day the power of the dark mage is to be renewed. Disrupt the celebration, and what will happen?"

"The Dark Mages will—" She looked at Jonna with narrowed eyes. "They will lose their power."

"Or the majority of it. In any case, their threat will be lessened, the elves will regain the forest, and the balance will be restored." He dodged a wooden box along the narrow path.

"They're still coming," Bob warned. "And gaining ground!"

"Bob, can't you slow them down with something?"

The pixie abruptly smiled. "Oh, that's a good idea!" He reached into his pocket, measuring out some pixie dust. "How about this? Ceres Bolium!"

The pixie dust flew, catching the wind. It spun and shifted with a life of its own. The moment it touched the debris behind them, the debris began to enlarge. Boxes doubled their size, tent poles became longer, and rocks turned into boulders. The security mages slowed their pace, forced to dodge the growing debris.

"After them!" Anos pushed on, struggling to avoid the obstacles, but everything around them continued to grow. The guards stumbled, turned, and fell.

Fighting to get past, Anos narrowed his eyes. He'd had enough. "Awiti Barbaros!"

Lightning streaked from the staff he carried, striking the items that barred his way. Heedless of his men, the obstacles exploded, sending pieces and parts in all directions. He paid no attention to the fallen mages.

Almundena remembered the map. "That way." She spotted the building Matthias indicated and pulled Jonna toward the street, plowing through the people.

A vendor dodged back and forth, trying to get out of the way of security, just as Jonna whipped past.

"Hectora," Anos shouted. The vendor froze in place, and the guards rushed around the human-turned-statuette.

"They're serious now." Bob chuckled. "Guess I got their attention."

"That you did." Jonna glanced back. "Thanks for slowing them down."

Almundena pointed at the narrow path the people formed in the center of the street. "More guards are coming from both sides."

"There." Jonna grabbed her hand and led them toward an alley. It was off the map but the only option left.

As they raced to the far end and turned the corner, all three jerked to a stop. A look of bewilderment crossed their faces.

"Dead end." Almundena released Jonna's hand. Panic danced in her eyes. "They're coming!"

Jonna spun around and tried to find another way out. "Bob?"

The pixie huffed. "Why are you asking me?"

"Turn us invisible or something!"

"Turn us invis—who do you think I am, the all-powerful Dorothy? She's queen of the pixies!"

There was no time for this, so Jonna reverted to the only thing he knew. "Unum-Clastor-Fillum."

Almundena looked at him, confused. "What are you saying?"

"Shh. Unum-Clastor-Fillum. Unum-Clastor-Fillum. Unum-Clastor-Fillum." Jonna grabbed hold of Almundena's hand. "Hold on! Unum-Clastor-Fillum!"

The security mages turned the corner, raising weapons in the trio's direction. Anos followed, stopped, and raised his hand as Jonna finished his seventh chant. "Awiti Barbaros!"

Lightning ripped across the darkness. It happened all too fast. Though both Jonna and Almundena were within the lightning's reach, it was easy to see whom Anos wanted to kill. Jonna jerked Almundena behind him in the split second before the lightning hit. A searing pain ripped through him. His mouth went dry, and his insides felt on fire. His only reassurance was the look on Anos's face as Jonna faded from view.

Anos ran toward them, screaming, "No!"

Then, Jonna fell, tumbling back into the familiar darkness of a spell misused. He struck the ground, gasping for breath, his body trembling and jumping as if connected to an electric wire.

Almundena moaned somewhere to his left. He had hoped to protect her by stepping in front. At hearing her words and the strength in her voice, he knew he had succeeded.

She breathed heavily. "Where are we?"

Jonna's teeth chattered. "So-some-somewhere else."

A light blossomed from the amulet Almundena wore. She searched the darkness to find him. Dropping to her knees, she put a hand to his face. There was quickness to her movements. It made him wonder what was wrong.

"You're trembling so badly, you've broken out into a cold sweat." She shook her head, and a sense of panic crept into her voice. "Without my herbs and potions, I have nothing to help. No magic I know of can contain this."

She seemed to be speaking to herself rather than him. Removing her cloak, she added it to his own and pressed her body against his, trying to keep him warm. Her arms became a pillow for them both.

Despite the trembling, Jonna felt a degree of comfort. The pressure of her body against his did make him feel warmer.

They lay there for a while, quiet in the darkness that threatened to overtake them. With a small sigh, she stilled herself, removing all emotion from her voice. "I—I can't lie to you, Jonna, and you deserve to know the truth. All lightning spells that meet their mark are fatal. If it does not happen at the moment of impact, then it will gradually over time."

She stopped and took a deep breath. "I should have taken the hit. Anos was aiming for me." Almundena looked down into Jonna's eyes. "Why did you do it?"

Still trembling, but feeling better, Jonna met her gaze. "Why wouldn't I?"

A tear rolled down her cheek. She turned to face the darkness. "It is not fair."

"Wha—" Jonna swallowed and then coughed to clear his throat. "What's not fair?"

The trembling had started to subside, and as long as his body did not go into shock, he should be fine. He could remember that much from the first aid of his own reality. Almundena had done all that she knew to do, which was good given she knew nothing about electricity. In his world, it would have been simple. Go to a hospital and have the emergency room check you out, right? From what he had read, if a fatality was going to occur, it should have already happened.

Why was she so pessimistic? He shifted the cloaks and placed a hand on her shoulder. "What's not fair?"

She jumped, turned around, and stared at him in shock. "You can move? You're not dying?" She leaned over, grabbed hold, and tightened her grip around him.

He chuckled, hugging her back. "What's a little lightning between friends? Besides, it was really getting warm in this cocoon you've put me in."

They both sat up. Jonna pulled her cloak from around him. As the cloak came off, she noticed his elvish clothes. It was impossible to miss the black mark on his chest. As she rubbed her hand over it, the black flaked off, revealing the untouched fabric underneath.

"I have no idea what saved you. You should be dead."

"Thanks for the vote of confidence," he teased, touching her nose. He took a deep breath, glad that the tremors were gone. "If I had to guess, because the spell that brought us here was in play before Anos said his own spell, the hit was not as bad as you think, and—" He tried to pinch part of the elven material. It would not wrinkle. "I suspect this armor is made of gold. Between its protection and me not being electrically grounded, the lightning did minimal damage."

Almundena wiped her eyes but still stared at him, unbelieving. A strange quality entered her voice as if she saw something far away.

"You are a strange one, Jonna McCambel. You should not have risked your life to save mine."

The words sounded foreboding, and Jonna could not help but remember what Bob had said. *Once a dark mage, always a dark mage.* He decided to ignore those words—at least for the moment.

He continued, "I bet we did phase out at the last moment." Jonna laughed, thinking back on the incident with the leprechaun. "That's becoming a habit with me."

She knew he was ignoring her words, but she let it slide. "I can tell there is a story behind that."

"Another time," he chuckled. "We need to think about getting back. How long do you think Anos will hang around?"

"Not long. Once they see we are gone, they will probably leave. However, they might post a guard or two."

Heavy footsteps moved at a distance, coming closer. Jonna remembered the minotaur.

Almundena heard it, too. "What is that?"

"Uh, we might have another problem."

Jonna reached for Almundena's right hand with his left. His other hand found the twigs in his pocket.

"Stay with me no matter what," he warned, and guided her away from the sound in the darkness.

"Jonna, where are we going?" Almundena put her hand around the amulet on her neck. It made the light shine ahead of them like a flashlight.

He smiled. "Nice trick. Did you use dark magic?"

"No." She laughed, though she looked a little taken aback. "Not all the magic I know came from the Dark Mages, remember? I told you about Lord Honorius."

He nodded, still walking, trying to figure out how to say what had to be said.

As they went, she watched the empty space around them. "So, where are we going?"

Jonna tried to minimize the problem without making her too concerned. "Suffice it to say, I left something in here that I'd rather not find again, at least until I know what to do with it." He changed subjects. "So Lord Honorius was a good man?"

"He helped me find the Light."

"That brings up an interesting point."

The thing moving behind them was now further away, but not entirely gone. Jonna's grip on both the twigs and Almundena never varied, but his mind was a whirlwind of thoughts.

A slight sigh left his lips. "We know that you're a Sarka. There is no debate. What happens when we confront the Dark Mages in their den?"

For a while, the question hung in the air. Jonna swallowed, dreading what he would have to do next. It was perfectly logical, but no matter how he played it out, she was only going to be hurt.

Almundena frowned, whispering, "I don't know." Turning to him, she pleaded, "But I want to help."

"I know you do." He paused. "And I want you to, but—" Jonna took a breath. "Almundena, I do trust you, but I also know you are controlled by something you cannot resist. When it comes down to the final battle—if you turned—"

She answered without emotion, the hopelessness of her situation sinking in. "You would destroy me." She turned away. "I can accept that."

"No." He shook his head, fighting back his own emotions. "And that is the point. I couldn't. No more than I could let you take that lightning strike."

Their eyes met, and they were keenly aware of each other. A strange feeling came over Jonna, a battle fighting in his very soul.

He closed his eyes, finally breaking the connection. "The point is, you cannot be there. I cannot take that chance."

They stood there, neither sure what to say. The things they had gone through in such a short time, yet covering volumes, went rolling through their minds.

"We are friends," she said at last in a stoic voice, pushing away the emotions and looking to the darkness in front of them. "Good friends, and nothing more."

The implication of the statement threw him. Were they talking about the same thing here? He had been referring to her staying away from the battle, but it sounded like she was going to stay away forever.

He had heard of this type of thing happening. A close bond shared between two people, because of an extreme situation, turning into something more, but this was a first for him.

Unfortunately, this was not the time to address it, nor did Jonna believe there would ever be a right time. Instead of correcting the possible confusion, Jonna left it alone. "Then you understand what must happen?"

"I do." She smiled sadly. "I will stay away."

His stomach dropped as he felt the finality in the air, but he pretended it did not exist.

"Good." Jonna felt relieved and conflicted at the same time. "Are you ready to head back?" He took her hand in his.

"Yes." But her tone was off. It was better to ignore that.

He spoke the chant seven times. As the darkness dissolved, they found themselves in the middle of a troop of security mages.

Bob appeared from nowhere. "You're back! As the lightning hit, we were separated, and I watched you fade away!"

"What in the world?" Two startled mages leaped back from Jonna, while another fell forward, tripping over his own feet. The man who fell into Jonna and Almundena broke the handhold between them. With Jonna's other hand on the twigs, he had no way of reaching her in time as a guard yelled out, "Hectora!"

Almundena froze, locked in place, her eyes still wide with surprise.

"You should have better manners," Jonna growled, releasing the twigs and leaping toward the nearest mage.

Inward blocking the man's right arm, Jonna sword-palmed him to the throat. The man gagged. His head tilted back. However, Jonna was not about to let this one get away.

The sword-palm turned into a hook, and he jerked the man toward him. After a knee to the mage's groin, the man groaned in pain as Jonna slammed him backwards with a heel-palm.

Jonna counted his opponents. One was easy, two not bad, and three were tolerable, but four or more? "Bob, a little help, please."

Golden glitters hit the air, falling in all directions. The swords and bardiches turned to rubber, slapping Jonna on every side.

"That was help?" Jonna grabbed one of the weapons and pulled its owner in. Ducking, he allowed the guard to flip over him into another.

One of the guards yelled, "Awiti Barbaros!"

Jonna dropped low, remembering all too vividly what had happened the last time. The lightning bolt streaked across, taking out three of the guards behind him.

The confusion turned the minor chaos into major calamity. More security mages poured around the corner, but no one knew exactly why.

"Awiti Barbaros!" Another bolt downed a second set of guards. Lightning bounced in all directions.

Jonna rolled to the right, coming up behind Almundena. "Bob, what can we do?"

"You're asking me? I use pixie magic!"

Pointing at Almundena, Jonna growled, "Do something to release her."

Bob barked back, "I'm thinking!"

Unexpected noises came from the alley around the corner, followed by exclamations, surprises, grunts, and flashes of light. A blue haze appeared, reaching up into the sky.

A voice Jonna recognized sighed. With a little smile, a mage stepped around the corner. "That's so much better." Väinämö turned and spotted Jonna. "New spell. Repeat after me: Unum."

"Unum—but—"

Väinämö shook his finger. "Clastor."

"Clastor," Jonna added very quickly. "What did you do to the guards?"

Väinämö waved at the blue haze above him and then pointed at himself. "Look at me, not the haze." He showed two fingers, brought them toward his eyes, and pointed at Jonna. "Now say, Pratima."

"Pratima."

"Now you know the words. Say them so they sound together."

"Unum-Clastor-Pratima?"

Väinämö waved a finger in the air. He looked like a song director, matching tempo. "Again!"

"Unum-Clastor-Pratima. Unum-Clastor-Pratima."

"Faster."

"Unum-Clastor-Pratima. Unum-Clastor-Pratima. Unum-Clastor-Pratima. This won't stop me from speaking again, will it?"

"Hush. Again."

A duplicate of Jonna took form, becoming more solid with each passing chant. The more solid the duplicate became, the more transparent the real Jonna appeared. He spoke the seventh phrase. "Unum-Clastor-Pratima."

Never before had he felt like this. He walked around his own duplicate body, throwing a glance toward Väinämö. "Can I speak?"

"Certainly." The mage stroked his own moustache. "Not too bad. But remember, you have to let it recharge."

"Or?"

"It won't work." The mage gave a belly laugh. "Also, I would suggest you not try it touching a second human being. This was meant to be used as a singular spell—one person only and that's it."

Jonna threw a glance at Väinämö while still shifting around his own clone. "Okay, wise guy, or what happens?"

"I don't know." The mage's eyes twinkled. "Remember, it was designed—"

"For one," Jonna finished. "What about Almundena?"

"What about her?" The mage looked at the guards Jonna had taken out. "Not too bad."

Could he never keep this mage's attention? "The girl is frozen!"

"She'll be fine." Väinämö tapped one of the guards with his right foot. "Out cold. Pretty good. What did you hit them with?"

Jonna was getting a little irritated. "My hand." You would think the mage could keep on track! "What about Bob?"

"Ask him." Väinämö touched one of the rubberized weapons. "Nice touch, Bob."

"Thank you." The pixie grinned. Now the mage was distracting

Bob!

"Bob, can you see me?" Jonna asked.

"Of course I can see you. I'm a pixie, remember?"

"But can anyone else?"

Väinämö laughed. "Not usually, and certainly not the Dark Mages." Apparently, the mage was at least half-listening. "It's beyond their perception," Väinämö finished. "One of the fallacies of dark magic."

"Only until they get a spell that corrects that." Jonna tried to stress the possibility.

"Tsk, tsk, tsk, don't be so pessimistic. Now, there are a few more things that you should know. The spell I've just given you only lasts for a short period of time. Once it expires, don't forget the rest period."

Jonna was suspicious. "How much time?"

"Let's see." The mage tapped his chin. "About an hourglass."

"You mean an hour."

"No," the mage countered. "An hourglass is the exact measurement."

Väinämö reached into the pocket of his robe and pulled out an hourglass that should not have been able to fit there. A portion of the sand had already dropped through. He held it in Jonna's direction.

Jonna made a face. "I don't want that. How am I going to carry it?"

The mage began, "All you have to do—"

Bob smiled. "I can carry it."

Jonna waved them both back. "Look, guys." He slid his sleeve up, showing his arm. "This is a watch. It measures time in hours and minutes."

"How curious." Väinämö leaned forward, studying Jonna's arm. "And those little needles show time elapsing?" He looked up at Jonna and smiled. "How impressive."

Lifting up the hourglass, he compared it to the watch hands. "I'd say you have maybe forty-five of those little needle movements left." He waved slightly at the watch and put the hourglass away.

"Now then, off to the Well of Tears." Väinämö faded away. "While you can."

When he disappeared completely, so did the blue haze over their heads. A large troop of security mages hurried around the corner. "Stop them! Hectora!"

Although Jonna stood by his body, he felt no effect.

Anos came from behind his men. "Excellent." He beamed, looking at Jonna's duplicate body and gloating. He turned to Almundena and frowned. "Take them both."

A small wagon rolled around the corner, and Jonna's duplicate, along with Almundena's body, was loaded into the back.

Jonna checked his watch. Thirty minutes remained. Pulling out the map, he made his way out into the city streets.

"Make way!" The wagon driver tapped the reins, and the horses dashed forward. In the process, they passed right through Jonna.

"Ugh!" Nausea rippled through his body. "What was that?"

CHAPTER 23
STEPHANIE'S PROTECTOR

Bob acted very scholarly. "It was the part of you still connected with this plane of reality intersecting with a solid object."

"While you're at it," Jonna teased, "stick your nose in the air and put glasses on. Since when did you know there were other realities?"

"Huh?" The pixie glanced at Jonna. "I'm just quoting Väinämö. What's a reality?"

"Never mind." Jonna studied the map again. "According to this, there are two ways in. One is through the main gate. The other is by a secret passage. Both lead to the Well of Tears." He looked at his transparent hands. "Why not take the main gate?"

"Sounds good to me." Bob sat down, enjoying the ride.

For some reason, the pixie was able to stay in contact with Jonna's ethereal body. Jonna would have to ask Väinämö how that could be. "Have you decided to tell me what you wouldn't say outside of Donovan's?"

The pixie shook his head sadly as his cheeks turned red. "As I said, it's too late now."

Jonna demanded, "What's too late?"

That opened the floodgate. "You told her everything in the cubbyhole. Now she can use it against you, as can all the other dark mages!"

Jonna frowned at him. "You're not back on that *you can't trust her* bit again? I told you, Bob, she is trustworthy. Is this why you wouldn't talk in front of her?"

Bob nodded. "If she knows, so do the Dark Mages. She is a Sarka. Once a dark mage—"

Jonna finished the phrase, "—always a dark mage. I know. You said it before, but I still can't believe it." Or could he? He, himself, had asked her not to help for that very same reason. Was he kidding himself?

"You don't have to believe me," the pixie stated smugly. "You'll see for yourself." Bob sighed. "I just hope it won't be too late."

At the end of the street, they turned left, coming to a large archway. Huge metal doors closed off the archway. There were arrow slits in both the right and left walls.

Jonna looked up toward the top of the doors at the symbol of a skull staring down. "This must be it."

Standing there, he took in the view. No one stood on top of the archway, nor could he see anyone behind the arrow slits, not that it mattered with him being out-of-phase.

"The magic rune must be on guard again." Jonna motioned toward the top. The runes at the main gate of the city appeared exactly the same as this one. "Are their functions identical?"

"What are you waiting for?" Bob looked around, trying to figure out what the delay was.

"What do you mean?"

"Well, you're standing outside the doors. It's not like they can stop you."

Jonna's voice rose in slight agitation. "I know I'm standing outside the doors. Maybe I want to understand how they work first."

"Why?" Bob asked, matter-of-factly. "Clear sky, no sign of rain, no crowds—"

"I'm waiting for someone to open the gates."

"Huh?" Bob shook his head. "Just walk through, man!"

"No."

"What do you mean, no?"

"I said, no."

The pixie stopped and thought. "Oh, I get it!" He slapped his forehead. "You don't like walking through objects!"

"Not at all," Jonna agreed. "That's a horrible feeling."

"Fine." Bob grinned. "Just stand there with your brain out of alignment and wait until they see you." The pixie folded his arms.

Jonna huffed. Bob was right. The likelihood of someone coming to open those gates was slim to none. "Fine."

He moved forward, put a hand in front, and stepped. That horrible feeling hit him again. The sickness crawled through his very core. Bob flew over the wall, came to the other side, and landed back on Jonna's shoulder.

"There." Bob chuckled. "Not so bad."

"Says you." Jonna swallowed the bile in his throat. "You're a bad pixie!"

"I'm a good pixie," Bob countered. "And don't you forget it." A mischievous smile crossed his face.

Jonna pulled the map out again and turned it in the right direction.

"There." He pointed. "The Well of Tears."

Directly ahead was an entrance to a church-like building. Pictures of mourning faces and various forms of punishment were carved into the outside walls. He walked across the courtyard, passing by a window with bars. It was set into a smaller building across the way from the Well of Tears.

"This looks like a prison." Jonna noted the guillotine and hangman's noose still in mint condition. "And they seem to take care of their equipment." Jonna cringed. "But where are the prisoners?"

"They only keep a few." Bob motioned toward the execution devices. "Probably for torture and information, and then—" The pixie pulled a finger across his throat.

"Thanks." Jonna glanced at his watch. "We have fifteen minutes before I show. Ideas?"

A door opened from a far building, and a man was pushed out with shackles on his wrists and ankles. His hair was unkempt. His beard was very long. When he slowed his pace, a security mage pushed him again. "Keep going."

Prisoners! The thought sank into Jonna's brain. That's where they took his and Almundena's bodies. His wife might be here, and maybe Elfleda.

"Jonna," Bob whispered, concerned. "What are you doing? I don't like the look on your face."

Jonna turned from the Well of Tears and followed the prisoner.

"Jonna, time is getting short!"

The prisoner was pushed into a bathhouse that apparently served as a restroom as well. His guards stopped at the entrance, turning their backs to the wall. Jonna walked in, making sure the area was clear.

"I need your help," he whispered to the prisoner.

The man jumped and turned. "Who's there?"

"Shh," Jonna cautioned. "You'll bring in the guards."

The prisoner sounded bitter. "How can I help you, wherever you are? For all I know, this place has driven me crazy. Can I open the doors and let you out? Then we both could be free."

This was going to be harder than Jonna thought. He expected a *where the heck are you*, or, at the very least, *give me more details on who you are*. However, there was very little time, and he would take what he could get. "I need to know who is kept here."

"They don't exactly give out that information, Mr. Hallucination.

They normally just take it in. It sort of goes along with the whole torture bit." He peered in the voice's direction but could not see anyone. "Not to mention, I have no idea who I'm talking to. If you aren't a hallucination, for all I know, you could be one of them, trying to play with my head." The prisoner indicated the two guards outside the door.

Sincerity dominated Jonna's voice. "I don't have much time. I'm looking for two women." He stopped and then thought back. "And possibly a man."

"Why should I trust you?"

Jonna took a deep breath. "I can't think of one reason you should."

Whether it was the tone in Jonna's voice or just the sheer crazy situation, the prisoner seemed to make up his mind. "Names might help," he prompted, voicing his choice. "Unfortunately, I've been here a long time."

"A lady with the first name of Stephanie?"

The prisoner shook his head.

"Elfleda? Princess of the—"

"I know that one."

"Really?"

The prisoner nodded, the rest of the sarcasm fading away. "But I've never seen her. Rumor has it they keep her at the far end."

"In isolation?"

"We are all in isolation," the man said bitterly. "If I ever get out—"

"I'm looking for one other," Jonna cut in. "A man, a brother of a girl called Almundena."

The prisoner stopped. "What did you say?"

"I'm looking for—"

"Tell me who you are, now!" The prisoner looked all around the room, searching every nook and cranny. "If you've hurt her—"

"I'm here to help her brother."

Jonna stepped back, avoiding the prisoner's search. Despite knowing he could not be seen or touched, he feared the man, who was acting crazy.

"I am her brother!"

"Okay, that's enough," one of the guards called inside. "Time to go."

Bob had been quiet long enough. "Jonna, the time!"

The prisoner jumped, having heard the second voice. "There are two of you?"

"He's a friend to help as well," Jonna whispered, noting that the guards were getting ready to come in. He looked at his watch. One minute remained. He moved to a side window and looked out between the bars.

The Well of Tears was too far to reach, and he was about to become visible. Almundena's brother walked toward the exit.

"I'll be back," Jonna threw at him, and purposely stepped into the wall. "This is your fault, Bob." He swallowed, trying to keep his stomach from coming up.

"My fault? How? I never told you to walk through that wall. I never told you to waste all your time talking to a prisoner."

Jonna held up a hand, noting how less transparent it had become, as he passed all the way through. He dove behind some barrels. As long as no one came from his right, he ought to be out of sight.

Bob didn't see much hope. His voice was a bare whisper. "What are you going to do? Maybe I can come up with something." He squinted as he tried to think.

As Jonna's nausea passed, his brain worked better. "I'm going to use the other spell."

"What spell? You don't mean—"

"No, no, I'm not going to send us back into darkness. I can't, anyway. There's only one human."

Jonna started the first chant, running through the phrases as fast as he could. His body faded.

"That's great." Bob smiled. "I didn't know you had to say a spell that many times, though. Is it every time? That seems annoying. Is that what you used at Thomas's house? I like that one. Can you go through walls?"

Jonna did not say a word, though Bob could still tell he was there.

"To the Well of Tears now, right?" Bob watched as Jonna changed direction, heading toward the main prison complex. "Jonna, where are you going?"

Jonna caught up with Almundena's brother and matched step behind him. The door opened, leading down a dimly lit hall. Most of the rooms were empty. If Bob and Almundena's brother were right, it would be surprising to see more than a handful of prisoners. That should make the search even easier.

241

The hall continued straight, but a flight of stairs went up. Almundena's brother ascended the stairs, stepped into the fourth cell, and watched as the oaken door locked with a loud click.

Jonna filed the information away. It was not time to free him. Right now, his main concern was to locate the princess and find his wife. A part of his mind kept watch for Almundena, though he knew she was too dangerous to have by his side. He would have to play the cards as the future dealt them.

Moving back down the stairs, he remembered what her brother had said. He found a hall that went straight and hoped it headed toward the far end of the building.

As he passed rooms on either side, the empty hall echoed. For the first time, he realized he could hear his own footsteps. That was not good. *Take it slower. Don't get in a hurry.* There was no time limit to this spell, but that was not the problem. Being this close to finding his wife, the stifled feelings of the last few days were making him lose his cautiousness.

He came to a crossroads with a spiral stair going down on his left. Which way to go? He moved slightly to the right but could not hear anything. She might be asleep, she might be sitting down, or she could be chained. How was he to tell?

"I see something," Bob whispered, pointing to his left.

Something reflected from around the corner, brighter than the torchlight. Jonna moved toward it, hearing a beautiful voice in song. The melody made even this drab prison glow.

"Winter is now almost over. Coming soon will be the dawn. Let us hold the candle closer. See the words pre-written from . . ."

The pitch and tone of the woman's voice floated out across the hall. It pushed back at the ugly darkness, filling it with light.

Small sparkles glittered, floating through the barred window set within an oaken door, but even they could not exist forever. As the sparkles touched the wall, they vanished.

No guards could be seen. However, it was easy to identify the magic sentinels carved around the entrance. The door swung back at Jonna's touch. The woman turned and whispered, "It seems you have learned a new trick."

Her voice went through him, just as he'd felt before. The troubles he had fought through, the things he had done, all were swept away.

"M□ 'lady." Jonna bowed on one knee, appearing as he spoke.

Bob's smile broadened to its maximum size. "Elfleda! You found her!" The pixie jumped up and down on Jonna's shoulder. "I mean, we found her!"

Her brief smile turned to sadness, and the light in the room dimmed.

"I am so sorry," Jonna began. "I—"

"There was no need to apologize then," she reminded him. "And there is no need to apologize now." Her eyes brightened. "It is good to see you, Jonna, but—" Concern crossed her face. "I fear the time is not yet right."

"What do you mean?"

"You have not retrieved the Rune Blade of Knowledge. Without it, my flight from here would be useless."

Jonna's heart fell. "And my wife?"

"If she wished to go, she could." Elfleda looked at him, her eyes boring into his soul. "You have changed, Jonna."

He frowned. "What do you mean?"

"You are different, somehow." She reached up, putting her hand against his chest. "You have been touched by dark magic."

"What are you talking about?" Jonna stood to his feet. "I have done no such thing."

Elfleda explained patiently. "You cannot be exposed to dark magic without it having an effect upon your heart. Even I, with the protection of the elves around me, have also been touched. Maybe that was why I could so easily refuse the throne."

"No." Jonna shook his head slowly. "Not you. You are a princess. You are to be queen."

"I am only elvish." She smiled. "Not perfect. Just as you are only human."

He turned away from her. "I am lost in this world of yours, Elfleda. There is nothing here for me but my wife. What do I do now?"

"Find the Rune Blade in the Well of Tears," she said softly. "Stop the Aatto of Ptah. Do this, and all will be brought into balance."

She held out her hand, which he accepted, turning back to face her. Her soft fingers gripped his, and his heart wanted to stop.

Elfleda smiled and then whispered, "Garbi Dorium."

A shimmering light appeared where their hands touched. It moved over Jonna's arm and covered his body.

She continued slowly. "I sense you have learned of our magic and know how to draw on its source. You are renewed. Use it wisely." She released his hand, but Jonna's hold stayed a moment longer than hers.

He pulled back and took a breath. "My wife. Can I see her?"

Elfleda studied him for a moment. "Is that what you really want?"

A pinprick hit his conscience, and he thought about Almundena. No, Almundena was a friend in an alien world. He needed to see his wife. "Yes."

Bob became nervous. "Jonna, I really don't think—" The pixie stopped, catching a glance from Elfleda. "Uh, I'll go keep watch." He took off, heading toward the door.

Elfleda resumed. "Would you risk the loss of everything, just to see your wife one more time?"

What was she trying to do? Was she trying to make him not want to find her?

"I don't understand." Jonna backed up in confusion. "She is here. I was told you knew how to find her."

"And that I do," Elfleda assured, trying to calm him. "But to do so now will bring attention to your presence. For the moment, you are hidden from the eyes of your foes by elvish magic. If I show you your wife, that will no longer be so."

To come this far and not see her? The thought was inconceivable! "I need to know she is okay," he breathed. "I need to know she has not been harmed."

Elfleda's face saddened. "Is not my word good enough?"

At her implication, time stopped, and a war raged within Jonna. His logic and emotion battled at one another with death grips on both sides. What was he to believe? What did he want to believe? A heavy weight settled in his chest. His breath slowed. "I just need—"

"Very well." Elfleda smiled sorrowfully. "Jonna, there are some things we must accept by faith in order to find the happiness that we desire, but—" A twinkle shone in her eyes. "I understand the yearning of your heart."

As Elfleda took a deep breath, her eyelids closed. In the room, the sparkles went out one by one, the radiant glow of elvish magic disappeared from the cell, and the elf was gone. Her body vanished as if it did not exist.

Elfleda spoke from somewhere above his head. "Quickly, Jonna. There is no time."

He turned his gaze to follow the voice, and there in the corner was

Stephanie, lying on a bench. She opened her eyes and smiled up at him. "Jonna!" But before she could find her feet, Jonna dropped to her side.

His voice shook. "Are you all right?" His eyes stayed on her face. "Have they hurt you?" With trembling fingers, he pushed her hair back over her left ear.

"I'm fine." She beamed at him. "And I'm glad that you found me." Looking in wonder at the room, she shook her head. "This is a whole different world from the life we led."

A part of Jonna relaxed. "You don't think I'm crazy? This, this place—" He could not take his eyes from her. "Tell me I'm not dreaming."

"You are here." She laughed, but there was sadness in her voice. "And I am the real Stephanie, but Jonna, there's something—"

Outside the cell, footsteps hurried in their direction. Bob appeared back on his shoulder. "We've got company!"

Jonna had forgotten about Bob. "Stephanie, this is Bob the pixie. Bob, this is Stephanie." His gaze darted between the two. He thought Stephanie would take meeting the pixie harder than this.

Bob bowed. "It is a pleasure to meet you." The pixie rolled his eyes toward Jonna. "But we really do have trouble!"

Elfleda's words came rolling back into Jonna's mind. He said aloud, "What have I done?" His eyes swept around them for something to use as a weapon.

Stephanie reached up and touched his arm. "Patience, my love. Listen to Elfleda. I will see you again." Stephanie faded in the same way Väinämö had.

"NO!" He reached out, watching as his fingers passed through hers. "God, please, no!" He turned around, eyes wide. "It's not fair."

"Jonna." Elfleda's quiet voice called to him, soothing him, despite what was coming toward them. "Use the spell. Reach the Well of Tears. Find the Rune Blade."

The spell! Jonna tried to think of the words, but his mind held only confusion. Heaviness took him, driving him down toward the ground. He struggled against the unseen force, but his arms and legs refused to respond.

"Jonna."

He heard the voice from far away. Was it Bob or Elfleda or Stephanie or Almundena? His mind swirled. What was happening? His throbbing head was going to explode. He picked himself up and started to mumble the first chant that hit his mind. As he spoke the last phrase, his head started to clear.

Elfleda returned, and with her some of the elvish magic—some, but not all. She appeared weaker, more vulnerable. Had he caused that? Had bringing forth Stephanie been a strain on her?

The brightness of the room became a shallow aura. Security mages rushed in, though what they expected to find, Jonna had no idea.

"You gave your word." The one in charge stepped forward. "You said you would not leave your cell."

"I did not," she snapped. Jonna could see that the very way she said it made the man regret his tone of voice. The man stepped back. "But you used magic."

"I am magic." Her demeanor made them cower. "We have our agreement. Leave the elvish kingdom alone, and we will not stand against you."

"You're in no position to bargain anymore," the mage said coldly, though he did keep his distance. "Tonight is our hour of power. Your elvish kind will no longer be a threat."

Elfleda smiled. "They never were."

"Shackle her!"

"No!" Jonna moved to intervene, but they passed right through him. Elfleda looked directly at him, shook her head, and said, "Go."

"What was that?" The mage nearest to her locked the first metal shackle around her wrist.

She cringed with pain, but said not a word.

"Pleading won't help." The mage laughed as the second shackle fell into place. She cringed again. This time sweat beaded upon her forehead.

Jonna screamed at all of them, "You're killing her! Leave her alone!"

"Who said that?" The mage in charge came forward, searching the room. He spotted Jonna's duplicate in the corner, lying on the floor, completely unmoving. "What is this, some kind of joke?"

He looked to Elfleda, but she ignored the question.

"Lock it in, whatever it is." The man turned back to the door. "Bring her along. The Elders do not like waiting."

The door slammed before Jonna got there, but he did not care. He pushed through the door, ignoring the pain, made it to the hallway, and ran to keep up.

Bob bumped into the door. Shaking his head, he flew up through the bars and caught up with Jonna.

"Jonna—" Bob flipped at his ethereal ear. "Well of Tears, remember?"

"I know, and stop that!"

Elfleda's captors turned the next corner.

"I have to find out where she's going!"

"We have to get the Rune Blade or knowing where she's going won't help at all!"

"Are you going to help or just try to nag me?"

Elfleda entered through a door. Her captors hauled her down a doublewide corridor and carried her over a bridge that spanned a small chasm. At the other side, two huge doors swung open, and the captors passed through them.

"Well, if you're going to catch them, you better hurry!" Bob took off, forced to follow the hallway, speeding up at the last moment to make it through the open door.

"Right!"

Jonna broke into a run, sprinting through walls as a shortcut. He reached the chasm, stopped at the edge, and moved back to the bridge. Across the way, the huge doors had begun to close, but abruptly reversed. Bob came back to his shoulder.

"Make way!" Several wagons carrying supplies rushed to meet the intercepting bridge. "Make way!"

The horses complained as the drivers reined them in, turning the corner quickly. The wagons went from four to two to four wheels, bouncing as they hit, dashing onto the bridge.

On instinct, Jonna leaped back and found himself suddenly off the bridge, arching through the air.

"Not good. NOT GOOD!" Bob watched as they both fell. "No ropes this time, buddy!" The pixie fought to stay on Jonna's shoulder. The formula was easy: add one downward descent, one whipping wind, an ethereal body, and there you had the problem.

"Bob, I'm falling!"

"No duh!"

Jonna dropped below the level of the bridge, reached out, but found nothing to grab. There was another small bridge below him. He shifted, headed in that direction, hit the bridge—and passed right through.

"What happened?"

Bob flew around the bridge, fought his way back against the wind, and when he came within range, he yelled, "You're going too fast. All it did was slow you down a little. We have to make you fall slower!"

As he stared straight down, it did not take much imagination for Jonna to finish Bob's thought. "Otherwise, I'll hit the ground, and—"

The pixie nodded. "Get stuck in it."

"Shoot!" Jonna changed direction again, focusing on another naturally spanning bridge. He hit, passed through it, but it was not enough. Bob swung out right before the bridge and then swung back right after.

"Ground's coming up!" Bob's eyes were wide. "I hate to say this, but I might have to jump!"

"Bob, you're a pixie; you're already flying!"

"Oh." Bob's cheeks went red, and he chuckled. "Sorry about that. I got caught up in the fall."

Jonna hit a third bridge and tried to find a fourth. The timing was going to be very close. If he missed it—he looked at his watch. Forty-six minutes left.

"There," Bob urged.

Jonna adjusted his position, then caught and passed through the fourth bridge. He could feel the pull this time, like walking through a wall. That was better, yes. But was it enough?

Until now, when Jonna looked down, all he could see was a mix of shadows and brief light, or maybe the occasional bridge that he was about to fall through.

But the scene changed. Instead of darkness, he could see the ground below. Bob kept mumbling back and forth, "Jump or don't jump? Jump or don't jump?" Jonna decided to help him. "Jump, for heaven's sake!" Throwing his hands in front of him, Jonna closed his eyes right before he hit.

CHAPTER 24
DAGURUNN THE DRAGON

He had stopped, but the pain going through his arms did not feel good. Jonna opened his eyes and found himself staring at the ground, arms in front and somewhere beneath it. Searching for Bob, he could not see from this position. "This is awkward."

Like pulling through molasses, he brought up one arm at a time, and then rolled over. He glanced at his watch. The spell would last thirty-four more minutes.

Where was he? Above his head, way above his head, was a small bit of light shining down somewhere around the first bridge. "How do we get back?"

"We?" Bob seemed a little aggravated. "If we hadn't been going in the wrong direction, we wouldn't be here!"

"Water under the bridge, Bob."

"No, Jonna and Bob under the bridge," the pixie shot back, and pointed at the sky above them. "Water has nothing to do with it!"

Jonna burst out laughing, and as Bob thought about what he said, he followed suit. Checking his watch, he realized only a minute or so had gone by. Jonna rose to his feet, glanced up, and sighed. "Which way shall we head?"

The pixie pointed at a large cave entrance. "That way."

"How do you know?"

"It is at least toward the Well of Tears."

"Good point."

They stepped toward the cave entrance, noting how the light did not seem to diminish. "Does the ethereal state I'm in affect how I see mica?" Jonna could see the rainbow sparkles reflecting in the rocks. Whatever the light source was, it gave off a spectrum of glow.

"No." Bob squinted at the area. "It looks the same to me, too." He peered back at Jonna. "And what's mica?"

"A type of mineral," he answered offhandedly. "Do you see a greenish tint?"

Reaching the cave entrance, Jonna looked in. His right hand felt along the wall, careful not to press too hard. A slight florescent green glow came off.

"Flora of some sort." Jonna rubbed it slowly between his fingers so as not to make it fall through. It spread like paint. "On a cellular level." He shook it off, watching as it dropped to the ground.

Apparently, he had some limited interaction with his environment, depending upon its makeup. Either that, or there was something in the green glow that bridged to his ethereal existence. Could it contain magic, too?

Bob stared at him. "I'm not even going to pretend to understand that."

"Oh." Jonna chuckled. "Yeah, sorry. I forgot."

"Forgot what?"

"You're not from my world."

Jonna moved all the way in, looking around the cave. The green light, combined with thousands of different colored gems, created an effect unlike any he had seen.

A shadow stepped out upon hearing their voices. A deep Renaissance voice boomed, "Why have you come?"

Jonna froze. Until this moment, he thought he and Bob were alone. "Come where?" he asked cautiously, trying to get a better view. "Is there a reason I should not be here?"

"This place is sacred." The voice deepened. "It is not for the eyes of mortal men."

Finally locating its outline, Jonna turned to face the shadow. "Then who is it for?" Unfortunately, he could not see anything distinctive. "Does this place belong to you?"

"I am a steward of the deep." The shadow moved toward them. They could hear the sound of rocks crushing into gravel. "I hear your voice but cannot see you."

Jonna laughed. "Then perhaps I belong here after all." As he thought over the situation, an idea popped into his head. "What do you know of the Aatto of Ptah?"

"Ptah?" The creature grew in height and roared, "You are a dark mage? You, who have stolen from us our power, dare to enter our abode?"

Jonna could smell sulfuric ash and something else combustible. "Bob, run!"

A wash of fire lit the room, changing the colors of the rainbow flashes. The golden-red flame went through Jonna's body like tickles on the outside of his skin. A moment later, the light and heat faded.

Jonna swallowed, getting his voice back. "My, my, we do have a temper."

Bob flew back to his shoulder and glared, still patting a wisp of smoke off his shirt. "A little more warning would have been nice!"

The creature turned, and rocks crushed into gravel again. "You're still here?"

For the first time, Jonna got the impression of some sort of reptile. It sneered at him. "Are you stupid or foolish?"

This time Jonna could see the creature. "How about naive and lost?"

With its huge pointed tail and nice sharp teeth, Jonna knew exactly what he was facing. "May I ask your name, dragon?"

"You may ask," it mocked with a low growl. "But I may not answer." It moved to the right, searching to find a better spot to see Jonna. "How is it a human becomes lost in these caves?"

Bob began, "Stupidity?" Then he stopped, seeing the look on Jonna's face.

Jonna challenged the dragon. "I will answer your questions if you will answer mine."

"Very good, human." The dragon sniffed the air. "But do not let me see you or burning I'll divine."

"I seek a weapon stolen from the elves."

Jonna watched the dragon's eyes, which shifted as he spoke. A burst of flame shot out, touching where Jonna should have been, and was, but the dragon could not see or touch him. He continued. "A Rune Blade taken by the Dark Mages. I simply want this back."

The dragon slithered around a large stalagmite, moving closer to where Jonna should be. His size was enough to make Jonna back up despite the fact he could not hurt him. "And if you had this blade, what then?" The dragon stepped forward, still trying to see him. In the process, it shifted its stomach above Jonna's head.

"I would use it to defeat the Dark Mages."

A moment later, the dragon's stomach dropped. Gag! It was not a pretty sight! Jonna closed his eyes and waited. As the dragon's body continued to slither past, he coughed. "When's the last time you ate?"

"Now that you mention it"—the dragon smiled invitingly—"I am hungry." He snapped the air, trying to find Jonna, and growled. "What trick is this?"

"That's three questions, and you owe me two." Jonna backed up from the stomach, glad not to look anymore. He moved to a flat area partially up the wall. "Now, you spoke of the Dark Mages stealing your power. How is that done?"

"Each Eve of Creation, Aatto of Ptah it is called, they gather in the great hall above these caverns. When the moon rises, the power of the earth renews, flooding magic into these caves. It has been this way for thousands of years before they came."

"I don't understand."

The dragon hissed. "Is that a question?"

"You didn't finish." Jonna laughed in response. He was not going to be tricked out of his answers.

The dragon chuckled. "When this time comes, they have devised a means of channeling that renewing power, focusing it not into the earth, but into a vessel of their own design. By a bonding ritual preformed, they make themselves one with this crystal and power."

"So that's why one mage would cancel another out if they fought," Bob whispered. "They all pull from the source!"

Jonna kept his voice low. "And why a Sarka is created when they suspect someone will turn. Matthias may be right. They may all be Sarkas."

The dragon moved its head back and forth. "What was that?"

"So through their own desire, they turn the magic evil?"

"Yes." The dragon smiled slyly. "And that is two questions. My turn."

"No, you asked another." Jonna stopped him. "I said—" He spoke louder. "That is why all Dark Mages are Sarkas. That way, they can't fight against their own kind."

The dragon turned, its massive body creating a huge coil, identifying where Jonna was. Jonna glanced at his watch. Fifteen minutes left. "Will you help me find the Rune Blade? I will end this taking of your magic."

The dragon paused, its eyes narrowing to slits that glowed yellow in the darkness. It saw the wall where Jonna was, yet still it detected no human. "How can I trust one I cannot see?" It sniffed the air.

"You have already warned me not to show myself. Give me your name, and I will."

The dragon laughed. "My name is as old as time itself. I came to these caves at the beginning of time. I feel the sapping of power from those thieving Dark Mages." He appeared to look right at Jonna, though he could not see him, and his anger continued to build.

"Uh-oh." Bob zipped away from Jonna, hiding behind the dragon. The reptile drew in air slowly. "My name is Dagurunn."

Dagurunn finished his breath and spewed fire, heating up the area where Jonna stood. In spite of the cold and hot temperatures, the crystals did not crack.

As the orange-red flames flickered out, Jonna smiled. "Then I shall show you, Dagurunn." He nodded in the dragon's direction, though he knew it could not see him.

Bob sped back around, coming to Jonna's shoulder. "Jonna, what are you doing?"

"Don't you see it?" Jonna whispered to Bob. "It's all here. The magic of everything: both good and bad, evil and kind, human and elvish—even pixie and sprite."

Bob huffed. "Now why'd you have to put us in the same class as sprites?"

Jonna shook his head. "You don't get it. This is the source of all magic in the earth. Väinämö told me at the beginning, but I just did not understand. This is why there is always magic." He waved his hands at the crystals. "Those of good pull from the excess. Those of evil steal from the source."

Bob scratched his head. "But what are *you* going to do?"

Jonna reached down, found two of the largest crystals, and placed one hand on each. He remembered the spell Elfleda had used with him, and how it renewed his strength. A glowing had engulfed him at its use. "If I am correct, I can prove to the dragon my intentions through his own magic."

He looked up at Dagurunn, and in a loud voice shouted, "Dagurunn, you wanted to see me. Watch carefully. *Garbi Dorium!*"

The cavern went silent. Only the drops of water echoing from further in the cave gave any sound.

Concerned, Jonna wondered if he had made a terrible mistake. Every time he did magic, he always said it seven times, yet he noticed that others in this reality said things but once. He suspected this was true because he was not from here. And that he was insulated against the magic due to his origins. If so, speaking the words seven times allowed his body to work as a capacitor, building up the charge until it finally performed its function.

Assuming he was correct, and the ability to use magic was in direct proportion to its source, then he had just hooked up to the mother lode, the strongest source of magic in this reality. All things being equal, he should only have to speak the words once. That is, if being this close did not burn him up. Unfortunately, this was his first opportunity to test the theory.

Sweat beaded on his forehead. With only minutes before the ethereal spell would finish, his stomach sank. Had he been wrong? Did he still have to say the spell seven times?

He started to release his hold when a tingling hit his skin. He jumped, heart beating faster, hair beginning to stand on end. Something shot up from the crystals, bathing his ethereal body in a power he had never known.

As Dagurunn watched, a swirl of energy rose. It started at the floor, spread, enlarged, and grew in color and light. It moved like a whirlwind, gathering around Jonna, showing an outline of his body standing exactly where Dagurunn had flamed.

He released the gems and staggered back from the sheer force of the magic. Something strong, stronger than he had ever felt, reached within his mind and soul. It searched, probing every thought. It hunted to find whether he was good or evil. The thought terrified him. Can one truly know their own mind? "What have I done?"

He remembered Elfleda's comment. Dark magic had touched him. What if—no. Magic was made dark by its use, and he did not want to use it for evil.

He could feel the searching of his thoughts, his being, hunting to find the truth. Thoughts, reasons, and methods: things that confused him before began to make sense. Intelligence was a misnomer. True intelligence was not dependent on what was learned, but what was done.

As the ferocity of the magic abated, his image disappeared from before Dagurunn. He slumped back against the wall, taking in gulps of air.

"I see who you are." The dragon's voice echoed around the cavern. "You are correct, you are not a dark mage, but what does that matter to me? I care neither for bad nor good." Dagurunn looked at Jonna. "That being said, what did you prove by showing yourself?"

Jonna flexed his hands open and closed, half expecting to see burn marks where he had touched the crystals. "That in spite of your best efforts, you could not destroy me. What does that mean I could do to you?"

Dagurunn continued to stare. Jonna could see thought behind those dragon eyes.

Bob glanced at Jonna's watch. "Two needle thingies, er—" He thought back. "Minutes!"

Jonna smiled at the pixie. "It doesn't matter now."

"What doesn't matter?" The pixie's eyes went wide. "In two minutes, he's gonna cook you alive!"

A faraway look dropped into Jonna's eyes. Never had the feeling been this strong. "No, he won't."

"Jonna?"

"Yes, Bob?"

"You're not playing with a human. You're playing with a dragon!"

Jonna's face relaxed as he grinned in Bob's direction. "I'm not playing at all. Unum-Clastor-Pratima."

Canceling the spell before it ended, Jonna appeared, standing before the dragon without his ethereal shield. Somehow, The Sight told him he could do that, though he did not have a clue as to how The Sight worked.

That was weird, Jonna thought. He hadn't said the spell seven times. However, there was no more time to contemplate as he called up to the dragon, "Do we have a deal, Dagurunn?"

There was humor in Dagurunn's voice. "Deal, little human." The dragon's voice boomed around the chamber. "On my honor and name, and on your life."

"Then shake." Jonna held out his hand.

The dragon uncoiled, stretching forth a single claw with the sharpened end glistening in the green light. When it reached him, Jonna stretched up and shook the end.

"There is a small passageway behind me," Dagurunn hissed in Jonna's direction. "Follow its path, and you will find your Rune Blade." The dragon turned, forming a figure eight as it moved off through the stalagmites.

"And that's it?" Bob glared. "Don't we at least get, *here, let me give you a ride*, or, *hey guys, let me eat those Dark Mages for you?*"

Jonna laughed. "Of all people, you should understand dragons."

Bob growled. "Ignoring the insult, I have never dealt with a dragon before!"

Jonna moved toward the passageway Dagurunn had indicated. "Just look what you can tell your grandchildren."

Bob froze. "My grandchildren? Now wait a minute, I'm not even married—" He squinted at Jonna. "Did you see something I don't know about?"

Stepping onto the path, Jonna laughed.

"No, really." Bob moved in front of him, flying backwards. "I can't stand secrets!"

"Welcome to the club." Jonna chuckled, moving up a small incline. Rivulets of water ran down the sides, gradually eating at the surface of the rock. At the top of the enclosure, another room opened up.

"No, I'm serious!" Bob fluttered in front of him, trying to look him in the eye but unable to decide which one.

Watching all the flying objects in the room, Jonna gazed about the smaller cavern. "Bob?"

"Yes, Jonna?"

"Duck."

Jonna dropped, catching himself at ground level. Bob, on the other hand, did not listen fast enough.

Swat! Jonna grimaced—that had to hurt. "Are you all right?"

Bob groaned, picking himself up. "You could have warned me!"

"I did warn you. Now turn around and tell me what we're going to do with those?" He pointed.

There were thousands of floating spheres, all moving in different directions, all of various sizes. The largest could swallow Jonna whole. They bounced this way or that until at last they found some crevice and squeezed their way through.

"What is it?" Bob moved closer but not too close. "It looks like—"

"Pixie dust." Jonna watched as huge pieces moved about the cavern.

Bob reached in his pocket, pulling out a little bit of his pixie dust. He studied its texture and shape. "Coarse and unfiltered, but you're right." He shook his head. "I don't believe it."

"I bet it's a byproduct of the magic further down, one of the many branches."

Looking wary, Bob slowly shook his head. "I don't think we should cast spells in there. If the stuff in my pocket is any comparison—"

Jonna chuckled. "We could have a force much bigger than we anticipate. It could possibly be the difference between a firecracker and a nuclear bomb."

Bob squinted at him. "There you go with the other-world stuff again!"

Noting where the largest portions came through the floor, Jonna studied the process. "It acts like bitumen when it floats in the water, coming up from beneath. When it hits the top, the magic in the crystal walls causes it to bounce."

"I think I liked you better when you didn't analyze." Bob sighed. "Can we go now?"

"Sure." Jonna stayed low, weaving through the maze of giant pixie dust. He stopped a third of the way in, looking back at Bob. "You coming?"

"I'm not so sure." The pixie glanced back the way they had come.

"No problem." Jonna ducked as a large piece floated by his head. "Tell you what, you head back out the way we came, go to the top, and find Elfleda. I'll get the Rune Blade."

Bob grew hot. "Now wait a minute. Do you really think I would leave you here?" He moved back, preparing to zip across.

"No, Bob. Walk!"

Bob shot out across the cavern, dodging the glowing dust. As he passed Jonna, he grinned, looking back at him. "Told you I could—"

Swat! Bob plunged into the middle of a nice, big yellow one disappearing from view.

"Bob!" Jonna leaped up, dodging three and jumping to the right of another. He was having a hard time keeping his eye on the one Bob had disappeared into. The huge piece of pixie dust bounced.

Down, up, over, step, jump, duck! This was never going to work. If the little pixie had just listened . . . Jonna leaped, avoided a particularly large one, collided with another, and—

"Wow." The whole world took on a golden tint, sparkling in every direction. Jonna reached out and touched the inside curved walls. A feeling of euphoria flooded his mind and body. *If only Stephanie were here,* he thought.

Something stirred within the bubble. A picture of Almundena appeared. It was the way she looked right after that night when— It changed to Stephanie in the cabin. It altered to Elfleda in the elvish city. The scene flipped to Artemis at the pool. It changed to—

"Stop!" Jonna held his head, trying to make some sense out of all the pictures: the wood sprite, the wind in the woods, the water sprite, Serena almost drowning, Väinämö, and Väinämö's home when it was ripped apart. What he had considered pleasant things had suddenly turned into danger, horror, and death.

"Let me go!" He struck out, fighting his way to the edge of the bubble. It bounced in the other direction, shifting him back toward the other side. It was too much magic. So much, in fact, that the human mind could not deal with it. It fed off every thought, every stray mental picture, cascading through the neurons in a living creature's brain.

Good and bad became lost. Jonna could not tell which side was up. If something did not change soon, both he and Bob might never get out. Their bubbles smashed together, and suddenly the pixie floated beside him.

"Bob!" Jonna reached over and shook him.

The pixie opened one eye. "Is that really you?"

Sighing with relief, Jonna nodded. "It's me. We've got to get out of here."

"My magic's useless." Bob shook his head, bewildered. "We were wrong. This much pixie dust does not make it stronger. It makes it unusable. It's like eating too much dessert and getting sick."

"You may be right." Jonna tried to spot where they were bouncing next, but it was not easy trying to see through the sphere. "I have an idea. On the next anticipated bounce, let's jump at a right angle."

"Right angle?" Bob had no clue. "As opposed to a left angle?"

Jonna closed his eyes a moment. The pixie dust was not only creating disorientation, but also a lack of patience. He spoke deliberately, without emotion. "Just follow my lead."

"That, I can do."

The bubble headed toward a wall, so Jonna placed his feet in the same direction. "Ready?"

As the bubble drew nearer, the jagged rocks did not look inviting.

Bob tensed, his eyes large and round. "Ready!"

"Go!"

The bubble hit, and he and Bob jumped. They broke through the surface and landed close to the far side on their backs.

Jonna flipped over. "Go, go, go!"

Scrambling on hands and knees, they slipped past another large bubble growing from the ground, dodged a second overhead, and rolled out of the smaller cavern into a hallway, both breathing hard.

"Jonna?" the pixie whispered, not getting up.

"Yes?"

Breathing quickly, the pixie said, "Don't let me do that again."

Sitting up, Jonna chuckled. "Deal." He looked from where the path had been to where the passageway led. They had definitely made it across. But to where? On this side was a short hall, and then it ended. He pointed at the dead end. "Does that look like a wall to you?"

CHAPTER 25
HEMMING ON THE WAY

Jonna rose to take a closer look.

The pixie opened one eye, saw the dead end, and turned to the left. He grimaced, pointing at the floating spheres. "No way. I'm not going back in there!"

Jonna reevaluated the trail from across the room to their present location. "This is the right way. So where is the passage?" He tapped the dead end in several places. "Secret door?"

Moving up beside him, Bob glared at the dead end. "I don't see one." He turned all the way around and scowled at the spheres. "I think the dragon lied."

"Why would the dragon—" Jonna checked the wall again. "Dagurunn didn't lie. He wouldn't."

"He kept trying to kill you every chance he could!"

Jonna shook his head. "He gave his name and thus his word. For him, that means everything."

"Until he can find a way to break it."

Remembering the stories of dragons from his own world, Jonna refused to believe it. "Not this time. There has to be something else."

He checked the dead end again, feeling a little frustrated. *To come this far, to be this close, and stop? No, there had to be something else.*

The dead end spoke in a female voice. "Okay, I give. Ask me what to do."

Jonna scrambled back, almost too far. He stopped on the border to the floating sphere room.

The dead end told them both, "I'm not really a wall, you know. I'm a hemming. Want to see?"

"Ah." Jonna took a breath warily. *What was a hemming?* "Sure."

The dead end laughed and immediately changed its form, becoming a replica of Bob.

"Hey!" The pixie frowned. "That's not nice. Although I do look rather fetching."

"Oh, all right." It changed again, becoming a rock sitting on the ground. "How's that?"

"Wonderful," Jonna congratulated it. "Do you live here all the time?"

"Well—" The rock sighed. "It has been a while. You see, I was originally sent here to guard the passage."

Jonna was intrigued. "Really? By whom?"

"You'd never believe me." The rock shook some of its pebbles.

"Try us."

"Well," the rock said in a whiny voice, "if I do, and you get away, you might tell, and well—"

Jonna asked, "Do you know what we are here to do?"

"Other than go up the passage?" The rock shook. "No."

"I have to stop the Aatto of Ptah."

"Aatto of Ptah! No way!"

"Yes way." He nodded. "And I have to do it very soon."

There was a whimsical note in the hemming's voice. "You're really going to stop it?"

Jonna and Bob both nodded.

The hemming questioned again, "None of this promising one thing and running off?"

Jonna and Bob both shook their heads.

"All right, on one condition."

"Name it." Bob grinned.

"I want to come, too."

Jonna thought about it. "You want to come with us?"

"Yes, let me come. I want to help."

"You want to stop the Dark Mages?" He studied the rock, and remembered it first took the pixie's form. If it could do that—

"Of course, who do you think put me here?"

Jonna nodded, glancing at Bob. "It makes sense."

"But we don't even know him." The pixie frowned. "Although, I did say *name it*."

"Her," she said, frustrated. "Why is it nobody ever knows the difference?"

Jonna hazarded a guess. "Maybe because you appear gender-free?"

"Ah!" She laughed. "That's right, I am. Let me fix that."

She took the form of a woman—one without any clothes. Jonna turned to face the opposite direction. When he glanced over and saw Bob still looking, he swatted him.

"Hey!" Bob grumbled, and turned around.

"Clothes please." Jonna waited.

"Oh!" She giggled. "Sorry, boys. There, how's that?"

Jonna glanced over his shoulder, nodding approval. "Much better." He turned around, extending his hand. "I'm Jonna."

"And I'm Crystilic." She beamed, shaking his hand firmly. "Nice hands. So warm." She rubbed them again. "Hanging around as walls and rocks is so cold-blooded."

"I bet." Jonna slipped his hand away.

Bob moved forward, hovering in the air. "And I'm Bob." He smiled happily. "A pleasure to meet you." He looked at her top to bottom. It was a little too obvious.

"Bob!" Had he been larger, Jonna would have elbowed him.

She giggled. "A pleasure to meet you, Bob."

"I'm not the one married," Bob told Crystilic, grinning widely. He looked at Jonna. "And I like her."

"Funny how you changed your tone when you found out she was a girl," Jonna accused.

The pixie waved it away. "You're just stuck on semantics."

"Shall we be going?" Jonna motioned to the upward slope.

"By all means." Crystilic moved up the path, taking the lead. After a moment, she stopped and waited.

Jonna came up behind her. "What's wrong?"

"Um." She looked a little embarrassed. "Do you mind if I walk beside you two?"

"Of course you can walk beside us. Why wouldn't you?"

"Well, my last master—"

"You think we own you?" Jonna sounded surprised. When Bob's eyes lit up, Jonna glared at him.

"Sure," she said seriously. "You found me and figured out how to get through."

"But you told us," he stressed. "We don't expect you to be our slave."

"But," Bob began. "If you'd like to—"

Jonna glared at him. "Bob."

"I'm just saying."

Excitement crossed her features. "You really mean it? I really am free?"

"Yes," Jonna assured her. "You really are free."

She leaped at him, putting him in a bear hug and wrapping her legs around him. Jonna struggled to stay upright.

"Thank you, thank you, thank you, thank you—"

"It's all right." He laughed. "You can let go now."

Crystilic released her hold, stepped back, and rearranged her hair. Disappointment filled Bob's face, but when Crystilic saw his expression, she reached over and kissed him on the cheek. "And thank you too, cutie."

He reddened. "You're—you're welcome." Bob barely got out the words.

Jonna chuckled. "Wow, I've never seen you so embarrassed."

Bob pinched his ear.

"Ouch!"

Jonna started moving up the slope, Crystilic keeping to his side—his right side, the shoulder Bob was currently on. That suited Bob just fine.

"So where are we going?" Crystilic bounced along, her head bobbing back and forth. They reached a crossroads that led in three new directions.

"The Dark Mages have stolen a sword called the Rune Blade of Knowledge. Somewhere above us, it is hidden. We need to find it."

"Oh goodie." Crystilic clapped her hands. "A treasure hunt!"

"That's exactly how I felt," Bob agreed, using any reason to look in her direction.

Jonna needed them back on track. "Which way?"

According to the dragon, it was up the path. He needed a few more details now. Jonna turned toward Crystilic. "Do you remember how you got here?"

She thought, frowning. "It was a long time ago." Her frown deepened. "Nope." She smiled and then frowned again. "Then again, maybe—"

She finally pointed. "That way." Her smile returned.

"That way?" Jonna followed her finger. She pointed directly at a stone wall. "They brought you through stone?"

She nodded. Her eyes were very serious. "It turned clear like water, and they dropped me through." She looked up. "Actually, I think it was above us."

Jonna followed her gaze, sighting a vertical tunnel going almost straight up, directly above the crossroads. "They dropped you?"

"I told you, it was sort of like water. I gradually floated down."

"Really?" Jonna tried to see some indication of what she was talking about, but it looked just like a rough-cut tunnel going straight up.

"Must have been a spell." Bob bobbed his head. "I can fly to the top. Shall I see what's up there?"

"You really want to do that?" Jonna looked surprised. Then again, the pixie really wanted to show off.

"Sure!" Bob shot up, disappearing into the darkness.

"Wow." Crystilic gazed after him. "That was fast!"

"Yes, he is," Jonna agreed. He listened, but could not hear anything from above. "What are the additional tunnels for?"

"Confusion, I'm sure." Crystilic peered down each. "Although, I do remember someone trying to go to the right."

"They look more like drainage tunnels." Jonna squinted, studying the sides. "All three are very smooth." He turned back to her. "Someone else came through from below?"

"Oh yes." She nodded quickly. "There have been others, but none of them wanted to help me. They all just disappeared, claiming to be after something called the Eye of Aldrick."

"Did they give you any more details?"

Crystilic frowned very hard. "It is green in color. It is very large." She frowned some more. "And it is supposed to be in the tunnel to the right." A beautiful smile lit her face. "How was that?"

"Geronimoooo!" Bob called out, coming in fast. He dropped down, swooped around them, and circled to a stop on Jonna's shoulder. He bowed to both.

Crystilic clapped, and Jonna laughed.

"So," Jonna asked Bob. "What did you find out?"

"There is a huge meeting room up there, but no one is in it."

Mulling over his report, Jonna nodded. "Okay. And?"

"What do you mean *and*?"

"There must be a few more details."

"I didn't stay that long," Bob emphasized. "You know, up there and back."

Jonna sighed. "So, we know about as much now as before you left. Didn't you see anything else?"

Squinting, Bob thought. "There was one thing. Remember those pictures we saw outside the Well of Tears?"

"Yes."

"They were on the inside of the room. And there were stained glass windows and carvings all around—"

"I thought you said you didn't know any more details." Jonna studied him. This show-off thing needed to come to an end.

"I didn't know you meant those details." The pixie looked sheepish. "At least now you know."

"Yes, we do." Jonna turned back to the crossroads. "Okay, straight or to the right?"

"What about the left?" Bob looked from Jonna to Crystilic.

"Beats me." She smiled and shrugged.

The pixie looked at Jonna, concerned they had learned something without him. "What else did *you* find out?"

"The Eye of Aldrick is the storage unit for the Dark Mages' power." Jonna took a tentative step toward the right side but stopped. "No." A funny feeling came over him. "We need to go straight, just as Dagurunn said."

As he stepped into the next corridor, the darkness changed to white. Jonna blinked but could not see.

Bob did no better. "Are you sure this is the right way?"

Crystilic shook her head. "Not for the Eye."

Jonna squinted against the light. He could barely detect the outlines of crystals set around the room. It made sense. He was certain the Eye of Aldrick was a crystal of some sort.

Moving further into the room, Jonna made out a path winding around the stalagmites. It moved from the center of the cave, approached the backside, and continued along the wall. The closer to the back of the cavern he moved, the brighter the light became.

Crystilic called out, "What is it?"

Jonna's eyes hurt the longer he kept them open. Even with his eyelids shut, the brightness was all too apparent. He reached the back of the cave, using his hands to guide him. On his left, the tips of his fingers encountered something huge, carved as one unit, slick as glass.

Opening an eye just a crack, he spotted objects undefined within. It took a while for his eyes to focus, and even then, the brightness gave him a headache. The distortion of the crystal's contents was not only because of its size, but also because of a liquid. Things splashed within it.

"It's a fish tank." Bob gawked in amazement. "Someone carved out a huge crystal and added water."

"Or some type of liquid." Jonna still tried to see what it contained, but the light coming from it was much too bright. Images, nothing more than changes of intensity in the light, darted about. "Can anyone see what is in the middle?"

"Not I," Crystilic answered, still just as bubbly.

Bob reached out and touched the surface. "Not me. I bet the walls are pretty thick."

Jonna traced the path along the back wall of the cavern. It wound its way gradually up, forming a spiral along the outside of the crystal-like structure.

As they neared the top, they encountered a stone door set with a pivot in the middle. Pushing it on one side, they all peeked through.

He spotted the carved decorations Bob talked about earlier. "We're in the Well of Tears temple," Jonna whispered. "It has to be. Maybe on a lower level."

Crystilic pushed forward behind him, bumping into the door. It flew from Jonna's hand, pivoted around, and slammed them into the hallway.

Cringing, she whispered, "Sorry."

In the silence, her voice sounded like a shout. Jonna stood up, noting the lack of dust on the floor. It was smooth and clean as if freshly washed.

He moved to the left, peering down the hall. It was then he noticed the floor vibrating.

Bob sensed it, too. "What's that?"

Small, well-rounded pebbles left on the floor, also clean, jumped and shook. A roaring met their ears. As Jonna realized what this was, he yelled, "Time to go!"

Going back down would be self-defeating. What Jonna feared was coming true. The tunnels below were drainage, designed to get rid of some type of liquid. If they got in those, they would certainly be washed away.

Bob and Crystilic met up with him. "What's going on?"

"We're about to be run over by a flood. Come on!"

They raced down the hall to the right. The hall ended in a multi-stepped cavern. Small stone bridges ascended. Plateaus were positioned at various heights with stairs leading to each. In the exact center of the room, cut into the ceiling, was a vertical tunnel going straight up. The beginning of a ladder extended out the bottom, but not very far.

Jonna saw it as their only hope. The rumbling grew louder—the shaking of the ground became worse. He looked behind him and caught sight of a huge wave heading in their direction.

"Down!" Jonna grabbed Crystilic's hand and ran her down the steps.

"What are you doing?" Bob glanced behind him in the direction of the water. "We need to go up, not down!"

Jonna exhaled between breaths. "We are going down to go up."

Reaching the edge, he and Crystilic leaped across a small pit, dropping onto the other side. They landed by the first bridge that went up.

The wave of water rushed into the room, its initial volume launching from the main floor, pouring into the pits below. The water level rose.

At the top of the first bridge, they leaped for the second and then climbed to the third. This placed them just above the main floor. The layout still did not make sense to Jonna. Channels under the city were filled with water and then drained off? "What is this place?"

Jonna climbed the next set of stairs leading to the fourth bridge. Each time they reached a new plateau, the path would change, circling, inevitably, toward the center. Granted, that was where they wanted to go, but it didn't explain why it was this way.

"Energy lines," Bob answered. "We pixies use the natural ones. The Dark Mages seem to create their own."

"Energy lines?" Jonna nodded, still climbing with Crystilic. "I've read about that in my own world. Some believe ancient people used them as power sources." Then, it hit Jonna. "The Dark Mages are going to use this to help focus the magic of the Aatto of Ptah."

He remembered reading about Druids who also followed the energy lines. It was all coming together.

Bob had an epiphany. "So that's why we didn't run back down."

The eighth bridge came into view as they noted the water level now covered the first. Jonna looked up. On the highest plateaus were chains secured to the sides by a bar. It did not take a scientist to figure out that at some time or another, they sacrificed living creatures here. Was drowning the preferred method of killing, or something else?

"Number eleven," Bob called nervously. Everyone kept watching the water rise.

Crystilic shook with the strain. All those years of being an inanimate object had not prepared her for an all-out run.

"Go, go, go," the pixie kept mumbling under his breath.

"That's not helping, Bob," Jonna reminded him. They leaped to the next bridge.

There were three more left. They followed the curve of the walkway, reached the next bridge, and jumped. Was it Jonna's imagination or were the walkways getting narrower?

"Two more!" The pixie could not help himself.

From their present position, it looked like they were in a huge fish bowl secured by the obscure walls of the cavern. Jonna leaped for the last bridge, barely reaching the edge.

Crystilic jumped, rolling in beside him. She stood up, smiling, holding her hands high. "We made it!"

"Not quite." Jonna moved to the edge of the last plateau.

By his calculations, even if he leaped out, he would be unable to grab the ladder taunting them above their heads. He bit his lip. "I guess we'll have to float up."

Bob pointed at the water. "Not a good idea."

The higher the level, the calmer it appeared, but things stirred beneath its surface. Crystilic tried to focus on one of the *things*, but just as it came into view, it flittered out of sight.

"Maybe it's not just drowning." Jonna voiced his suspicion.

"What did you say?" The pixie kept staring at the water.

"Any ideas?" Jonna turned to the others. He looked pointedly at Bob. "Surely you have a spell for this."

"You're the human. I'm just a pixie."

"Boys, boys." Crystilic moved closer to the water. Without a pause, she leaped backwards. As she fell, her body changed, formed a raft, and landed with a huge splash.

"Get on," she called, creating a mouth to speak. She had two female knotty eyes near one side of the raft.

Jonna took a tentative step onto the raft's surface. It was solid.

"I'm safe, silly." She giggled. Her eyes moved across the raft from one side to the other. "But you better hurry!"

They floated closer to the ladder, watching the last bridge and plateau disappear. The raft bounced. Jonna leaped up but could not reach the ladder. "Almost there."

"Good." Crystilic sounded worried. "There is something in the water trying to poke me on the bottom."

The raft bounced sharply. Jonna dropped to his knees, shifted his weight, and tried to hold on.

"What is it?" Bob was wide-eyed as he stared at the water. "Maybe I can stop it."

"You don't want to go down there." Crystilic shook her eyes. "It doesn't look pretty, and—" She sent them to peer quickly under the raft. Seconds later, they appeared back on top. "There are more of them than you."

The raft bounced up in two different places, shifting dangerously toward one side. Jonna started to slide, fighting to stay toward the center. Dark shadows loomed all around the raft, hiding under the water's surface.

Two handholds appeared, and Jonna grabbed them. Crystilic winked. He looked up, checking the distance to the ladder. Another inch or so more, and he could grab the bottom rung. "Ready?"

Time slowed down. The creatures struck the raft again. Jonna, preparing to leap, gauged the distance. "Now!"

CHAPTER 26
RELUCTANT GUARDIANS

Jonna leaped, catching the rung. It was not as easy as it looked. He pulled himself up, one rung at a time, until finally resting his feet.

Not far up the tunnel, he could see a metal grate. He checked how it was secured, noting it appeared to slide back.

Crystilic screamed, "Help!"

Jonna shifted, spotting Crystilic's raft. The creatures were attacking from all directions, knocking her body about. They seemed to be trying to eat her.

Working his way back down the ladder, he hung by one hand and extended the other. "Can you jump? I'll catch you."

He thought about trying a spell Väinämö had taught him, but how would that help? They were purely defensive. He remembered some of the dark mage spells, but as Almundena had pointed out, he was not a dark mage, nor did he want to be. According to her, he could not do their magic. An idea hit him. "Can you change into a fish?"

"Yes," she grunted, absorbing another hit. "But what would that—" A crafty smile appeared. "Oh, I see. Change into a fish, swim down, and leap up. You'll catch me!"

"That would work." Something about it seemed a little too simple to Jonna. He added quickly, "But nothing too small."

"Done." She transformed into a perch, dropping into the water.

Jonna stared after her. She was so small, something was bound to swallow her, and he could not let that happen. "Unum-Clastor-Pratima!"

By habit, he started to speak again, but watched as the first chant completed the whole spell. It still seemed strange, but he could get used to it. "Bob, she needs a distraction. Push my duplicate off the ladder."

The pixie backed up, centered on Jonna's duplicate, and plowed into it full steam. The hold the duplicate had on the ladder broke, and both watched it plunge toward the water.

There was a huge splash. Black shapes converged with a flash of speed. The duplicate was ripped to shreds before it sank below the surface. Jonna swallowed. There was only one thing left to do. "Bob, you better stay here."

"I can go if I want."

"Okay." Jonna grinned. "Have fun with the fishes."

Dropping from the ladder into the water, Jonna sank without a single stir. Bob watched him go and then dropped toward the water himself, only to shoot back up. Three of the water creatures leaped into the air, smashing into each other. Had he been just a little slower—

Searching frantically beneath the surface, Jonna yelled, "Crystilic!" His voice upset the water creatures. They swam through him multiple times but could not seem to find him.

A commotion stirred deeper in the water. Crystilic swam in rapid zigzag patterns. Unfortunately, the number of creatures chasing her grew by the moment.

"Help!" she called out again, dodging those who tried to cut her off.

"Up here!" Jonna caught her attention, but the creatures swarming around her blocked the way. What could he do, other than stand there and watch? While he was unaffected, or relatively so, the spell also stopped him from interacting easily with the world at large.

Crystilic was about to be boxed in. If she slowed her speed, they would surely catch her.

"Change," Jonna shouted, trying to think of something larger. "How about a dolphin?" Did she know what a dolphin was?

"Good idea." Her voice held an edge. "But I want something even bigger. It's payback time."

Water volume pushed aside as the level rose drastically. The things chasing her rammed nose first into the tough hide of a—whale? Some bounced off and sank to the bottom, stunned. Others zipped back in fear, watching from a distance.

Crystilic turned to Jonna and smiled. "Thanks!"

Surprise lit Jonna's face. "You can see me?"

"Yep." She swam in his direction, flipping her tail just to make sure any stragglers got whacked. Moving under him, she lifted up slowly. Too fast, and he might fall through.

As they reached the surface, Jonna grabbed hold of the ladder, meticulous about the climb up. How fast he moved determined whether he passed through or not.

"Unum-Clastor-Pratima."

He was back in the normal plane. Crystilic leaped out of the water, having resumed her perch form. Jonna reached out to catch her, but Bob beat him to the punch.

"I gotcha," Bob exclaimed, tagging her back fine. She changed form back to a woman, grabbed a ladder rung, and kissed him on the cheek.

Her smile was genuine. "Thanks!"

Had Bob not been flying, he would have fallen over. As it was, he flew sideways. Jonna stopped him before he hit the wall.

"And now for the grate." Climbing as high as possible, Jonna checked the sides, trying to rock it back and forth. It was no good. Something kept it from moving, but he could not see what.

Bob shook his head, coming to his senses. "How about some pixie magic?" He stared at the grate, tossing pixie dust up in the air. "There."

When Jonna reached up, the grate felt like soft rubber. "That's pretty good." He tugged, ripping down the rubberized grate one piece at a time. It dropped into the water and immediately vanished beneath the surface.

The top of the ladder was not far now. An artificial light from above illuminated their way. As they surfaced from the vertical tunnel, all three heads popped up just above the ring. No one else was in the room.

The pixie pointed up. "Look."

They saw an identical vertical tunnel directly over their heads.

Jonna speculated out loud, "There has to be a purpose for all these vertical holes."

He climbed out and looked around, followed by the others. The smooth floor was made with different colored tiles. The colors formed symbols that could only be seen from above.

Thinking back, Jonna considered. "There was one at the crossroads. There is one beneath us. There is another directly above. I bet there's one in every room." The picture of a circuit board went through his mind. "Circuits," he mumbled. "Connections and the flow of power. Air components, such as these rooms, perform individual functions with symbols on the floor. These work like components on a circuit board. When the water fills the lower tunnels, it completes the circuit, captures the magic, and conducts it to the Eye of Aldrick."

Bob cleared his throat. "Uh, Jonna, what's a circuit?"

Turning away from his thoughts, Jonna grinned. Bob's expression said it all. He laughed. "Sorry about that. In my world, we use a thing like magic, only we call it electricity. Circuits are what we use to harness that electricity."

"Wow." Crystilic's eyes widened. "So there are Dark Mages in your world, too?"

It was not the metaphor Jonna was after, but now that he thought about it, it was close. "You could say that."

"So where do we find the Rune Blade?" Bob landed on his shoulder as Crystilic moved to his side.

"Yes." Jonna nodded. "The Rune Blade." His memories stirred as he remembered the first time he had encountered the weapon in the elven hall. It was not so much hunting for the Rune Blade as feeling where it was. When he had entered the elven hall, he had seen the Rune Blade for the first time and was immediately drawn to it.

He closed his eyes, thinking back. If he pushed everything else away . . .

Crystilic moved closer to him. "Jonna?"

"Shh." Jonna tried to refocus. If he pushed everything else away, he might even . . . there. He could see the Rune Blade. Even at his thought, it began to pulse and glow.

Bob grabbed his ear and whispered loudly, "Jonna!"

Jonna opened his eyes. "I've found it." His eyes opened even wider as he stared around the room. Forming a perimeter around them were four-armed, upright, weapon-carrying snakes about Jonna's height. They stood on two legs, using their tails to help balance.

"They're nagendra," Bob whispered. "Dark Mage guardians!"

The nagendra in front asked, "Who are you?" This one carried a spear while the rest carried swords.

Though surprised, Jonna was not shocked. He had run into a talking snake when he had first left Väinämö. How much different could one that walked on two feet be?

"I am Jonna McCambel." He bowed. "A pleasure to meet you."

"Maybe not ssssso pleasssssurable," the spear-carrier hissed. "Why have you disssssturbed our abode?"

Jonna thought about what to say, how to say it, and how they might react. It was very apparent they had no idea why he was here. That could play to his favor, maybe.

"I seek to restore order in magic." Jonna studied the one with the spear. "I seek to bring down the Dark Mages."

"Human," the leader sneered. "Do you not know we are allies with the Dark Magesssss? Their sssssssuccessssssss issssss oursssss."

"And if they fall? Will you fall as well?" He looked around at the circle of nagendra. "Tonight is the eve of their power. Tonight they will lose the magic they hold so dear."

The leader hissed, testing the air. "You act sssssso cccccccertain for one who isssssssss about to die. I ssssssmell fear from you."

They needed to get to the Rune Blade, but they could not do that unless they could dump the nagendra.

Jonna went through his arsenal of two spells, plus the others he had heard. None of them seemed adequate to the task, unless . . .

There was the first spell Väinämö had mentioned. Two humans touching at the same time were sent to the darkness, but what would happen with a human and a hemming? In any case, it was worth a try.

"You confuse fear with cautiousness, my friend." Jonna bowed to all around. Like a magician about to do a trick, he kept their eyes upon him. At the same time, he took hold of Crystilic's hand and prayed his guess would work. "Warn your people," he declared. "I have no quarrel with the nagendra, only the Dark Mages. Unum-Clastor-Fillum."

He and Crystilic vanished. Jonna put his finger to his lips, warning Crystilic to be quiet. Just like when he used the ethereal spell, she could still see him, though how, he was not sure.

The nagendra panicked, warriors turning this way and that. The one with the spear searched around, checking the vertical tunnel. "Find them," the leader shouted. "Find them now!"

Through a gap in the circle of guards, Jonna stepped away from the nagendra, leading Crystilic toward a doorway. They dare not speak, and he knew he had taken quite a chance.

Väinämö had been explicit about the spell. It was designed for one human. Two humans were sent someplace else. However, Crystilic was a hemming, so it would not work the same. Right? Thank magic he had been correct!

Again, it was strange to say the spell only once, but he would not look a gift horse in the mouth. All the changes in how he could do magic did make him wonder if the recharge time for the second spell would still be necessary. After his actions in the dragon cave, everything seemed different.

Jonna found the main hall and headed toward a split corridor. He had seen the Rune Blade in his mind, felt its presence, and knew the direction to go. His mind was like a metal detector. The closer and larger the object, the more he could tell it was there.

The nagendra seemed especially upset. The news that their coalition was about to end, and not in their favor, certainly did not sit well. Of course, Jonna still had to find a way to carry out his warning, and a lot might change before it got that far.

Bob called from his shoulder, "There it is."

"Oh my," Crystilic exclaimed before anyone could stop her.

The moment she spoke, they both appeared, standing at the entrance to a small room. In the room was a large crystal ball. In the center of the crystal ball, the Rune Blade shone. As Jonna approached, it glowed even more.

Bob flew around the room. "Jonna, we don't have much time. Break the ball." The pixie kept one eye on the door.

Jonna looked around for something to hit it with, but the rest of the room was empty.

"They're coming," Crystilic warned with just a little bit of panic in her voice. She changed form, becoming a solid wall just like when they had met her, and positioned herself over the doorway. "I'll do my best to hold them back."

Jonna circled the ball, looking for a way to open it. The Rune Blade responded, glowed brighter, and sparkled in the room. It reminded him of the elvish magic that danced around Elfleda. It also reminded him of Stephanie, the bright light in her eyes when she looked at him. He reached forward to touch the sphere.

A flash of light lashed out, knocking him backwards. Hitting the wall, he bounced to the floor. He heard a laugh outside Crystilic's protective wall.

"You cannot reach it, human." The voice sounded like the nagendra who carried the spear. "In sssssspite of your clevernesssss, you have no placcccce to run."

Crystilic's eyes went wide. Something struck her on the outside of the doorway. "Ouch." She looked at Jonna. "That hurt! I don't know what they're doing, but—"

"They're going to make it in." He nodded. "I know." He got off the floor, looking back at the sphere, and noticed writing on a small slab at its base.

He read softly, "World without ending caged now eternal, held by the finger of God in his power. Destiny waiting, now for the coming. How to haste open when men do all cower? Listen now closely. Seek now the answer. Finding it will be as snow covers rain. Patiently lifting, holding suspended, breaks up the walls where foundation is gained."

It was signed with a C. The writing brought up a whole bunch of questions, but the only important one was, *What does it mean?*

Bob scratched his head. "Whoever wrote this had more imagination than me."

"But—" Jonna reread the writing. "It does suggest they expected someone to figure it out."

"Or it's a trick." Crystilic grunted and then sighed. "I can't hold them much longer!"

"World without ending," the pixie quoted. "Easy: the sphere itself."

Jonna nodded. "Caged now eternal—that demonstrates the connectivity of the sphere, maybe even referring to the item inside."

"Held by the finger of God in his power?" Bob looked around. "That seems sort of obvious. It knocked you off your feet!"

Jonna laughed nervously. "That it did, and I'd rather not repeat it. I am grateful it didn't kill me, but then again, I don't think that's what it was designed to do."

He continued with the verse. "Destiny waiting, now for the coming." Jonna moved closer to the inscription, but not too close. "The author expected for someone to open it." He paused in thought. "The author knew someone would open it." *Was he reading too much into this prophecy thing?*

Bob came to Jonna's shoulder and read the next line. "How to haste open when men do all cower? The inscription knows the solution is not simple."

"Guys!" Crystilic groaned, still holding the door. "Soon! Pleasssssee!"

"Listen now closely . . ." Jonna skipped the next few words. ". . . Snow covers rain . . ." He sped to the last verse. "Patiently lifting, holding suspended." He looked at Bob. "Can you make us both, me and the globe, float?"

Bob blinked. "I think I can, but why?"

"Energy has to have a ground." Jonna thought back. "If we are both floating, no ground."

Bob shook his head. "I don't get it."

"Help!" Cracks formed upon Crystilic's rock exterior. "Do something fast. I can't hold much longer!"

Bob tossed some pixie dust on the globe and Jonna. "Ne Atalante." They rose from the ground, suspended about a foot.

Jonna repeated a part of the verse. "Breaks up the walls." He shoved the globe. It spun around, striking the side of the room furthest from the door.

The chamber exploded in light. The pieces of the globe faded away as the energy it contained dissipated. The Rune Blade touched the wall, bounced back, and fell to the floor.

Jonna's heart soared. He had been right! Without thinking, he said, "Atalante." He slowly lowered to the ground. Staring in amazement, he realized he was not the only one shocked.

Bob's eyes were wide. "I didn't know you could use pixie magic." He blinked. "And without the dust, too."

Although Jonna knew there were different forms of magic, so to speak, he never really thought about the difference. Why shouldn't he be able to use all magic? It all came from the same source. He shrugged. "Me neither. It just sort of popped into my brain."

Crystilic groaned. "Well, keep popping. I can't take any more. Ready or not, here they come!" She fell backwards, transforming into a rug.

The nagendra shot forward as a group and immediately became pinned in the entrance. They squirmed back and forth, hissing at Jonna, unable to get in and unable to get out.

Jonna reached down and picked up the Rune Blade of Knowledge. The grip melded with his hand, changing to a perfect fit. It pulsed with a life of its own. He had the sword, but how were they to get out?

He searched the room for ideas, turning toward the nagendra. The sword's brightness blinded the nagendras' eyes. "Now what?" With a sudden thought, he realized Crystilic was beneath them. "Crystilic!"

She changed into a serpent, slithered out from under them, and shaped back to a woman. "I'm fine, but sheesh." She shook. "Yucky things!"

"What are we going to do with them?" Bob counted how many had tried to force their way in. "They're all jammed tight."

"You could just start hacking." Crystilic brightened. "It would cut a hole right through the nagendra blocking the door."

The nagendra stopped and then began to squirm frantically backwards. Bob laughed evilly, adding to their fright.

"Well—" Jonna looked around the room. "Tempting as that might be, since they were trying to kill us, we need to find another way out."

Bob made a face. "Aw, come on."

Shaking his head, Jonna frowned, realizing Bob could be right. It might be the only way. There was only one door. However, as his eye caught where the globe had struck the wall, he noticed fractures at the point of impact.

Following the lines, he traced them to their point of origin and pushed with his hand. Pieces fell outside the room. Jonna stared, a grin forming on his face. "That's it! Come on, everyone, help me with the wall."

Bob huffed. "The other way would be easier." He left Jonna's shoulder to dash back and forth, knocking a few pieces of the wall out himself. Crystilic, deciding it was easier to follow Jonna's example, pushed them out.

Hoping the wall was weak enough, Jonna backed up and slammed his shoulder into it. The cracks spread. The second time he struck, larger chunks fell out and away.

"Ready?" He looked at the other two, who nodded. "On three: one, two, three."

The leader of the nagendra roared in anger. "You fools, let me in!" One by one, the nagendra jerked back and disappeared. Those left struggled to their feet.

The trio hit the wall. The impact sent them through. They tumbled out on the other side.

The nagendra with the spear jumped into the room and saw the globe gone and the back wall destroyed. He rushed to follow the trio.

Bob flew forward. His momentum carried him further than the others. He screeched to a stop in midair. This was no place to take a large step.

They stood on a ledge overlooking a deep ravine. Turning back to Jonna, he raised an eyebrow. "Okay, wise one, now where?"

"They're coming!" Crystilic glanced back, watching as the lead nagendra worked at making the hole big enough for his frame.

Jonna turned around, looking the leader in the eye. "Maybe we should take a stand."

"You challenge me?" The nagendra laughed, knocking out a few more pieces of the wall. "You are no match, human. I will kill you, and my hordesssss will dessssssstroy your friendssssss."

"You still have the choice of leaving us alone." Jonna smiled as he made the offer. "How about a deal? I defeat you. You show us the next level out."

"Why sssssshould I make a deal—" The leader stepped through, motioning his warriors to hold their place. "When I already own your life?" He flipped the spear from right to left. "I have a sssssspear. You have a sssssword. Even by weaponsssss, you are no match."

He struck out at Jonna, missing his head by a mere inch.

"Good." The nagendra nodded. "You're making it a little more interesssssssting."

"Only a little more?" Jonna lifted the Rune Blade with his right hand, holding it back and keeping his left hand forward. His eyes never wavered from the leader. The intimidation worked, if only for a moment.

"Ha." The nagendra shook his head. "The mind trickssssss of a human on a nagendra?" He swung at Jonna's feet, curved around, and thrust.

Jonna leaped, remembering there was a ledge somewhere behind him and landed softly. He caught a portion of the spear's shaft and jerked the leader forward. A grunt escaped Jonna's lips. *Boy was he heavy!*

A second later, they stood within five feet of one another, exchanging blows and countering thrusts. The nagendra's four arms certainly gave him an advantage, as he could easily switch from one to another. Jonna was beginning to tire.

The leader chuckled. "You have done well, but it isssss only a matter of time. I told you, no human can bessssst a nagendra."

"I don't want to best you." Jonna cut back, slicing close enough to nick one of the nagendra's knuckles.

Surprised, the nagendra slid his hand away along the shaft. "No?"

"I want to disarm you."

Jonna stepped to the right, dodged a downward blow, and struck, catching the arm that the leader favored. It sliced clean through.

"You sssssstupid human! You will pay for that!"

Jonna struck the other way, the Rune Blade slicing into one of the arms on the left side.

"Arraagg!"

The warriors behind the broken wall pushed through, but the leader waved them back.

"NO, he isssss mine!" His spear came up, heading for Jonna's neck.

Jonna turned, pulled back at an angle, and sliced off the end of the spear. He spun around, cutting into the leader's tail and knocking him off his feet. In the briefest of seconds, the Rune Blade of Knowledge stopped, frozen, inches above the leader's throat.

The leader rasped, "Kill me! What do you wait for?"

"I spare your life." Jonna stepped back, sword held in the ready position. The broken spear was at his feet.

"You are a fool," the leader cried out. "I would have killed you." The anger in his voice was undeniable.

"You're right." Jonna caught the nagendra's eye. "But my battle is not with you. I seek the Dark Mages. Lead me to them." He motioned to the broken wall. "And we will spare their lives."

"Uh, Jonna," Bob whispered at his shoulder. "Did breaking the crystal smash your brain? There are hundreds!"

"You couldn't." The leader tried to speak the words harshly, but his strength was leaving as his wounds bled. Uncertainty crossed his face.

"You said I could not best you." Jonna spoke without emotion. "Yet this I have done. You said I could not retrieve the Rune Blade, yet we have. Do you think I've traveled this far for nothing but a silly piece of metal?" He held the Rune Blade up for all to see. "This is the magic of the elves."

In response to his words, the sword glowed brightly. As he turned to face the nagendra warriors, their weapons came to attention.

"Enough," the leader called out weakly. "I would have no more of my kinsssssmen hurt!"

"Good." Jonna kept his eyes on the warriors. "So we have a deal?"

The leader paused, his anger trying and failing to come. He roared in pain, "DEAL!"

Jonna lowered his sword, moving toward the leader. He stopped three feet away. "Bob, heal him."

"What?" Bob floated around to face Jonna. "I don't know how to heal a nagendra!"

"You know something," Jonna countered. "Heal him."

The pixie made a face of distaste. "I only know about pixies and humans, and not so much on humans. To heal, you need to understand how they work. Anything I did might kill him."

There was no time to argue. The nagendra grew weaker by the moment, and soon it would be too late. Jonna stared at Bob until the pixie turned away.

"Oh, all right!" Bob floated toward the wounded nagendra and tossed a glitter of pixie dust into the air. "Lasona!"

CHAPTER 27
AN UNEXPECTED NAME

As Jonna watched, the nagendra's wounds closed and his slashed arm regrew. The anger on the leader's face gradually abated as the wounds healed up, to his disbelief. When his arm finished, he rose to his feet. "Why? I am a nagendra, and you are a human. Why should you care if the nagendra die?"

Jonna thought about that as Bob moved back to his shoulder. Why did he care? He did not know these creatures, and all they had done was try to kill him.

"Because—" He looked the nagendra in the eye. "All life is precious, be it nagendra, human, or any other. It is the Dark Mages' abuse of power that threatens life."

There was silence as the nagendra considered this. Though his followers did not lower their weapons, they too considered the words.

The leader finally spoke. "You are an honorable opponent." He gave a single nod. "And your wordsssss have merit. They are not unlike one of our own, Cato, who hassssss spoken againssssst our allianccccce with the Dark Magesssss. He, too, believesssss assss you." The nagendra paused, and more silence was followed by a final nod from the leader. "I accccccept your offer of friendssssship."

Having never negotiated a treaty—that was not part of his degree plan—Jonna wondered what to do next. "So I take it we are no longer enemies?"

The leader raised his chin. "Nor will the pact we've made with the Dark Magesssss continue." He bowed. "Mosssssst humanssssss run from our very sssssight. How isssss it you do not?"

"I am honor bound to save the elves." Jonna held the sword up, the glowing metal shining in all directions. "I, too, have family to save."

"Then ssssssso be it." The nagendra leader extended one of his hands. "I am Gernot, leader of the nagendra who hold thesssssse habitationssssss. From this day forth, you have my friendssssssship."

"As you do mine." Jonna shook the extended hand. "I'm Jonna McCambel."

Bob whispered behind his ear, "Give him a name."

Jonna looked at Bob, not sure he heard that right. "Gernot already told me his name. What are you talking about?"

Leaning closer to Jonna's ear, he whispered, "It will seal the treaty between you and him. Give him a name!"

"What name?"

Bob thought quickly and nodded. "Algar."

"Algar?" Jonna repeated. It came off his tongue easily enough, unlike some names he heard. "What does it mean?"

Bob smiled. "Elf spear."

"Perfect." Jonna turned to Gernot. "By the power of might and ability—" Jonna really hoped he wasn't dressing this up too much, but come on, he had never done this before. "I give you a symbol of the trust we have. In my world, you will be known as Gernot Algar!"

Gernot listened, playing with the name on his snake lips. He translated the combination. "Sssssssmashing Elf Sssssspear, I like that." He looked Jonna in the eye. "And you sssssshall be known asssss Xun Ove, The Fassssst Blade."

Jonna glanced at Bob and smiled. "That's sort of cool." He looked at his watch. Although times in this place did not correspond to the hours he was used to, he knew they had better get going. "Will you lead us?"

"I would be honored." Gernot Algar bowed. He spread his hands, and the warriors parted, making a path.

As Jonna and his group came forward, most of the nagendra bowed in honor of the agreement. Here and there, a few showed reservation, but when they saw Gernot, they ducked their heads.

As they passed through the wall and out through the room where the Rune Blade had been kept, Jonna saw that the hallway was crowded with spectators. Rumors had spread fast. Small nagendra children peered from between parents, trying to see the strangers who came from below.

At the end of the last hall, they entered an area with guard quarters on both sides and a central group of buildings not unlike a city square. Gernot turned, raising his hands, about to speak. The nagendra filled the room to overflowing.

An old voice called from the ranks of those around them. "Gernot!"

"Who callsssss?" Gernot could not see the speaker. When the person did not come forward, he waved his hand, calling those around him to move away.

It was an old nagendra. His mouth was gray. His skin was much more dry and scaly. One of his hands gripped a staff. The other hand

284

held a round orb.

"Sssspeak, Cato." Gernot bowed in his direction. "Why did you not approach?"

"How can I come to one who would dessssstroy the world we know?"

"Thessssssse—" Gernot motioned to Jonna's group. "They are not our enemy. They sssspeak the very wordssss you have tried to convincccce ussss of. When another foe might have killed and let die, they have offered friendssssship and mercccccy."

Cato raised his voice, the waver of old age suddenly gone. "Do you hear him? Do you hear him? Do you hear the one who would sssssteal the magic from your homessssss?"

A rumble of voices started in the back of the crowd. It moved as a wave upon the nagendra lips. Was this true? Had Gernot betrayed them?

"Sssssilence!" Gernot calmed the voices, but the feeling in the room had changed. He looked to Cato in amazement. "Old friend, you have alwaysssss expresssssssssed great wisssssdom to thissssss people. You have alwaysssss ressssssisssssssted the movement to work with the Dark Magessssss. Why, now, do you go againsssssst your very own teachingsssss?"

Half the people turned to look at Cato. The other half continued to watch Gernot. Nervous tension hung in the air. If things did not shape up, the mob of creatures would be impossible to fight off.

Jonna's group shifted their gazes from one to another while Jonna spotted a place of safety should things go wrong.

"My teachingsssss." Cato nodded. "Yessss. Age hassss a way of changing the foolissssh mind." He waved around, catching the eyes of the people. "And today'ssss eventssss have opened my eyessssss to the greater good!"

Voices of confusion threatened to drown out any answer. Having been reminded of Cato's teachings, the people shifted in dismay. From what Gernot had told Jonna, this did not seem like the Cato the nagendra had described.

"Something's not right." Jonna moved closer to Cato. He looked just like a nagendra, but—Cato's eye was quick to spot Jonna's approach.

"Why do you come, human?" Cato took a step back, holding his staff like a shield.

"I wish only to hear your great wisdom." Jonna bowed slightly. "I am no threat to you."

"No threat?" Cato almost shouted. "You come to our cccity from the depthsssss of the cavessss. You invade our home, attack our people." Cato motioned to the Rune Blade. "And ssssteal from our treasuresssss. And now, you tell usssss you are no threat?"

"I reclaim only that which was taken. I refrained from hurting your people, and we restored your leader. What else can I do to show we come in peace?"

"You can die!" Cato struck his staff on the floor.

Lightning shot into the upper reaches of the chamber, arced down, and hit the ground all around Jonna as if deflected by an unseen force. Jonna guessed it had to be the sword.

Cato roared, "No!"

Gernot stepped to Jonna's side. "Do not do thisssss." The nagendra looked into Cato's eyes. The pupils flickered. They were human, not nagendra. "You are not Cato!" Gernot's spear came forward, aiming at the elder nagendra's chest. He roared out to those in the room, "Thisssss issssss an imposssssster!"

"That issssss true." Another Cato appeared, moving through the crowd. He came to Gernot, standing by his side, looking at the fake Cato. "*Phanessssss*," the real Cato called out, pointing his staff in the fake's direction.

The air around the fake wavered like water, and the illusion of Cato changed, revealing a dark-headed mage.

"Fools! Cowards!" The fake spun around, aiming his staff at those watching. "You dare to betray the Dark Mages? You dare to stand against those who share their power?"

"In exchange for guarding your precccccciousssssss ssssssecret," Gernot shouted back, "you barely give usssss enough to ssssssurvive!"

The dark mage's eyes flamed. "You were hunted, driven from the sight of most humans. We accepted and helped you. We keep you from dying."

"You placed usssss in prissssson," Cato said evenly. "You ensssssslaved our people. It issssss time for the children to leave the nessssst."

The dark mage turned and glared at Jonna. "Not today. Awiti Barbaros!"

Lightning lashed out, heading in Jonna's direction. There was nowhere to run, and avoiding the blow would only get other nagendra killed.

Jonna lowered the Rune Blade, praying that whatever had diverted the lightning before would do so again, and waited for the strike. He had no desire to die but would have no one else die in his place.

Cato, as if he had all the time in the world, waved his hand. "Ne Barbarosssssss." The lightning vanished.

The dark mage glared in shock. "You have grown stronger." The mage sneered at Cato. "It is an unexpected surprise. Perhaps you are not such idiots after all." With a sly voice, he bowed and said, "May I speak further?"

"We have heard enough." Gernot stepped forward, but Cato held him back, nodding.

"Let the dark mage sssssspeak, for even now he feelssss hisssss doom." The dark mage stared, his eyes growing wide. "What have you done?"

"By taking my form, you have called forth retribution. You have violated the treaty between the nagendra and the Dark Mages. I allowed you to do thisssss, though you were unaware, knowing what you would bring to bear."

"NO." The dark mage spun frantically around, looking up. "Stamato Zaman!"

The room froze, and all the nagendra with it. Only the dark mage, Jonna, and Cato remained mobile.

"You have only delayed what will happen." Cato put his staff in front of him, looking into the dark mage's face. "You can't win."

Cheeks burning red, the dark mage aimed his staff at Cato. "And neither will you. Baqir Janus Tillo Cassius!"

A black portal appeared in front of the evil mage, sucking in air, pulling in stray objects. The longer it existed, the stronger the pull became.

Jonna called to Cato, his hair and clothing blowing in the massive wind, "What is he doing?"

The wind grew stronger, making it very hard to stand. Cato stood against the wind, but he, too, had difficulty. Raising his voice, he answered, "He hasssss created a vortexxxxx. He intendsssss to dessssstroy all in thisssss room."

Jonna moved forward, raising his sword. With no idea what the sword could do, and no idea how to stop this vortex, he had to try something. If he could slice the black portal, would magic counter magic?

Cato's staff tapped his shoulder. Jonna turned back to look, seeing the nagendra shake his head. "No good. We have to sssstop the mage himself."

Jonna struggled to turn, the force of the vortex growing in strength. He fought against it, coming within arm's length of the dark mage, but when he tried to reach him, he hit an invisible wall. The personal firewall surrounded the evil mage's body.

"Too late." The dark mage laughed. "By the time I'm through, the hero of the elves will be gone forever!"

Jonna's feet slid, pulled toward the vortex. There was nothing on the floor to grab, and his shoes seemed to have lost their grip.

"Can't you cast the reverse spell?" Jonna shouted toward Cato. "Like you did with the lightning?"

Cato, also slipping toward the vortex, was not doing much better. "That wasssss a different type of magic. Thisssss isssss unique unto itsssssssssssself, like demon magic."

That was what Lilith had done, but even then, Jonna had found a way around it. He had an idea. "If we can't stop it, can we change it?"

Cato thought and then nodded. "If we knew a word to alter itsssssss effect."

The word Serena had used to call the magic tunnel came to mind. Both it and the vortex had the same basic principle. Both allowed things to move from one location to another, though this one was certainly nastier about it. In any case, it was worth a try.

"Baqirum," Jonna shouted, praying he remembered the word correctly.

The room shook. The black portal distorted as the darkness altered its shape. It formed the tunnel Jonna remembered, leading to Lilith's lab.

The drag of the wind ceased. The evil mage roared. He dropped his personal firewall and rushed in Jonna's direction. With more fear than threat, he shouted, "You cannot win! You cannot!"

The dark mage swung his staff, the end even with Jonna's head. Jonna brought the sword up and watched as it cut cleanly through the wood.

An explosion of light burst out, blinding his eyes and knocking Jonna backwards. He felt himself slam into a wall where no wall was before. As the explosion continued to blind him, he noticed other unusual things.

Where was Cato? Where was the dark mage? He blinked, but the brightness would not go away. It seemed like he was somewhere else. "Where am I?"

A familiar voice chuckled.

"Väinämö?"

"In the flesh, er—" The mage continued to chuckle. "More like the spirit."

Jonna expressed his concern again. "Where am I?"

"Right now?" Väinämö seemed to look around, though how Jonna could sense it, he did not know. "Let me see."

After a moment, the mage answered again. "Well, it seems you're somewhere between light and dark."

Worry lines showed on Jonna's face. Thoughts of people dying and showing up in heaven came to mind. At least it was better than the alternative, right? However, that could not be right, since Väinämö was here. Not that he was implying— "All I see is light. What do you mean?"

"Let's study the facts." Väinämö smiled, raising one hand up and extending one finger. "One, you cut a staff of power." He extended a second finger. "Two, it was in the middle of a suspended time spell." He extended a third finger. "And three, doing that has really strange effects. Can you see now?"

"I see." Jonna nodded and then stopped. "Actually, I physically can't see." He shook his head, feeling just short of exasperated. Figuring out what this mage wanted was not always easy. "What does this mean?"

The mage smiled broadly. "I'm taking advantage of the power you unleashed to help you. Repeat after me."

"Uh, okay." Jonna kept blinking, trying to pick up anything, but the light was too bright. It forced him to close his eyes.

Väinämö did the little musician thing with his finger. "Menes."

"Menes."

Väinämö was very careful to stress the "Ol" at the beginning of the next word. "Olwen."

Jonna repeated, "Olwen." Then inserted, "Why don't you ever tell me what they mean?"

Väinämö grinned. "Why do I need to? You find out soon enough.

Now, pay attention. Milburga."

Jonna sighed. "Milburga."

"Now, say it all together." Väinämö took a big step back from Jonna. Again, it was *felt* and not seen.

"Did you just step away from me?" Jonna tried to look in the mage's direction. "I don't think I like that, especially when I'm about to say a spell."

Väinämö huffed. "Just say it. Why do you have to be so difficult?"

"Me?"

"Say it!"

"Menes Olwen Milburga."

A swoosh sounded around him, and little tingles started in his body. Jonna's eyes went wide, despite the light. "What was that?"

"Hmm." Väinämö studied him and frowned. "Something happen that I don't know about?" The mage squinted at him. "Now, say it seven times."

He waited, tapping his foot. At least Jonna knew the mage was not all-knowing. "I don't have to do that anymore."

"Really?" Väinämö sounded like a kid with a new toy. "This makes for an interesting story." It sounded like Väinämö pulled up a chair and sat down. Did spirits use chairs?

"Could I at least get my eyesight back?"

"Oh no, can't do that. It's against the rules." Something sounded in Väinämö's direction, and he looked at his arm.

"That sounded like a watch chime." Jonna turned his head this way and that. "Did you create a watch?"

Väinämö tapped the small item, humming proudly to himself. "Just a little contraption I devised. It is not quite as small as I'd like yet, but I'm working on it. After seeing the thing you carried—" Väinämö sighed. "Oh, well—" He stood up, and Jonna was sure he heard a chair push back. "Time to go. Remember what I told you. You'll need it for your battle with the Dark Mages." Väinämö faded away.

"Menes Olwen Milburga," Jonna said again, trying to make sure he remembered. The swoosh sounded again, but this time instead of little tingles, bright light pulled from all directions. Something told him the spell had nothing to do with coming back. Väinämö had helped him with that. However, that begged the question, what was the spell for?

He bumped across the floor, backing into the nearest frozen nagendra. He could see the dark mage falling toward him, staff severed at the end.

The dark mage threw up his hands, his body landing on the Rune Blade still held in front of Jonna. He screamed. The moment he touched the tip, the mage's whole body dissolved.

"Help me," the man screamed, but before he could speak another word, he vanished from view. Time abruptly resumed.

"Cato!" Gernot went to the elder's side, helping him to his feet. He checked to make sure the older nagendra had not been hurt.

"I'm fine. Let me go." Cato turned around, spotting Jonna. "And help that human up, too." Multiple hands picked Jonna up and put him on his feet.

"Uh, thanks." Jonna grinned at those around, though it might have been easier without all those green hands. "Thanks a lot."

Bob came to his shoulder angrily. "Where did you go? You aren't supposed to—"

"I didn't do it." Jonna hushed him. "But I did see Väinämö."

"Where?" Bob looked in both directions almost at once.

"He—it's hard to explain."

"Fine, don't tell the pixie." Bob feigned offense but smiled. "We were worried!"

Cato moved next to Jonna, bowing slightly. "If it issss to be assss the prophecccy foretold, you musssst hurry. The nagendra'ssss continued exxxxisssstencccce will depend upon your ssucccccccccessssssss."

At the mention of the prophecy, Jonna locked eyes with Cato. Knowledge from The Sight filled his head, and he knew who had written the verses on the bottom of the crystal sphere. "You knew I would get the blade. You knew I would protect your people."

A slight smile lit Cato's face but quickly went away. "Perhapssss. What I knew wassss that the perssssson who could retrieve the blade musssst be the perssssson of prophecccy. Nothing more. But there issss sssomething elssssse on your mind, eh?"

If that did not add pressure, nothing would. Jonna nodded. Now he was responsible for another whole race, and all he wanted to do was save his wife. He looked at the nagendra around him and then back to Cato. "I need a way into the Dark Mages' level without them knowing."

"They already know." Cato appeared unconcerned, as if this, too, he had foreseen. "But to what exxxxxtent, I cannot sssay. When the

291

dark mage frozzzze time, it ssssstopped him from communicating with hisssss brothersssss. However, they already know you are coming. They already know you have the Rune Blade."

Did the Dark Mages possess telepathy as well? It was a question for another day. "Show me the best route."

Past the gates, toward the right side of the wall, Cato tapped a section with his staff. The small section wavered, revealing a key hole. He reached into his pocket and pulled out a shiny gold key.

"Doron," Cato said. He tapped the key and inserted it into the lock. It twisted to the right with a single click. As it did, the stone vanished, revealing stairs that led toward the upper level.

The elder nagendra pointed to the stairway. "Thissss will lead you passsst the normal entriessss. At the end, you will find a corridor of mazzzzessss. It issss by thessse mazzzzessss that the Dark Mage roomssss do breathe. From there, it issss up to you."

"Thank you, Cato." Jonna shook all four of his hands, then turned to Gernot and did the same. "Thank you, Gernot Algar." Jonna bowed.

Gernot gave a nod. "You are mosssst welcome."

As Jonna started to turn, Gernot held up his hand. "Wait, I have a gift." Gernot handed him a small, flat stone.

"What is this?"

"It issss a Mariah sssstone. It hassss been marked to my persssson. If you ever find yoursssself in need, rub the sssstone and call my name." It looked like an ordinary stone to Jonna, but in this world, who knew?

"Thank you." Jonna placed the stone in his pocket. "Farewell to all."

He stepped into the small tunnel, heading up the stairs. As soon as they were all inside, the door vanished behind them.

"Uh, lights?" Crystilic looked around. "Granted, I could just change into a bat."

"That's right." Jonna seemed puzzled. "The green glowing algae are not here."

He felt the wall to his left, his eyes adjusting with the pixie sight. Yep, Bob's magic was still doing its job!

"No bats," Bob said firmly. "They make me nervous."

Jonna moved up the stairs. "Why is that?"

The pixie began, "When I was younger—"

"Guys!" Crystilic still stood at the base of the stairs. "You want me to turn into a bat?"

Jonna glanced back and chuckled. "Sorry about that."

"I'll take care of—" Bob started to zip back.

"No." Jonna held him up. "Let me try something." Pulling out the Mariah stone, he closed his eyes and thought back. Both Väinämö and Almundena made objects glow simply by saying a spell. Could he do the same? Why not? "Erebos illumini!"

CHAPTER 28
HANGMAN'S NOOSE

Jonna held out the Mariah stone. Light shone in all directions.

Bob huffed. "Now you're getting like the pixie females: always showing off with their entourage of fireflies."

"Bob, you know that's not true. You just wanted to hold Crystilic's hand as you led her up the stairs."

The pixie's face grew red. "Well, uh, maybe."

In the glow, Crystilic came to join them. She kissed Bob on the head. "It's okay, Bob. I appreciate the thought. You can still hold my hand if you'd like."

Bob's face brightened. "How about, instead, I whisper sweet nothings in your ear?" He flew to Crystilic's shoulder. She giggled. Jonna laughed, shaking his head, as they continued up the stairs.

"Jonna—" Bob frowned as he stopped whispering to Crystilic. "When did you start doing magic? When I saw you in the elvish palace, you didn't know a stick from a wand."

Jonna chuckled. "Good question. Actually, I didn't. I just did what Väinämö told me to do. And then—" He went silent for a few steps. "Bob, do all humans do magic?"

"I don't think so." Bob glanced at Jonna's sword. "There is something different about you. Something not normal to a human of these lands."

Jonna frowned. "I'm not from these lands, remember? Väinämö says anyone can do it."

The pixie shook his head. "He tells you that as encouragement, but believe me, the average human is stup—" Bob caught his tongue. "Er, sorry about that." He looked away sheepishly. "I did say *average*."

Jonna laughed at his embarrassment. "No offense taken."

They continued their upward plod, coming to a flat, square area that dead-ended by a wall. Jonna pushed at the wall, watching his hand go through.

"I bet it's one-way." Bob zipped through and tried to come back. "Yep. Tag, you're it."

Jonna exhaled. "Bob, don't do that. We do not know what could have happened. What if you got in trouble, and we couldn't get through?"

"Aw," Bob called from the other side. "He cares."

Sighing, Jonna shook his head. "Of course I care. No more taking chances, got it? Now, before we come through, what do you see?"

Spinning around, Bob studied the room. "Holes. Lots of holes. But no dark mages."

Crystilic watched Jonna. As soon as he nodded, she passed through, finding Bob on the other side.

Bob glowed. "At last, alone!"

"Silly." She stepped away from the wall so Jonna could come after. A moment later, Jonna was there.

"And here is the maze of tunnels." Jonna moved around the open area. "Now which way?" Why did no one ever give detailed directions?

He went to a smaller opening and listened. In the distance, he heard children playing. In another, a couple spoke in quiet conversation. And still another, the pounding of hammers on burning steel echoed back. However, none of these seemed the way to the Berk Hecktor.

Crystilic moved from one hole to the next, listening as she had seen Jonna do. She held up her hands. "I have no idea."

Stepping back to the center of the small room, Jonna closed his eyes and listened. From this position, the room worked like an echo chamber, and he could hear in all directions at once. There were thousands of people speaking. If only he could find one voice—

"Leave me be."

That voice sounded familiar, though he had only heard it once. Jonna turned toward the sound, following it to a large hole. "That sounds like Almundena's brother." He listened again. Chains struck against the wall, and Jonna nodded. "I know how to find Berk Hecktor."

The pixie's face fell. "Wh-what?" He shook his head. "No!"

"We have to go back," Jonna countered. "It is the only way to find the path. Besides—" His eyes narrowed. "I have a promise to keep."

"If you keep that promise, we're as good as dead," the pixie growled. "We have to go forward, not back!"

"By going back, we will go forward."

Crystilic's head bounced between the two as they spoke.

Bob turned toward her. "What do you think?"

"I don't know." She smiled. "Go. Come. It doesn't matter to me."

"You're not helping." Bob huffed. Crystilic laughed.

Jonna dropped to his hands and knees, crawling into the larger hole.

Two small, beady eyes glowed from a distance. When he moved forward again, something squeaked and ran.

"Great," Bob exclaimed. "Rats."

Crystilic looked frightened. "Rats?"

"What are you afraid of rats for?" Jonna moved forward and looked back at Crystilic. "You're bigger than they are."

The pixie swallowed. "I'm smaller."

"Well," Crystilic thought. "I don't think I really am afraid, but this form I'm in seems to think so. So—"

"You pretend?" Jonna laughed. "Not all females are afraid of those things." He chuckled some more. "You don't have to be, you know."

"You mean—" Crystilic kept pace, watching those in front. "It wouldn't make me less attractive not to be afraid?"

"No." Jonna shook his head, still being careful to shine the Mariah stone so she could see. "Of course not. Although, that's how some men get a boost to their egos."

"Jonna," Bob cautioned. "That's enough."

"I see." She grinned. "So, if a woman wants to get a guy's attention, she should pretend not to be able to do something." She giggled. "How silly!"

"But it works." Jonna could see a light at the end of the tunnel, literally.

Bob grunted reluctantly. "He's right. Some males are like that."

"Some," Jonna continued. "There are those who simply like you for what you are. I would suggest you be yourself."

"You mean it?" Crystilic looked around, a mischievous smile on her face.

"Jonna—" Bob caught the expression Jonna could not see. "I don't think that's a very good idea."

Crystilic vanished. A floating mass of brilliant colors floated in her place.

"Oh my!" Bob swallowed. "Jonna!"

Jonna looked over his shoulder, pleasantly surprised. "This is your true form?"

"Yes." Crystilic's words were more like chimes. "Do you like?"

Jonna nodded. "You're beautiful."

"Really?" Her voice was giddy, the chimes raising an octave at the compliment. She moved forward, bathing him in color.

Bob sneezed twice. "I think you're tickling my nose."

"Sorry." Crystilic backed up, allowing him some breathing room. She whispered something in Bob's ear, just low enough that Jonna could not hear. Bob turned red.

Jonna watched her colors change. "Can you be hurt in that form?"

"Yes." Crystilic morphed, once more appearing as a woman. "And no. Once they see me in that state, though they cannot harm me, they know the type of creature I am. They can cast a spell to capture me. That is how I came to be in their service, if you catch what I mean."

"I do." Jonna reached the end of the tunnel and found a grill covering the exit. "Bob, will you do the honors?"

"Certainly." Bob moved forward, dropping a little pixie dust, and said, "Malthasso."

"That's different."

Bob looked around. "What?"

"You spoke a spell to do it this time." Jonna reached down, grabbing one end of the grill, and ripped. The grill, now rubber, detached from the wall.

"I can do magic with spells if I want." Bob stuck his nose in the air.

"I'm sure you can." Jonna laughed. "It's just the first time I've seen you do the same spell in a different way. What does the word mean? Why is it always rubber?"

"Well—" Bob thought. "I think the word means 'to soften,' but the only thing I can think of that's soft is rubber." He shrugged.

"So magic is not so much by the word as by the thought?"

Bob shrugged. "How should I know? I just do what I was taught. The words are a medium, sort of like a mage's staff or pendant." He pointed at Jonna's weapon. "Or a sword. Most mages can only use one form of medium."

"I see."

Bob's brow wrinkled. "Didn't Väinämö teach you that?"

"We've not had much time." Jonna passed the rubber grill to Crystilic, who put it somewhere behind her. "Ready?"

He stuck his head out upside down. They were in the corner of a hallway, and no one else was about. Pulling back, he brought his feet over and dropped through the hole, landing on the hallway floor.

Bob floated down. As Crystilic dropped in behind him, she whispered, "Now what?"

The runic symbols carved into the walls caught his attention. They were just like the ones that guarded Elfleda's cell, and he was no longer

298

cloaked by magic.

"Hide the stone." He handed the Mariah stone to Crystilic. There was no time to reverse the spell on it, and he was afraid it would shine through his pouch. "I think we need to hide." He grabbed her hand. "Unum-Clastor-Fillum."

Security mages ran around the corner, their weapons drawn and ready. They hunted in all directions. The trio dodged, slipping between the armed men, and walked toward the front of the prison. They searched for Almundena's brother's cell.

They found the cell at the top of the stairs, just like Jonna remembered, but it was empty. As they headed down, the clatter of wood caught their attention. Moving to an outer prison door, they spied a rope dancing on a hangman's platform. Thankfully, it was empty.

"Tonight—" Jonna recognized Anos's voice. "All will be accomplished. We will no longer have a need for you."

Jonna and Crystilic slipped through the outer door someone had left ajar. There, by the hangman's noose, was Almundena's brother. They had shackled him to a tall post, leaving him to sweat in the later part of the evening sun. Jonna glanced up at the sky. Had it taken that long to find his way back from the dragon's cave?

Still invisible, they headed toward the prisoner, trying to find a way to free him. Several problems had to be addressed. One, there were four guards posted around him, and not a single direction in which they could escape unseen. Two, there were the shackles. Although Jonna had a good idea what they could do about them. Three, the moment they broke him free, every guard across the field would be alerted. The odds were not in their favor.

Jonna thought about waiting until after dealing with the Dark Mages. At that time, it would be possible to free him at their leisure. However, that assumed his team would be the victor, and things were never as simple as they seemed. A feeling in the pit of his stomach said he had to free him now.

Was it connected to The Sight? Maybe. But he got the idea that, somehow, Almundena's brother would be a key factor to the upcoming battle. So then, how were they to free him and keep the guards off their tails?

Anos checked the hangman's platform, verifying all was in order. Satisfied, he turned away from the prisoner, heading toward the outer gate.

Standing beside the pole to which the shackles were secured, Jonna noted what they used to tie him down. It was some form of rope, wrapped multiple times around the pole, and part of a chain. He traced the end of the securing rope, locating where it tied off with a knot. He wanted to communicate with the prisoner, but if he did, the invisibility would go away.

His hand still holding Crystilic's, he worked his way under the hangman's platform. Stepping into the shadows, they hid behind a series of thin supporting poles.

"Bob," Jonna whispered, causing the invisibility to fade. As it did, their hiding place did not look as good as he thought, though none of the guards had noticed them.

"What are you doing?" Bob looked around. "They can see you!"

"I need you to deliver a message."

Bob listened, not sure if he should agree. "And if something happens, and we don't get there in time?"

"We'll make it," Jonna assured. "As long as everyone plays their part. Are there any questions?"

"And you want me to be a—" Crystilic thought a moment. "A wooden box tall enough for two people to hide in."

Jonna nodded. "I need your texture to match the wood under this platform. Can you do it?"

"Let me see. I normally only emulate things that are in one solid shape."

Crystilic closed her eyes, thinking about the construction. She opened them only briefly to look at the wood grain around her. Her eyes lost focus. Her shape changed, flowing out first one way and then another. She filled up a small corner, creating a door in one side. "Does that look right?"

"Perfect," Jonna congratulated. "Now Bob, remember. No words. Just pixie dust. Got it?"

"Got it." A mischievous smile crossed the pixie's face. "This will be fun!"

"Yeah." Jonna showed enthusiasm for their sake. For the plan to work, they all had to do it right. "Ready?"

Jonna opened the door to Crystilic and stepped in.

"This is cozy." She giggled. "I've never had someone step inside me before."

"Focus, Crystilic. What's going on with Bob? Can you give me two peek holes to see with?"

Two small hollows appeared in the wall, and Jonna looked out at the prisoner. He caught sight of Bob moving toward Almundena's brother. Why wasn't he invisible? At any moment, the guards might see him!

As Bob vanished from sight, Jonna sighed with relief. Now, if he only had a way to hear what was going on. Jonna remembered what Bob told him about magic. It was not so much by word as by thought. The words, pixie dust, etc., were all just mediums used to focus the magic. So, did that mean he could make up a spell of his own?

He thought back to the unusual words he had run across in his history and language studies. If he changed the ending just a bit and tried to give it some flare— "Accruium Emit Ergo." It would not win a Latin contest, but . . .

At first, there was nothing. He thought he did something wrong. But then, Bob's voice formed loud and clear.

Bob whispered above the prisoner's head, "What shall it be? Green beans or rice?"

"What?" The prisoner looked up but saw no one.

What was Bob doing? That wasn't the script!

"Er, sorry. Private pixie joke." Bob grinned. "We've come to help!"

The prisoner looked up but could not see anyone. "Who's *we*?" At least the man seemed saner this time.

"Remember the bathhouse?" Bob waited a moment for the words to sink in.

"Yes," Almundena's brother whispered back.

The guard directly in front of him turned around, snickering. "Praying for mercy, are we?" The guard chuckled. "It won't do any good." He turned back around, still laughing to himself. Jonna exhaled. Thankfully, the guards were not paying close attention.

Bob reached into his pocket, adjusting the amount of pixie dust in his hand. "When I tell you, run under the hangman's platform, got it?"

"The hangman's platform?" The prisoner looked to his left. "That's the last place I want to go."

Bob put more emphasis on the words. "Just run under."

"I'd rather get a weapon from a guard." The prisoner's eyes focused on the nearest one. "I'd really like to take *his* away."

"You would only get a few feet before they caught you," the pixie

301

warned. "It's under the platform or I go away."

It took a moment, but Almundena's brother conceded. "Fine. Tell me when."

Bob tossed the pixie dust up into the air. It sprinkled down on the shackles. "Pull!"

The prisoner jerked, snapping the shackles that had become rubber. He ran through the nearest guard, knocking him aside, and raced to reach the hangman's platform.

"Do you think they'll let us go to the event?" The security mage in front of him turned at the noise. "Stop right there!"

Almundena's brother rammed the next guard in the back, knocking him forward from behind. The guard's weapon went flying, landing under the platform. The prisoner rolled, having lost his balance, regained his feet, and slipped into the shadows.

"Stop!" Three guards rushed in his direction.

The prisoner whispered, "I'm here, now what?" The guards were almost to the platform.

Jonna swung the door to Crystilic open, grabbed the man by the shoulder, and pulled him in. Bob zipped in behind them.

"This isn't going to hold them long."

"It doesn't have to," Jonna said quickly. "Listen, I'm going to cast a spell, and you will suddenly disappear and gain the ability to walk through walls. When you do, I want you to do exactly what I say."

The guards reached the platform. Confused voices reached Jonna's ears.

"What's this?" One of them tapped the outside of the wooden box. "I don't remember this being here." He tapped it again with his weapon.

"That's because it wasn't there." The second guard's eyes narrowed. He walked around the box.

"Jonna," Crystilic whispered, seeing the four walk around her. "However interesting this experiment is, you do realize—"

"I know." Jonna focused on Almundena's brother. "Can you do it?" His gaze stayed on him.

The man nodded. "I'll do as you have asked."

"And you, too, Bob?"

"Of course!"

Jonna sounded doubtful. "Are you sure? Last time—"

"All right, all right!"

"Good."

One of the guards hit the door with his shoulder. Crystilic grunted against the strike. "Ouch."

Jonna made sure the prisoner stood apart, though he did not think it would matter. He focused his mind on Almundena's brother alone and spoke the spell. "Unum-Clastor-Pratima."

A strange sparkle leaped in all directions, fading away into the air. Abruptly, there were two prisoners: one appearing to be frozen, and the other walking around himself.

"Holy Moly." The prisoner stepped back, comparing himself to his statue. He reached out, passing his hand through his own image. "That's amazing."

"It is, isn't it? I felt the same way."

Two guards struck the door at the same time, bulging it in.

Crystilic groaned. "Jonna, please."

Jonna touched the inside of the wooden wall. "It's all right," he reassured. Looking back at Bob and the prisoner, he added, "Remember what I said. Unum-Clastor-Fillum."

The two guards backed up again, put their shoulders together, and slid to a stop. The wooden box had disappeared. Their prisoner stared at a support beam, not paying any attention.

The nearest guard walked up, gawking suspiciously, but was still unwilling to get close. "What's wrong with him?"

Crystilic morphed, still invisible, back into a woman. The touch Jonna made on her wall morphed into a hand. Jonna, holding Crystilic's hand, led her around the guards.

The trio made their way to the prison door. Unfortunately, Jonna's plan held certain unknowns. One, would Almundena's brother truly do as he was asked? And two, while Almundena's brother could pass through things, they could not. Nor could they communicate with him or Bob without becoming visible.

They stepped up to the prison door but found it locked. A security mage stood just inside with a group of keys held at his waist.

Jonna watched, hoping Bob kept to the plan. Pixie dust dropped from nowhere, glittering over the guard's head. Bob swooped down, untied the key loop, and took the keys to the lock. A few keys later, the door clicked open.

CHAPTER 29
EYE OF ALDRICK

Opening the inside door, the three started down the hall. Almundena's brother was waiting, and so far, had not spoken, keeping to the agreement. If all went well, it would just be a matter of timing.

What was the plan? It was not the easiest by any means, and it really depended on things going just right. Bob was their only communicator, and as Jonna noted earlier, he did not always do things according to instructions.

"This way," Bob whispered, turning the corner.

It was strange how Jonna could still see them: Almundena's brother in ethereal form, Bob with pixie invisibility, and Crystilic made invisible by magic. The others he understood, but why could he see Bob now? Did it have something to do with his own cloak of magic? Only Väinämö would know. Perhaps it was because he was the one who had cast the invisibility, and it was similar in nature to Bob's spell. If that was the case, then all a mage had to do to see another mage was become invisible himself.

It was a good theory, but this whole magic thing was a little too new for him. Going into battle against such odds, with people who were untried as a team, with weapons he was not sure how to use, and against people whose capabilities he did not know, really seemed foolish.

But what could he do? Someone had to rescue Elfleda and Stephanie—Jonna pushed the thoughts away.

A part of his brain had hit upon a truth that confused him. Every time he tried to think about it, his brain went to something else. Right now, he could only deal with one thing at a time.

Bob stood waiting. "Jonna, we're here."

Before them was the bridge Jonna had fallen from. As he stared at it, he felt a shiver. The first time he had been in ethereal form. If he fell from it now, he would not be that lucky.

Shifting thoughts, he focused on the other side of the bridge. No guards were stationed outside, but he knew they had to be there. He nodded to Bob, trusting he would improvise correctly.

The pixie moved forward over the bridge. They reached the metal entry doors and paused as Almundena's brother passed through.

Almundena's brother returned and whispered, "There are three security mages on the inside, but they're not really watching. The outer metal doors are held by three wooden bars. A room or so down, there is a lot of activity."

Jonna moved up to the metal doors, studying the thin crack between them. He could see the bars: one in the middle, one below, and one above. Here's where the plan would depend upon everyone following his directions.

He knocked on the door. Noise from the inside told him someone was shifting things. A smaller metal window opened. A security mage looked out. "Who's there?"

Bob slipped in through the open window as Almundena's brother passed through the door. Jonna released Crystilic's hand just out of sight of the guard. She became visible and stepped into view.

"A servant to help with the preparations." She bowed before the guard.

"A servant?" The guard's eyes grew wider than before. "You don't look like a servant."

Crystilic had changed her clothes. They accentuated her figure, catching the guard's eye. She moved closer to the window, touching his fingers lightly. "Then maybe I could make the time less boring?"

The guard looked both ways. Seeing no one else around, he nodded. "Maybe you could. Just a moment."

The small metal window closed. With a slight rumble, the bars slid back. A moment later, the door swung open. Jonna walked in behind Crystilic.

"Boys, we have a visitor."

The guard turned back but saw his two comrades lying across the table asleep. Jonna had to smile. Bob had done his job well with the pixie dust.

"Guess they're busy." The security mage grinned as he turned back to Crystilic, enjoying the view. "Maybe it's for the better."

"Maybe it is." Jonna appeared in front of him. He knocked the weapon from the guard's hand. Grabbing the security mage's arm, Jonna elbowed to the guard's solar plexus, chopped to the throat, and rammed the guard's head against the wall. The guard went unconscious.

Crystilic gave a gracious smile. "Thank you."

"You're welcome."

Jonna checked the unconscious mage's pockets but found no other keys. Then it hit him. He still didn't know what to call Almundena's brother. He turned to him. "Don't you think it's about time we learned your name?"

"I suppose it is." The brother moved closer to them. "I guess the moment never came up before. I'm Aias. Thank you for your timely rescue."

"You are welcome. I'm Jonna." He pointed to the others. "This is Crystilic and Bob."

"Well—" the pixie corrected. "Bob isn't exactly my real name."

Rolling his eyes, Jonna glanced toward the pixie.

Bob grinned. "I know. We need to focus on the mission." He looked back at Aias. "It is a little complicated."

"I'm sure." Aias frowned. "Is this the whole team to rescue the princess? I'm not knocking what you've done, but beyond this area—"

Crystilic whispered to Bob, "I bet I could say your name."

Jonna cleared his throat, bringing the two back on track. "Have you been here before, Aias?" He sat the Rune Blade down inside a small storage room while he searched the guards, removed their weapons, and hid them. Seeing his intent, Bob and Crystilic helped.

"Only once." Aias tried to help too, but his ethereal form made him useless. Frowning at his hands, he asked, "Shouldn't I become solid again?"

"Are you ready to?" Jonna kept watch down the hallway. So far, no one inside the complex had noticed their arrival.

"Maybe not yet." Aias considered. "I might be of better use if I can get more information."

"Good idea. How about you scout ahead, but be cautious. Your time in that form is limited. As a matter of fact—" Jonna thought about how to phrase it. "You've probably half an hourglass left."

"I understand." Aias turned, moving quickly. "I'll be back." He disappeared through a wall.

They finished moving the guards away from the main hall into the smaller storage room. Since he had been able to cast a spell on Aias and himself with Crystilic, he assumed he should be able to do the same to the guards. Was there a limit to the amount of magic a person could draw? Väinämö had implied there was, but for whatever reason, Jonna had not reached that limit. Could it have something to do with his actions in the dragon's cave? Focusing on the three guards, he aligned his thoughts. "Unum-Clastor-Fillum."

The three guards vanished. There was nothing, no ill effects, though this time he could feel the change when the magic activated. That was new.

Crystilic moved to the door and looked out into the hall. "What if they wake up and start walking around invisible?"

Jonna shrugged. "We hope for the best. The moment they speak, they'll become visible, but at least the spell will hide them for the moment."

As they stepped into the hallway, Jonna remembered the Rune Blade lying inside the small storage room. He turned around to get it.

A man standing in a grayish robe and holding a leather-bound book appeared from nowhere and demanded, "What do you think you're doing?"

Jonna and Crystilic froze, slowly turning to face him.

"And where are the guards?"

Jonna thought fast. "They let us in and disappeared."

The man huffed. "Can't find good help anywhere. Come on, both of you." He frowned at Crystilic's clothing. "Child, that's not the way we dress in here. And you—" He glared at Jonna. "Where did you get that ridiculous clothing?"

Grabbing them both by the arms, he shoved them toward a different room. "You must change at once. When the ritual begins, it will be too late." The man pushed them through a door. "Hurry now." He walked off.

Jonna reached for two of the grayish robes. He handed one to Crystilic and kept the other.

Crystilic looked puzzled. "Why didn't he suspect anything?" Checking the robe's fit, she shook her head. "It needs to be taken up right here." She motioned at her waist.

"I think the idea is not to show off the figure." Jonna grinned. "And I'm not sure why he didn't suspect." He adjusted the robe, tying it off. "Unless he feels so safe, the idea never crossed his mind."

They stepped into the hallway, spotted other gray cloaks entering another room, and moved quickly to follow. If nothing else, under this disguise, they could at least look around.

"Hurry, all of you," a gray cloak with a medallion around his neck exclaimed, motioning for them to step it up. "Place the candles and move out quickly. We must be done within the hour."

Jonna and Crystilic watched as each person around them picked up a wrapped stack of wax candles. Doing the same, they followed them out the back of the room, through a thin, winding corridor, and into another smaller room.

Here, each person undid the wrapping, separated the candles, and placed them on the top of tall brass candleholders. The holders were carried to a closed door and left standing beside it.

Jonna stepped toward a window. It was a one-foot slit cut into the wall. Looking through, he could see a large arena below that contained at its center a circular plateau. In the center of the plateau lay a hole filled with darkness that descended out of sight.

The Eye of Aldrick—the name jumped into Jonna's mind. Somehow he knew it would be placed above the hole in the plateau. He glanced up and saw a circular cutout in the ceiling. By looking carefully, he could see the sky.

"Hurry up, we don't have all day." The man with the medallion grabbed Jonna by the robe and shoved him back toward the corridor. Jonna reached the room containing the wrapped candles. He picked up another set.

Aias whispered, "Jonna, we need to talk."

Jonna shifted closer to Aias.

"The princess is here." Aias nodded. "Held in a room off the main arena."

Crystilic came near, as if trying to decide which candle set to pick up.

Jonna frowned. "Is she alone?"

Aias shook his head. "They've more guards there than any place else. And another thing, they plan on killing her as the event begins."

"Then we don't have very much time." Jonna's frown deepened. "My Rune Blade is still in the small storage room by the entry to this building."

"I'll get it," Bob announced, leaving Jonna's shoulder.

"But how are you going to carry—" Jonna stopped. Bob was a pixie, after all. "Never mind."

As the pixie took off out the door, Jonna glanced at his watch. "You're about to change back," he whispered to Aias. "I suggest you go to the robe room. It's the next door down."

"Good thinking." Aias headed out, halting in the doorway. "Which way?"

"There." Jonna placed his bundle of candles down and pointed, watching as Aias took off. Jonna turned around, almost running into the man with the medallion. The man growled in his face, "And what are we doing?"

Jonna kept his voice even. "Helping someone find the robe room."

The man looked out and down the hall but did not see anyone. "I think you're lying. What's your name?"

As other gray robes slowed to watch, the room filled up. Before Jonna could stop, the words popped into his head. "Xun Ove."

"Hmm." The man studied Jonna. "Xun Ove, eh?" The supervisor chuckled. "Been studying up on the prophecy, I see? That is quite a joke. Do not worry. There will be no *Xun Ove* here tonight. The elders have seen to that."

The chatter of voices increased dramatically. The man with the medallion turned around and clapped his hands twice. "Back to work. All of you!"

As Jonna turned away, the man caught his shoulder. "And you better start working. We all like a joke, but there's work to be done." He poked at Jonna multiple times. "Don't slack off again."

"Yes, sir." Jonna reached down, lifting a group of candles.

Crystilic came up beside him, carrying her load, and whispered, "That was the name Gernot gave you. What was that about?"

"I don't know." However, something inside Jonna said he did. For the first time, it confirmed to him he was doing exactly what he should.

They returned to the room with the candlesticks and finished their placement. Aias came behind them, wearing a grayish robe. The three stepped apart from the others.

"I'm ready," he announced as he slipped the Rune Blade from under his cloak and handed it to Jonna. "Bob told me to give you this."

Jonna stashed the sword out of sight. "Why didn't Bob come?"

Aias shook his head. "He just hurried away, following a group of security mages."

"Maybe he's trying to find another route in?" Crystilic suggested.

"Maybe." Jonna was not sure. He did not like it when the pixie vanished, and right now was not the best of times.

The man with the medallion hurried into the room. "All right." He took in all those gathered and pointed at Jonna, Crystilic, and Aias. "You three, over here."

As they stepped into the middle of the line, the man went to the closed door Jonna had seen earlier, released a locking mechanism, and pushed it. A cold breeze came out, flowing around the room and down the hall. The man gave instructions. "One by one, single file. Each of you grab a candleholder and follow Phel." He touched the head of the grayish robe in front. "Place your candleholder on the ground around the plateau. They are all marked. When you are done, follow the others and return to the gallery for seating."

The man pointed at them all. "Do this well. Not many graduates get this honor. Go!" He stepped back and watched as Phel began walking. The others followed.

They descended a series of winding stairs. Every ten feet or so, a door would appear on the inside wall. However, Phel bypassed them all until finally reaching the base. At the bottom, he swung open the final door and marched into the arena.

They headed toward the large plateau in the center of the arena. On the ground floor, a long, circular line of interconnecting tables spread out in a ring. The tables went around the plateau, with chairs spaced every two or three feet. Behind the chairs were markings on the floor. Phel placed his candlestick in the first marking and waited while the others filled in around the circle. When the last one came, they had three extra candlesticks. Without making an issue, Phel led them to the stairway again, went to the first door above ground level, and guided them into the sitting area. All sat except for the last three gray robes. Jonna was glad it had not been them.

"What is the meaning of this?" One of the security mages approached the man with the medallion. "Do you want to draw attention?" He motioned to the three gray robes still standing with their candlesticks.

"It was a slight miscalculation." The man with the medallion nervously instructed the last three to place their candlesticks beside the wall and take a seat.

The security mage growled, "There can be no miscalculation tonight. We've already had disturbing news that a prisoner, Aias by name, has vanished from the prison." The security mage drummed his fingers against his weapon. "As well as other *unusual* happenings."

The man with the medallion turned pale, recognizing the name. "Almundena's brother? The Dark Mage counsel won't like that." He shook his head quickly. "I remember Almundena coming through training. Her grasp of magic was uncanny, which is why she caught the elders' attention. Her brother was taken to keep her under their will." His nervous eyes caught the guard's eyes. "When did this happen?"

"Only a short while ago. One moment they had him shackled, and the next he vanished, leaving the shackles unopened."

"Jonna." Crystilic leaned toward him in a whisper. "Did you hear that?"

Jonna nodded, whispering back, "It probably happened when the spell stopped." He tried to look in the direction of the two mages without appearing obvious.

"I want a check of all the personnel," the security mage continued. "No one comes within yelling distance of this arena until we know they all have the mark, do you understand?"

The man with the medallion jumped. "Right away." As the security mage went down the stairs, the man turned toward the students. He wiped sweat from his forehead and addressed those sitting. "There appears to be a few issues that need to be taken care of. I need all of you to show your identification mark. Phel, check them. Start from the back."

Phel came forward and showed the man his own.

"Very good. Proceed."

Phel moved to the last in the group. One by one, he watched as they revealed their identification mark.

"What's he looking at?" Crystilic noticed that each of the students showed him a spot above their right breastbone.

"A symbol, the shape of a skull," Jonna whispered. "If you don't have the mark, you aren't one of their initiates."

Crystilic looked back, catching sight of another person's mark. Without so much as stirring, she said, "How's that?" Shifting her robe slightly, she showed the tiny skull mark.

"That's good." Jonna nodded, impressed. "Now all I have to do is fix Aias and me."

Phel was still a few rows away, but that did not change the fact that Jonna had no idea what to do. Magic might be able to make the mark appear, if only he knew how. A word! He needed a tool to channel the spell.

He went through a series of Latin words he had learned but could not make up his mind. No wonder mages studied long hours working out magic. It had to be the right combination that brought confidence to the user. So far, Jonna had been lucky that his magic worked at all. Then an idea hit him, and he whispered, "Illudere."

Aias checked his shoulder. "I don't see anything."

"You won't," Jonna whispered back, only slightly nervous. "I put the spell on Phel."

Phel reached their row, checked those to Jonna's left, and worked his way down. He reached Jonna and smiled. "That was a good joke with the name in the room." He chuckled quietly. "I'm surprised you didn't pretend to have the elvish sword, too." A wide grin crossed his face as he nodded. "Okay, show me the mark."

Jonna tensed. It was one thing to know he had done magic, but to be unable to see the results made him nervous. He moved back the grayish robe.

Phel nodded, realized he had forgotten Crystilic, and checked her as well. Aias exhaled after Phel passed him, too.

Once Phel was off their row, Aias leaned toward them. "They know about your sword?"

"I guess so." Jonna shrugged. "I'm in the dark as much as anyone about this. If we could get a copy of that prophecy, it would certainly help."

Bob's voice spoke in his ear. "How about this?"

Jonna looked to his shoulder but could not see the pixie. "Where have you been? I was afraid—"

"Aw, I'm touched." Bob laughed, though he was still invisible. "I overheard a mage talking about that same thing, so I followed him to the library, and—"

Moving from beside Jonna's head, the pixie dropped to hide between Aias and Jonna. A rolled-up scroll appeared as if out of thin air. As Jonna took it, keeping it out of sight of the other gray robes, he noted the edges were old and faded. He opened the scroll. Whatever dialect it was in, he had no idea how to read it.

"And?" Crystilic leaned next to him. "What does it say?"

"Bob, can you read this?"

Bob returned to his perch on Jonna's shoulder but shook his head. "It looks gnomish. It also could be something else."

"Let me see." Crystilic turned Jonna's hand a little. "Not gnomish. I've seen gnomish. I don't think this is a language."

Aias leaned toward them. "Let me see."

Jonna carefully passed Aias the scroll, watching for others who might be listening. "Maybe elvish?" He handed the scroll back.

Ever since Jonna had his first encounter with Sir Verity and came to this land, he had been able to understand, speak, and read any language he had seen. He did not understand why, though subconsciously he *knew* the difference from one to another. This was the first item he could not read.

"Not elvish." For some reason Jonna knew that. He scanned down the lines of text, recognizing the name Xun Ove, although it was not spelled exactly right. "It is a language, you can see the patterns, but it must be some unique form—" The Sight suddenly hit him, and he realized something more. "It's not of this world."

A cold feeling settled into his bones, and Jonna knew exactly from where it came. It was from his world, and this implied something even darker. Could the first dark mage have come from his reality?

Suddenly, the layout of the Well of Tears made even more sense. There was no way he could explain all this to those around him. He rolled up the scroll quickly, and then said as a cover, "Either that, or it's encrypted."

"Encrypted?" Bob looked at him. "What does that mean?"

"Secret. Hidden." Jonna tried to think of a word that might describe it while knowing he was hiding the truth. "How about scrambled?"

"An unscrambling spell might work then. Hmm." Bob thought. "Let me think about it."

Jonna handed the scroll to Bob. "Keep this safe."

Bob did the little stomping spell. Jonna grimaced. The scroll vanished.

Someone in front of them pointed toward the arena. "What's going on down there?"

Mages in grayish robes, all wearing golden skull medallions, moved from several different entry points onto the arena floor. They approached the candles. In one voice they spoke a single word. "Ziyo!"

As they seated themselves cross-legged on the floor, the candles burst into flame, glowing around the plateau. Security mages entered the arena, rolling a large wheeled platform. They positioned it equidistant between the arena wall and the plateau.

When they stopped, a ramp was set up to access the top of the wheeled platform. A chopping block was carried to the top of the platform and placed in the center. As the security mages left, the mages around the center chanted.

A greenish haze rose over the floor, drifting up just short of the seats where Jonna and the others sat. Two mages carrying golden horns stepped onto the auditorium floor directly opposite each other.

"Up, everyone." The man with the medallion came back, prompting them to stand.

The golden horns played. The music was sorrowful, creating magical scenes in the greenish glow. It told of a time when dark mages did not exist. Chaos held their land. It swept through the creation of the first dark mage magic, building in tempo, moving faster and faster, and then stopped.

Silence dropped over the entire assembly. Slowly, new notes played from the horns. From the arena entrances came dark-clothed mages. Their black capes stood out against the greenish light. They moved past the grayish-robed figures, each taking a chair and sitting down.

The horns stopped again. In the silence walked a single black-robed figure. The golden thread used to stitch the robe together glistened in the light. A golden skull had been embroidered on the back of the robe. The black-robed man reached the plateau, moved up the single set of stairs, and stood before a small podium.

"The Aatto of Ptah is upon us," the dark robe's voice boomed, echoing around the arena. "It is time to renew our power and our strength. But more than that, the celebration tonight will be of a special importance. For the first time in our history, the ancient prophecy will be fulfilled!"

Two large doors that led into the arena burst open. In walked a troop of security mages. In the center of the group, Princess Elfleda walked sluggishly, her elven sparkles far more diminished than they had been before. The light around her pushed back against the green glow, defiant, even as it waned against the Dark Mages' might.

CHAPTER 30
AATTO OF PTAH

The mage on the plateau boomed, "See our enemy? Tonight, we shall conquer all!"

A roar went up from the stands as the new graduates jumped to their feet. Even those circling the plateau stood up. Jonna, Crystilic, and Aias followed suit, trying not to look suspicious.

The mage on the plateau boomed again, "Let us bring forth the Eye of Aldrick!"

A hum came from the dark-capped mages. The grayish-robed figures on the floor joined in. The green mist in the air sparkled with bursts of light. A vortex of spinning, pulsing light centered over the hole in the plateau.

Wind shot up in all directions, whipping hair and fluttering robes. As they watched, a huge green gemstone rose from the hole's depths. Rising up above the plateau, it spun in the air, its revolution slowing over time. As the last gleams of sunlight struck its surface from above, Jonna knew the stars shined.

The Rune Blade beneath Jonna's robes hummed. He could feel it against his body. As long as the Dark Mages chanted, the humming could not be heard, but if they stopped—suddenly, the room went silent.

At first, no one paid attention, caught up in the excitement. But then, the hum became obvious. A few of those dressed in grayish robes glanced back in different directions. Jonna and the others did the same. He needed a spell, something that would cover the sound at least for the moment. The man with the medallion, sitting with the graduates, rose to his feet and searched.

In desperation, Jonna remembered the spell he had made up to hear what Bob was saying and whispered, "Ne Accruium Emit Ergo."

The humming stopped. Frowning, the man with the medallion went back to his seat. Had everyone heard the noise? If so, they seemed to have forgotten it now.

The mages around the plateau chanted again. The Eye of Aldrick glowed, casting a brighter light around the room. It washed all gray to green, black to dark green, and pushed away the shadows as the light bounced in all directions.

Elfleda's brightness fought against it, but it too began to dim. The green light of the Dark Mages shoved in upon her, trying to smother the elven magic.

She raised her head and stared in Jonna's direction, as if she knew he was there. Their eyes locked, and then all at once, she collapsed.

The mages unshackled her unconscious body, picked her up, and placed her on the platform, positioning her head on the chopping block altar. They then turned and left the arena.

It was now or never, but what could Jonna do from this far away? He could feel the excitement all around him. He knew they waited to watch Elfleda die.

The chanting rose in volume. The panic in his chest grew more intense. If she died, so did any hope of finding his wife.

Grabbing Crystilic's and Aias's hands, he whispered, "Now's the time. Unum-Clastor-Pratima."

Jonna tensed, focusing on the group. The power ripped through him. Had he waited long enough since last using the spell? His body shook. He was unable to stand.

Crystilic, on her feet, gazed at herself in the ethereal. "Wow," she whispered. "So that's what I look like?" Her eyes opened wide as she noticed Jonna. "Are you all right?" She helped him rise, but the sickness in his body did not get better.

"I—I don't know." He struggled toward the door, passing through everything: people, seats, and walls. Finally, he stopped on the stairway and glanced around to see who was still with him. When he turned to locate Bob, the pixie was in ethereal form also. "You too?"

"Apparently so." Bob chuckled. "I don't know what you did, but—"

Jonna swallowed. "I don't either."

A stab of pain struck, starting at his stomach and moving toward his chest. He gasped out, "It seems we can interact with each other since we are all in the same spell."

Jonna fell forward, released their hands, and tumbled down to the next level. The warning Väinämö had given him, the warning that spells have singular and plural forms, came rolling through his mind. Not only had he included another human with himself, but also a hemming and a pixie. On top of that, he still was not sure the proper rest period had elapsed.

Aias, Crystilic, and Bob rushed down the stairs. They helped him to his feet. Crystilic looked him in the eyes and frowned. "You don't look very well. I think you better cancel the spell."

"I can't," Jonna barely got out. "If I do, you'll all be discovered."

A roar of dismay went up inside the arena. Security mages hurried down the stairs. With Crystilic on one side and Aias on the other, they helped Jonna reach the bottom floor.

The stabbing pain eased. Perhaps it was a fluke. He held up his hand. "I'm good, I think."

He stood up straighter and smiled. With a single nod toward the door in front, they all passed through.

Security mages hurried in from all points of the arena. Patrols watched nervously at the exits. A guard stepped out from behind them and addressed another. "What's going on?"

"The crystal's changing," the other said in awe.

Jonna looked up. The Eye of Aldrick had changed color.

The dark mage beside it roared in anger. He spun toward the arena and demanded, glaring at the crowd, "Who dares to use other magic during the Aatto of Ptah?" His eyes narrowed on Elfleda. "Kill her. Kill her now!"

"NO!" Jonna tried to run, but his strength was not there. He dropped to his knees, unable to get up. In desperation, he looked around, trying to find something, anything that might help.

Security mages climbed up on the platform and held her still. One of them raised a large bladed axe.

"NO!" Jonna could not let this happen. She was the only link to his wife. He reached a hand forward. "Unum-Clastor-Pratima!"

The world spun. He found himself falling sideways. In slow motion, he hit the ground, still staring at the platform.

Up and down no longer mattered. His vision blurred. Sounds came from everywhere and nowhere. They created a volume of pure noise.

"Jonna!"

It sounded like Crystilic, but he could not be sure. The pain in his body rippled through him. Strange images floated into his mind, and he wondered if this was what a battery felt like when it was about to die.

"Battery." He heard himself chuckle. "Batteries aren't alive."

Väinämö's familiar face appeared. "And you won't be for much longer." As the rest of the mage's body faded into view, he frowned at Jonna. "Why do they never listen?"

"Väinämö," Jonna croaked out, feeling pain but struggling to push it back. "What's happening to me?"

Väinämö sighed, shaking his head. "My boy, you can't go around violating the very principles of magic and expect it all to work. Look at you! Why do you think it takes years to become a mage?" He stressed the next words by tapping his staff on the ground. "To keep things like this from happening."

Jonna could not see anything short of Väinämö. That scared him. "Is—is Elfleda safe?"

Väinämö looked somewhere over Jonna's head and walked around him. "You seem to have succeeded. She has attained an ethereal form." He looked at Jonna seriously. "For the moment."

"For the moment?" Panic filled Jonna. He felt numb as the pain was shoved away from his body. "Have I failed?"

"If you don't destroy that gem the second before Aatto of Ptah begins, all this effort will be for naught."

Jonna could feel sweat running down his forehead. Did that mean it was too late? "But I couldn't let her die," he gasped between stabs of agony.

"No," Väinämö said thoughtfully. "I guess you couldn't. Although—" He shook his head. "No, you'll have to deal with that later."

"What are you talking about?"

"I've got to go. Do you remember the last spell I taught you?"

Jonna nodded, using the motion to distract himself from his nerve endings that felt on fire.

"The second before you strike that gem, speak those magic words. Do you understand?" Väinämö reached down and raised Jonna's head. He looked him in the eye, making sure he could still comprehend.

Jonna groaned and nodded again.

"Good. Now, I'm going to let you go. Please, don't do anything else stupid."

"But—" The pain came back worse than before as Väinämö faded from view. The spinning world slowed to a slight twist. He could see the security mage with the axe standing on top of the large platform, towering over Elfleda's body. The dark mage's blade dropped down.

Rage went through Jonna. He received strength from a source he had never felt before. With all the pain now gone, he stood and screamed, "Awiti Barbaros!"

Lightning leaped out, knocking the security mage off the platform. The mage's body spun and then slammed into the wall. Yet it did not stop there. Jonna's anger lashed out. Even if Elfleda was in ethereal form, they had no right to touch her.

"Awiti Barbaros!" he called forth again, lashing out at the others gathered around the platform.

Multiple strikes tore through the air. Mages screamed and died. The green mist that had been so dominant before changed into a deeper red.

The leader on the plateau boomed, "Who is the dark mage who fights against us? Who is the one who betrays his own people?"

Jonna closed his eyes and thought, *Dark mage?* The leader's words tried to seep through his anger. *No!* The anger gave him the strength to go on. He had to hold on!

Elfleda's soft, musical voice came from somewhere behind him. "Jonna."

He turned around, kneeling before her. "Elf—Elfleda, you're all right?"

She nodded, but her eyes held sorrow. "You cannot fight them with their own power. You will only strengthen what you seek to destroy."

Jonna stammered, shaking his head, "I—I'm not. Magic is neither good nor evil—"

Elfleda nodded as his words fell off. "You are correct, Jonna McCambel. It is the person who makes it either good or evil. It is the source they draw upon. It is the reason they do the things they do. If we use magic based upon fear, anger, or revenge—" She lifted his chin up to catch his eyes. "We further the dark mage and his devices. If we use magic based upon hope, gentleness, and beauty, we bring blessings to the world at large. Do not allow this evil to win. If you destroy the stone using dark mage magic, you will cast a greater shadow upon the world." She paused. "And upon your own heart."

The anger waited for Jonna's decision. The strength it gave promised more of the same. But she was right. He could feel that in his heart.

Jonna let it go. As he did, the red tint that tried to take the room resumed its normal green. The peaceful calm he so often felt came rolling back—and with it the pain. Jonna collapsed into a ball, bordering unconsciousness.

Elfleda knelt down beside him. "Be of good cheer, my hero. All is not lost. Garbi Dorium."

At her touch, the pain ebbed away. Jonna gulped down air into a body that could breathe.

"Now." Her eyes jumped with excitement. "Create for me a spell of light."

Jonna stood up slowly. Though his body still ached, his strength had returned. With narrowed eyes, he knew just what to say.

"Hove," he spoke, looking in the direction of Elfleda's double.

A bluish glowing dome dropped over the platform. The security mages moved back in terror, and Jonna laughed. He was sure they had never seen that before.

The word was from an ancient text he remembered reading in college. It meant *shield*, or something similar, and was perfect for the task.

"That really wasn't necessary." Elfleda fought off a smile and forced on a stern look. "I'm here. Remember?"

"I know." He couldn't help the grin. "But I feel better about it. Aias and Crystilic, are you ready?"

Both moved up beside him.

"And me, too." Bob appeared on his shoulder. "Good to have you back!"

"Good to be back." He took a deep breath, happy to breathe without the feeling of needles stabbing his lungs. He looked at his watch. "We still have time to kill, and the mage—"

"His name is Cassus," Bob chipped in.

"—Cassus," Jonna added, "to defeat. It's too late to play the waiting game. I'm sure, even now, they are trying to figure out what is going on."

Security mages rushed toward the bluish shield, trying to find a way to get in. The blue dome stood as a beacon against the dark green magic. As confused voices rose, panic ensued around the arena.

Jonna stepped forward. "I want all of you to guard Elfleda." He looked up at Cassus. "I have to destroy the Eye of Aldrick."

Jonna wrestled with the robe, finally tossing it from himself. He held the Rune Blade out in front, his right hand finding the twigs in his pocket. His watch showed less than five minutes before the ethereal spell would stop. Jonna ran.

Pressing quickly around the plateau, it took him a moment to find the stairs. Once at the top, he passed unseen through the layer of guards, stopping near the podium.

Väinämö had said the gem could not be destroyed until the second before the eve was upon them. That meant they simply had to defeat their enemy and wait out the time. Right? He laughed. For such a difficult task, they were such simple words.

The watch hand seconds counted down. Five, four, three, two— Five feet behind the dark mage, Jonna spoke. "Cassus." From the corner of Jonna's eye, he saw the first of the guards catch sight of Crystilic, Aias, and Elfleda.

Cassus turned, watching as Jonna faded into view. The ethereal spell had passed. The dark mage spoke with an expectant smile. "The infamous Jonna. I wondered who was causing all the trouble with the gem."

"And now, you know."

Colors flashed in the greenish air as Elfleda's group defended and attacked.

"Indeed." Cassus looked at the Rune Blade in Jonna's hand. "So the rumors were true. You did retrieve the Rune Blade."

Jonna gave a single nod. "And I'm going to use it to destroy your gem."

"We shall see." The dark mage placed his staff in front of him. "How does the mighty Jonna deal with this? Janus Govadium."

The air around Jonna swirled. Small puffs of air exploded on every side. He was heaved upward, rising above the top of the gem and staring at the battle going on below.

Elfleda, Crystilic, and Aias had their hands full fending off those who attacked from every side. Streaks of magic launched in their direction. Elfleda's flashes deflected the blows, turning them back upon their senders. Explosions of light dazzled the eyes, creating multicolored effects throughout the arena.

Jonna stopped moving up, the winds that held him suddenly gone, and he fell. He commanded, "Ne Atalante." Remembering the spell Bob used, he hoped it would counter whatever the dark mage had done.

His downward movement slowed, and he floated just a foot or so off the floor. A final time he said, "Atalante." A moment later, he touched.

"Impressive," Cassus mocked. "Maybe you're not a warrior at all, but a wizard in disguise. Phero Orphne."

323

Black wisps of smoke crept over the edge of the pit beneath the gem. They reached out, surrounded, and grabbed hold of Jonna's feet. Like vines growing around two posts, they bound his legs together. Jonna slashed with the sword, but the brief cuts he created simply merged back as one.

"You see," Cassus taunted, gloating, "as a dark mage, I have not yet reached the end of my spell knowledge. Have you?"

The dark mage laughed, watching Jonna struggle. As slithery as snakes, the black wisps worked their way up, securing his left arm first and heading toward his right. Like the white fingers that pulled him down the stream, there seemed no way to shake them.

Think, Jonna, think! Since the Rune Blade passed right through them, force could not be used. Like the vortex he had turned to a portal, the wisps had to be turned into something he could fight.

Jonna remembered two words from college. He altered their endings, as The Sight seemed to suggest, and slammed the two into one phrase. Roughly translated, the phrase meant, *to become solid.* If his ability to do magic was based more upon thought than the actual words— He crossed his fingers and said, "Hawhy Ethan."

The wisps of black smoke froze, taking on volume and mass. As he moved his arms and stepped forward, the vine-like wisps snapped apart.

Cassus stepped back. "I've—I've never heard of such a spell. Only the first dark mage could—"

Fear grew upon the dark mage's face. He glanced toward the battle taking place below, but his eyes came back to the Rune Blade held in Jonna's right hand. Cassus's eyes narrowed. A slight growl issued from his throat.

Jonna advanced, pointing the Rune Blade in his direction. "Do you yield?"

"Yield?" The mage laughed. "I am the greatest of all living dark mages." He stressed the next words one by one. "I—do—not—yield. Heng Awiti Barbaros!"

Lightning leaped from the top of Cassus's staff. It snapped like a whip at Jonna. The Rune Blade slashed with a mind of its own, battling the magic as it sought to find its target. Strike and counterstrike, blow for blow, the two magical forces leaped this way and that.

The strain took a toll on Cassus. His face turned red and sweat trickled down his brow. Cassus put both hands on his staff, forcing the magic to continue, increasing the speed of the strikes.

Jonna's eyes were wide open. He seemed more like a guest than a driver. The Rune Blade responded to Cassus's spell with increasing speed. He almost fancied he could let go and watch, but he did not want to take the chance.

A battle cry came from behind. Several security mages rushed toward the plateau. It was hard for Jonna to think about anything else as his sword fended off Cassus's magic.

Unable to turn around, he reached into his right pouch and touched Snovipa's twigs. *I wonder,* he thought, as he remembered the word he used to protect Elfleda's body. Without further hesitation, he said, "Hove."

A blue glow engulfed both him and Cassus, cutting off the advancing troop. The muffled shouts of angry mages sounded outside the dome.

Cassus's eyes darted nervously as his hands started to twitch. Was Cassus experiencing overextended magic? Jonna repeated again, "Do you yield?"

With his own arm beginning to ache, he, too, looked for an end to this contest, but it did not seem to matter. The Rune Blade never slowed from catching every strike.

Hatred burned in Cassus's eyes. Jonna could tell the man's breaths were becoming more labored. In a final push, Cassus thrust the staff at Jonna, and a surge of power leaped out. There were no more tricks, no more delays, no more testing back and forth. Cassus made a last-ditch effort to end Jonna's life.

The Rune Blade sliced forward, dividing the energy into two separate strands. The energy crackled in rebuke, showering explosions as both strands touched the shield. But unlike Cassus's earlier attacks, these strands did not disintegrate. Instead, like two conscious beings, they rebounded, turned, and came at Jonna from behind.

Cassus cackled, watching Jonna squirm. "What think ye now, oh Jonna, almighty?"

Jonna shifted to the right, the Rune Blade slicing into one of the strands. It was a clean cut and should have stopped it cold, but it did not. Each time Jonna struck one strand, the strand turned into two.

They were alive, and Jonna knew it. Somehow, Cassus had designed heat-seeking magic that actually fed off the energy of his Rune Blade. If the strands were anything like the missiles of his time, they would not stop until they found a legitimate goal.

The strands circled, turned, and twisted to catch him. Each time they did, they came a little closer, and the Eye of Aldrick glowed brighter. Pulsing faster, it pushed against his blue protective shield.

The whole room was bathed in greenish light. The mist shone. The guards pounded on the dome.

Jonna leaped, lost his footing, and rolled, coming back to his feet. Since his options of dodging had dropped to nil, he backed up quickly.

Two attacking strands missed as he split a third. With the blue shield behind him and the Rune Blade in front, there was no place else to run.

But what could he do? To strike the strands made them stronger. Dodging had lost its charm. To fight them—he stopped and then noted the dark mage's movement. Cassus carefully made sure that Jonna was the closest to any one strand.

It was his opponent's actions that revealed the answer. Jonna stood perfectly still. He watched as the strands sensed his location, turned toward him, and homed in. The energy crackled in anticipation. Its target had chosen to stop. If the magic could have smiled at him, it would have gloated all the way.

Reaching into his pocket, Jonna wrapped his fingers around the twigs. It was risky to wait until the last moment, but anything else, and Cassus would suspect. As the strands got close, Jonna met Cassus's eye and grinned. Jonna passed backwards through the shield.

The energy strands hit, but not their intended target. With Jonna on the outside, Cassus was the only one left within. The strands pounded against the inside wall. The waves of energy shot back, homing in on the nearest warm body. They headed straight toward Cassus.

"NO," Cassus screamed only seconds before his coming doom. He glared at Jonna and started to speak, but before he could, the strands hit.

He let out a horrible wail as flames erupted around him. Everyone stopped, attacker and defender, as his cry cut through the arena.

A hush fell. Security mages on every level stepped back, watching as Cassus died within the blue shield. The dark mage leader gave a last flicker and was gone.

Running toward the exits, grayish-robed figures around the plateau bolted to escape. Those in black robes stopped their attack. Shocked filled their faces. The graduates in the stands hid in fear.

Jonna's voice echoed through the chamber. "Ne Hove." It cut into the hearts of those who dared to stand their ground.

The blue shield vanished. Security mages fell back. Jonna looked at his watch. It was almost time. He moved to the spot where Cassus had stood before the Eye of Aldrick, raised the Rune Blade above his head, and waited for the final second.

A soft voice from his right whispered, "No, Jonna."

He turned, lowering the sword, and watched a black-hooded mage come toward him. Even before the hood dropped back, he knew who spoke. Almundena.

"If you do this, you'll kill us all."

Jonna's eyes narrowed. He started to lift the sword again.

"Jonna," she pleaded. "You'll kill me."

He froze. Part of him knew this was a psychological game. The Dark Mages wanted their power to continue, and without the Eye of Aldrick, their reign would be over. And yet those words, spoken from a person whom he did not want to hurt, cut deeper than a knife. She knew that, she knew him, and she was playing it for all its worth.

Touched by the dark magic. Elfleda's words echoed through his mind. Almundena had been touched as well, and even more, there was a bond between him and her that reached the point of lovers. *No,* he denied what he felt inside. *Not lovers,* though the feelings were still there. It was a spell brought on by dark mage magic designed to twist him from his goal.

She could not have known. She would never have done that to him. Almundena was . . . There were footsteps running up the plateau, and Aias called out, "Almundena?"

Almundena turned, her face a mask without recognition. "Who are you?"

"I am Aias," he said in wonder. "Your brother. What have they done to you?"

There was no emotion in Almundena's voice. "I have no brother. He died a long time ago."

"No." He came forward, moving near her. "You are not one of them. You are my sister, Almundena. Jonna has come to set you free."

"Stop." She extended a hand toward both Jonna and Aias. "Stop, or I shall kill you both."

Aias's intervention had given Jonna time. Jonna drew back her attention. "You cannot hurt me, Almundena, nor could I ever see you hurt. No matter what they've done, no matter how they've tricked you, you know that truth within your heart."

"No," she snapped toward Jonna with eyes that were not her own. They were wild, like that of a cornered cat, as her fingers curved in claws.

Jonna raised the Rune Blade, though he knew he could not use it. The feelings he shoved away stabbed back, damning his soul. The Rune Blade lowered to the ground slowly. If she attacked, he would not defend.

Aias pleaded, "Almundena, listen to him!"

"Stay away," she warned in a crackling voice. Moving her hands in a system of symbols, she shouted, "I call upon the power of the gem, for by its might the Dark Mage wins. Though you would try to stop me now, you'll fail as those who always cower." Eyes flaring, filled with a green light, Almundena pointed at Jonna. "Rid me of this infidel!"

"NO!" Aias leaped forward toward Almundena. Almundena spun as the green light left her body. It struck her brother, tossing him like a rag doll across the plateau.

Jonna dropped his stance and rushed to Aias's side. Checking his pulse, Jonna relaxed. He was still alive. As Jonna looked at Almundena, his emotions tore in two directions.

CHAPTER 31
A DUBIOUS RESCUE

Jonna stood up slowly and walked toward his friend.

"I trust you, Almundena. I told you that before. What have they done to you?"

"Stay back," she hissed, green flames still in her eyes. "Or your fate will be the same!"

Jonna shook his head. "I don't think so."

He moved closer, studying her. Her eyes were terrified. Her hands trembled. Whatever type of spell had taken hold, she was trying to break free. Jonna laid the Rune Blade on the floor, stood back up, and reached out, taking her by the shoulders.

"Almundena, look at me."

"No." She turned away, looking toward the arena. Her eyes were wide open.

His voice softened, but he demanded, "Look at me. Fight it. Don't let them win."

"No!"

Her head snapped the other way, and she gazed at the Eye of Aldrick. Its pulsing slowed, and the green mist lessened, but the brightness was still there.

Jonna moved his hands to touch her face. Clammy, damp skin met his fingertips, but he could feel the power of the Eye of Aldrick coursing through her veins.

It called to him, promising power beyond his wildest dreams. Yet, it was more than that. He remembered the anger he had felt. He remembered seeing the Eye turn from green to red. If he were to touch it, if he partook, the dark mage cult would be the least of this world's problems. With a firm but gentle hand, he turned Almundena's head to face him.

"Look at me," he whispered. "And remember."

Her glowing green eyes met his. "Join me, Jonna, and the world will be our throne."

From the depths of her eyes, he sensed her soul. His breathing stopped as he felt the consuming passion that joining her would bring.

Closing his eyes, he clung to the only thought that saved him. Stephanie. He had to save his wife.

Jonna whispered, "This is not my world."

Almundena's hands suddenly found his throat. Green wisps coiled from them. With incredible strength, she squeezed.

"I told you not to come near. I warned you not to save me." But the voice pleaded. Behind the green, behind the taint of the Eye of Aldrick, Almundena longed to be free. Feeling her fingers squeezing tighter, he knew that she could fight it.

"Almundena." He pulled her closer despite the pressure on his throat. As he stared into her eyes, their foreheads touched. "Do you really want me to die?"

"No," she whispered weakly, although her grip did not lessen. "Kill me, please. Kill me now." Abruptly, she released her grip, taking his hands and putting his fingers around her own throat. "I can't get them out of my head," she pleaded. "I don't want to do these things!"

"I know you don't," Jonna reassured. He could feel the battle within her. "I know the person you are. You are not this person."

Almundena gasped as sweat beaded on her forehead. Her chest heaved, and her heart beat frantically.

Jonna took her hands, torn by the battle she could only face alone. She was one on one with the dark mage magic as it battled to keep control. Her body shook.

"Listen to me." He tried to give her focus. "Listen to my voice."

There had to be more. He needed a thought, a word, anything that might help her. It was as if she suffered under hypnosis, forced to remember what she did not want to know. In his world, under that circumstance, the hypnotist would have woken her up.

"Daw," he said, remembering the ancient word from a study he did at the university. It simply meant "awaken," but when combined with magic it would be good enough.

Something stirred behind her eyes, and the green glow faded out. As if coming from a nightmare, she collapsed against him, gulping in gasps of air.

"It was killing me," she sobbed. "They refused to let me go. There was a child. And when you told me to leave . . ."

It all came bubbling out in no coherent order. Jonna held her, knowing the time was ticking away. Aatto of Ptah was just around the corner. Yet, it did not matter. He had to help his friend.

Her memory came flooding back. Emotions rippled across her features. She pulled away from his grasp, although she refused to release one hand.

She blinked as she held his gaze. He could see her remembering all she had done. In fear, her eyes went wide open. "Aias!"

She let go of Jonna and hurried to her brother. Kneeling down, she searched his body for life. "What have I done?" Almundena looked up at the sky, agony shaking her body.

"He's alive," Jonna assured her. "You didn't kill him."

Almundena leaned over and listened, placing a hand on her brother's chest. Now, she could hear the shallow breathing. His lungs expanded slowly but true.

"You never gave up," she whispered to her brother, tears coming to her eyes.

"No, he didn't," Jonna said quietly, noting her burning determination. Whatever happened, she would make this right. If the spell that had controlled Almundena remained even the tiniest bit, she could certainly fight it now.

The sound of sliding metal caught Jonna's ears. He turned around and saw the shiny Rune Blade of Knowledge held by another. The security guard holding the blade spat the words, "Missing something, Xun Ove?"

It was clear to Jonna the man knew the prophecy. This dark mage just did not believe it. Jonna gave him points there. He could not believe it, either.

The guard tossed the sword behind him, allowing another to pick it up. He spun his spear like a well-tuned instrument. "I've a spear and you have nothing. Are you willing to take the chance?"

Jonna glanced at his watch. There was barely any time left.

"Your leader is gone." Jonna did not smile. "And your order is destroyed. What do you have to gain now?"

The man bared his teeth. "The satisfaction of knowing you'll have joined him."

The guard leaped forward. He struck, spun, and thrust with the spear.

Jonna leaped from the leg strike, dodged the spin, and pinned the thrust with an inward block-catch. The spear no sooner stopped than he followed through with a back-knuckle and jab to the throat. The guard fell backwards, red-faced and gagging. Throat barely working, he croaked, "Throw it!"

The guard behind him tossed the Rune Blade high. It arced toward the hole in the plateau.

"No!" Jonna leaped, though he knew he was too far away. He watched the blade bounce off the side of the gem and then fall toward the edge of the hole.

He scrambled toward it, bulling through the man who had thrown it, stepping on fingers as he fought to grab the handle. The Rune Blade dropped, falling into the darkness. Without a second thought, he leaped in behind it.

"Jonna!"

He could hear Almundena's voice somewhere above him, but the darkness took over the light. Unable to see the sides of the hole, he felt like he was dropping in slow motion, although he knew he fell much too fast.

Jonna reached out. His fingers barely touched the pommel. They inched up the handle that threatened to slip away from his grasp.

One, two, three fingers encircled the grip, drawing it closer. His second hand grabbed on tight. The sword conformed to his grasp and cast light in all directions, a flame in the pit of doom.

How he had caught it, he did not know. Clinging to it with both hands, he flipped his body over.

The Eye of Aldrick shrank away from him. He had to do something quick or the power of the Dark Mage might never be broken.

Yet, what could he do? What could he say? Väinämö's last spell flowed into his mind. "Menes Olwen Milburga!" He threw the Rune Blade upward with all his might, but he knew it would not be enough.

Two words from his past popped into his mind. Their meaning was simple, but they might just do the trick. As a final note, he added, "Hermes Alkaios! Speed mighty!"

A surge of power hit him. His entire being focused on destroying the Eye. Though it was dark, light leaped from all directions, coming toward him in a vortex of color.

The light shot up, illuminating the darkness, draining every drop of his strength. As the magic hit the Rune Blade's handle, he felt a quiver at its touch.

Crystals of various colors embedded the walls, and Jonna knew where the magic had come from. He was a tool, a lightning rod, and he had just been struck.

The Rune Blade glowed ever brighter, as if his hand still held it. With a sudden thrust, the blade shot up, arcing toward its target.

As the edge of the Rune Blade found its mark, the Eye of Aldrick trembled. Green became red, red became blue, blue became yellow, and yellow became white. As the white cleared, the gem became transparent and fell.

Moonlight washed down through the hole. It struck the Eye as it tumbled. The Eye pinged, cracked on every side, and then, all at once, it shattered.

Jonna could hardly move, rotating slowly as he fell. It was just as well that he could not watch, for at any moment, the broken shards would hit, slicing through his body.

Whatever he had done zapped every bit of his strength. Even endeavoring to think of words took more effort than he had.

He continued to drop, though how far he could not tell. His eyes tried to close in sleep. His head could no longer formulate thoughts. He found himself staring into darkness.

Somehow, he rotated over again and saw a dazzling light dropping from the hole above. It bathed the darkness in rainbow colors, lighting the crystals and warming his skin. Was this the magic of the earth returning? It was beautiful.

Jonna rotated one more time, and the ground came up to hit him.

CHAPTER 32
WAKING THE DEAD

If not for the thumping, he would have slept forever.

Jonna squinted, trying to open his eyes. One of them was sealed shut. The other would only open halfway.

"Awake, are we?" Dagurunn's voice was very deep, more of a roaring than a voice at all. The dragon stopped tapping its foot.

Jonna fought to get one eye completely open. He tried to move an arm, but it did not want to respond. He croaked, "W—what happened?"

Surprised at the sound of his own voice, he tried to breathe deeply. Something was not right with his lungs. He could not seem to get enough air. A puff of flame hit somewhere beside him, and Jonna could hear the crackle of a fire.

"You kept your end of the bargain, human," Dagurunn said. "The magic has returned to the earth. I am impressed."

"If I kept my end of the bargain—" Jonna tried to clear his throat, but it did not work very well. "What's going on with me?"

"Oh, that." The dragon chuckled. "You had a slight—mishap?" The dragon studied him closer. "Nothing too serious, I think."

"Too serious?" Jonna tried to roll over but could not budge. After several tries, he was able to get his left hand to function. Small crystal shards lay on top of him and on the floor. "Why can't I get up?"

"I've been trying to fix that." The dragon sighed. "But I'm afraid I'm not too good at fixing humans. I normally eat them." He snickered, giving a big, toothy smile. "*Inside* joke, you know."

"I—I see." Jonna coughed. There was a funny metallic taste in his mouth, and his legs felt cold. "Uh—" He coughed again. "Dagurunn, I think I'm dying."

"Really?" Dagurunn looked closer. "You might be right."

The dragon pushed down on Jonna's back with one claw. Other than noticing the bounce of his body, Jonna felt nothing at all.

"That might explain it." The dragon nodded. "I think a few crystals cut through your spine."

Jonna's eyes went wide. He coughed again. "That would explain no pain."

The dragon nodded sadly. "I've had to do that to a few victims. It kept them from screaming." He looked down at Jonna. "What would you like me to do?"

"Call for help," Jonna suggested. "Soon."

"I take it that dying is not in the plan?"

Jonna groaned. "I hadn't scheduled it in." A very cold feeling crept up his body. "But—" He took a shallow breath. "I'm not so sure I have a choice."

"We all have choices." The dragon raised an eyelid. "Do you want to lie there and die or do you want to get up?"

Jonna tried to move but could not. "Does it look like I have a choice?"

"No." The dragon turned his head, studying him with one eye. "But then again, you're not just a human, are you?" The dragon puffed a few smoke rings, watching them float away. He gave a big, knowing smile.

A spell—Jonna needed a spell. He thought back to what he knew. Unfortunately, he was not very good at medical terms. Playing doctor had not been in his degree plan.

He thought through what Väinämö had said, and all the spells he heard along the way. Bob had told him about the healing spell, but he also said you had to understand what you wanted to heal. That should not be a problem. He could still remember biology class.

He pictured the diagrams from his text books: how the spine connects to the muscles and nerves, and how the veins run through the skin. Unfortunately, the cold feeling in his legs grew worse.

If he could just remember—he tried to say the word Bob had told him, but his lips did not obey. He coughed again as the cold feeling reached his stomach.

It's time, he thought. With barely a whisper, he mumbled the word, "Lasona."

Jonna closed his eyes.

~

He blinked, hearing a voice. It sounded like Bob.

"Of all the stupid, ignorant, selfish things to do—" Bob stood beside his ear, yelling. Jonna flinched, pulled his hand up, and blocked out the noise.

"Bob, please." His heart pounded in his ears.

"He's alive!" Bob shouted out, jumping up and down. "Over here, he's alive!"

336

The pixie launched upward, shooting out flares of pixie dust. Larger hands reached out and rolled Jonna over, washing away his pixie sight with the light from a glowing amulet.

Jonna looked up. Aias and Almundena fearfully studied him from head to foot, their faces pale. Jonna blinked several times. Thankfully, the headache was going away.

"What's wrong?" he asked as Bob hovered off his left shoulder. "Do I look that bad?"

Almundena attempted a quivering smile. "Of course not." She sat down beside him on the right, with Aias on the left. Tears ran down her cheeks.

"Hey," Bob called out. "Watch the pixie!"

"Sorry." Aias shifted, trying to see where Bob was.

"Why are you crying?" Jonna looked up at Almundena. "Aias looks fine to me." His voice sounded better now, much better than when he had first woken.

"Now who's being stupid?" Almundena adjusted the torn material of his elvish clothing. "Those crystals should have gone right through you." She checked his back, shock, relief, and surprise on her face. "They did!"

Jonna lightly laughed. "That's what Dagurunn said."

He stretched cautiously, remembering his limited movements from what felt like only a moment ago. In a strange way, it was as if his body had woken from a dream.

Aias and Almundena said at once, "Who?"

"Dagurunn, the dragon."

Almundena looked around. "Jonna, there are no dragons in this part of the cavern. It's cut off from all the rest. That's why the magic was taken from here."

"O—kay." He looked around. Where he remembered Dagurunn starting a warm fire, there was nothing but crystals. "I could have sworn—"

"And most do." Aias nodded. "Especially when they've just survived a fall like that."

"But he—" Jonna sat up slowly. "I know he was here."

Bob flew off and scanned the cave, following the walls.

"And we believe you," Aias added quickly, prepared to grab Jonna should he fall over. "But I think you ought to take this slow."

More of Jonna's surroundings sank in. "How did you two get down here?" His fall came back to his mind, very vividly.

"I am a mage." Almundena pretended to be hurt but smiled. "I do know a few tricks, Jonna almighty."

At the name, Jonna laughed. "You heard that, too?" His internals felt a little sore. He rubbed his side. "I guess that cure spell takes time." Another thought crossed his mind. "What about the Dark Mages?" He glanced up, steeling himself for more bad news.

"The Eye of Aldrick is gone," Almundena assured. "The power of the Dark Mage is broken forever."

She smiled at him. Their eyes met in a look that said more than words. "With the breaking of the gem, the spells they held over the people were released. I am no longer a Sarka. We are truly free."

Bob flew over from the other side of the cave carrying a shiny object. "Look what I found!"

"The Rune Blade." Jonna reached out and accepted the sword from the pixie. Its glow lit the area brighter. "It's still in one piece." He looked around, and his face fell. "Where's Elfleda? Is my wife okay?" Jonna's gaze shot to Bob.

Bob pulled out some pixie dust and dropped it over their heads. "Come and see." Reaching out, the pixie made them all join hands. "Hold on!"

They found themselves rising like a hot air balloon gaining speed toward the sky. Jonna's heart beat faster. Was the journey finally over? Surely he could find Stephanie now! Mirroring his anticipation, the Rune Blade grew brighter, casting a sphere of light in all directions.

They rose above the hole and then dropped slowly on top of the plateau. The arena had changed. Instead of the greenish light, the room was brightly lit. The sun shone through the opening above them, revealing a sky of aqua blue.

So how had the moon appeared above the hole? Then it hit him: Aatto of Ptah matched a solar eclipse. He grinned. "Aatto of Ptah is over." As Jonna looked around the arena, he saw very few people still milling there.

"Not over." Almundena smiled broadly. "Gone. Aatto of Ptah is gone forever. When the Eye of Aldrick was destroyed, the dark mage magic was lost."

Something about that did not seem to fit. Maybe it was a lingering doubt, or perhaps it was the experience itself that tainted his heart and soul. Or maybe—he remembered the story that the inchworm had told him. No, this was not over, not by a long shot.

His mind snapped back to why he was here. "Where is Stephanie?"

Almundena smiled, a hint of sadness on her face. She turned away, looking out across the arena floor. "I'm sure Elfleda knows," she said quietly.

Aias moved beside his sister, giving her a hug. "It's a new dawn." He brightened at the thought. "The shadows of the past have been swept away."

"Thank you for helping—" Jonna became distracted by a shadow coming from behind him. He turned quickly, Rune Blade ready, and heard Azazel's voice.

"Well, well, you did survive."

The rest followed Jonna's lead and spotted Azazel Sampo Elam, ruler of Chernobog, as the man strolled to a stop.

Jonna's eyes narrowed. The Rune Blade glowed brighter in his grasp.

"Hold!" Azazel looked at the sharp, glowing Rune Blade. "I come in peace and to keep the deal we struck." He bowed to them all. "As was agreed, the city has been spared. They can all go home without my interference."

Bob launched from Jonna's shoulder, holding pixie dust in both hands. "Okay, Azazel, I want my duel!"

Azazel stepped back, frowning. "Haven't you heard, my friend, all my dark mage powers are gone. Although, I might know enough other magic to suffice. If you insist—" A wand appeared from beneath his robe.

Bob growled, "Don't call me friend, you pixie-box-stuffer!"

Almundena stepped forward, putting herself between the mage and the pixie. "Stop it, both of you!" Her gaze snapped from Azazel to Bob. "The fighting is over. The Dark Mages have lost. That war is done."

She glanced toward Jonna, noting how quiet he had become. "Jonna, you can back me up at any time." All eyes turned toward Jonna expectantly.

The problem was, Jonna agreed with Bob. He remembered his own promise to make Azazel pay. He remembered the dark magic the mage cast upon Almundena and himself. Azazel did not deserve a truce. But could Jonna attack a man visiting under the colors of peace?

Jonna shook his head, addressing Azazel. "I don't like you, Azazel.

However, Almundena is right." Jonna threw a nod at Bob. "Let it go, Bob. This is not the time or place."

Bob growled at Azazel, "Another time, mage!" He flew to Jonna's shoulder.

Azazel bowed amiably. "At your choosing." He walked toward Almundena, giving her a wolfish grin. "As a matter of fact, the job of seeing all the people leave Chernobog is somewhat tedious to me. With my demon gone—" He threw a raised eyebrow toward Jonna and Bob. "I have no one to help with their return. That being said, I find myself in need of a new liaison. With the way now open for travel back and forth, it is important we have the right relationship with the travelers." Azazel looked Almundena in the eyes. "Or is the call of your old job with Lord Honorius holding to your heart?"

Jonna suspected the ex-dark mage had done that just to spite him. Watching Almundena, Jonna knew it was none of his business, but surely she would not agree.

Almundena shifted toward Jonna. Their eyes met. They both remembered when he had told her she had to stay away.

"My thoughts are my own," Almundena warned Azazel. "However, now that the Dark Mage influence is gone—" She looked away from Jonna. "We'll see."

"A possibility, then!" Azazel smiled broadly, turning toward Jonna. "And what will you do now? There's always room for two. And with your particular talents—"

"I'm going to find my wife," Jonna answered curtly. The fact that Almundena even considered working with Azazel did not sit right with him.

"Oh, really?" Azazel's eyes lit up. "But I thought—"

"You thought wrong," Jonna countered, a little angry at his implication, and angrier at himself for not containing that anger.

Almundena stepped in, physically placing herself between the two. "It was all a farce, including the clothes thrown around the room."

"What?" Aias looked from Jonna to Almundena. "Am I to understand—my sister?" His gaze snapped back to Jonna. "What did you do to my sister?"

Jonna sighed, turning away. "Nothing. It was all a ploy. Now, if you'll excuse me, I want to find my wife."

He headed down the plateau stairs and reached the main floor. It was time for them both to get out of this crazy world. How was he going to find her?

Bob chimed in, "We have to find Elfleda." The pixie hesitated. "She holds the key to seeing your wife."

Jonna thought back, not paying attention. "She should be in the cell." He mentally traced his path back up to the floors above them, to the front of this building, and across the bridge. "We can start there."

Bob said nothing.

Jonna cringed. "In all the excitement, she would have been forgotten."

He ran, reached an arena door, threw it open, and climbed the stairs as far as they would go. At the top, he stepped into a smaller room, followed a narrow corridor, and merged into the main hall. Thankfully, as the saying went, all roads lead to Rome.

"Jonna—" Bob tried to reason with him. "No one would leave your wife in the cell."

"But she was there. I saw her."

Jonna remembered when Elfleda had shown her to him. He remembered the protection Elfleda had thrown up to hide her. All this time his wife could have been there, invisible, protected, or hidden in some way he could not understand.

The Sight hit him, and his steps slowed briefly. That thing, the thought at the back of his mind, tried to come out. However, his immediate focus washed it away.

Reaching the main doors, he saw that the three crossbars had been removed. Jonna crossed the bridge at a steady pace and threw back the prison door. He shouted, "Stephanie!" His voice echoed down the corridor, bouncing from room to room.

Inside the main building, he continued to search, calling time after time. The more empty cells he passed, the quicker his steps became. He rushed along.

Bob pinched his ear hard. "Jonna, stop!"

"What? That hurt!"

Jonna saw nothing but empty cells. He found the cell where Elfleda had been, but there was no one inside. His heart fell, and The Sight showed him the truth. Stephanie was not here.

"Where is she?" Jonna stared at Bob. "I have done all that was asked of me. I have survived the trials, the temptations, and the strangeness of a world that is not mine. I deserve to find my wife!"

Bob swallowed. "Elfleda," he pleaded. "You have to find Elfleda!"

Jonna glared, his jaw tightening. "Where is she?"

"I—I don't know," Bob explained quickly. "Last I knew, she was going back to the elvish city."

Jonna looked down, finding the amulet still hanging around his neck. Somehow, through it all, it had never left his person. Then it hit him—at any time, he could have returned. At any time, he could have abandoned the quest and been free of the hardships. Yet, he kept going, moving through the mire of trouble, pushing forward with one goal in mind.

"I will find Elfleda," he promised. "She will bring me to Stephanie!"

He put his hand around the amulet, closing his eyes. Remembering the things he learned of magic, this time Jonna tried a different thought.

The instructions were *see the city of your mind*. However, right now, he did not want a city. He wanted a person. His mind focused on Elfleda. Light sprang up in all directions, and a portal opened where none had been before. He stepped through, feeling the change in the atmosphere.

Going from dreary prison to bright-lit forest, he blinked his eyes. The wind blew through the trees. The birds chirped in the branches. The strong smell of honeysuckle assaulted Jonna's nose. Bob sneezed.

Elfleda's musical voice chimed behind them. "There you are, and just in time."

CHAPTER 33
THE DUEL

Elfleda reached forward, taking Jonna's hand. She pulled him toward a tent-like structure. Before he reached the door, he glanced behind him. Some sort of jousting area with peasants and nobles alike had been set up in the field.

"What's going on?" He attempted to stay angry, but her countenance made it hard to keep his resolve. "What is this place?"

Her voice held the promise everything would finally be over. "It is time for the duel. It is time for you to save the kingdom of the elves."

"I thought I just did that?" Jonna tried to glare at her, but her beauty forced him to look away. "No, I—I can't. I want my wife. You know where she is."

"Jonna—"

He felt her hand touch his shoulder.

"Your wife is safe. Complete the task, and save the elves."

"What is it with all of you?" He removed her hand, staring into her face. A part of him wanted to turn away, but his anger had surged again. "From the very moment I found she was gone, all of you" He threw a glare at Bob. "All of you have kept some sort of secret. I played along, thinking it would explain itself, but it hasn't, and I'm really tired of playing games!"

"Jonna—"

Elfleda put her hand to his face. He could feel the tingling of her soft touch. He could hear the calming song of her words. "Remember."

For a brief second he tumbled into the past. A memory of a young girl came to mind. Her hair was golden, shining in the sun. Her face was happy, full of life. He shook himself. The scene was so real, he felt like he was there again.

"The face in the water." He exhaled as the memory faded. A look of wonderment crossed his face. "You were there. You were the little girl."

Elfleda nodded. "I was very young then." She laughed. "Not knowing the ways of humans in your world. But I never forgot our first meeting."

Her last sentence seemed to be hinting at something. Jonna

frowned. "There were more?" *Surely he would have remembered that!*

With a smile, Elfleda nodded. "Off and on. When you least expected."

Part of him believed her, and part of him did not. This wasn't making a whole lot of sense.

"M'lady—" An elven soldier stepped in through the curtain. "We are ready to begin."

She nodded, granting him permission to step out. Elfleda turned back toward Jonna. "Will that suffice until after the duel?"

Jonna watched her face. "Then you expect me to win?"

"Of course." She laughed, sounding like tinkling bells. "Why else would you be the Queen's Champion?"

Jonna noted the change in words. "That doesn't answer my question."

"That's why I'm here to help," Bob declared. "Or you might not! And if you're ready, we have a guard outside waiting."

Jonna sighed. What could be tougher than what he had already faced? The Rune Blade hummed, glowing in his hand. He turned around, pushed the curtain back, and stepped to the nearest guard.

"Here, sir." The guard led him to the edge of a sand-filled arena. He paused long enough to make sure Jonna stopped there and then hurried away.

"What's with him?" Jonna looked around but did not see his opponent.

Bob whispered, "He knows what's next, and it ain't gonna be pretty!"

A herald called out, "Jonna McCambel!"

In the commotion of the crowd, Jonna spotted Elfleda making her way to a large stand filled with many seats. Instead of one royal viewing box, there were two, with the queen in one and the king in the other. Elfleda moved to join the queen. Oddly, the king sat in shadow, his features undefined.

The herald called again, "Jonna McCambel!"

"I am here." Jonna raised the Rune Blade. Half the crowd roared.

When the multitude quieted, the herald called another name. "Anim Yspaddaden!"

Knocking sand into the air, a huge foot stomped into the area beside Jonna. The sand rained down on a portion of the spectators, yet all that was visible was the footprint.

The herald coughed, using a handkerchief to wipe his face. "Anim Yspaddaden!"

A voice boomed, thundering down, "Here!"

Another part of the crowd roared. Anim's large mass faded into view. He was a giant, reminding Jonna of the story of Jack and the Beanstalk.

A huge boo came up from part of the stands. Soldiers were dispatched to silence the ruckus.

"You know the rules?" The herald looked up at Anim and took a step back.

Anim nodded. Jonna shook his head.

The herald never took his eyes off Anim. "Good, let the game begin!" He put the horn to his mouth.

"Wait a minute." Jonna took a second look at his opponent. "I don't know the rules."

Bob whispered, "You don't have to."

"You don't have to," the herald answered with authority. "Only the incumbent has to know the rules."

Jonna swallowed. "Incumbent? What is this, a presidential election?" *Talk about big shoes to fill.* "Hold it, if he used to hold the position I'm holding now, why in Sam Hill am I fighting?"

The herald laughed. "Not very bright, are we? The queen accepted you. When the queen accepts a new champion, the incumbent goes to the king. Since you guard her honor, you are not the incumbent."

That did not answer Jonna's question, but he wasn't sure the herald could. "Okay." Jonna frowned. "I guess that makes sense. However, if the new guy doesn't get to know the rules, and the new guy becomes the incumbent when another new guy is accepted, then nobody knows the rules."

Bob nodded. "The herald's right. You can't be the incumbent."

Jonna fought to control his voice. This was like arguing with a rock. "I don't care if I'm the incumbent. I want to know the rules!"

The herald started to blow the horn again.

Though Jonna was not sure if it would matter, he interrupted a second time. "Wait a minute. Doesn't it seem just a little unbalanced here? I mean, think about it. A huge giant who can go invisible at will is facing me, a human?"

"And?" The herald stared at him, unblinking.

"I—" Jonna took a deep breath. "I don't even know what I'm

supposed to do."

The herald smiled, put the horn to his lips, and blew.

The giant turned toward him, grinning. "I can help with that." His massive club came swishing down.

"Jump," Bob screeched, deafening Jonna's left ear.

Jonna leaped to the side as sand shot up in all directions.

The giant hefted the club again. "Aw, I missed. Your turn."

"We take turns?" Jonna gazed up at the giant, trying to estimate how much downward force Anim had generated.

"Forfeit, eh? You want me to go again?" The giant grinned. "Sure."

This time the club swung sideways, taking out a section of runner within the jousting area. Boards flew. The crowd cheered. *Which side were they on, anyway?*

Jonna ducked, going as flat as he could. The swish over him felt like a hurricane, but what was he to do? How do you take out a giant?

One of the spells he had learned came to mind. Without thinking, he held up the sword and shouted, "Awiti Barbaros!"

"Jonna, no!" Bob closed his eyes as he waited for the inevitable. The lightning arced up, touched the giant, and rebounded straight for Jonna.

"Shoot!" Jonna leaped, rolling to the side. The lightning struck the ground, sending sand in all directions.

"He's magically resistant!" Bob yelled out, trying to stay on Jonna's shoulder. "And how in the world did you do dark mage magic with the gem gone?"

Jonna rolled, looking up. He responded in reverse order. "What? Now you tell me!"

The club came down again, striking the sand. With Jonna on the ground, the wave almost buried him. This was not going to be easy. By inheriting a huge, magically resistant giant, the king certainly knew what he was doing.

Jonna came to his feet, ducked between the giant's legs, and stood underneath him. He needed time to think.

"Ho, ho." Anim chuckled. "The old hide-beneath-the-giant trick."

One of the giant's feet lifted up. A second later, it came stomping down.

Jonna wobbled, trying to stay on his feet. However, the ground had not stopped shaking. When it settled, he focused on the giant. It was time to find a way to fight back.

He spun through different ideas, staying under the giant but away from the feet. The crowd cheered on both sides. For whom, Jonna could not tell.

"Bob, a little help might be nice."

Jonna stepped behind the giant's heel, making it harder to be seen. At least the giant did not attempt to kick backwards.

Bob looked offended. "Oh, I can't do that."

"What do you mean, you can't do that?" Jonna started around the foot but quickly stepped backwards as the giant turned.

"I'm only here in an advisory position." Bob shrugged, watching sand move as the giant's foot changed location. The hunt was on.

"Then advise," Jonna growled.

So far, Jonna had stayed out of the giant's sight, but the crowd had begun to boo. For all he knew, they might start telling the giant where to step.

"It's all a matter of perspective—" the pixie began.

"Perspective my foot." Jonna slipped, caught himself, and stood back up. An idea hit him. "Perspective?"

He looked from the giant's foot to his own. If the giant was resistant to magic, he was not. Jonna remembered the spell Bob used on the boxes. "Ceres Bolium!" he announced, and then moved quickly backwards. He enlarged, growing in stature behind the giant.

"Where are you?" Anim boomed, frustration filling his voice. He hit the ground, turning around. His eyes opened wide.

"Well now." The giant grinned. "That's better!" He swung his club at Jonna's head.

"Yes, it is." Jonna parried with the Rune Blade, driving the club back. The giant grunted, muscles bulging. His face reddened.

The two weapons wavered. The crowd went mad.

"Bob, you still there?" Jonna had to drop the volume. He sounded much louder than usual.

"Yes," a tiny voice called, almost out of hearing. Jonna glanced toward his shoulder but could not see the pixie.

"I'm here," Bob called again. "Give me a moment." The pixie moved closer to his ear, sitting down inside it. "That better?"

"Yes."

The weapon thing was getting nowhere. Jonna shifted his weight, brought up his right foot, and stomped down on the giant's toes.

The giant howled in pain. "No fair! No fair!"

As the giant dropped his club and grabbed his foot, Jonna deflected the giant's weapon, knocking it out into the forest. He stabbed his own Rune Blade into the soft sand, placing it safely out of reach. Grinning at the giant, he chuckled. "Now we play."

The giant roared, throwing a left hook. Jonna deflected with a right outward block, hooked the giant's arm, and kicked his opponent in the groin.

The giant's eyes opened wide. His right hand dropped to protect himself as he bent forward, putting his chin in the perfect position. Jonna heel-palmed his chin, stepped behind the giant's leg with his own, and threw him toward the ground.

Soldiers on both sides ran in all directions as the giant's body slammed downward, squashing what had been Jonna's tent. As the giant's body stilled, Jonna dropped with an elbow to the solar plexus, driving it home.

"I yield," the giant wheezed, fighting to speak. The last strike had paralyzed his lungs. He tried to breathe, but his lungs just would not function well.

"Did I hear a yield?" Jonna's eyes narrowed. "I better see a nod or I'm coming in for more."

The giant nodded as much as he could manage. Jonna stopped pinning him, checked the giant's raspy breathing, and nodded. "You'll be all right. Give it a moment."

Standing up, he stepped—with a single stride—back into the arena and pulled the Rune Blade out of the sand. Holding it up, he called out the spell, "Ne Ceres Bolium."

Bob leaped out of his ear as Jonna's size diminished. For the first time, Jonna could hear the crowd cheering down below.

The herald motioned for him to stand before the king and queen. "Jonna, come forth!"

Together, the king and queen made a very handsome couple despite the fact that Jonna could not look directly at the king. Every time Jonna tried, something forced him to look away. Neither appeared disappointed at the outcome. So what was the earth-shattering duel about?

"Kneel," the king commanded.

Jonna went to one knee.

"You have won the duel. You have saved the elvish people. You have returned balance to this land. You are its holy protector. What is

348

your wish?"

A flash of light glinted off the Rune Blade, reflecting in the sunlight. Jonna looked around at the forest, seeing for the first time the faces of many he recognized.

Sir Verity nodded with pride. Dorothy floated with the fireflies around her. Väinämö acted like a father who had just seen his son graduate college. O'Conner McBear still looked wishful of getting back the amulet. Thomas, Janice, and Phillip all stood as a family again. Elpis, next to Phillip, caught Jonna's gaze. The small girl moved toward the fence, grinning from ear to ear with a sparkle in her eye. Naida Perdita, Serena Magnus, Deela, and Artemis all stood within the crowd. Azazel Sampo Elam and Matthias Omid waited to one side, watching without comment. Although Jonna thought he saw a smile escape Matthias's lips.

Crystilic appeared and winked as she changed from a flagpole, sporting the queen's insignia, into a woman. The flag had shown Jonna's name on it. Gernot Algar saluted him, while Cato cast a blessing. Even Anim sat up, watching the ordination, finally able to breathe more easily. Jonna saw respect in the giant's eyes.

"What do you wish?" The voice no longer belonged to the king, but to Stephanie, who was coming toward him. His heart tried to beat out of his chest. She was back. He was back. They could go home!

Yet, as he looked up, he saw something he had never seen before. Her appearance changed. Her hair became softer, sparkling in color. Her voice took on a musical note. She moved her long hair to one side, and he could see her elvish ears.

"Jonna." Elfleda stood before him, looking steadfastly into his eyes. "Do you not recognize me now?"

Jonna's heart stopped. He had just watched his wife, Stephanie, change into the elvish princess, but his mind could not believe it.

"I don't understand," he whispered, though he knew in his heart he did. The Sight, even now, confirmed what he had not seen before.

"Stephanie was my human form, taken many years ago." Elfleda smiled, still watching his face.

Jonna's eyes narrowed. "That's not possible."

"Why do you resist the truth?" She stepped toward him.

"I—" Jonna's eyes swept the crowd. Most watched him with joyous expectation. His mind spun in a million directions. His heart beat faster than it should. "Why?" His eyes went back to hers, gaining focus.

"I was an elven princess, and I saw a little boy who drew my heart. In order to be with that boy, I had to take on a human shell." She came closer. "Don't you understand?"

He heard the words, but the voice confused him. That musical voice that drew him in now shook his world.

"There is no Stephanie?" He shook his head, fixing his eyes on the ground. Jonna's thoughts raced in all directions. His memories, memories of the times they spent together, were not real? Their college years? Their marriage? Their home? Had it all been a lie?

Stephanie appeared to read his mind. "No, not a lie. Those things were real. We experienced them together. Yet, when trouble came to my land, I was forced to return. I had to take my native form." She shook her head. "Don't you understand? In my absence, the world, my world, had fallen into chaos. I could tell something was wrong, but until we came to the cabin, I never knew to what extent. Once I knew, I had to come back."

Another thought entered Jonna's mind. It was a truth he had suspected but pushed aside. "We can't go back to our reality?" His eyes came up to meet hers.

"No." Elfleda smiled sadly. "I can't go back. Once I was forced to return, I had to give up my human life in order to save my people. I had to accept my role to become the next queen."

She extended her hand. "If you agree, I would do that with you."

Her eyes sparkled as she waited for his response. A strange sensation dropped over Jonna. He felt deceived and betrayed. "And if I don't?"

Had he been duped into coming here? Had he been tricked? He looked at the Rune Blade attuned to him. It responded to his presence. The attunement was no mistake. Someone had done it on purpose.

All he ever wanted was a normal family with a wife and kids. How could they have a normal family here?

"If you don't"—Elfleda's gaze dropped toward the ground, and her smile faded—"you have the choice to leave."

Jonna's thoughts stopped. He could see everything going on around him. He could hear the voices of the crowd as if from very far away. The sound of his heart beating in his ears boomed loudly. Conflicting emotions crashed against each other.

This was an alien world, different from his own. This was Elfleda's home, and she could no longer leave. Moreover, the last realization slapped him in the face harder than the rest. Stephanie and Elfleda were the same person.

Remember. The word came to his mind, taking him back through everything that had happened. The learning of magic, the trusting of allies, and the taint of dark magic that tried to claim his heart. He had chosen to continue based on one simple thought: he had to find Stephanie.

"What do you wish?" The words echoed from the back of his mind. The ideal picture of his life exploded with this turn of events. A normal family he could never have in the comfortable world of his origins. His dreams and goals would become a thing of the past.

Or would they? Changes happened all the time. Discovery was a part of time itself. He could still have his family. He could still pursue a career. It would just be in another time, another place, far from the world he first called his home.

Yet, in the end, none of his expectations mattered. Only one thing was important, and one thing alone.

He reached out and raised Elfleda's chin, gazing into her eyes. The love was still there—the thing that had drawn them together from the very start. That love had kept them together through all their troubles.

The body was different, but the person was the same. Nothing could force a change in how they felt about each other. It was their choice.

He saw the sparkle in her eyes. She longed to be in his arms. His heart ached to hold her close. He had to tell her it would be all right.

Jonna spoke softly, though the words sounded loud in his ears. "I am here to stay."

He stepped forward, his lips touching hers. His arms went around her and held her close.

Time held still as the kiss lingered on. He closed his eyes, thinking of nothing but her. After a moment, his grip relaxed.

Reaching up with his right hand, he moved back her hair and then stroked her cheek. "I love you."

She opened her eyes and looked into his. "I love you, too."

The End

For the next book in the series, read *Partition Majik*, Book 2 in the Xun Ove Series.

ABOUT THE AUTHOR

James William Peercy fell through a portal into the publishing biosphere in 2012. Previously, he had been observing his own world and recording it since the age of 10. James continued writing while attaining a degree in Computer Science, getting married, raising dogs, and starting a business. Since all worlds exist simultaneously, he has added three book series, the Cliff Fulton mystery series, the Xun Ove fantasy series, and Ivan, Universal Space Tech series. He's also a New Apple Solo Medalist Winner in poetry for "Within the Heart of Silence", which he collaborated with author and photographer, Jacqueline E. Smith, who provided the photographs for the book. With a mind constantly moving, he devotes his downtime to writing, enjoying a bit of travel, and adoring his wife, Claudette.

If you like poetry, fantasy, sci-fi, steampunk and mystery check out his website.

http://www.JamesWilliamPeercy.com

http://www.StoriesToTell.com

https://www.facebook.com/jameswilliampeercy

https://www.facebook.com/jamespeercy

https://www.instagram.com/jameswilliampeercy

https://twitter.com/JamesWPeercy

If you like the book, drop him a line. If you don't like the book, drop him a line anyway. He will appreciate the feedback. As in the words of J.R.R. Tolkien, 'May the hair on your toes never fall out!'

Made in the USA
Lexington, KY
05 November 2019